PRAISE FOR *THE SECRET ATTIC*

"*The Secret Attic* is creepy and atmospheric with a sprinkling of dark humor, exploring the horrors involved with sifting through one's past and confronting grief. Conradt captures the toxic mother-in-law dynamic effortlessly, then takes it to a whole new level of disturbing. I couldn't put it down!"

—Miranda Smith, author of *Smile for the Cameras*

"Think your mother-in-law is bad? Just wait till you meet the MIL from hell in Chelsea Conradt's creepy whirlwind of a novel. The perfect read for bullied daughters-in-law everywhere."

—Alma Katsu, *New York Times* bestselling author of *Fiend*

"A deeply chilling exploration of the complex bonds formed by love and lies, *The Secret Attic* is at times as heartbreaking as it is frightening. You won't be able to stop reading."

—Christina Henry, author of *The Place Where They Buried Your Heart*

"*The Secret Attic* is clever, unsettlingly immersive, and emotionally complex. This book simmers with suspense and an ever-growing unease that will have you checking over your shoulder—if you can tear your eyes away from the page long enough to do so."

—CJ Dotson, author of *These Familiar Walls*

"Chelsea Conradt expertly mixes toxic family dynamics, the lasting impact of grief, and horror vibes in her newest release. Through turns that are both atmospheric and perfectly disturbing, *The Secret Attic* winds its way through your nightmares to deliver a chilling new twist on a revenge thriller. Do not miss this one!"

—Darby Kane, #1 international bestseller of *Pretty Little Wife*

"Claustrophobic and packed to the rafters with menace, *The Secret Attic* is a house of horrors filled with ghosts, lies, and the trauma we swallow to keep the peace for the sake of family."

—Tanya Pell, author of *Her Wicked Roots*

PRAISE FOR *THE FARMHOUSE*

"A fresh start becomes the stuff of nightmares... A slippery slow burn of a haunted tale."

—Christa Carmen, award-winning author of *The Daughters of Block Island*

"Haunting and atmospheric, Chelsea Conradt's debut thriller led me on a chilling ride to a deadly crescendo. I did not see that end coming!"

—Nalini Singh, *New York Times* bestselling author

"*The Farmhouse* is a thought-provoking, action-packed thriller with a gripping plot."

—Lisa M. Matlin, author of *The Stranger Upstairs*

"An unputdownable novel. A smart, chilling, ferociously feminist thriller."

—Kristen Simmons, Bram Stoker Award nominee

"*The Farmhouse* twists together the threads of rustic dreams and pastoral nightmares, creating an atmospheric read that will haunt you long after the story is done. Conradt's thrilling debut is not to be missed."

—Lish McBride, author of *Red in Tooth and Claw*

"Wholly gripping, chilling, and compulsively addictive... Conradt masterfully crafts a fast-paced, eerie thriller."

—Rachel Fikes, author of *Keeper of Sorrows*

"*The Farmhouse* will leave you looking over your shoulder... Satisfyingly layered."

—Jaye Wells, *USA Today* bestselling
author of *High Lonesome Sound*

THE SECRET ATTIC

CHELSEA CONRADT

Poisoned Pen Press

For the moms. I hope no one asks you for a snack while you're reading this book.

Cover design by Sarah Brody/Sourcebooks
Cover image © Dave Wall/Arcangel
Inside cover and character art by Simon Mendez

Published by Poisoned Pen Press, an imprint of Sourcebooks
1935 Brookdale RD, Naperville, IL 60563-2773
(630) 961-3900
sourcebooks.com

Cataloging-in-Publication Data is on file with the Library of Congress.

Printed and bound in the United States of America.
PAH 10 9 8 7 6 5 4 3 2 1

AUTHOR'S NOTE

This is a story about family dynamics, what we'll do for those we love, and motherhood. The journey to becoming a parent isn't always a straight line. Prior to the start of this novel, the main character, Addison, suffered an early-stage miscarriage. While it happens months before this book begins, it's central to Addison's sense of loss and drive to connect and seek justice. As a mom of a rainbow baby, it's important to me that readers know miscarriage is part of the journey of the book. Be gentle with yourselves.

Chelsea Conradt

CHAPTER 1

ANYONE WHO COMPLIMENTS YOU ON BEING "GOOD IN A crisis" will let you flounder with your feelings in the aftermath. Fortunately, I'd married out of the obligation of being the solid one in the family. My husband Luke never asks more of me than I can give.

Or he hadn't, until his mother died.

A dark cloud loomed over him for weeks following her death, and for the first time, Luke needed me to carry him through the bad times. So when he asked me to help him navigate the estate preparations, I took a block of time off from the accounting firm, and we flew north. Every trip to the tiny dot of a town on the Oregon coast where Luke had grown up had been miserable for me, but I'd go one last time to prepare his mother's house for sale.

Because there's nothing I wouldn't do for Luke.

Fog slithers over the road ahead, sliding in from the ocean. The gray obscures the water, too. It's one thing I like about coming to Oregon with Luke. Every morning it's like the sea reaches inland to wash away worries and let the land start anew. He'd grown up with it, so he is less impressed by the daily clean slate.

Our home in Austin has a lush lawn and easy access to Zilker Park. The quirky bubble works for us. Great local restaurants, festivals every weekend, and a town big enough that we rarely run into people we know when grocery shopping.

We absolutely will have to talk to people Luke went to high school with while visiting Rockside Bay.

We turn onto a graveled driveway, and Luke's childhood home comes into view. Despite the decaf in his to-go cup, my husband is vibrating.

I press my palm to his thigh, giving it a little squeeze. "We've got this."

"One weekend," he says, still trying to convince himself he can unload decades of deluge from his mom's place in a couple days.

"It takes however long it takes." I lean over the console to press a kiss to his shoulder. "Taking the time away is good."

The three-story house is as impressive as the first time I drove up to it with Luke ten years ago. Apprehension cinches around my chest. This time is different, I remind myself. The home is magnificent with craftsman styling and forest-green shutters open around the numerous windows. I half expect to still see my mother-in-law Barb peering from behind the sheers on the second story. She'd never picked us up the from the airport, but upon our arrival would simultaneously hug Luke with the same gusto as a baggage claim reunion and chide me for taking so long to drive the two and a half hours from the airport. It'd never mattered if Luke had been behind the wheel.

At least I wouldn't have to deal with that today.

This house is objectively stunning. Tall, imposing, and wrapped in ivy. Maybe it stood out as a stark, powerful image at the edge of town because it is this pristine white place overlooking the gray churning ocean. Whereas most homes in the small town nearby are bungalows, and while greenery is prevalent here, the ivy carries a hint of prestige that had brought Barb pride.

We inch up the unnecessarily winding road, gravel crunching an announcement. This might be the last time we visit this house. *God willing.* Because no matter how beautiful the exterior is or how Barb could present the first-floor common spaces during a party, the inside would forever give me the ick. This place is crammed with everything Barb had ever touched or owned. It's as though she needed to keep every item, like some ridiculous display of her wealth.

Not that I would say that to Luke.

Some people collect mementos. Other people collect oddities. My late mother-in-law did neither; she simply *amassed.*

And a tiny part of me relishes the petty joy of getting to throw it all out.

But I need to shove that shitty part of myself aside. Being there for Luke comes first.

His mother may have hated me. But she had loved Luke. This is going to be hard for him, and because I love him, I have to think of this cleanout as more than pitching a hoarder's garbage. This is about letting go of who his mother drove him to be and beginning the path toward accepting her loss. Those are journeys no one should have to tread alone.

The steps groan as we approach the back door of the house. Every bit the welcome I am used to at my mother-in-law's house. Luke hesitates; his keys are poised to grant entry but just rattle beside the door. The plain brass key had been on his ring when I'd met him. The silver one for our front door, the gold one for his office, and the fob for our car back home all swing beneath. Luke had left Oregon at eighteen, but that key had remained on the ring.

"We don't have to do this right now," I say, softly resting my hand on his arm.

"I'm good, Addison. Really." The keys on Luke's ring jingle, that expression of nerves so telling.

I press my hand more firmly against him, like I can read how much he needs a hug by touch. "We could find a hotel. Rest a moment. And come back here after we've eaten maybe?" I don't want to be here, but I want to see Luke hurt even less.

"We don't need a hotel. This town doesn't even have hotels. And the last thing I'm going to do is stay at Betty Johnson's bed-and-breakfast or a roadside motel. This was my mom's house; now it's mine." He sighs, the exhale pure conviction. "We need to stay here."

His key slides into the lock as if that is punctuation on our conversation.

The door swings inward, silence spilling forward. Had someone hit the hinges with WD-40? I swear the last time I was here, the damn thing screamed when I walked through the door. Maybe that was just Barb. She'd had that effect on me.

The drapes have been drawn. The home we enter is nothing but shadows. Charcoal gray sketches the frames of the windows on the far wall. The curtains nearby should be varied shades of cream with pastoral flowers. Why Barb thought that was *the look*, I never knew. But lingering in the doorway with my grief-stricken husband, I see none of the lightness that this room normally held. Dust lingers in the air, and every breath is thick with grief and tension.

Even with our contentious relationship, this place feels wrong without Barb. Or, I guess, *more* wrong? I'd never been comfortable here. Or more aptly, I'd never been welcome. But the first few steps into the kitchen, it's almost as if hands clasp my shoulders, shaking me, shoving me. I'd always wanted to leave this place, but this is the first time I feel like I need to run.

Luke hesitates. Is he overwhelmed with the same sudden urgency to flee to the car? But when he steps forward, it's all smooth confidence. He flicks his fingers against the light switch, the same move he's been making for decades. I move forward and slip my hand into his, giving him another quick squeeze.

"If you're sure you're ready for this..." Am I asking him if he's ready to process his mother's death? Am I asking him if he's ready to go through her mountains of garbage? Yes? Maybe? Letting him fill in the blank is safest.

I'd been struck by loss only six months ago. Not only me; both of us. And now we stand here together with Luke buried in it again. He took such gentle care of me, and I am determined to do the same for him.

When he nods and releases my hand, we don't speak. Just go to work. I open the curtains throughout the first floor. Diffused sunlight spills through the overcast sky. It brings no warmth, but it lifts a chill all the same.

Even if grief isn't rotting the air around us in every room, being in Barb Lowe's home turns my stomach.

Look, I know my mother-in-law hated me. The dirty looks, the snide comments, the terrible Christmas gifts. Blatant "I'm enduring you" moves. For *years*. But nothing proved it more than her dying and leaving her estate for me to clean out. A three-story house full to the brim of stuff. *Pure torture.*

Luke's worth it though. He's wearing his pain now. Prickly chin, rumpled T-shirt, mouth so often pulled into that tight pout, like he's about to deliver bad news. Before this though, he laughed in a way that made every person in the room chuckle too. As a partner, he is that rare gem that brings me flowers every week, finds festivals for us to day-trip to, and makes me laugh so hard I cry. Luke can't clear this house alone. He might be a damn fine lawyer and okay on a pickleball court, but OMG the man would find any reason to keep old magazines or kindergarten scribblings... Just like his mom, he's terrible at letting anything go. I, however, am so ready to pitch Barb Lowe's amassed garbage. And donate the quality items to people who will actually use them.

Every item on the first floor of the house is carefully curated. The rooms are designed to draw your eye to elite items and Barb's idea of pristine perfection. She'd been deeply involved with her community, and honestly, the woman had loved to host a party. Though most were excuses to boast about her successes. I'm trying to remember a time when we had a Thanksgiving where her "What I'm thankful for" was more than a list of her son's accolades.

This first floor lies to us. There's easy estate work to do here. It pretends—like Barb would—that it's organized and simply needs a good dusting and a coat of furniture polish to be maintained. Anyone walking in would believe we truly could complete this home cleanout in one weekend. Only I've been to this house before. What awaits upstairs includes more boxes than I can count, pathways to get to the rooms, and zero labeling. Nothing about this trip is easy, but loving Luke is, I remind myself. Pictures of him line the walls. Special moments captured in film and set in silver frames. Graduations, birthdays, family trips, and even a newspaper clipping or two. Those I want to keep. I understand Barb treasuring looking back at those moments, wanting to hold on to a part of Luke all the time. Though I've never actually enjoyed staying in the Museum of Luke Lowe. Maybe this time will be different.

Luke walks back to the kitchen. The door between the dining room and the kitchen is one of the swinging ones. The kind you'd expect to see in restaurants and old movies, but also somehow fit in really fancy houses. Unlike the other doors, it announces its movement. The soft whine of its sway makes sure I know where my husband is.

I follow him. Luke stands in the center of the room. Bewilderment steals his features. Wide eyes, narrow mouth. He slips his hands into his pockets, then pulls them free. He turns toward the door leading to the deck and Barb's prized garden. But instead of going outside, he pivots yet again and opens the refrigerator door.

There are fourteen bottles of white wine inside the refrigerator. Twelve had been opened and recorked. Look, it's near wine country, although who wouldn't pick a local pinot noir? And perhaps hosting requires a great amount of booze. But, good lord, the woman had been tiny. How much had she been drinking?

Luke closes the door. His attention flits around the room, but lands on nothing. "All these condiments need to go."

"Cleaning out the refrigerator is no problem. Do you want me to handle that?" We haven't discussed how exactly we are going to clean out this house.

Luke nods as though in a daze. Had I looked like that? My heart still aches from losing the potential of becoming a mom. How long had I mourned? Am I still mourning? I scrub the heel of my palm against my chest. The motion has become second nature, but it doesn't really help.

"I don't know where to start, Ads," Luke admits. Then softly, he says, "I need you so much."

"Oh, babe."

Behind me a box thwacks against the floor. Luke jerks back at the sound. I turn to find the box of old baking supplies spilled onto the floor. Flour and sugar settling into the grooves between the hardwood planks. A canister of baking powder rolls toward me.

"Maybe I shouldn't have brought you here—" Luke starts.

I shut that down. "We're a team. Always."

Ignoring the mess, I wrap my arms around him and squeeze until I can pour my calm into him.

"I love you, Addison."

"I love you too. Now, why don't you look around downstairs, and I'll clean this up." We may not have made a plan for purging this home, but then that is my role. Luke can handle contracts. Luke can handle negotiations. But me? I handle feelings. Inasmuch as *handling* means understanding how to shove them into boxes I can stack neatly away for another, better time. I can manage the world as it falls apart if it means I can dodge my emotions.

Not that anyone cared why I was so good at it. Or that I ever really thought about what made me become so skilled at subverting crises in the first place.

CHAPTER 2

BARB'S KITCHEN IS A FAIR PLACE FOR ME TO START OPERATION Purge. For whatever reason, it bewilders my husband, but also we need a place to put groceries. I pour the excess wine down the drain and load my arms with as many empty bottles as I can carry.

I carefully haul the load out the back door and to the recycling bin. *When is trash day?* The crunch of gravel pulls my attention down the drive. A well-loved station wagon rolls toward the house. It's a light blue and has a sticker for a local church on the back window. The woman who steps out is perhaps a decade older than me. She's in luxe joggers and a crop top, but her loose curls suggest she didn't come from the gym.

"Oh, hi," she fumbles upon seeing me. "I thought Luke would be here."

"I'm his wife, Addison." I extend my hand to her. Her handshake is so light, I'm not certain we've actually clasped hands.

"I'm Meg," she says. "I have a quick favor to ask of Luke, and then I can get out of your hair."

Despite the polished exterior, Meg's eyes glisten with worry. I need to run defense. "He's resting, but I'd be happy to help you, Meg."

She licks her lips but then decides to plow forward. "It's silly, but I brought a dish to one of Barb's parties. She said she'd washed it for me, but I never got it back."

"Barb let you bring food to one of her parties? Impressive." Even when I stayed in the house, I wasn't allowed to so much as help prep carrots for a salad.

Meg's smile is weak. "I surprised her. My family's cherry crumble is legendary."

"I'm sure we can find your dish for you." I turn toward the house, letting Meg follow me.

"It's a ceramic baking dish with a red rim and cherries hand-painted on the inside."

"Easy to spot," I say, like I don't expect to encounter dozens of dishes in the kitchen.

"Thanks for this." She climbs the stairs behind me. "I'd offer to make you one, but our family orchard has been hit by one pest after another the last three years."

Inside the kitchen, I start opening cabinets and checking Barb's meticulously organized bakeware. A chill skates down my spine. I roll my shoulders against the sensation and focus on Meg. "That's awful. Is that your family's business? The orchard, I mean."

She nods but looks somber. "My brother moved up to Washington State to start a new orchard. It's thriving up there, but the one here in Rockside Bay is… You don't need to hear my sad story. I'm sure you and Luke are buried in your own drama." Red rises on Meg's cheeks.

I cast a quick glance in her direction. How much does she know? How much does this town know about what we've been through? The cabinet door snaps shut on my thumb. I hiss and hold my injured hand to my mouth to keep from making more of a spectacle.

"Oh, goodness. I'm so sorry."

"It's truly fine," I say, probably too quickly. "But unfortunately, I don't see your dish in here."

Disappointment radiates from her. "We're probably moving up north with my brother soon. I'd hoped to get it back, but thanks for looking."

"I can keep looking for it. Here." I hand her my phone. "Give me your number, and I'll text if I find it."

"You'd do that?"

Her surprise stings. Does she think I must be like Barb, or had my mother-in-law convinced every person she met that her son had married down?

"Of course," I reply as cheerily as I can. "We're going through this whole house. The cherry bakeware should be easy enough to watch for."

She types in her digits and then texts herself so she has my number. "Luke married a good one."

"He's a good guy." I hope I'm sparing him by keeping Meg here instead of bringing her farther into the house for him to chat with.

Meg hesitates by the door. Is she going to ask to search the place herself? Had I misread this lady? Her gaze flits to the stairwell. "Do you think your daughter might come help us look?"

I sputter, "Excuse me?"

It's a miracle I don't swear at this woman.

Pink shame floods Meg's cheeks. "I shouldn't push. I just saw her in the window upstairs, and teens have this way of finding *everything* they're not supposed to. My niece is totally like that."

Panic grips my chest like it's readying to throttle me. The carefully stacked blocks barricading my loss wobble. *I will not cry in front of this woman.* "We don't have a daughter."

No matter how much I wish we did.

Meg's brow twists with confusion. "Oh, I didn't mean anything. It was probably the sunrise on the window."

I nod as if we both don't know that the clouds are slung low across the sky. My rib cage is so tight, my lungs struggle to fill, crushing every little box of feeling I've hidden there. *Change the subject. Distract yourself.* "I'm definitely not old enough to have a teenager." I laugh it off. "But I am going to dig through this whole house. So should there be a cherry pan, it'll come back to you."

We both smile, but sorrow has settled between us. My thumb throbs.

"I'm so sorry I haven't met you sooner," Meg says. "After that last party, it's been one thing after another, and I haven't made another of Barb's events."

Meg clearly has a way of stepping into unseen minefields. I'll forgive her for asking about a child. I'm thankful this woman is unaware she'd deeply offended my mother-in-law. Barb had so many rules about how events should run, how meals should be served, what people were allowed to do in her home. This nice girl tried to be kind, and I'd bet my shirt that Barb had made a point to not let her come back.

"I'm truly sorry for your loss, Addison. Please let Luke know I'm here for him. The whole town treasured Barb, and we grieve with you both," Meg says before heading back to her car.

I watch her leave through the kitchen window. An invisible pressure digs into my neck. The weight of the moment or the resurgence of grief, I can't be sure. Something about Meg twists me up. Why wait so long to come back? Why not ask Barb to return the dish? I thought everyone in Rockside Bay loved her, but I'm not the only one who can read a room. Perhaps I'm not alone in having been wary of my late mother-in-law after all.

Who had Meg seen in the window? Worry wells in my empty belly. The urge to check on Luke pushes me out of the kitchen.

"Good lord, Mom," he's grumbling as I rap my knuckles against the doorframe of the office.

"That bad, babe?" I hope my wan smile is comforting. Seeing *him* is the balm I need.

Luke's broad shoulders slump, making him look smaller than his six-foot stature. He still tries to match my smile. Bless him. "Nothing is organized."

How very Barb. "Not even the file cabinets?"

He shook his head.

"Good thing you're great at deciphering mountains of paperwork?" I try.

Luke's lawyer skills have to help here, even if he's not in his signature black suit, crisp white shirt, and seriously shiny shoes. The tailored maroon zip-up jacket he's in had been a gift from me but is one hundred percent his style.

He lifts a handful of papers and lets them flop back down onto the desk. "I can figure it out, yes, but Ads, this is going to take so much time."

I step behind him and dig my thumbs into his tight traps. He groans.

"Luke, we're a team, right?" I remind him gently.

"This is too much, Ads, especially after everything—"

"I'm doing okay. Let's focus on you and processing this, and when we get back home, we can worry about building our family again." My sincerity almost convinces even me.

Luke pulls my hand forward and presses a kiss to it. "You're too good to me."

"Taking care of each other is what we do." My heart squeezes with the truth of it. He's carried me so much this year. Even after my car accident and the loss, he never once blamed me. Luke took on the sticky emotions for me, and I'd do the same here.

I don't grieve Barb—which slicks my sides with self-disgust—but I can take the weight of Luke's sorrow and help shepherd him through this.

"We could still hire someone to handle the estate," I offer, already expecting his reply.

"My mom would have hated that."

"She wouldn't have wanted you burdened." Whether it's true, I'm not certain.

"I can do this, Ads. With you."

Guess I'm stuck purging this house.

The first day of cleaning out Barb's hoarder mess of the home turned out to be...not that terrible. Focusing on Luke certainly helped, but if I'm being honest, it has more to do with the fact that neither of us is willing to venture up the stairs. The first floor is easy. Barbara had staged each room with a goal. She'd strategically placed mementos of Luke's successes throughout the space, making it easy to center him in conversation, even when he lives more than two thousand miles away in Texas. In the last few years, she did the same thing with items from her charity work, although to a lesser degree. Her deep involvement with the local food bank was the one thing about her that I truly respected, if you don't count raising the man I love. I suppose I should count that more.

The living room holds framed pictures of children I don't know. Sample backpacks for kids' weekend meals rest artfully on a side table. Not a single picture of me. The photo from our wedding day hangs askew on the wall. I'm not in the image. It's Luke and Barb dancing and laughing. She may have had me photoshopped out of the background for all I know. I straighten the frame. Sharp, molten heat bites my finger where it touched the decorative metal. I yank my hand back to my chest, but my finger looks fine upon inspection. Not burned. Not nicked.

Pull yourself together, Addison.

Even with Luke and me tackling the "easy" rooms, my body aches. My muscles bear the strain of fresh stress, like I've taken up Olympic weightlifting. Sure, I'd carried a few books around the room, sorting them into first editions and a donation pile, but standing by my husband's side might have been the most difficult part of the day. Guilt sluices down my neck, scratching a stiletto fingernail over my spine. The shiver that racks my body isn't cold. Quite the opposite, it lights me with fiery regret.

I'd only been eight weeks along when I lost our baby. Just two weeks of even knowing that I was going to be a mom before it was taken away. And yet, those fourteen days meant everything. They'd been packed with hope and dreamy images of Luke's and my future. And then I lost control of my car on the way to the office. I'd been called in to help *on my day off*. There hadn't been water on the road, but the car had skidded into a barrier as though hydroplaning. And with one violent, painful afternoon, it was gone. My doctor said the fetus hadn't been viable and the car accident was a fluke. She said I could get pregnant again easily.

I cough on a bitter laugh. *Easily.* Sure.

A hollowness had settled in my chest back then. This empty space where what could have been resided. A space that remains. One that cracked wider again when that woman asked about our daughter. No matter how many nights I cry or how many times I lament the unfairness of it, Luke carries my pain. He wraps his arms around me each time, as if to contain my sorrow. He wept with me. He bore my loss and his own with such grace. And here I am beside him after he lost his mother. The woman who had raised him is gone, and I have the nerve to be stressed. I need to get my shit together, because I am not going to be that asshole.

We should have gone upstairs to the second-level guest room to sleep last night, but we'd crashed on couches. We'd each stretched out on the light-brown leather sofas in Barb's living room. I refuse to call it the sitting room like she had. My husband had found the perfect streaming radio station, and we'd both fallen asleep listening.

Luke is still sleeping when I wake. The sun is cresting the horizon, but all I can see is captivating fog beyond the window. *Maybe we should make this place into an Airbnb*, I think. Lots of people would pay good money to feel peaceful seclusion here on the edge of Oregon. It's with that thought in mind that I brew my coffee and carefully step onto the back deck. I ease the screen door closed to keep from waking Luke with the wooden clap. I know all too well the exhaustion that comes with loss, and his is so acute.

The air is perfectly crisp. Salt and ozone tangle around me. It's as though I've stepped inside a cloud. I set my coffee on the small bistro table and tug my hoodie a little tighter around me before sitting on one of the two chairs. This is one of the rare spaces in Barb's home that isn't set up for entertaining. And perhaps, the one space that she and I both enjoyed. Because, out here, there is peace; there is tranquility. While gray clouds dance beyond the fence line, I'm in a small bubble where I can view everything objectively. Dew dapples the verdant green grass, and along the back wall is Barb's precious garden. Roses of rich red, deep fuchsias, and the palest pink mingled with dahlias and sunflowers and so many varietals that had no business snuggling together. Somehow my mother-in-law had made it work.

But the best part? Perching atop the wooden fence behind those flowers is a full murder of crows.

The beautiful black birds hop and caw at my arrival. One—and then two—swoop down to the lawn, pecking and chattering. I watch them with delight, and the longer I observe them, the more I realize they're taking me in as well. I lift my coffee mug to them in a silent salute. One, the largest, tilts its head as though it is considering my coffee.

"I don't think caffeine is good for birds," I say, hoping the crow understands.

She bobs her little head. I don't know why I've decided she's female, but she clearly is. She bounces around, edging closer to me. I have to name her.

"Nixie," I say, like a patient parent. And OMG. That's perfect. "Are you looking for snacks?"

I watch the bird, expecting her to, I don't know, ignore me. She is a bird. But crows are supersmart. Maybe I'm projecting, but I need a friend now, and Nixie is going to be it.

Once again, she cants her head. *Okay then.* I slip back into the kitchen to the tote bag full of snacks. I'd like to tell you that I packed the snacks in advance of our flight out here. That would be a lie. I'd stuffed the novelty black bag with a change of clothes as a backup because I will not be caught with lost luggage again. But both Luke and I succumbed to great offers on candy bars and trail mix and seeds, both at the airport and at the car rental station. The drive from Portland to Barb's house is not fast or smooth by any stretch.

I bring the half-empty bag of sunflower seeds back to the deck. My new friend Nixie has not moved. The other birds still gather around Barb's garden, on the fence or the edge of the flower bed.

Is there a set technique for feeding these birds? Tossing seeds for the crows can't be that different from tossing toast out for ducks at a park, right? I pour a handful of salty sunflower seeds into my palm and walk toward the edge of the deck. Nixie stands her ground but lifts her hooked beak like she's sizing me up. Best to stay on the deck then. I fling the seeds out onto the lawn. I have never been good at games that require throwing to a specific location. Skee-Ball, cornhole, that game at carnivals where one chucks a Ping-Pong ball at fishbowls, all not for me. But the seeds scatter over the grass, and Nixie dips her beak to snatch up the treat.

At least I'm getting approval from someone. The intrusive thought breaks through faster than it should. *That is unfair*, I chide myself. I press backward in my chair until the metal slat at my shoulder blades pinches sharply. Regret is bitter in the back of my mouth. I douse it with coffee, but it doesn't purge the taste. *Get your head on right, Addison. It is a new day, and I am here with Luke.*

For Luke.

I gulp down half my coffee. The caffeine is fuel for devising a plan and subverting this mess. We need to map out this house and get to hauling things out to the trash cans. The sooner we complete this cleanout, the sooner we can be home. And that means having

Luke back to myself. It might even mean trying to get pregnant again. We'd planned to, and even had started trying, but then Barb died. Trying to create a new life while mourning the loss of another twisted a dark tangle in my husband's mind. Like a warning bell chimed when he realized we were on the path to building a family when his had been rocked again. I hesitated too, because—and I hate that I think this—a tiny part of me worried I'd open the door to tying our child to Barb's memory forever.

But we both deserve some joy, and perhaps we can find some of it in going through Luke's childhood home together. Barb kept everything. And I do mean *everything*. If I didn't get at least a handful of great Christmas ornaments crafted by elementary-school-aged Luke, then I'd keep all of Barb's bone china. I inhale the chilly air, coughing against the cold. That is how we will navigate through this: mementos.

Luke hip-checks open the door and staggers out onto the deck, hair mussed, coffee gripped tightly in both hands. He drops into the chair next to me, his mug clattering against the bistro table.

"Morning," he grumbles. There aren't any bad morning vibes though, as his hand reaches over and grips my leg. He needs the connection. How many times have I fallen back against his chest on the couch and given away my loneliness? It isn't just the warmth of his palm against me that ignites our bond, it's the way he wiggles my leg back and forth as though moving my body will jog his own brain into action. Moments like these remind me how special it is to have someone who loves you unconditionally.

"You have the most epic bed head right now," I say, unable to contain my laughter.

He presses it down, but there's no embarrassment ruddying his cheeks. "Ah, well, I don't have anywhere to be today."

Luke casts a long look toward the kitchen door. Is he imagining his mother plating cherry Danish on one of her countless crystal platters? *Or a pilfered one from the orchard family.* Maybe I should run to the local bakery and pick up some pre-made breakfast treats.

"How's the coffee?" he asks, attention still focused over my shoulder, at the house.

"Coffee is coffee," I say. Luke's mom surprised me with her coffee maker setup. This lady with, I kid you not, at least fifteen crystal platters for freaking Danish, had a simple Mr. Coffee on her countertop. Everything about this house screamed *bougie*, but when it came to coffee, it was a tin of Folgers in the cabinet and a pot-by-pot situation. It worked for me. Drip coffee and a couple nondairy creamers got the job done.

I'd expected her to upgrade to a French press to appease Luke—he struggles without his daily Americano and preferred beans from specific South American countries—but she'd held steady on the standard appliance.

He says as much. "I wouldn't go that far, but it's drinkable."

Nixie and her friends have flocked back to the fence at the farthest edge of the yard. They must've eaten all the snacks. I grab the small packet of sunflower seeds and pour another allotment into my palm.

Luke's hand closes over mine. His grip is tighter than it should be. "What do you think you're doing?" His tone is harsh, dangerous, as if I am about to slam my open hand on a lit stove burner.

"Excuse me?" I yank my hand from his, spilling the sunflower seeds all over the table and a little bit in my coffee. Great. I don't need caffeine anyway. "What is wrong with you?"

That sleep-mussed softness that wrapped Luke when he sat down evaporates. His gaze hardens the longer he stares at me. His hazel eyes—so like his mother's—sharpen until steel cuts through them.

Through me.

His next words drip slowly, distinctly. "Don't feed them, Addison. Don't encourage them. And don't trust them."

Panic pinches in my chest. That's his courtroom voice. Full of power and edged in darkness.

My husband is hurting, but is he for real? Is this grief or a side effect of being in this house?

I choke back my judgment, but still have to say, "Trust them? They're *birds*."

Luke shoves back from the table, the chair scraping sharply against the freshly stained deck. He stands and sweeps all the spilled seeds into a small pile on the table and scoops them into his palm. It is like he doesn't even want errant sunflower snacks to be available for the crows. Oh, right. His mom had such a beef with these birds. I don't get why my mother-in-law hated them. They're smart, they're beautiful, and they clearly aren't interested in messing with her flowers.

Barb had plenty of quirks, but hating some of the smartest birds in her neighborhood was an exceptionally eccentric one. Luke had placated her. Or so I thought. Did my husband hold the same silly superstition that crows could hold a grudge and exact revenge?

I must be wearing my emotions on my face, because Luke's narrowed gaze eases. His mouth softens. "I'm sorry for grabbing your hand like that." He sits back down, still gripping the sunflower seeds. "You didn't grow up here, but those crows are not your friends."

Ouch. Had he been watching me earlier?

"Is this the thing about your uncle?" I ask. I honestly thought that was a joke. Tension vibrates off Luke. Not exactly the time to dismiss his mom's beliefs.

Luke rolls his shoulders like he can shake off whatever bad vibes have taken over the deck. "I suppose. And I know you're right that they are simply birds, but they attacked my mom nearly every time she gardened. So...often."

"I'm not your mom." Well, that is the most obvious statement I've ever made.

My husband slides down in his chair, almost like he wants us to be eye level. But when his gaze lowers to his clenched fist, the weight of our conversation, of Barb's invisible presence here, and the *overwhelm* are clear.

"I'm sorry." Regret tangles my apology into a whisper.

We sit there together for long minutes. The shushing of the waves stretches between us until a neighbor's lawn mower drones in the distance.

"They took his eye." Luke's voice is reedy, lower than usual.

I cradle my coffee mug, even though the liquid is now tainted with discarded sunflower seeds. "Your uncle?"

He nods solemnly.

Barb had told me the story countless times. Each time getting more irritated when I tried to speed her along by filling in the facts she'd given me the last time.

For the first time, I ask to hear the story, because Luke is in his head. "Tell me what happened."

"You've met my Uncle Stan, right?" Luke pauses and waits for my nod. Then continues. "So back when Stan lived in Rockside Bay, he'd been in real estate."

"Why did he leave?"

Luke shrugs. "Falling-out with Mom."

She ran her own brother out of town? *Interesting.*

"Anyway, Uncle Stan rented out several of the buildings downtown. Mostly retail spaces, but there was one he'd built out for food service."

"Good business here, then," I prompt.

The throbbing vein in Luke's neck is fading the more he talks. "Yes, but he didn't really know much about restaurants. So he sold that space to Paul Abernathy."

Luke's habit of dropping names in conversation leaves me at a loss. "Have I met him?"

"Not Paul, but I think you met his son Tyler a couple years back. Nice guy. Owns a running shoe store." Luke is my context king.

I gesture for him to continue. "So what happened with Paul?"

"Uncle Stan sold Paul the building, and they both went on their merry ways. Until six months later, when Paul did some remodeling for what would become that vegan place we like."

Barb never gave that detail. "We should order from there tonight."

Luke's smile warms me. "That could be good. Anyway, Paul rips up the floorboards and finds mold. He says Stan knew about it and that's why he sold."

"Wouldn't a building inspector catch that before the sale?"

"That's what I said!" He squeezes my leg. "But they must have missed it, because the mold was pervasive. Took almost another six months before Paul could get the place cleaned and approved by the town."

"And this resulted in your uncle losing an eye?" Hard to picture the nice guy at the vegan joint stealing eyeballs.

"The crows clustered at that place. Until the mold. Once Paul sued Uncle Stan, they flew here. Small claims sided with us, and the birds started swooping the next day."

"Isn't that what birds do?" Even in my supportive role, I need to say it.

"My mom swore the Abernathys were in league with the birds. Plying them with food or drugs or who knows what."

"You think Paul drugged or trained crows?" I could take playing along with family legends to a degree, but c'mon.

"What I know is a crow poked its beak right into Uncle Stan's left eye, and then that bird never came back."

Crows chat and hop in the garden. Zero malevolence.

"I can't believe that happened."

"It did," Luke says harshly. He takes his hand from me and cradles it around his coffee mug.

Way to step in it, Addison. "I should have said that differently. I believe you. It's just mind-blowing."

"I'm not here to say how Paul made it happen. I'm just here to tell you that crows can be cruel, and they're dangerous. They hold grudges longer than any lawyer I know." He attempts to smile, but sadness still fills his eyes.

I shouldn't have asked for this story. "I'm so sorry about your uncle," I say softly.

"It was a long time ago." It's the expected reply, but Luke's gaze goes hazy as he stares out at the birds.

Old memories become new in this place. The more we dig, the more it'll come to the surface.

The flock remains perched on the fence. A few appear to be dozing. Nixie's attention is on me, but with a quick bob of her little head, she swoops down onto the other side of the fence. Maybe there are better snacks back there.

"It's such a terrible story. I understand why it hits you so hard, but I promise these crows are simply standing around being beautiful."

"Hardly. They're rats with wings," he mutters.

I don't bother correcting him that he's thinking of pigeons, who *can* be trained and are probably also smarter than he'd give them credit for. Now isn't the time to dig into Barb's—and apparently Luke's—whacked beliefs.

I turn away from the crows, making my body face only Luke. "The only thing that matters to me right now is you. What do you need?"

"To be done here?" He nods slowly, to himself, like he hasn't realized how much this place burdens him.

"Then let's get as much done today as we can. We'll be back home and having a stay-in-our-robes Sunday before you know it."

His smile warms me from nose to toes.

We've been together for nearly a decade, but he has stories to surprise me. Being here will help me know him better. Who he had been in Oregon might not be the same man that I know in Texas. If I can leave this place understanding him better? This trip might not be a total pain.

One thing is certain: It will only make me love him more deeply.

CHAPTER 3

WE COULDN'T CONTINUE AVOIDING THE UPPER LEVELS OF the house. The sooner we face the cluttered corridors above, the sooner we'll be back home. Luke says as much. We walk up the narrow stairs together, Luke avoiding the step that creaks. Plastic storage bins and slumping brown boxes line both sides of the hallway. The path isn't exactly straight, but after the first few steps, light spills into the hallway from an open door. The guest room.

Luke pauses in front of it. "I can go through the guest room real quick so we can sleep here tonight."

I'm not confident anything in this house can be done quickly, but I agree. "It'd be nice to have a room cleaned out for us."

"It wasn't too long ago we were here last. So I'm hoping she didn't add much." He leans into the room and then looks back at me. "The lamps have multiplied."

Laughter bubbles from my chest. "You say that like they've procreated."

"It almost looks like it." He shakes his head. "I'll bring the spare six downstairs, and we can donate them."

Spare six? This is going to be a journey.

Luke lingers.

"What is it?" I nudge.

"Can you do Mom's room?" Sheepishness is odd on Luke but disarms me.

"Whatever you need, I'm here."

His brow furrows. "I just... I can't go in there."

"Don't think on it. I'll handle her room and find keepsakes for you to look at." It was as good a plan as any. Besides, I love that Luke is putting himself first. His heart can't take that room, but there's no question Barb would hate me stepping in here.

Everyone wins.

Luke disappears into the guest room. Even from the hallway, his little bear cub sighs reach me. He makes the plaintive noise when he's not feeling well, and never notices. He's making a space for us, which means it's time for me to do the thing I promised: endure Barb's things in the name of love and kindness.

The boxes my mother-in-law stashed in her hallway crumple at the lower levels, the weight of age and stacked contents smushing the past toward the floor. I sidle through the narrow path at the end of the hallway. Barb's bedroom door is closed, the warm oak framed by aged cardboard and a stack of law review journals that must go back a few decades. The doorknob chills my hand. Ridiculous nerves. I twist it, push inward, and am smacked with the scent of flowers and clean linen. Barb's signature scent. It's so strong, I half expect to see her stroll out from the en suite bathroom and chide me for daring to step into her private space.

This room is more cluttered than most others on the upper levels of the house, but there are signs of life. Plastic bins, tote bags, and luggage tower around me, but Barb's footsteps have worn a small groove in the narrow walkway to her bed. Dresses drape over the tops of piles, and closer to the bathroom door, she'd piled a stack of blankets.

For a home that never came off as cozy, Barb had every type of blanket imaginable. Fleece throws, knit bed blankets, chenilles that would look lovely draped over an armchair, but have instead been sandwiched between heavy shearling options. The air is stale in here, and it isn't just from disuse since Barb's death. I wouldn't be surprised if the HVAC vents were blocked by detritus at this point.

She even hoarded air. A bubble of laughter rises in my chest, popping in a sound loud enough that the walls bounce it back to me.

I clap my hands to my mouth like I can swallow back the noise. Shame pours down my throat. Coughing against the regret doesn't change a thing. Mocking the dead? I should be better than that. I stagger backward, bumping into Barb's bed. My knees give and my rude ass bounces on the extra-firm mattress.

A plastic bin topples to the floor. Dozens and dozens of nail polish bottles clatter on the floor. Reds, purples, blues, pinks, greens, and even black roll toward me. None of them leak.

Silence stretches around me. I stare at the ingredients separated inside the polish bottles. And I wait.

And wait.

And wait.

I don't dare breathe, as though my inhale would somehow rouse Barb's memory and send her son rushing to me.

When my chest burns in a plea for oxygen and there hasn't been a single creak from the old oak floorboards in the hallway, I gulp in a rush of air. The cloying floral scent stings my sinuses.

"Luke?" I say his name so quietly, I doubt if I even spoke.

My husband doesn't pass the portion of the doorway I can see from here. A few breaths later, his heavy steps emanate from the stairs. Carrying a batch of donations? He's trying. I should be doing the same.

In this room, though, Barb's luxe perfume is suffocating. This whole house carries her memory, of course, but this room? It is like needles are jabbing into my back, scraping my neck, and telling me to get the hell out. Probably how Barb felt every time I walked into this house.

I slip off the bed to the floor and gather the small bottles. I count them as I return to them to the bin. Two hundred and forty-eight. Why would a woman who hit the salon every two weeks for a gel manicure have *hundreds* of bottles of nail polish? Goose bumps march across my forearms.

I stand, though the sensation doesn't fully abate, and survey the room. Now that I'm in the center of the room, there's better visibility. A dresser with a vanity mirror presses against one wall. Clutter obscures the mahogany surface with drawers below, but the detailed frame of the mirror affixed to the top is clue enough. Dozens of jewelry boxes are stacked up on the right side of the dresser. The other side has brown cardboard shipping boxes from beauty stores. Unopened. Makeup or skin care or who knows what. My mother-in-law loved to talk about the latest trends, the best brands, but I'd often wonder how she even had time to try everything, much less recommend it. Apparently, the truth is she had time to buy them. Probably. I grab a box from the top. The postage label is nearly two years old. No wonder the packing tape is dusty. It's a surprise it's still sealed.

I reach for the next box but can't make myself grab it. My hands hover, shaking. My hesitation only makes the chips in my purple nail polish more glaring. Barb would hate this. I hate this. Even dead, the woman rattles me.

"Can't even keep your hands presentable."

I spin at the backbiting words. "What the—" I say under my breath. Great. Now I'm hearing Barb's voice in my head.

Barb is very dead. This room is far from empty, but it certainly doesn't hold a single other person. I slowly turn to survey the room as if I'm unaware of those facts.

Alone.

"Luke?" I call. Half wanting to hear he is near me, and half needing to know he wouldn't have said such a crass thing to his wife.

Silence. Of course. Because he is in the guest room making a comfortable place for us to crash. Or he's given up and returned downstairs to dive into his mother's records like he could paperwork his mother's death into logic. And he's always liked that I painted my own nails at home. They don't last as long—or really endure the ten-key life—but the freedom to change them whenever

I liked mattered more to me. Plus, just because you could spend money didn't mean you had to.

I stand still. Swallow. That thought might as well have been spoken in *my* mother's voice. She treasured the belongings she had but would only spend when it mattered. "Keep a rainy-day fund," she'd say. "Keep a second stash that only belongs to you," she made me vow before I married Luke.

Had his mother given him a similar talk? We don't have a prenup, but I could imagine Barb suggesting one.

Barb never spoke negatively about my mom. At least not in front of me. But she also wanted to host, plan, and control any party or celebration that would involve family. She even tried to commandeer my bridal shower. That backfired. My aunts still bought lingerie that made Barb uncomfortable as hell. I didn't want the crotchless panties, but watching Barb squirm had been the ultimate gift.

"You'd probably feel the same way about me having to go through all your unopened packages," I say, as if my mother-in-law is here with me.

I flip off the bed. Just in case I'm truly not alone.

No response. I must have been in my own head too much earlier. The fog remains thick beyond the bedroom window. Forest-green vines frame the view. New sprouts stretch toward the center of the glass. Were we supposed to prune those? It doesn't matter. We won't be here long enough to need to trim hedges, vines, or tend the flower beds.

Right. Empty the room. Empty the house. Get home. That's what I need to be focused on. Not dwelling on the past.

I set the beauty boxes in the hallway unopened. Anything with a postmark more than a year old is getting pitched. No point in wasting my time digging through Barb's expired makeup. There are seven boxes added to the hallway chaos in minutes.

I'm going to be done in no time at this rate.

CHAPTER 4

LUKE RAPS HIS KNUCKLES AGAINST THE DOORFRAME SOME-time later. I am kneeling near the night table with a tissue in one hand and my shoe in the other.

"You going to war over there, Ads?" Humor softens his tone, warms my chest.

"In a matter of speaking." I stick my tongue out in focus, leaning closer to the baseboard I've exposed, and swing the shoe hard.

I lift the sole to reveal zero dead spiders.

"Damn it." I yank a tote bag full of art history books from the wall. The books spill all over the floor. The hardy brown spider scurries forward. Is everyone and everything in this house taunting me?

"Babe, let me." Luke takes the tissue from my hand, ignoring my implement of arachnid destruction, and smushes the spider on the first try.

"Thanks," I mutter.

Luke just nods and takes the tissue to the hall bathroom—though the en suite would have been faster. The toilet flushes, and then he reappears in the doorway. "Are you doing okay up here?"

His skin is more pallid than it was this morning. Sweat dapples his temples. He needs distraction. Probably a better one than a rogue spider.

"It was going well until that little spider kept escaping me."

"He's gone now." Luke tries to smile, but the muscle in his jaw is ticking. He glances back into the hall every few moments; this room—and maybe the lingering scent of his mother—is overwhelming him.

"Thanks for that, but I would have gotten him eventually." I brush the dust from my knees. "I'm making good progress up here, and it'll be easier to tackle those pests once I have more room to work."

"Yeah." He sounds miles away. "Saw the boxes in the hallway. Are those keepers?"

"Trash 'em."

Luke turns toward the stack beyond the door, offense flaring his nostrils. "But they aren't even opened."

"They're expired makeup." Most likely. "Not something we can use or donate."

Luke pulls back, face scrunched. His toes are back behind the threshold again. Outside the bedroom. "How do you know that?"

I tilt my head to the side. "My wheelhouse, honey. I promise I'm going to be careful with your mom's things."

He stares at the spilled stack of books. "You didn't even open them."

"I know what's in a Sephora box."

"She might have reused boxes."

He has to hear he's reaching, right?

"And resealed them?" I say as gently as I can.

Luke shrugs. "If you want, I can go through them—"

I don't let him go there. He might be playing me, but when you're mired in loss, you aren't logical. My detail-oriented man is fixated on the wrong pieces, but that's okay. Normal. I can help him through this.

"I'll take care of all of it." I employ a tone that skates closer to caregiver than I prefer with my partner but gets the job done.

"Really?" His relief is obvious.

"I've got it. Now go. I won't throw anything out without opening it."

"Thanks," he says but doesn't bother hiding his wariness. Perhaps he's too tired to, but it's for the best. I don't want him hiding things from me.

I try not to lie to my husband. It is the type of move that makes for big arguments, bad feelings, and the kind of distance that makes people more roommates than spouses. I want none of that, but I also know what it means to grieve. I haven't been able to shake my own sorrow fully despite the months that have passed.

Luke needed to hear me say I would open every sealed package in his mother's house and carefully collate their contents. And, honestly, I could carefully review the contents of each with enough room. Something Barb's bedroom lacks majorly. Moving those first few boxes into the hallway gives me working space on the dresser. If I could sort all this junk into groups and shove some of this shit out into the hallway, I could get a space to actually open and assess her various pack-ratted goods.

And so I heave eleven NPR tote bags into the hall. Each filled with books. The first floor's built-in bookcases are exquisite. Like "Luke should make me some" kind of gorgeous. Barb could have shelved these there, but they don't carry the same panache as the high-brow selection appropriate for visitor viewing. There isn't a cracked spine on a single paperback here. I should thank "viewers like you" for buying the bags with the primo stitching, but OMG my arms. I cluster the bags in one area; the local used bookstore is about to have a field day.

My box cutter gets a workout as I slice tape strips on packages from luxe department stores. A pair of brand-new loafers are still wrapped in the crisp Dior paper. Barb and I were not the same size in anything—dresses, shoes, ego—but when I shift the box to move to the donation pile, the size flashes at me. *My* size. A chill grips my sternum. This had to have been a mistake. The cognac color is all Barb, but...fuck it. I toe off my sneakers, remove my socks, and slip my feet into the designer duds. Buttery soft, totally cushy, but also structured to make my feet somehow look daintier than they are. I stand and walk the narrow gauntlet paths my mother-in-law had made in her bedroom.

There's a pinch at my shoulder, my nape. I squirm and ignore the bite. These shoes are perfection. A whisper of icy breath kisses my ear. I spin, but there are only the stacks of discards here. I slip the shoes off but tuck them aside for myself.

Cocktail dresses, sheer blouses, red-soled shoes, silk scarves, and jewelry Barb had never worn piles up. I condense the goods into the largest box and chuck the cardboard in a trash pile. She'd bought all this and yet had never purchased me a good gift. Because there's no way she intended those shoes for me. That they're my size is an accident; their color is proof.

Don't be an asshole, I chide myself. I never needed *stuff* from Barb. Respect? Yeah. But, geez, if the lady had been willing to buy all this but not get me a comfy pair of shoes or a good hand lotion or a book I'd love, her need to buy me the same ugly scarf every year is certainly willful. I'd suspected it for years, but finding proof pinched right behind my breastbone. I scrub at my chest in the same clockwise motion to soothe the sharpness.

"Guess we're both assholes, Barb," I mutter to the room.

I'd spent several years making peace with the fact that my mother-in-law hated me. I hadn't even cried the last trip here. It had never been about *me*. Any girl wouldn't be good enough for Luke in her eyes. That was a mom thing, I suppose. Those couple weeks I experienced as a would-be mom before we lost the baby, the two when I knew the little cluster of cells existed, I'd pictured what life could be like. Not just the way our family would come together or how Luke would be a doting father, but how Barb might finally be able to bond with me. We'd both be mothers.

Powerful common ground.

I miscarried before we'd told Barb. Perhaps I'll understand her better after we finally grow our family. The loss still carves my insides, as if reminding me of how I've failed somehow. I couldn't have done anything differently. The doctors assured me. I guess I could have not driven that day. *I hadn't even planned to go in that day. If my boss hadn't called me… No, stop that thinking.* We're going to try again, but Luke's grief at losing his mother remains thick. Loss is a sticky tar pit. Some people can linger at the edges, but for others it consumes. I am Luke's towline. I'll bring him back. We can return to our life together.

After we get this hoarder hell house emptied.

I've been at it for hours, and yet there are still stacks of gift bags and cards and drawers and—oh, hell—the closet. I haven't even really noticed the damned offshoot. A tower of Bloomingdale's brown boxes had been stacked in front of the door. With them cut down, the crystal knob to the closet winks at me. The chaos clustered in front of the doorway must have blocked dust collection too, because the door itself has the brilliant shine of a recent polish. Most of the doors in this house are a farmhouse white. This one, though, boasts the original oak. Stained to keep its warm color vibrant.

I push up from my spot on the floor and shuffle toward the door. It could be the long time sitting, or the dust or exhaustion, but the draw to the door is magnetic. The clear knob is cold beneath my palm. Not like cool because no one has touched it in who knows how long, but like pressing my palm against ice.

I grip the handle tightly and twist. I jerk the door open, bumping the wood into my careful stack of shopping bags. They scatter all over the newly cleared space on the floor. Inside the closet…

More boxes.

Disappointment flicks the back of my skull. I shake it away. This is why we're here. What was I expecting from Barb?

I sigh loudly enough it practically echoes in the walk-in. The other bedrooms in the house have modest closets. Enough room to hang a seasonal wardrobe and a shelf for off-season storage. Barb's, though, extends at least six feet deep. Between the cracks of the box wall at the entrance, I spot a single bar on the back wall where clothes would hang. There might be a coat or two back there, but from here—my admittedly garbage point of view—it appears oddly empty. If there is available space at the back of the closet, why are these boxes flush with the door?

I groan. Hell, why did she need to stack old magazines next to her bed? Who knew why Barb did anything?

I return to the same task I've been toiling at for hours: moving boxes, opening boxes, sorting boxes. My biceps ache. *All the things you bought, Barb, and you couldn't get yourself a hot tub?* At this rate, a pharmacy run for Icy Hot and ibuprofen is imminent.

The boxes in the closet are older. The cardboard gives easily under my hands. I have to hold them from beneath to keep the contents from crashing onto the floor. At least they're light. I peek in the first one: fabric remnants.

Well, if that isn't proof this woman collected random items

simply for the sake of spending money… Barb hadn't been the type to sew her own *anything*.

I plunk the box out in the hallway and return to the room. I should focus on the main area, keep making space, but a flash of gold catches my eye. Beyond the boxes, in the back of the closet, a glimmer demands my attention.

CHAPTER 5

I PULL BOXES—NO BAGS, NO STACKS OF READING MATERIAL or unworn clothing—from the closet in a fever. I don't sort. I don't open more after the first one. Just grab, lift, twist, drop. I swear I care about all of this, about the possibilities of precious memories, about finding gems we can donate. And, well, the fabric remnants are strange enough to pique my curiosity, but it's more than that. More than my obligation to handle this for Luke. There is *something* important hidden in the back of this closet. Certainty chimes in my chest, hardening my resolve.

Grab, lift, twist, drop.

Gold glimmers in the breathing room between the boxes. Every time it flashes at me, it's like a frigid fingernail is clawing straight down my spine. A chill erupts from deep inside me. This is more than a heebie-jeebies goose bump affair. It's like my bones themselves are frozen. Moving forward is the only way to keep the ice from seeping into my marrow. I'm not about to be left frozen in the worse possible place: my dead mother-in-law's bedroom.

And so I shuck boxes faster. Only the cardboard deluge is less overwhelming than expected. In fact, it's almost as though Barb had merely stuffed things here to block the main door. For a hoarder, she'd really dropped the ball on packing her closet. Score one for me?

As I clear the closet, the icy anxiety abates. Boxes don't typically trip my dread alerts, but nothing about this is standard. I take a deep breath, coughing against the stagnant air.

The oak floor is scuffed and dusty but bare in the back half of the closet. I tap my toe on the hardwood, tentative, waiting for a dart to fly at my head or some other terribleness. OMG, would Barb have booby-trapped her best items? The woman had countless hang-ups about her belongings, but trapdoors had been beyond her skill set. Then again, I'd found fabric. Maybe she had been handier than I realized?

My stomach twists with each light step forward. The floor is solid—not so much as a lone creak beneath my weight—and yet dread pours down my throat. The bitter taste is nothing compared to the way it clogs my airway. I gasp. Fear trickles past my sternum and settles in my belly, burning the entire route.

I don't stop. I can't.

A low buzz settles in my ears. If Luke is nearby, I don't know it. I don't hear music from the first floor, or the vines scratching the windowpanes, or even my own heartbeat. Only an unsettling *uhnnn-nnnnnnnnn uhnnnnnnnnn* like an off-kilter fan on its highest setting.

Coats hang from the lone bar on the rear wall. Furs and belted trenches. I shove them to the side. There, thigh height, is a small door.

This is not fucking Narnia. There will be no talking animals on the other side of that gateway.

The door is barely three feet tall. It's the size I expect for a crawl space entry, but Barb's house has a robust attic. There are four panels on the door itself, as though an ornate front door has been shrunken to miniature. Peonies, feathers, ocean waves, and what I can only describe as a medieval tower decorate it. Had Barb picked this design? Who would pay for this type of ornamentation to hide behind clothes and boxes?

I run my fingers over the flowers carved into the white wood. The ridges are neat but smooth. The dainty knob is a brilliant gold. The longer I stare at the handle, the more its shape shifts. It's an orb; it's an oval; it's dripping. I blink once, twice. *It's a normal handle*, I tell myself. But everything about this little door is wrong. Its placement, its careful art, its gilded handle.

And yet.

I have to know what's behind it. Luke grew up in this house. Did his childhood bedroom have a weird little door in the back, too? I could check before bed tonight, but only once I open this one. Because of course I have to open it. I hesitate. Luke probably knows what's here. I should ask. Only I can't make myself turn away.

I move as though encased in molasses. The universe stretches this moment, allowing bitter dread to congeal in my belly and screw with my balance. I squat lower, in a move my former personal trainer would have been proud of. *Ass to grass, Addie.* Kneeling would have been easier, but I refuse to crawl in his mom's house, because even though she's dead, I won't risk letting his mom see that.

I grip the delicate yellow knob. The metal sings against my palm. Hot. Electric. My mind blanks. I forget how to operate a handle… or my mouth…or my lungs. White creeps in the edges of my vision, but I don't let go. Or I can't. I'm not even sure anymore.

Finally, I twist my hand. The zing through my palm, through my brain, is gone. My vision clears, but the heady need to know what the hell Barb would hide in here is as strong as ever. I open the little door. Beyond is an inky darkness. The stale scent of disuse and cedar stuffs my nostrils. Thank god for the cedar.

I peek over my shoulder. The jerky motion has my neck muscles yelping. Barb's bedroom is bright. Diffused sunlight stretches in from the windows. Even sliced by the vines, it illuminates the room. The overhead light—four bulbs beneath a slowly churning fan—add a honey glow. There is no one in the room. Just boxes and bags and stacks of Barb's belongings that are going to a charity.

Okay, Addison, you can do this. Go in the weird door hidden in the back of Barb's closet. Having hyped myself as much as I'm capable of, I suck in a big breath and enter.

I crack my head on the doorframe. That stockpiled breath hisses free. Gritting my teeth changes nothing, but I double down and haul myself the rest of the way through the passage. I exit into darkness. Not the half darkness of late nights in the city. There's no ambient glow softening the experience. It's harsh and disorienting. If not for the golden glow behind me, the cyclone in my chest would have me spun in the wrong direction. I grope the air, stretching, skimming, reaching at anything for contact, for orientation, for a damn light switch.

Thwack. A swear slips from my lips. More air gone. I flip my hand upward, ticking the lights on, and then cradle it to my chest. The sharp cry from my bent fingernail does not ebb. I slip the injury between my lips as though saliva can absolve the sting.

The pair of two-by-fours that hold the switch I've slammed myself into don't match the rest of the house. They aren't ornate like the little door or period perfect like the rest of Barb's house. They are simple, utilitarian. New.

Okay then.

I finally turn, and the pain in my hand is forgotten.

Boxes. All brown cardboard. Miles of them. That has to be an exaggeration. This is a three-story craftsman house, not a sprawling villa. But wherever the back wall is hidden, I can't see it. The uniformity of the room is more than a surprise; it's unnerving.

I step forward. The floor groans—*squishes*?—but nothing shifts. I rise to my full height slowly. My five-foot-two frame rarely has to worry about headroom, but given I already cracked my skull once, precautions are warranted. Only the ceiling stretches far overhead. Where is this place? The ceiling is practically vaulted. Heavy wood beams brace the sides of an A-frame pitch overhead. The lights hang from each beam. Four pendant lights on each. Structured. Precise. Planned.

This is no crawl space. Why has Luke never mentioned this? He must not know, I tell myself. This is Barb's secret, and I've found it. Am in it.

Holy shit.

I exhale, and dust motes dance in the glow before me. The boxes are arranged in neat rows. Text is scrawled on the sides of each box in black marker. I'd placed Barb's unused label maker in the donation pile yesterday. Clearly it had been underutilized.

I approach the first set of stacked cardboard. The heat in the room is near oppressive. Strange. One of my universal grumbles about visiting this house in the winter is how cold it remained. Even in the summertime, it was never hot in Barb's place, while I admit we have different barometers for "hot." Austin has full-on roasting summers, but Luke's hometown has the more consistent rainy and cold vibes that everyone expects on the Oregon coast. The actual attic—should I call it the main attic now? This is an attic, right? A hidden giant closet at the top of the house had to be an attic. Just, I don't know, not connected to the rest of the attic or easily accessible. Though Barb clearly hadn't had trouble.

Sweat clings to my nape. I swipe it.

"You're overthinking this," I tell myself. "They're boxes."

I have to announce this in case they aren't just boxes and Luke pops up in a second telling me not to touch something again.

"Lord. They're just fucking boxes." I'm such an idiot.

I stride to the box wall and begin reading.

Beverly Polson.

Katy Colter.

Kathryn Wall.

Evelyn Caputo.

Meg Haltom.

Ellie Watts.

All names. All *women's* names. One on each box. Had Barb been keeping files on people? My mother-in-law might have been a gossip, but I hadn't thought she'd go full investigation on her friends and neighbors. Was this my mother-in-law's dark secret? She'd amassed burn book files on everyone in Rockside Bay? Maybe she'd stored others' secrets here.

Man, is it terrible that I hope so? I'd take some rude joy in knowing this whole time she'd been untrustworthy among her friends. Had she hosted every party because no one wanted her in their house?

A tiny bubble of laughter slips out. Then another. That dark humor has a way of doubling, tripling. I laugh and laugh until my cheeks ache and tears spill. Better here than in front of Luke. He's managed enough of my tears.

I shuffle the boxes, making new stacks. The second row has more of the same. I settle inside the ring of boxes I've pulled free and tug a container close to my knees. This one is labeled *Cassidy Warren*.

The name tickles my mind, but I don't know why. Like I've heard this name, but the particulars—why, when, or how I'd know her—elude me.

The lid is tucked closed, but the corners are well creased and open easily. Not the first time by a long shot. I wiggle my fingers, half dispensing the anticipation, half ignoring the aches setting into my muscles. Excitement pulls at the edges of my mouth. And I hate the effervescence building in my chest.

I'm here to help Luke. Not gleefully dig through a hidden attic... but I *did* promise him I'd go through every box.

If Barb stored secrets in this space, am I any better than her for wanting to see them too? I pause, resisting the urge to peer inside the box. I'm here to get things done. To solve problems. To be the empathy queen.

I enjoy solving problems, but there's no denying it's a survival skill. Keeping the peace in a crisis flipped me back to the little girl who ran the house. I'll manage the crisis downstairs, but here I'm alone.

And Alone Addison gets to worry about herself. She gets to find a flaw in her too-perfect mother-in-law. The one who had hundreds of guests at her funeral. The one who people told us "held this town together," but whose death resulted in few condolence cards. The one who had a concealed attic packed with secrets. Right now, I need the cheap thrill of opening these boxes.

"I never met your standards, Barb," I say to the room. "But I also don't have a hidden room full of boxes with women's names on them. That's some Miss Havisham shit." I cackle and push up onto my knees. Time to unveil one of Barb's secrets.

I lean over the box, and all that joy evaporates.

What.

The.

Hell.

Deep in the big box are only a handful of things. I lift a small maroon hooded sweatshirt out. Beneath it is a friendship bracelet, the kind with bright beads. Hot pink, white, and neon green. I look straight past it, though, because under that bracelet is a doll. Its porcelain face stares at me, haunting eyes locked on mine. Its gaze tracks me even as I stumble backward.

My best friend in elementary school had an American Girl doll. Samantha, I think. This doll reminds me of it. Only smaller and clearly handmade. This doll's hair is blond and stretches long past the shoulders. It wears a miniature version of the sweatshirt I pulled from the box. Folded notebook pages peek from beneath the doll. I don't touch them.

I don't touch the doll.

I edge closer to the box again, hovering. *It's just a doll.* And a weird collection of, I don't know, belongings? Yet lowering my hand into the box at all ignites a vibration in my sternum. The doll's blue eyes are eerie, the outfit a creepy coincidence, but there's a black object poking from the doll's closed hand. I reach for her. A caterwaul rises in the back of my mind. I still, frozen, though sweat dapples my lower back.

Caw caw caw.

I whirl, seeking the crow announcing itself. The rafters are empty as far as I can see—and I'm not venturing farther in now. But the sound echoes as though the birds from this morning have set up shop beside my eardrums. I heed the lizard-brain warning, and instead of grasping the toy, I pull the box beneath the closest overhead lamp.

A feather. The tiny lifelike doll is gripping a single crow's feather.

My face flashes hot. My teeth chatter.

Nope. Too fucking weird.

Why did Barb have a doll like this in a box? Why did she have it hidden?

Luke's name flies from my mouth. He can't hear me, though. I'm in the hidden attic, and he's probably burrito-wrapped himself in paperwork.

I drop the hoodie back in the box, close it, and haul it back to the small door. The whole time keeping my fingers away from the flaps and chanting *just a doll* in my head like it'll stop my hands from shaking.

The crow cry silences.

I push the box through first. I need to show Luke what I found. Maybe there's a logical answer. He's great at those.

He might know who Cassidy Warren is and why Barb wrote her name on this box.

I crawl through the doorway, banging my knees this time. I close the door behind me and relax at the satisfying click of the latch settling into place.

I zigzag through the half-sorted work in the bedroom and the piles in the hallway, clutching the Cassidy Warren box like if I release it for a second, it'll disappear.

Luke is halfway into a BLT at the kitchen table when I find him. I drop the box on the other end of the table.

"Addison?" Worry creases his brow, but it's the slow way he says my name that tells me how panicked I must appear.

"Sorry," I say on reflex. "I found this box upstairs, and I don't know what to do."

What an understatement.

"Oh." His genuine surprise stings. He's been so good at supporting me. I'm supposed to be the rock this time, but I've forgotten what it is like to have requests for help met with bewilderment.

"It's, um, a doll." How am I to explain this? In the daylight, is this going to look like a normal thing? Preemptive embarrassment twists my hands into fists.

Luke rises and carefully peels back the cardboard flap to open the box.

His upper lip twitches.

"It's nothing." There's an unfamiliar hardness to his voice.

I bite the inside of my cheek. Maybe the doll really is unremarkable in the cool sense of the day. I peer around his arm. The doll is every bit as unnerving here. It's clearly a doll but also looks *too* real. I squirm away but can't escape its gaze.

Luke edges his body between me and the box. "I'll get rid of it."

He snatches it from the table, twisting toward the door. His yelp is the only warning I have to step back before the box thumps onto the floor. Luke flaps his hand, a litany of swears slipping on his breath.

He's hurt himself. Somehow. I should care. I do. It's just...the doll.

Cold blue eyes cut my heart to ribbons. *It's pretend*, I tell myself. A child's toy. And yet the doll is watching me. Like she knows something. Knows me.

It takes me several tries before my voice is solid enough to speak. "Who is Cassidy Warren?"

Luke's shoulders curl forward, but he doesn't speak. He swipes a kitchen towel from the table and shoves the doll back into the box fully. He storms out. The screen door bangs. Moments later, the clap of the trash barrel lid echoes.

He returns quickly, sweaty and gaze focused anywhere but on me.

"Luke," I say his name. I need to understand what is happening. When he finally looks at me, I push. "What the hell was that?"

He has the gall to shrug. "Mom probably had the doll as a gift for someone."

I'd hate to be the recipient. "Right. Cassidy Warren. Her name is on the box."

Luke makes this rough sound deep in the back of his throat. Not an answer.

Fine. I'll ask again: "Do you know who Cassidy Warren is?"

A flush rises on my husband's neck but never reaches his face. His throat bobs. "Sure. Our family has always been close with the Warrens."

I wait for a bigger explanation. A muscle ticks in Luke's jaw.

Finally, he says, "You remember Kim, right?"

His high school sweetheart. Of course I do. She posts on his Facebook damn near weekly. "Sure."

"Cassidy's her little sister."

How big is the age gap there? Kim is at least thirty. The box is old, though. Barb could have gotten this forever ago and then never gifted it. That would track with everything else in this house. Only Luke pitched it like I'd brought a dead rat in here.

"Was your mom in the business of making gifts for your ex's little sisters?" She sure hadn't sent a gift to my sister.

"Oh, um, no," he stumbles. Ruddiness dapples his cheekbones. "We've been at it all day. You must be starving."

Luke doesn't acknowledge his twice-bitten sandwich waiting on the table. Much less the debris of emotional fallout surrounding us.

The need to keep arguing hangs around my neck, but about what? A box and a doll that creeped me out? Luke has earned leeway. "Shower and food would be amazing. Maybe we could find a funny movie to watch later? Something light?"

He nods. "Why don't I pick up some pho for us while you shower?"

Pho is my comfort food. There's a decent little local place for it here, too. It's my go-to need whenever we visit.

"Perfect," I agree. I could save the rest of Barb's bedroom—and whatever else—until tomorrow.

Luke drops his sandwich in the garbage, puts his plate in the sink, and is out the door in less than two minutes.

It isn't until I'm halfway through washing my hair that I remember why Cassidy's name is familiar.

Cassidy Warren is dead.

And has been since she was fourteen. Back when Luke was dating her sister.

CHAPTER 6

DWELLING IS A HOBBY FOR ME THESE DAYS, WHICH MAKES it hard to discern if I'm overthinking a situation. Quiet moments are dangerous. No distractions and too many memories ready to rush to the forefront. A few months ago, Luke had found me in the spare bedroom in our house—our would-be nursery. Just hovering at the entrance. Dried tears leaving tacky traces on my cheeks and splotches at the collar of my shirt. I could picture the chair I would have put near the window, the crib right beside me. The imagined weight of a tiny perfect human in my arms would fill my heart with hope for that fraction of a moment until I remembered that we didn't need to move the bed or the treadmill out of the space. Because I'm not pregnant anymore. The what-if hit me hard when there wasn't a distraction.

I'm better now. Really. I stay busy; that way the overwhelm can't wallop the same way, but I can still picture how it can all go wrong.

A car cutting me off in traffic is more than a mule kick of panic to the chest. It reignites my loss, my grief. Not that I'd even seen the car in front of me when I rolled my small SUV. *That was the problem. You blanked out. Shouldn't have gone to the office on a Sunday. Never should have been in the car. You'd be another person, a better person if you hadn't.* I blinked against the cruel thoughts. There shouldn't have been water on the road. The other vehicle shouldn't have braked so hard. There was no steering out of it. But I still was childless all the same. Grief was etched on my heart.

A quick trip to the grocery store twists me up now. And if I'm alone in the car—and don't tell Luke I admitted this—I imagine what would have happened if the car had hit me. Not like a fatality—I very much want my life—but I think about the trauma and recovery. The broken limbs, the pain, the punishment for the mistake. Physical injuries are like math. There's a finite answer, a clear process to repairing the damage. I can imagine the penance of healing.

Heartache is an art. Your point of view and mine are not the same.

Which is all to say that it's entirely possible that cracking open the Facebook app on my phone to look up my husband's high school sweetheart could very well be normal…if you squinted.

Kim Warren had still not accepted my friend request, but she didn't hide her life. I'd locked my profile down. If I don't know a person, they can see that I exist. That's it. It had been Luke's suggestion—he does the same thing. He doesn't need clients or opposing counsel in his personal business.

Kim is blond, leggy, and has the flawless makeup of an influencer post–beauty tutorial in every photo. I scroll her page like there'd be anything useful here. She's two years older than me—ha!—just like Luke. That makes sense. Her wall gives me more frustration than clues. Plenty of posts to Luke's page, though. Inspirational quotes offering him strength and peace and whatever. The little lone heart underneath each is from Luke. He's being polite, I remind myself.

I try clicking into her "about" section, but the family listed are all older. No Cassidy. Was she too young to have bothered with Facebook? I rarely get hit with a case of the olds, but holy shit.

I could look up her name online. A quick search would tell me if that name was meaningful, right? But Luke had told me it was nothing. He'd told me who Cassidy was, and I might not even be remembering correctly about her dying. Barb buying gifts and withholding them—or even forgetting the purchase, if I am being generous—is completely plausible.

A rotten pit forms in my belly. I pull my foot up onto the kitchen chair, tucking my knee beneath my chin. Cradling my phone in one hand, Kim's perfect profile picture stares at me. I roll my eyes. How could that have been Luke's type at one point? My deep-brown hair curled like it was crouching for a fight in this weather. I'd learned to tame it into an echo of cuteness here, but that level of veneer isn't my style anyway. More reason for Barb's disappointment. *Oh, well.*

Gravel crunches outside. Luke's back. I drop my phone to the table, hot guilt rushing up my throat. I grab a bottle of water from the refrigerator and down half the thing before my husband walks into the house with the white paper takeout bags.

"This was a good call," he says instead of greeting me. Tension still pinches his shoulders in a way that makes him look smaller.

He has enough on his plate without me worrying over either Warren sister. At least for now. The pit of warning hardens and embeds itself in my stomach despite the comfort of my spouse. May the hot broth he's brought me dislodge it.

Luke pulls open the bags and sets the Styrofoam containers out.

"Didn't realize how hungry you were until you left the house?" I say with as much of a breezy tone as I can muster.

"Kind of," he hedges. "I needed to be out of the house for a minute."

At least I wasn't alone in being weirded out by that doll. "Ah, a 'touch grass' situation?"

He shakes his head, like he's disappointed in me, but his sly smile says otherwise. "I didn't go for a hike, Ads."

Maybe he should. I mean, in the legitimate fresh-air way. "We could, you know. I'd be willing to walk the beach in the morning."

"Tempting." He is not the least bit tempted. My man is cracking open some local beer and settling in for some noodle-y goodness. "But I expect we're getting enough of a workout moving Mom's things around here."

"Facts." My shoulders ache, and my head still throbs from my foray into the hidden attic.

I open my soup, and then I realize my water is nearly gone. "Did you pick up a six pack of those?"

I don't mean it to be accusatory, but Luke is the guy who brings ice cream without asking, who picks up my favorite coffee because "the shop is on the way."

"Oh, shit. I'm so sorry." He scrambles out of his chair and gets me a cold one and one of his mom's fancy pilsner glasses. "Here, babe."

"It's really okay. I just could use a little alcohol to shake the stress off today."

Luke shakes his head. "Of course. Of course. Of course," he over apologizes, which only sparks a fresh twinge of guilt for questioning him. Great. "You're doing amazing. You know I couldn't do this without you?"

I do know that. "You'd manage, but I'm glad that I can help you with this."

"What did I do to get a girl like you?" He taps the neck of his beer bottle to mine.

My beer foams over, but Luke is ready with a paper towel.

"You pretended that you liked concert hopping on Fifth Street." Humor softens my heart, and his, I hope. Our first date was perfect in that Luke did whatever it took to make me smile. It'd been the week leading up to the Austin City Limits festival. I'd lamented that the tickets were sold out, but lots of smaller bands filled the clubs downtown. Luke picked one that he thought I'd like and took me.

"I liked it!" he protests now.

I incline my head toward him, seeing straight through him. "You asked where the chairs were."

He ducks his head. "Sure. I would have liked it more without the standing."

"And?" I prompt.

"And I would have liked to take you home earlier than three a.m."

"You wanted a shorter date? Imagine that, Mr. Lowe. You'd have missed out on that time with me." I fake clutching pearls, spilling a little pho in the process.

"I didn't say taking you to *your* home." Luke did that devilish eyebrow thing that had to be a trick they taught guys in hot guy boot camp.

Dinner is...nice. Luke is charming, sweet, present. Yet I can't fully relax. I laugh at his jokes and easily banter about how we should have packed robes to at least have a semblance of our normal Sunday this week, but I can't shake the trickle of doubt slipping down behind my right ear. The longer we sit at the kitchen table, in fact, the louder it whispers to me. I glance toward the back door. Eat a little. Look over there again. Nod along with Luke's story. Check the door again.

"Is there something out there I should be worried about?" he asks, twisting in his chair to look at the same door I'm watching like it's plotting to rob me.

It's one of those with a window in the top half. A gauzy cream fabric swoops over the glass, providing the illusion of privacy.

"It's nothing." I answer so fast, he shouldn't believe me.

"You good?" It isn't the right response. I try to remember a time—any time—when Luke didn't intuit what was going on with me. This is new territory for us, but I can't expect him to be normal right now.

Nothing about this is normal. Nothing has been normal for months.

"I'll be fine." Even as the words tumble from my mouth, the tartness of the lie stings my lip. The sense of being watched, sized up for an attack, presses more firmly.

I take a hearty swig from my IPA. That unnerving sense has lingered from the freaky doll. The one bought for a dead girl? Was the eerie need to check the door coming from her?

I set the bottle down harder than necessary, earning a small instinctive grumble from my spouse. Drowning demons isn't my style, nor is imagining ghosts.

I focus on the soft hazel of my husband's eyes, his slightly disheveled hair, the burgeoning stubble peeking at his jawline. This is why I'm here. Him. Luke.

"I'm pretty sure I'm the one who's supposed to be asking how you're doing, babe." My teasing lilt earns a smile. Good.

Luke waves a hand in a wide circle over our heads. "I'll be fine when this is taken care of."

He won't, but I understand the need to feel that way. Tasks help. Step one to proper compartmentalization. Not that I want him stuffing his feelings in boxes. One of us could be good at that—*hi, it's me*—and one of us should have a healthy relationship with processing feelings.

"You made it through the guest room quickly." I'm happy to have a space carved out for us already.

He nods. "Mom didn't keep much in there."

Since when? Every nook in this house is packed with *stuff.* "That's unexpected, but I'm glad for it."

"I think she wanted us to visit more." Luke pokes his chopsticks at the noodles like they owe him money. "The room was mostly ready for us."

I place my hand on his, stilling the noodle damage. "I'm glad we're here together. I know she'd be proud of you and honored that you're taking such care of her estate."

Even if Barb would have hated the bonus of her daughter-in-law being here.

Luke kisses the back of my hand. "I love you, Addison."

I blush like it's the first time hearing those words. We return to eating, but the silence in the house scratches at me.

"Is it strange to go through her paperwork?" I ask. He'd been in the office the majority of the day.

"No." He slurps another bite of food and then continues. "I reviewed most of the contracts for her before...yeah, before."

Oh, I know. Barb loved to call at 10:00 p.m. and ask Luke to read through a forty-five-page legal document for her. Buying property. Selling assets to a museum. Whatever. I never asked for details, because the less I was in Barb's business, the better.

A tiny cough of a laugh escapes my lips. I clap my hand over my mouth like it can truly act as a sound barrier.

Luke's eyes flare white, and his hurt hits me solidly in the chest.

"Sorry sorry sorry," I sputter. "I just realized that I'm now also reviewing her things, and I never thought I'd be in that situation."

He nods slowly, leaning back into his chair. "Yeah. She would have..."

He isn't going to say it. I will. "I wouldn't have been her first choice for going through the house."

"No, but you're my first pick. Always, Addie." He stretches his hand toward me on the table.

I take it. Squeeze it. "And you're mine."

We sit there for a long moment. Ignoring our food and drink. Ignoring the chittering animals outside. Lingering on the moment of connection, of support. There is comfort in knowing we are both surviving together. His grief and maybe mine too. Still. I pull myself up to my full height, inhaling along the way like the air can bolster me. I'll make sure he gets through the painful journey of emptying his mother's house. He'll keep me from losing my shit here, and when we get back home, we can go back to taking turns catering to one another.

"Mom's office is overwhelming, if I'm fully disclosing," he says like this admission is revelatory. His shoulders finally ease. "But I want to get the office review complete so I can speak with the estate attorneys and keep everything on track for them."

That is fair. I create plans, focus on the numbers, the math of how to solve a problem. Luke finding comfort in contracts and clauses makes sense.

He pushes his takeout container away. I resist asking if he is going to eat the leftovers tomorrow. He's still got half a bowl.

"Your pho not great?" Mine is bonkers delicious.

"Same as always. I'm just not that hungry." He rises and opens another beer. So, thirsty then.

I shake off the thought. He's mourning. Had I wanted to eat after the miscarriage? No. Not for like a month. Luke was the one there with subtle nudges like, "made you a grilled cheese" and "Tuesdays are now hot-fudge sundae days."

This house is messing with my mind. Maybe I need to get outside too. Only now it's dark, and I don't know anyone here other than Luke, and he's already stretching like bedtime is imminent.

Luke reads me well though. He's a morning-shower kind of person, but he claims he needs to "wash off the day." A quick shower will rally him to stay awake with me. This leaves me in the kitchen with our trash and not much to do. *Unless you count a houseful of junk to organize.*

Being alone in this kitchen is strange. It's not that it had never fallen quiet, but Barb had never let a person linger in her kitchen solo. If I pulled open the pantry door, I would half expect her to bustle in behind me with a "I'll handle that, Addison," my name curdled milk on her tongue. But no one rushes in here now. I pitch our take-out containers into the garbage bin she kept there. The cupboard is already stripped to its bones. Aluminum foil—for baking, never storage at Barb's—and freezer bags. Ceramic storage containers nest in the back, their lids leaning on the side. We should wash them. Who knows how long they've been stored here, and I *am* a leftovers person.

I carry them to the sink. I plan to rinse them, but when I lift the first bowl, twin black feathers are pressed to the center of the second one. *Crash!* I drop the offending white bowls like they've burned me. The larger one breaks.

They are feathers, *Addie. Get yourself together.*

No matter how much I say that to myself, my stomach continues to twist tighter. Except now I've made more work for us. Broken ceramic in the sink would stymie the whole "relax together" event I'm hoping for. I tug the trash can over and toss the pieces of pottery inside. My thumb grazes one of the feathers, and the chill that shoots through me is bone-deep...and totally in my head.

I shake it off, tie the bag shut, and haul it outside. The garbage bins out back are already teeming with refuse. All in the name of progress. I turn to hustle back into the house, but the soft sweetness of flowers gives me pause. Barb's garden is across the yard. A pale moon peeks from behind blotchy clouds, bathing the yard in grays so appropriate for coastal vibes. It's the kind of snapshot appeal that draws people to this place.

Light flashes from the garden. I still. It flickers again. Is it a sputtering solar light? We'd put those along the path in our yard, and on gloomy days, they are never as bright as I like. I start again, nearly to the steps up to the deck, when the light catches me again. I can't explain it, but it's so much like my sister flicking her little makeup mirror to distract me back when I was ten and she was annoying. We'd thrown away so many items today. A shiny something could have blown into the garden. I should go pick it up.

My heart rate eases as I move toward the dahlias and lilies now cast black. My fingertips tingle. Smooth paver stones line the bed. I drop to my haunches and lean in toward the garden, no longer getting a brilliant flash but still needing to know exactly what it was. I push petals and leaves aside, then scuttle to the right and do it again. The garden didn't seem dense this morning, but in the post-twilight hours it takes a new tone.

Flash. There. A tiny glimmer peeks from behind feathery leaves. I grasp it without thought. Like it couldn't be sharp. Like it couldn't be filthy. Like it couldn't be dangerous.

Like I don't know what I'm doing.

It's none of those things but also more discomforting. A tiny toy arm is in my hand. A doll part. My skin goes numb beneath the plastic. Delicate play jewelry gems are strung around the wrist. They'd waved at me. My stomach flips. I grip the little arm and empty my dinner onto the grass.

Bitterness coats my mouth. My knuckles ache, but the rest of my hand might as well have disappeared. There's no sensation of the plastic piece in my palm. How the hell is there a part of a doll out here? I've been to this house dozens of times and never seen a hint of my mother-in-law's interest in children's toys—unless they were Luke's. And he was a Hot Wheels kid. No, that doll I'd found had been made for a dead girl.

A doll that Barb had hidden away in her attic. One that my husband couldn't have thrown away faster. He pretended Cassidy Warren's name was a mere echo, but standing in the dark garden with a part of a child's plaything, a piece of me broke. What happened in this house?

Was it her toy reaching up at me, or were there more?

I redouble my search efforts in the dirt. I pull my phone free and toggle on the flashlight, but there isn't another part of a doll here. Only this lone forearm and hand, yellowing with age and marred by the dark silt.

I turn toward the house slowly. The lights in the kitchen windows glow brightly. Dark vines squeeze the upper levels. A soft hum fills my ears the longer I stare. I blink and blink until I finally look away. The trash bins aren't visible from here. How did this piece of a doll get all the way over here? I've been ready for secrets—drinking problems, high school love letters, a metric ton of commemorative plates. But not this. Not gifts for a dead girl. Not doll parts in the fucking dirt. What did Luke know? Had dread not welled in his heart when he looked at that doll? Hell, was this arm from the one for Cassidy?

The longer I held it, the more sweat pooled at the small of my back. The more I wanted to squirm. I should walk it back to the garbage, but what if it finds its way back?

I swear I'm not a litterer, but I shoot darting looks over each of my shoulders and then chuck that doll arm right over the fence.

If you find lone doll parts in your dead mother-in-law's garden, you're allowed to throw that shit off the property.

CHAPTER 7

I TRY TO EXPUNGE THE NAME CASSIDY WARREN FROM MY mind, but finding a piece of a doll has reignited a worry in my gut. The strangeness of it all scales my bones like poison ivy. Not thinking about that box and its contents is harder than I expect. The image of the sweatshirt replicated in miniature, then the yellowed plastic arm outside rise in my mind, and a shiver ripples down my body. I clench my jaw, thankful Luke's back is to me.

I'm here to solve problems, not be one.

Luke pulls a silver tin from the keep pile we're amassing in the dining room. It's a dominoes set. The kind with the little multicolored trains. Barb loved to bust that game out at her smaller gatherings. I have not played in years.

"Only enough room for six players, unfortunately," Barb would say, the glimmer in her eye giving away her pleasure.

Luke is already opening the lid. "Are you up for dominoes?"

I'm being invited to play. Finally. At Barb's house, no less.

I'll take the distraction from remembering the chills down my spine from earlier. I glance at the china cabinet and the stiff armchairs at the end of the room. I scope the bar cart too. The decanter is half full of amber liquid. No doll parts here. I need to let it go. Luke is supposed to be my focus. I cling to the thought and settle at the table kitty-corner to him.

A sharpness strikes my neck. Like the quick jab of a needle. I pretend not to feel it, but then it happens again. I skim my fingertips over the spot, hovering at the top of my spine. There's no bump, no sticky blood, not even a tiny mosquito to blame.

Ceramic tiles clunk on the polished wood. I flinch, but Luke doesn't notice. A smile tugs at his mouth. We don't even own this game. Oh. I guess we do now. I had no idea it would bring him this much joy.

I grew up in a hand-me-down Yahtzee house. The red cardboard box had been worn at the corners to reveal the brown layers beneath. Original barrels for the dice had been replaced with cups from Happy Meals. What type of toys did kids get these days? Not place settings. Someday I'd find out, I supposed, though Luke and I hadn't been drive-through people since his grad school days.

"How long has your family had this game?" After I say it, I worry about breaking his reverie. Good compartmentalization requires ignoring the feelings we've sealed away.

But Luke's smile widens. "You know, I honestly don't know." The single-breath chuckle that escapes him is warm, comfortable, like I've unlocked something special. Thank god.

"It's always just been a part of get-togethers?" I prompt, needing this distraction too. The needling at my neck starts up again. I shift in my seat. It's as though the sensation is coming from overhead. Like that attic is tracking me. *What else is in that hidden room?* I blink rapidly, flushing the ridiculous thought.

"You know we get it out at holidays." His delight dims. Is he thinking about how he had to offer to play as a team every time?

I pivot away from the sadness. "Was that the case even as a kid? No wonder you're so good at it!"

He sets up the game. "Just luck of the draw," he says like he did after he won every Thanksgiving we spent here.

"If I recall, you get lucky a lot." I mean the game, but a snicker slips out.

"Mrs. Lowe, are you propositioning me?" Humor dapples his cheeks. I love it.

But not in his mom's house. "First I have to see if I can kick your ass with a pattern of dots."

Luke laughs now too, the sound honey thick and just as sweet. "You think about your strategy, and I'll grab us beers."

"I thought this was about luck," I call to his retreating back.

Yahtzee is a luck game. You can trust dice to be equal opportunity. I expect this is why Luke would always be a blackjack guy at a casino, and I'd be ready to win or lose quickly at a craps table. Or at least a younger version of me would have been. Now I play cards for a bit before I start scrolling on my phone for a good show with available tickets.

I've had enough of trusting a good time to the fates in my life.

The family Yahtzee game now lives at my sister's house. That game of luck had been through three owners before my aunt gifted it to us on a camping trip. The smooth metal container for the dominoes game before me gives no hints to its past. There aren't any random marker doodles on the side, no creases from the time my sister Mallory stumbled over discarded jelly shoes and toppled onto the lid. The dominoes box hides its secrets. It remains polished, stalwart, presentable. How very Barb.

Okay, and maybe a little Luke, but he couldn't not have a flavor of that, given he grew up in *this* place.

Does he know about the weird attic space? Had he recognized the doll? Would he be surprised there was an arm plunked in Barb's garden like a decorative gnome? The questions fill my mouth, but then he plops down next to me looking happy for the first time in days. I swallow the sharp taste. I can't steal that. He deserves the reprieve. He's given me so many.

"What color train do you want?" he asks as he passes me my drink. He answers for me: "Yellow."

I accept the little train he hands me. It's cute and sunny. I chug it across the table until Luke shakes his head at me.

"You give a girl a train, she's going to test the locomotive's power."

"I don't think that's a standard thing." He shakes his head again, all amusement.

"Good thing you picked the weird girl." A spike slams into my back, sharp, cutting. I leap to my feet, a tiny cry squeaking free.

"Hun?" Luke might be giving me the wild eyes. I don't know. I'm busy wheeling around, hand held high like I'd slap someone away. But there's no one behind me. There's no one in this house aside from me and my grieving husband.

I roll my shoulders, but the echo of the pain radiates throughout my body.

"Addison?" Luke squeezes out my name. Enough to cut through my panic.

I lower myself slowly into my chair, as if moving like molasses will somehow conceal how rattled I am. My hands shake; I slip them beneath my thighs.

"Sorry." I wish that one word could carry more power. There are times when the admission hits like an anvil. This is not one of those times. There's no explanation in the breath of apology.

"What just happened?" Luke isn't looking at me. Not really. His gaze lifts to the ceiling behind me, above me, and then back down. *He knows about that room.* No. It doesn't matter.

"Just had a really sharp shiver." The reply isn't true, but my embarrassment is.

"A shiver made you jump from your chair?" He raises his brow. It's a move that can really punch people during his contract negotiations. It's the "should I drag you on the carpet, or do you want to admit it" face, and I do not care for him using it on me one bit.

"Stow the look, Lowe."

Humor softens him. "Fair enough, but seriously, Addie, what's going on?"

Do I tell him his mom's house is nightmare fuel, and no one would think finding a box with a dead girl's name on it is normal? No. I can be honest-ish though. "I'm still thinking about the doll—"

"Let it go, Addison." His sharp tone returns, and once again he's being weird about the doll.

I reel back. "You asked."

His sigh ruffles the little black napkin he placed beneath his drink. "I did. Sorry."

He doesn't have the bandwidth for this, but he'd hate me lying even more. "You were weird about it..."

"I overreacted. Anything related to that time in my life is hard, and I'm not at my best right now."

That time in his life? "Thought you loved high school," I lightened my tone. This is a safe space. Well, *I* am a safe space. This house is another thing altogether.

The corner of his mouth ticks up. "I like my life now much better. Thank you. Now, are you sure you're okay?" Fatigue tugs at the corners of his eyes.

"I'll be fine. It truly was a chill. My nerves are a little on edge right now."

He nods knowingly.

I do not correct him on how little he knows.

"You know I really appreciate you doing this with me, for me, right?"

"I would do anything for you." The reply is automatic. Fervent. True.

"And I you." He laces our fingers together, and we stay locked like that while he studies me. There isn't a sexy undercurrent to the way he surveys my body—it's like he's looking for damage. Joke's on him; I keep all of that on the inside in a steel lockbox.

"We can do this, Luke," I say, moving back to the more comfortable caretaker role.

He nods, the consternation pulling his eyebrows together dissipating until his gaze fills with what almost looks like relief.

"It really is going well, and I'm so happy you've already found mementos to bring home with us." I don't want Barb's shit in my home, but I do want my husband to have good memories.

For all her faults, Barb had been sentimental for anything Luke related. Every track meet ribbon, every piano recital program. She'd kept them all.

"It's been therapeutic," he agrees, the words distant. Like we are holding hands but mouthing words on opposite sides of a pane of glass.

I grip his hand tighter, determined to restore our connection. Pull us closer. Back to normal.

Not that anything about this situation is normal.

A series of soft raps against the back door breaks the spell.

"I'll go check that." I release his hand and push away from our labyrinthine domino layout.

"It's nothing." Luke waves it off. "Stay."

The sound doesn't repeat, and I pause, waiting for another knock.

"Addie, it's fine. Just the wind."

They must have special Pacific Northwest wind. I try to hide the thought from reflecting on my face.

"We'll be back in Austin in two days, tops. We can do this, my beautiful girl." Luke's playfulness, his hope are every bit the man I married, the man I knew. Yet, he isn't looking at me. His attention is over my shoulder, as if he can see more behind me than I want him to.

I nod and rejoin the table. "I'm sure you're right."

"We should get some sleep." He throws back what's left of his beer and then meticulously sorts the dominoes by number to place back in the tin. I try to help, but Luke brushes my hands away.

Hurt burns behind my eyes, but Luke's attention is focused on the tiles. He doesn't mean to dismiss me, but that's what happens here. I'm not allowed to touch. I'm not supposed to speak my mind. I'm cut out. I clench my jaw. Is this like the office? Something that is only for him and his mom? What keepsakes has he already found, has he not yet shared with me? What is it with this house and secrets?

I try to bury the thought, but tears are welling. I need out of here. "I'll clean the kitchen and then meet you upstairs."

Luke nods, still focused on the game. For the best. If he sees me crying, it'll make it all worse.

I rinse our utensils in the deep basin sink, letting myself cry while the water runs. The rote task should still my mind, but even selecting a dishcloth from Barb's mountain of linens ignites my ire. My tears dry. We aren't getting out of this house in two days. My super-plush bed at home probably misses me. The only way to expedite our exit would be to get Luke to help with more than the office.

Guilt sloshes in my stomach, my demons swimming in the alcohol I'd poured in it. I'd come here to handle this. I could—would—handle it. The lingering sadness rattling in my bones would still be there next week, next month. The wave of loneliness cresting with Luke stepping away is an easy fix. Getting home would cure it.

This house is merely a math problem I need to find the formula to solve. I mentally tally the number of rooms upstairs. Allocating equal time for each won't be accurate. But maybe I can give each one hour, and shove all the unopened boxes and obvious garbage into the hallway, pitch it, and then return to the rooms for a second round with more space?

I make a mental note to call the garbage service to see about extra pickups or their dump policy.

The floor behind me creaks. I drop the damp cloth and turn, the corner of my mouth already tightening in preparation to tease my husband about startling me.

Only he's not there.

No one is.

Scraaaaaaaaaaaape. Clack clack. Skrittttch.

I freeze. The sound shears the air, cutting into the room from the window to my left. The one next to the pantry door. This room is elevated enough that no person could be standing outside the window. At least not without a ladder.

I close my eyes. *You are alone. You are safe. You control your body and your reactions. You can do this.* The mantra I've used for the last six months steadies my racing heart, but only until the skittering, scraping sound shocks the room yet again.

Whirling on a window like I'm ready to rip off hoop earrings in a bar is not my finest moment, but it's that or break down in tears. And I'm not supposed to be the one crying anymore.

A thick green vine snakes across the panes. Or at least in the daylight, it'd be green. Now the plant clings to the window like a wicked serpent covered in poisonous spikes. But it is not that, I remind myself. It's a plant, and the stupid wind is powering it to creep me out.

Bedtime is the answer. Lying next to my husband and shutting my brain off can cure my jumpiness. I'm almost out of the kitchen when I catch Barb's visage in my periphery. Her face in that window. I stumble back, cracking my hip on the kitchen table. I clap a hand against the future bruise and spin to face my mother-in-law.

But she's dead. And gone. And I'm standing in a kitchen staring at nothing. No vine. No face.

FML. Tomorrow I'm speed purging this place. The sooner I get rid of Barb's garbage, the sooner I can quit losing my shit.

If only it were so simple.

CHAPTER 8

THAT NIGHT I DREAM OF A TEENAGE GIRL. HER LONG BLOND hair whips over her face from where she stands on the craggy beach. I don't know her, but in the same breath I do. I'm not this girl, but I also am in the way that only makes sense in dreams.

I wouldn't have walked barefoot on the rocks, even in my youth, but I am trapped in her body and rocked by the fear billowing from her pores. She clings to a golden rod. The light pulses enough to push the foggy clouds away.

Then the light ebbs, illuminating only the girl.

Only me.

The light is now in my hand, nails painted scarlet. A friendship bracelet encircles my wrist. Hot pink. Neon green.

Why is it all so familiar? *Because dreams, Addison.*

Thunder snaps through the air. Rocks tumble from the cliffs. The ground roils beneath my bare feet, rocks cutting my soles. I drop the golden light.

The dream dips to obsidian. At my feet though, a lone flame flickers. Beside it is a tiny doll in a maroon sweatshirt. The doll from the box I'd found.

Cassidy Warren.

I wake slicked with sweat and with a dead girl's name on my lips.

I should get Luke up. A ripple of panic skates over my damp skin, and I reach for him instinctively. My palm slides across his chest. His soft snore stutters. I inhale a shaky breath. The guest bedroom is frigid, and the cold air burns my lungs. Luke's forearm is flopped over his face, like he's hiding even in sleep.

He's the one in crisis. Clenching my jaw until my back teeth whine dulls my panic, but my guilt quickly fills the opening. He'd evaded my questions about Cassidy last night. She looked *just like the doll.* I hadn't given a second thought to the bracelet before. I slide off my side of the bed, crumpling to the cold floor. The bracelet had been on the tiny arm I'd found outside. Just like the one I'd found in the box in the attic.

How had I seen Cassidy Warren in my sleep? I'd never met the girl, but my heart broke for her. For her family. For her mother. Why had Barb kept these things? What is Luke holding back about it?

His grief, my conscious provides. The man needs time to process.

I tell myself this is the only reason I don't wake my husband, why I don't ask about Cassidy Warren again right now.

But when I stand, the pressure of this place—to be perfect, to be refined, to belong here—scrubs my skin like sandpaper.

You don't get to control this, Barb.

I tug on a pair of joggers and kneel next to our open suitcase on the floor. It takes longer than it should to free a fleece zip-up. I yank it on and head out the door, being sure to close the bedroom door carefully. Not so much as a snick of the latch.

If Luke sees me like this—sweaty and wide-eyed—he's going to worry. And it's clear he's not ready for that again.

Hell, I didn't like him doing it before. The first time he'd brought me a cold compress after a crying jag, I'd gotten up in the middle of the night to mop the floors. As though it evened the scales. I handle my business. My life has structure and plans, and they make emotions manageable. We'd planned the pregnancy. Luke made partner, giving us added stability. My solid schedule at the accounting firm would ease me toward motherhood easily. As long as I didn't give birth right before tax filing season. I should have been picking out furniture and little mommy-and-me outfits. The next phase of my life is supposed to be now.

But I'd flipped my fucking car, and now I am in a holding pattern. Future stolen and left standing in Luke's past. The thought sears my mind like it's not my own. Cruel and cutting. This atrocious house is scraping my fears free, but I *do* have a plan. Delayed plans are not forgotten ones, I tell myself.

I'm going to Barb's bedroom of my own volition. If worry about Cassidy Warren is so wedged in my mind that I'm dreaming of her, then I need to douse it with some old-fashioned logic. Shadows cling to the hallway. I keep my head low and hurry along the narrow path we've excavated toward the main bedroom. The door is open, and I flip the switch, bathing all my remaining work in pale-yellow light.

I trip over totes and what looks like an early 1990s Caboodle—do they even still make those?—but make it to the closet with minimal swearing. The door doesn't pulse or shimmer. The art carved into the wood is merely decorative. The wave isn't truly cresting. It's all fine, I assure myself.

There are no dolls or their lost limbs anywhere in the closet. I triple-check.

The door opens without a sound. No whine. No creak. No whisper of movement. Inside is...nothing?

There are no boxes inside the attic. I reach inside, and my fingers graze a wooden wall. Dust litters the narrow inlet. A crawl space. Luke had said that's all it was, but... I blink. No boxes.

My heart thunders in my ears. This can't be happening. Every box vanishing? My brain sputters that *it doesn't work that way*, but my youth says it does. I still remember the time when we were living in an apartment—before Grandma let my mom take over the family home—and when I came home from school, the whole place was empty. Not just no one home, but furniture gone. My toys, my bed, my life had been removed while I'd been at school.

My soul tumbles back to that moment. The fear, the sense of loss, of being left behind dumps over my head, the sticky emotions splattering on the floor around me, splashing up on my shins, scalding my skin.

I close my eyes and grit my teeth. I'm in Oregon. With Luke. We want this house to be empty.

I slam my hand forward, clapping it against the warm wood. Those boxes mattered. The ache in my bones, the dream, all of it say they matter. My eyes burn. *They can't just be gone.*

I blink again.

More nothing. But I'd carried a box down from here. I'd found the doll. And there had been dozens, maybe hundreds of boxes in that room. I beat my palm against the wall, like it'll change anything.

What is this house doing to me?

"It was here." I want to convince myself. Because I'm the one who has it together. Now. I'm the one who is supposed to be aware. I cradle my head in my hands. "I actually thought I'd seen Cassidy. My head is playing tricks. Barb would have loved that."

I exhale hard and pull my damp hands away from my eyes. A cedar breeze brushes my cheeks. When I stare forward, the boxes are back.

Rows and rows of them.

Stacked to the ceiling.

Stretching back and back and back.

The names on the boxes blur with my tears, but they're here. I crawl through the small door and pat my hand on box after box.

"What is this place?" I wonder aloud.

The cardboard doesn't answer.

I grab the nearest box and take it with me. I need caffeine to deal with this, but also proof.

I reach the second-floor landing, the cold floor chastising me for not bringing bulky hiking socks. Why couldn't Barb have put a thermostat upstairs? My toes catch on something rough, sticky, thick, and I fly forward. My hip crashes into the narrow accent table beneath the window. The box from the attic tumbles. My palms catch my weight before my face can plow into the worn rug. Wood and metal clatter around me. My hip screams, my toes are throbbing, and I can only clench my teeth and curse a dead woman's house.

I shift to my butt. I haven't flipped on the hallway lights, but diffused gray moonlight is filtering through the window. Just enough to see the fat vine stretching across the floor.

I'm not a green thumb, which should make me ideal for making these vines die a quick death, but I will hand this task over to Luke today. He needs a more mindful task than paperwork. Yard work could be meditative, right? Perhaps he can deal with rogue toy parts this time.

I kick the vine, but it has the weight of heavy-duty cables and bounces against my foot. The gummy sensation gives me a full-body ick.

I need coffee to survive this. The box I'd pulled from the hidden space upstairs waits in a heap at the bottom of the steps, the sealed bottom up in the air. Small pieces of porcelain litter the edge of the landing. I rise, gather bits of the broken doll, and walk down the stairs. Slowly this time.

The banged-up cardboard's contents are heaped beneath it. Chunks of ceramic are tangled in locks of brown hair, each curled with that perfect Hollywood bounce and secured with a barrette. A white knee-high stocking lies atop the mess. A green eye watches me from where it'd rolled across the room. *Guess those are glass.* The shiver that steals my senses doesn't abate until all the bits are shoved back in the box with the flaps closed.

Am I going to dream of this girl, too?

I roll my shoulders and try to rally. I turn the box, ignoring the sharp pinch at the back of my neck. The ink is lighter, but Kathryn Wall's name is clear enough.

Not Cassidy Warren. Not the dead girl I dreamed of.

Get it together, Addie. You're in better control than this, I scold myself.

Am I though? Being inside this place is twisting my insides. I need out. Even if for just a moment. I carefully traverse up the stairs and back down again, now with my sneakers on and double knotted.

I write a quick note on the small notepad affixed to the refrigerator. The sun hasn't woken yet, but there's no accounting for when Luke might. I drop the broken doll and her box in the overfull trash bin and tug it out to the end of the drive.

I'm on the beach in five minutes, and the ocean's heavy sigh is my own. Salty air fills my lungs, and it's energizing. There's more than the obscene amount of *stuff* in Barb's house that makes it suffocating. Making me feel small had been Barb's favorite hobby, but *she's not here*. No, instead there are boxes with women's names on them. Women—*girls*, I correct myself—that fill my dreams.

My slow walk turns into a jog. No vines here to trip me. The mermaid purses, the kelp, the driftwood, all of it obvious. But every step in Barb's house makes me test the ground like I'm expecting a bomb.

Who are these women? Barb had known everyone in town, but what was the point of the boxes? Did she have one for me? No, making me a gift would have been abhorrent to her. Fine. Those dolls are fucking ugly anyway.

And now I don't have to worry about her gifting nightmare fuel in porcelain form to my child someday. The unkind thought sours my stomach, but alone on the beach, I don't regret it.

Hell. Where am I? I slow, letting my lungs catch up. I must be miles from the house now.

Silver moonlight bathes the sea. The water is agitated here, noisy. Here, I'm not lashed to all the bad Barb memories.

Or I shouldn't be, but a tiny scraping sensation at the back of my neck won't let me forget the reason I woke early. Cassidy Warren. I sit on the cold sand, welcoming the numbing. What is it about *her*? Luke would probably say this is me trying to find a problem to solve. A distraction. But I have plenty on my plate right now without borrowing any new worries. Honestly, how my brain made space for this is really rather impressive. My thoughts swirl every night with worry for Luke. *Is he processing his feelings? Is his work truly okay with all this time off? Is he ignoring anything important that I should be covering? Should we have hired a company to clear the house to keep him from this burden?* And that didn't even include my own problems. *Will we have a family? Can I get pregnant again? What if I'm pregnant now? Will Luke want us to name our kid after his mom? Will it break him when I say no?*

See? I have no shortage of worries without thinking about the name scribbled on a box in Barb's creepy little hidden attic.

My breath fogs the air. *I am heat. I am fire. I am galvanized.*

"Hey! Are you okay?" A woman calls from far enough back that she's just a slender silhouette in a bulky hoodie.

I wave. "I'm good, thanks!"

"I didn't want to startle you. No one walks this early." She's coming closer. The woman is shorter than me, and I get the sense she's boxy beneath the bulking sweatshirt. Her brown hair is likely lighter in the day, but now it's a dark knot atop her head. "It'd freak me out if someone just walked up behind me."

And yet here she is doing that very thing. I stand and dust the back of my joggers.

"Goodness, you're Luke's wife." She takes a half step back as though she needs to see my full body.

No one has ever looked at me like I'm a celebrity. I kind of wish it wasn't while I'm running from my problems in Oregon.

"You know Luke?" I ask. If Barb's memory catches me out here, I may scream.

She shakes her head slowly, her bright smile plain, even in the low light. "Everyone does."

Is she starstruck by my husband? That's…nice. Deserved.

"I'm Katy Colter, by the way."

"Addison Lowe." I nod in her direction, and she gives me a knowing smile. I lower my guard, try to ignore the chill creeping in. "I'm guessing you went to high school together?"

"Oh, more than that." Her voice projects right out to the ocean, probably waking fishermen invisible from here.

I arch a brow. Had Luke Lowe been a high school lothario? What would Kim think?

"Oh god. Not like that." Her offense delights me. "We were rivals."

"Rivals," I repeat. There's no way I heard that right.

"Debate is one of those teams that is made up of individuals winning. He and I spent our senior year battling it out at every competition for top spot." A dash of bitterness seeps in her tone. "We both qualified for State."

There's a reason my husband is a shark of a lawyer. Details, meticulous research, and you do not want to argue with him. The fact that it still rubbed her that Luke beat her in a high school debate suggests she needs to get out more. "He's a natural at that for sure."

Katy nods. "He is, but I wouldn't mind getting to go up against him in the courtroom."

"You're a lawyer too?"

"You don't have to sound so surprised. Someone has to be around to help with legal needs in Rockside Bay." She shakes her head, and mostly to herself says, "If I hadn't crashed that bike, who knows who would have won?"

"You missed the competition?" Gossip—even distilled by time—can be a balm. Everything this morning can be pushed aside as I remind myself it happens to us all.

Katy starts walking south, and I go with her. It takes me back toward the house anyway. "I had to."

"What kind of bicycle accident puts you out for a debate meet?" My bluntness surprises even me. "Sorry, I need coffee to be a polite human."

"I don't mind directness." Her smile warms. "Most people, if they flip over their handlebars and crack their collarbone."

"You didn't?"

"Oh, I sure as hell did." Her fingers seek her clavicle, like the remembered wound is still fresh. "But the handlebar twisted somehow and caught my throat."

She got throat punched by a bicycle? How do you survive that?

"Yep. That look on your face is right. Weird as hell."

"But you're okay now?" I ask, no longer wanting to wallow in others' bad memories.

She nods. "Tip-top now. But it took three surgeries and a vocal coach."

Three...surgeries? As a high school senior. "That had to be devastating."

"Oh, I flopped hard, but my mom raged like no other. Got me to a great specialist in Portland and"—she gestures to her neck—"voilà!"

"That's wild, Katy." Like, unreal wild.

"Eh, wild stuff happens in Rockside Bay all the time. Keeps me in business." She shrugs it off, but I don't think I can. "Speaking of, condolences for your loss."

"My loss?" I fumble.

That sly smile steals her face again. "Mrs. Lowe. I mean, Barbara's death."

The late Mrs. Lowe and the living Mrs. Lowe. Barb. Me. The fire of upcoming tears kindles at the corners of my eyes. This small town is going to hear I don't grieve their beloved charity queen. "Thank you," I choke.

"It's okay. Mrs. Lowe, er, Barbara, had complicated relationships." No one had ever said that before. Not to me.

"Is that so?" Please tell me it's not just me.

"My parents were on the board at the food bank but somehow never were invited to parties at her home."

"Never?" Even the orchard girl got invited once.

"Well," she hedges. "Perhaps when I was young, but in high school, it was Luke versus me in class, and Barb over everyone outside of it."

I swallowed hard. Katy's free spirit spoke to my own, but I caught the horizontal scar at the base of her throat. She'd fought for it. What is it about this town that makes people claw for happiness?

"Did you ever think of moving?" I ask her.

"Why?" There's no offense in her tone, but it's as if she's never considered it.

"Different people, a different life, more opportunities?" The list is long, but I'm not here to judge her. Hell, I've only just met her.

"This is my home." Katy slows. "Can I tell you something?"

Part of me craves it; the rest fears it. "Shoot."

"Barbara Lowe did immense good for this community, but I don't think you'll find many who would describe her as a having a kind heart. So...don't feel alone there. If you are."

Am I that obvious? "We're complex creatures."

"That we are." Katy stops and hikes a thumb over her shoulder to a path. "This is me, but it was good meeting you, Addison."

I nod. "Thanks for sharing your perspective."

I begin to move on, but Katy calls after me. "Hold up." She hands me her business card. "In case you and Luke need a local to help with estate stuff."

Katy Colter, Attorney at Law.

I have never accepted another lawyer's card, but this feels like a gift for Luke. A connection to his past, to his town. A sign I'm trying. I pocket it with appreciation.

CHAPTER 9

LUKE IS SOUND ASLEEP WHEN I GET BACK TO THE HOUSE. I RIP up my *I'm out* note and brew a pot of coffee. The run helped, but now I'm back to being the only person awake in a dead woman's home.

The soft dripping of the coffee maker completing its task pulls me back to the kitchen. I fill my mug nearly to the brim, splash creamer on the top, and take my coffee and a cozy blanket to the back deck.

I pull my knees up, curl my busted toes at the edge of my little seat at the bistro table. I drape the heavy blanket around my shoulders and tuck the edges under my feet until I'm in a cocoon of shearling and flannel. I sneak out a hand to capture my coffee, cradling the ceramic mug and letting the heat permeate my palm.

I nurse my coffee more than a woman with so much to do today should. Nothing glimmers in the garden, thankfully. At home Luke is the early riser. But now the sun crests the horizon just for me; the sounds of the world waking slip over the fence. Cars on the road.

The clap of a screen door in the distance. The rustling of early birds after worms and whatnot.

My conversation with Katy replays in my head. I've met many of Luke's classmates on our visits here, but this is the first time it's felt like a friend for *me*.

The first crow perches above the garden as I rise to get a second cup of coffee. Maybe if I clatter around in the kitchen, Luke will appear and join me at the little two-person table setup. It'll be like one of our Sunday-robe mornings back in Austin. I'd told my sister about it once and she'd called it bonding time. She'd been poking fun, but when I don't have that time to reset and reconnect with Luke, it does create distance between us.

A darkness oozes down my sternum. I press the still-warm mug against my breastbone like it can melt away the familiar sense of self-disgust. Worrying about routine comfort touch points with Luke while we're amid all of this? Shameful. He'd let me sleep through more than a few of our couch-robe sessions. He'd brought me coffee or hot cocoa in bed. He'd even dropped off a plush armadillo one time. And here I am in his dead mom's house, while he's forced to face the loss, thinking about how I want cuddling and for him to bring me coffee?

I hate how much this hurts him. I hate myself for not being hurt. Barb was the worst to me but not to her kid. I have to be here for Luke. Even if it's awkward.

I should make *him* coffee. I take a mug upstairs to him, but when I softly say his name, the response is simply a man who is very much *out*. He needs rest, and I will give it to him.

I carefully go back downstairs. No more tripping. I pour out Luke's coffee—too much sugar for me—and linger at the sink. Unspent anxiety jostles my legs, but this stone of apprehension presses on my chest, holding me in limbo. One more cup of coffee, I tell myself, and then I'm purging this house like I'm aiming to be a house-cleaning influencer. It's enough to get me moving, at least.

I bring my phone out to the deck along with the freshly brewed Pike's Place blend. I will not doomscroll. I sip and then—avoiding social media and the news apps—search for the sanitation information in Rockside Bay. We either need a bigger bin for this mass cleanout or for the garbage pickup to at least double this week.

I open my Notes app. I'd listed a few of the names from the boxes here. This is dwelling, and it will only serve to bring me back into a bad move. I am going to click out. I swear. Close the app. But then a name strikes me. It punches me so hard in the face, blood should stream down my chin. How had I talked to Katy Colter this morning and not remembered her name?

She's on my list. Her name is on a box in the attic. Barb's messed-up doll boxes include one for Katy. Who couldn't recall ever being in this house. Who wasn't close with Barb. Who definitely wasn't going to get a special handcrafted porcelain doll from *the* Barbara Lowe.

What the fuck is going on here?

A trio of caws resound, snapping me to the present. Barb's garden is packed with deep-green leaves and riotous punches of fuchsia and yellow. It's beautiful, but not as much as the birds hopping at the edge, dipping their beaks in the soil.

"Do y'all know about Katy Colter?" I stage-whisper. "You'd like her, but I can't believe Barb would have."

Sharpness scrapes my back, and I rocket forward in my chair.

The crows titter.

Oh, I'm a terrible bird friend. I forgot to bring out the seeds for them. I'm about to do just that when the tallest of the crows lands on the bistro table. He—I somehow know it's a male—tilts his head at me. The inspection is undeniable. *Maybe he does know Katy?*

"I have snacks for you," I say, like I've ever been this close to a crow.

He cants his head to the other side, sharp black eye tracking me.

Barb and Luke both detested these birds. How? The stunning black feathers shimmer with a subtle blue even in this heathered light.

"I'm off today. Sorry about that. I don't know if birds dream, but I had a shitty one, and I gotta be honest, I'm having *a time*." Talking to the bird, who I mentally name Eddie, is nice.

His little head bobs. *See, he gets it.*

"Let me go grab some seeds for you." I move to stand, but Eddie wiggle-walks close enough we could share the coffee.

"Eddie, coffee isn't good for birds. Probably. It's not great for me, and I'm way bigger. So no go there, friend."

He taps his beak against the mug. Is this crow asking for coffee? Is this a Pacific Northwest thing? I know they're into caffeine here, but even the birds?

Taking the coffee cup away from the bird is the kind of task that requires slow motion, I decide. I can sense the other crows watching us. There's more of them now, but no one is dive-bombing me. Eddie tracks my motion but doesn't move to peck me.

I edge the mug back toward myself. The crow lowers his beak and raps against the table. When all I do is watch him, he taps the glass tabletop again and then hops to perch on the backrest of the other chair.

On the table between us, next to the echo ring of my drink, is a hot-pink bead. It has the letter *C* in crisp white.

Fear freezes my bones. My stomach clenches, whether to hold the coffee in or pitch it out, I'm not sure.

"Luke threw that bracelet out." I mouth the words. Steam escapes from my lips, but I'm silent.

I swallow like it takes back the acknowledgment, like it changes anything. Time stretches thin and long, but I manage to glance Eddie's way. The crow bobs his head once and flies to his preferred perch on the tallest fence post at the back of the yard.

What is happening here? I forget the birds and look to the table. To the bead from a friendship bracelet. One that hadn't been broken. One that had belonged to Cassidy Warren. One that my husband threw in the garbage yesterday.

The hot pink is going to sear my retinas, but I can't stop staring.

Tears track down my cheeks. I let them.

I linger on the deck long enough that my coffee chills and the air warms to where I no longer need the blanket. The hot-pink bead and its damning *C* stare at me from the tabletop the whole time.

Did the birds simply collect whatever they found? I thought crows went for shiny objects. Paper clips and coins and the like. This bead is not flashy in that way. It's bright to me, but what had that bird seen that made him bring it to me? Is this how that doll's arm had arrived in the garden? What will I find in Katy's box upstairs? Would the crows bring its contents to me too? None of this makes sense, but the warning wail in my chest refuses to quiet.

The screen door behind me whines, and it might be a gunshot for how I leap from my seat. I bang the table forward, my coffee spilling.

"Oh, shit. Sorry, Addie, I didn't mean to startle you." Luke's warm palm presses against my upper back. Solid, steady, doing the job I should be doing.

I scramble. "No apologies needed. I was space-cadetting."

"Deep thinking is good, if you're not dwelling. Isn't that what you told me?" He says this playfully, but it still feels like a dig.

"Yeah, but sleepy zoning is just a sign I need more coffee." Three cups are probably too many, but caffeine consumption is low on my list of concerns.

"I've got a new pot brewing," he says, all comfort and kindness and mine. "I'll pour us both cups."

"That would be good. I was up early."

"Don't tell me you've been downing coffee for hours?" It's not about the coffee. He glances at my hands like he'll catch me fidgeting.

"No, I went for a walk on the beach." Well, a jog.

He frowns at the horizon. "Did you wait for dawn?"

"No, but you're the one who always tells me how safe Rockside Bay is."

"Yeah." Distance creeps into his voice. "I'm sure it was peaceful."

It'd been good to leave here, but then... "Mostly. I made a friend."

His smile is thin but real. "Anyone I know?"

"You know everyone, but it was Katy Colter." A chill skitters down my spine as I speak her name.

Luke blanches. "I haven't heard that name in ages."

"Do you remember her?"

"Sure. We weren't close or anything, but smart girl." He's retreating toward the door.

Katy classified Luke as a rival, but does that count if the other person doesn't feel that way?

"I see the asshole birds are still hovering over mom's garden." Did he just subtly flip off the crows? I'm losing it.

"I like them." I hope Eddie and his friends hear me.

"You shouldn't. They're predatory." He stares out at the birds, making eye contact with Eddie as he says it.

"I think you're thinking of vultures, babe."

"You didn't grow up here, Addison. Just trust me, okay?" There's a warning in his tone. A reminder of our varied pasts, of his expertise, of trauma he hasn't exposed to me yet.

I don't push. It's okay to have family secrets. Shame is available at every class level.

So I nod. "I'll clean up this mess and then be in."

I pocket the bead after his back is turned. I don't know why it matters. Why I want to keep this colorful bauble. Why I don't share it with him.

We drink our coffee like I haven't lost time on the deck and he hasn't been flustered by some birds.

"Are you up for today?" I ask, knowing I should be supporting him and not the other way around.

Luke lifts a lone shoulder. "As ready as I can be."

"I made a plan for today..." I start.

"Of course you did. Is there an itinerary, because I would support your guidance here." He isn't even joking.

"I think we can be more efficient today and move through more of the boxes." And I'm not going to find any more of those little doors at the back of closets. Or, I guess, if I do, I'm not opening them. That's a problem for future tenants.

I pause, waiting (hoping?) for Luke to ask where he should start. But he finishes his coffee and rinses the mug, leaving it in the sink for later.

"Do you want to start with me this morning?" I prod.

Whatever it is that clouds his gaze now isn't about me. Had he dreamed of a dead girl too? He'll tell me when he is ready, but asking while he is hip-deep in processing the loss of his mother would be an unkindness not worthy of his wife.

My husband tilts his head back; fatigue swallows his features. Whether he's staring at nothing or picturing the upper levels of the house, there's distance when he speaks. "Not yet. I need to do a bit more in the office; then I can help with the rest."

I can't believe the office requires more than one day, but then I'm also fine with chucking boxes quickly. "I can help if you want. We could spend the day together."

He settles his attention on me. "Thought you said divide and conquer was the way to go?"

I kiss his cheek. "It might be faster, but that doesn't mean it's best for us."

Luke gives me a squeeze. "It's okay. *I'm* okay. I've got to check in at the firm. This Pacific time zone thing is killing me, but I'm sure we'll get lots done with your plan."

He doesn't mean to be patronizing, but I can't resist assigning him work. "Do you think you can get the garage emptied today?"

Luke already has his phone in hand and is texting. He answers without looking away from the screen. "Do we need something from it?"

Other than for him to move on to a task that will get us out of here faster? "I stumbled over another one of those vines this morning."

He swears under his breath, and while I don't recognize the word, the intonation is clear.

"I don't mean to make it a thing—"

"No, it's not you." He pockets his phone and then reaches for me, pulling me close. I take the hug, sink into it. "Mom put in those vines when I was in first grade, and they overtook everything. I should have helped her purge them years ago."

"I don't mind them as long as they're outside the house." Kinda like bugs, I believe they should stay in their house, and I'll stay in mine. "I don't know how they keep getting in."

"I'm sure we just missed one. Besides, they always seem bigger in the moment. It could have been a little one Mom had been propagating inside that we somehow missed."

I've been digging in Barb's things. This house is swollen with unused items, but there is nothing green inside unless we're counting peridot and emerald.

"Didn't you see it on the way down here?" I hadn't cleared it.

"I'll gear up and head out to the garage. I can get it organized and get the tools we need to handle the vines. No more of my wife going ass over teakettle." Luke is a professional question dodger.

I slip from his embrace. "Okay. I'm going to work on the second floor this morning."

"You finished Mom's room?" His fingers flutter at his sides.

I shake my head. "I'll come back to it. I think there are some areas we can get through quickly to clear more space."

As I'm answering him, Luke pulls his phone from his pocket again. He is nodding, I think to me, but also is typing on his phone. The dimple on his right cheek appears.

"Everything okay at work?" I hate that they won't let him have bereavement in silence.

He thumbs the lock button and waggles his phone at me. "This is no big deal." He repockets the device. "You, however, are the best."

He steps around me to head toward the living room, swatting my butt on the way past.

"Garage is out back," I call after him.

"Jacket's by the front door."

CHAPTER 10

I GET TO WORK. I PROMISE MYSELF THAT THE FASTER I GET through Barb's stuff, the sooner I can go back to my own bed and kitchen and life. It's a fact I hold firmly.

The landing is clear when I go back upstairs. I try not to think about my tumble or Luke's reaction to it. Though I find the bead in my pocket and roll it between my fingers. It's only reassuring in that it's solid and undeniably real.

None of that confidence boost stops me from averting my gaze from Barb's bedroom door when I walk past. Just in case that golden glint from the closet tempts my attention. No lures for me today, no new troubles. I don't need to look in the box with Katy's name on it.

But even thinking her name leaves my mind itching for answers. She hadn't been close to Luke. That bicycle accident had to be one of those one-in-a-million type things. What is it with Rockside Bay? Cassidy going missing Luke's senior year and this other girl impaled on a bicycle handle? It's...bonkers. I try to put it out of my mind and focus on cleaning this stupid house.

It shouldn't be possible to have so much stuff in a four-bedroom house. It's not the first time I've thought it, but every time I pull a box free in this place, it's like four more replace it. It's the *Space Invaders* of deep cleaning in here.

Tackling the oddly bountiful linen closets should be easier. No boxes to multiply on me. There are three official closets for towels, sheets, and the like; Barb also has a freestanding one at the far end of the hall—an armoire shoved to one side.

I open the armoire first. White sheets. Cream sheets. Three shower curtains. Pillowcases of varied sizes. Some embroidered with feathers. Nothing says *allergy warning* like putting pictures of feathers on your pillowcases. I'm not the only human allergic to down feathers, but Barb sure acted like it was hardship to allow down-alternative anything into her home. But then admitting me into the family had been a struggle too.

Before Luke and I were engaged, Barb visited Austin regularly. She'd been coolly indifferent to me in general. The three of us would go out to dinner, and she'd only speak to Luke. I'd get nods and tight smiles. And she'd shift the subject back to Luke. They were close though, I told myself, and I was a new third wheel during her time to catch up with her son.

Why I'd thought that would change with a ring on my finger...

Luke had proposed in early November and then whisked me to coastal Oregon for the first time later that month at Thanksgiving.

I'd been ready to show Barb my ring. To talk about my vision for the wedding. To generally let my love for her son spill all over the place.

She'd gripped Luke tightly upon arrival and then offered me a curt, "Oh, right. Hello, Addison." As if I were a surprise guest instead of her future daughter-in-law. Our first night there had continued in that same stilted fashion. My existence offensive.

Luke had gone upstairs to shower after dinner; I'd taken to the kitchen to tackle the dishes. Desperate to score brownie points wherever I could find them.

The swinging door leading to the dining room announced Barb's entry.

And yet I hadn't been prepared for her snarl. "You going to pocket that?"

"Pocket?" The word tasted foreign. I'd set the crystal water goblet I'd been rinsing on a makeshift drying station of a folded kitchen towel.

Barb glared at me. "I see you for what you are."

"What I am? You mean the girl who is desperately in love with your son?" I sputtered.

"Love?" Her laugh was sharp enough to cut to the bone. "You're greedy. Unworthy of him."

"Greedy? What on—"

"You steal all his time. Take him away from his work." She didn't say it, but the *from me* was clear.

"I only want to support your son, Barb."

"You don't get to use my name," she snapped.

That would make life incredibly awkward. I scrambled. This was not how gaining a mother was supposed to go. "Mrs. Lowe," I tried, "I only want to support Luke. Whatever he needs, I'll give it. Joining your family is an honor—"

"You aren't joining our family."

I choked on her words. I peeked down at my hand to confirm I was, in fact, still wearing an engagement ring. It was an obscenely huge solitaire that was unnecessary, in my opinion. Barb clearly agreed.

"Luke and I are going to get married. I love him, and I'm sure when we get to know each other better, we can build love too." The water pipe hummed nearby. Why was tonight the night Luke had to take a more than five-minute shower? I swallowed hard. Vulnerability is how one built connection. I gave her some. "I lost my mother a few years ago. I had hoped you might want to help me plan the wedding."

Barb clucked her tongue in disgust. "I'm not your mother."

No shit. "No, but you're going to be my mother-in-law, and our relationship is important to Luke."

She narrowed her gaze on me, scrutinizing every wayward strand of hair, each too-large pore. "Luke will come to his senses."

She stalked away from me, like there was finality in her word. Perhaps there often was, but she didn't get to choose who her son loved.

"Mrs. Lowe," I called after her. She paused but didn't turn around. I needed to try. "This is happening. I want to find a way for us to enjoy each other's company."

She tsked at me. "No."

Barb remained cold but polite to me whenever her son was in the room. She'd never hide her passive aggression, but Luke pretended not to see it. But when we were alone, she'd never miss an opportunity to suggest I was less than. She'd make snide comments about my sister. About my late mother. About Texas. About me. And I'd swallowed them for years.

For Luke.

And now I'm sorting her sheets. I pull an armload from the armoire and drop all the neatly folded items onto the floor. The trifold crispness lost in the flop. *Here I am, ruining your things again, Barb.* It gives me less joy than I hoped. When the freestanding dresser is empty, I give the built-in the same treatment. Forty-seven decorative hand towels. I have to count them out of sheer wonder. I've never seen any of these towels before. Had Barb even used them?

Someone would. I bring some nice boxes to the hallway, and what the...? The sheets are gone. I whirl around like I'll find Luke with an armful of old linens, but I'm alone. I drop the empty boxes on the floor and return to the armoire. The doors are closed. Had I closed them? I can't remember. I open the cherry-stained wood door. The sheets are stacked inside. Crisp corners.

No, I think, *I pulled these out. Threw them on the floor.*

But there they are, back on the shelf like I hadn't touched a thing. Whatever. I snatch the first stack and drop them into an open box. Two white marbles roll forward from the back of the newly emptied shelf. I try to catch them, but gravity is faster. They clack on the floor and roll toward the stairs. Guess this place is built on an incline. I chase the marbles like catching them matters, like I'm not going to simply toss them in the trash.

They slow in front of Barb's bedroom. *Great.* I grab them. Cracking a joke about losing marbles is too easy right now. I shake my head and then open my palm to see what Barb had hidden in the back of the armoire.

The marbles stare at me. A ring of soft brown around a black center. Disgust rebounds through my body. I drop them and hustle backward until my butt hits the wall. The marbles stay put. Settled in front of Barb's door.

Not marbles. Doll eyes.

I knew Barb hated me, but hiding fake eyeballs around the house before she died was a next-level bitch move.

The realization stokes a darker part of me. I snatch the creepy glass balls from the floor, shoulder-check Barb's bedroom door open, and storm right into her closet. The marbles chill in my palm, growing colder by the second. I squat before the small door in the back wall. There's no time to worry about what I have or haven't seen in this place. Barb's disturbing doll fascination belonged in her strange hidden room. I open the half door and chuck the marbles into the attic with all the strength I can muster.

Barb doesn't get to unnerve me here anymore.

There's no satisfying crack when they land though. Disappointment thumps in my chest. I wait, but it's just me and the soft whirr of the ceiling fan behind me in the bedroom. There's too much in Barb's secret stash room to allow the tossed marbles to land on anything satisfying, I suppose.

They're gone. That's what matters. Or at least that's what I choose to believe. Except when I turn, I see someone. Just from the corner of my eye. A round face surrounded by a muddy haze. My heart attempts to flee my body, like it's had enough of my bad choices.

I look back into the attic fully, but the face is gone. A soft shush fills my ears. I clench my jaw like it's an off switch for the sound, but it doesn't work. Tightness steals my shoulders. I fight the invisible grip and make myself go inside.

I stub my toe on the way in. I flick on the light switch, but there is still no one here. Only me and mountains of boxes. Including the one that's sitting at the base of the post holding the switch.

It's Katy Colter's box.

Only who had put it here? The sound in my ears grows louder. Dread drips like a leaky tap overhead. *Plink plink plink*ing anxiety onto the crown of my skull.

I nudge the box with my other foot. It's not heavy, but also why is it by the door? I lower myself slowly, back rigid. I can run if I need to. *But it's only a box.* The tangle of clean linen and soft florals fills the air. Barb's perfume is cloying.

The cardboard flaps fold back easily. The doll inside is, thankfully, lying face down. Its brown hair is pinned up in a French twist. An ill-fitting tan suit hangs off the small form. Beside the doll is a standard-issue black-and-white composition notebook. The top right corner is rolled forward like its user had a favorite spot. Katy's name is written in cursive on the cover in simple black ink.

My mouth goes dry. I swallow, but that only makes my throat scratch. I don't want to pick up the doll, but I'm compelled to do so. I met this woman just this morning, and here I am back in Barb's emporium of weird belongings looking at another doll. One that looks like the teen version of Katy. What does this mean? Was Barb up here shoving needles into dolls like pincushions? No, they're porcelain. There are so many women's names listed up here, it's like she was keeping track of the town.

I grasp the doll carefully under its arms. It's heavy; I brace its legs on my other hand and turn it to face me. It's Katy. Down to the same sardonic smile. Only the doll's neck is mottled black and purple. Red paint slips from the doll's right nostril down over its mouth. This is a doll of Katy postaccident.

Crows caw in the distance. Louder and louder. There's a rattle of glass behind me, back in the house.

I set the doll back in the box gently. She doesn't need to be broken any further.

The box wobbles. I push it back toward its cardboard brethren. A slender green vine pokes through the floor near me. I stomp on it as I retreat from the attic.

What had my mother-in-law been playing at? Weird dolls are enough, but what would possess her to create a doll like *that*? To capture the image of her son's debate rival—good lord, who cared?—at her most traumatic in porcelain?

Maybe it isn't such a bad thing that my mother-in-law hadn't liked me. Except how did a person with this kind of sick hobby turn out a human as amazing as Luke?

I close up both the attic and Barb's room and retreat.

If only I could do that with everything else in here. I can't leave until we clear this place. And Barb's omnipresence in this place is all in objects. Creepy ones, sure, but it's simply memory. Deep breathing has me solid again. If I work fast, I won't have to look at another one of those damned dolls, I tell myself.

I move to the far bedroom. It's packed not only with *stuff* but also with the vibe of home gym ambitions. The handlebars and screen panel of a treadmill peer over a collection of clear plastic totes near the window. A shudder rocks me. Handlebars to the throat. Katy. The wounded doll. I shut my eyes tight and will the thoughts away. When I open them, I focus on the knobby ends of two handles from an elliptical—probably?—jutting up from a sea of slick grocery totes. The local store Shipley IGA intended them to be reused there, but Barb clearly kept buying them each time she visited. *Ever hear of sustainability, Barb?*

At least the room doesn't reek of rotting avocados. Whatever she'd chosen to store in here, it isn't going to harm me. Well, except potentially my feelings.

I employ my new plan. Shoving as much as I can out into the hallway. The bags and boxes in this room are heavy. I quickly work up a sweat and have to tie my hair up, curls quickly sneaking free. *I'm totally the first person to sweat in this room.* Effervescent humor tickles my throat. I unearth more fitness gear, all with tags intact.

Barb had been limber, fit even. The fact that her heart had given out floored us. She wasn't a smoker, unless it'd been in secret. She'd eaten a metric ton of red meat, but the lady had balanced it out with activity. Or maybe not? Barb had to be *seen* working out for it to matter to her. She'd hit the lunchtime yoga on the lawn in front of the community center five times a week. I'd been invited plenty—usually after Luke had given her another talk about accepting me—but only attended once. It was enough.

So why had she bought all of this? Were these pity purchases? Could she not help but spend? None of it made sense, but I'd never pushed Luke for an explanation of his mother's *collecting*. He isn't one to part from items either. He finds sentimentality in so many objects. It's a beautiful trait.

We went to this local pizza parlor on our first date. Luke had shaken the parmesan over our pizza, and the lid loosened, fell, and left a mountain on our pie. He'd returned to the restaurant after I accepted his marriage proposal and bought one of their shakers. It's still the only one he uses.

That's different from this, right? Those are one-offs. Those are things that mean something. Things we use. Not a room shoved full of expensive equipment and how-to books and architecture magazine back issues stuffed in totes and stacked atop more of the same. The room is overwhelming and sad and one hundred percent not my future.

My heart flutters erratically, and I press my palm to my chest. My shirt is already damp. Why am I so sweaty? It's not like seeing Barb's hidden junk means I have to start hoarding copies of *ELLE Decor* like it's my job.

Luke raps his knuckles on the door in a musical rhythm. "Hey, gorgeous. How's it going?"

His hair is damp and cheeks are ruddy. My face is surely glowing with sweat too. "Hot and dirty, but okay. You?"

"Same." He frowns. "Not sure I like us doing hot and dirty separately."

I snicker and then spread my arms wide. "There's plenty of hot and dirty work in here for me to share with you. Take your pick, handsome."

He steps into the room, and the space instantly shrinks. My vision tunnels in on Luke. His hands graze my hips, pull me up against his body. His shirt is bordering on wet, but I press into him anyway.

"Can I pick you?" His roughened words kiss my ear.

Heat curls through me, distraction and hope chasing the lust like Luke is my tether to all things good and sane. I push to my toes and kiss him. He welcomes it, gripping me tighter. He deepens the kiss, and then we're stumbling. Luke collides with a box tower, and it clatters to the ground. Shattering ceramic echoes through the room, like bad decisions stomping on a reverb pedal.

Luke releases me. I step back. Our connection severed. Loss freezes me, and I wrap my arms around myself like it'll bring back his warmth. We never get sexy at Barb's house. Now we start and break shit? Lovely.

"Aw, hell," Luke grumbles.

"I'm sorry," I say as if this is my fault. It's not.

"What?" His genuine surprise is soothing. He pulls a pale-pink ceramic elephant trunk from the box we'd knocked over. "I wasn't swearing at you."

There's this note of incredulity he gets that burrows beneath my skin. It's a rare flash of annoyance from my husband, but when it happens, it hurts. It's like he's perceived a slight against him, and my feelings are the culprit.

Emotions are high, Addie. Give the man a break. My sister's voice is sound in my mind.

"Yeah," I say to fill the gap. "What did we break?"

"Elephant bank." He is staring into the box like there's more to it than just a bank. The little trunk is still in his hand.

"Yours?" Barb had been a traditionalist about gender roles—and had too many opinions about my husband cooking and cleaning up after himself like a grown-up. There is no way she gave Luke a pink piggy bank.

"No, I had a big gray pig. You've seen it." His back is to me. Still.

I edge forward, half to comfort him and half to see what's in the box.

I lift my hand, readying to rest it on Luke's back, but frigid nails dig at my upper arm. I whirl around, but it's just me, Luke, and the hoarder's den. I fold my arms across my chest and sidle next to Luke. The cold bite at my arm sharpens, sinks in, the longer I ignore it.

I peer into the box that has captivated my spouse. More shards of the elephant bank and I would guess its contents. There are four black buttons, roughly the size of quarters. They're not metal but almost look like the type of old wood one finds on a hike in a forest. Damp and darkened by age and rot and tiny living things.

"What are those?" Though I speak softly, Luke startles.

He tosses the trunk back into the box; a small piece breaks off. "It's nothing. Just more of Mom's junk."

The icy grip releases me. "Are you sure—"

"I've got it." He folds the box lid closed and hustles out into the hallway.

I'm right on his heels. I don't know if this is grief or a greater emotion, but if Luke's unnerved, I'm unnerved.

"Luke," I plead.

He pauses, giving me the same smile he gives to potential clients he's going to decline. "It's no big deal. I can pitch this on my way out. I need to run into town for a ladder. Mom's is missing."

Forty-seven hand towels and no ladder? Strange.

"I only came up to check in and see if you needed anything," he adds like it helps.

It doesn't, but I let it slide. "Okay. I'll get to a stopping point around lunch. Maybe we can get good takeout sandwiches?"

"Maybe." He's already going down the stairs.

"You want me to come?" I ask.

He's already out of view, but his comment rebounds in my chest all the same. "No, the car just stresses you out. Back soon."

The thoughtless slap like my trauma is a nuisance leaves a fiery print at my core.

What the hell just happened? I step into the bathroom and splash cold water on my face. I use one of the regular towels in the bathroom to pat my face dry. In the mirror I catch the small sickle marks on my biceps. Four little black arcs. Like someone marked me with soot from their fingernails.

I touch the bead in my pocket again. What is going on in this house? When Luke gets back, I'm asking him about his mother's bedroom. I'm asking about the surprise attic. About the doll.

Cassidy Warren. I can clear this place out, but I have to know what I'm up against.

I've expunged a decent amount from the bedroom I now thought of as the "aspirational home gym," but when my dumbfounded ass returns, it's like the boxes have reproduced while I was gone. No, we can't stay here. I'm not doing this. I'm not sure how long it'll be until Luke's back, but I start grabbing boxes and taking them straight downstairs. Right out to the trash pile. We can donate the equipment—a local community center will love them—but the rest of it can go to the dump.

I expect to see the box with the broken bank and the eerie coins at the top of our heap, but it's nowhere to be seen. Maybe Luke had other items to throw away, and it's under them?

I turn around, looking toward the garage. The door is open, but I can see a deluge of garden implements from here. Did Luke take a load to the dump too, on his ladder journey?

I glance to the garden. Two of the crows remain. They watch the flowers; they look toward the sea; neither is particularly interested in me poking at the trash.

Fair.

I fetch nuts and seeds from the house and then toss them into the grass. "Thanks for keeping an eye out. If you see anything weird, give a holler."

I say this like the crows are watchdogs. As if they're my friends. Like I'm alone here.

I try not to think about why I feel so isolated. Both at this house and in Oregon.

CHAPTER 11

I'VE JUST FINISHED MY TWENTIETH RUN TO THE TRASH BINS when I hear the purr of the rental car coming up the driveway. I slow at the threshold, gripping the screen door frame like it'll pause the moment. Like I'm not about to get caught pitching his mother's precious items into a trash heap. Only Luke parks the car and doesn't so much as glance at the amassed garbage. He strides toward the side of the garage. Does he even notice me? He's grumbling, but none of the words carry far enough to make out. I wait, deer-meet-headlights, as he stalks around the backyard, phone out, fingers flying.

Unobserved, I slip into the house, slowly easing the door closed behind me so as to not disturb him. But I watch, because of course I do. Is this anxiety? Grief? Did something happen at work, or is this another frustration? My tummy twists. All I want to do is to help him, but the longer I watch him, the deeper the gully between us becomes. Asking him what's wrong would only underscore that distance.

He tucks the device into his front pocket before turning toward the house. Is that a kindness meant for me? Politeness? Is he keeping his own secrets? He returns to the car—opening the door and then shutting it again—before finally coming inside.

I hug him in greeting, and while his arms wrap around me automatically, there is little warmth.

"Did you want to go get lunch together?" I ask. We try to always have meals together. It's not like he brought sandwiches back, and the fridge is lacking.

"I grabbed a bite while I was out." He's already pulling his phone from his pocket again. Distracted. "Sorry, babe, I need to take this."

And then he's out back again.

And we're both alone. Again. Silence is dangerous when mourning, but he doesn't seem to want the company. And I don't know what to do with that.

My stomach offers an audible protest to the situation.

I get my coat, fully capable of driving to the one McDonald's in town. When I step outside, Luke is cradling the phone to his ear. Shoulders hunched, he's pacing a circuit in the shorn grass. His tired, cold, exhausted posture dulls my hangry mood.

"Now isn't a great time. Let's talk later, okay?" he says to the caller. He quickly hangs up and turns his attention to me.

I wave sheepishly. "I'm going to get myself a Happy Meal. Back soon."

"You don't need to do that." Regret coats him like veneer.

"Who was calling?" *Who did this to you?*

He shakes his head. "Doesn't matter. I'm sorry I forgot about the food. Let me go get you something or take you to a sit-down place."

On the whole, I'm not someone who gets embarrassed easily. I'm too clumsy for that. But the idea of sitting in "Barb's town" and having people she surely told stories about me to watch me eat while my husband sits there is more cringe than I can take.

"Drive-through is fine," I say.

He doesn't invite me to come with him, but I do anyway. I'm not sure either of us need to be alone right now.

Quiet car rides are lovely. This is not one of those. The road hums and clacks beneath us. The wind lashes the windows. And there's this unspoken question between us that I don't know how to approach because I'm not even sure what it is. The longer we sit there, the more grating I find every soft *frrpt* of his phone vibrating with a notification. *Is it work? Is it friends? Should he be shutting people out?* He just made partner. That makes it hard to disconnect. I'm trying to understand, and he knows that. Only now my head is all scrambly. The unknown takes root in my mind, festers until I want to squirm from the itch.

The road into the town proper takes us along the shore. The water is foamy today, crashing against the craggy gray stones. Rain begins to pelt the car, blurring the view. Eventually we pull into Rockside Bay's downtown. Hodgepodge cottage-style storefronts commingle with modern glass-and-metal-body affairs. Each spot, though, carries an artisan air. Outside of a Walmart on the far end of town and our destination, McDonald's, every business is a local one.

I mark the names of the businesses as we drive. None of their bags litter Barb's hidden caches. She may have lived here for decades, participated in all the civic events, donated to their charities, but she spent her money elsewhere. Why?

There's a line at McDonald's, which I find comforting for the first time in my life. At least I'm not the lone out-of-towner going to the only chain eatery. Self-consciousness settles in my belly. Oregon visits have always gotten to me, but this one has rattled me more than most. I'm thankful not to have to bear Barb's backhanded digs the whole time, but I'm also literally steeped in the woman's life. She's everywhere, and Luke is...not.

He orders for me—we rarely hit fast-food joints, but I get the same thing every time—and gets himself a drink. A Coke from them hits different. I get it.

A man with a long mustache waves us down before we can exit the parking lot. Luke pulls up beside him and rolls down the window.

"Luke Lowe!" the man bellows. He's roughly our age. His red suspenders are for fashion as his jeans seem to fit just fine. "I heard you were in town."

Luke flips on the charm. "Just got in."

"We thought we'd see you down at Frankie's last night. Drinks on us if you want to come on by tonight." He nods to me then. "And bring the pretty girl. We always need more pretty girls here."

Luke laughs. His real laugh. "She's spoken for, Waylon."

"I'm not in the market either." He wiggles the ring on his left hand at my husband. "Have to think your mama for that one."

"Barb played matchmaker?" I blurt. I thought she'd only wanted to do that for Luke—and mostly to get rid of me.

Waylon's belly laugh brings genuine humor to a five-mile radius. A joy I am jealous of. "In her way. Peyton pissed off Barb at the food bank."

"How does one cause problems at a food bank?" Luke asks, clearly already judging the girl.

"She wasn't. Barb got all in a snit about 'an outsider' starting that triple-bean stew without getting permission from her."

"How'd she know to make it then?"

"Peyton volunteers there all the time. She didn't realize Barb was in charge, even if she didn't work there."

Now that sounds like my mother-in-law.

"So how'd you end up with Peyton?" Luke shoots a quick glance at the clock but continues smiling.

"Barb kicked her out back with me. Told her she could break down boxes." He beams. "We spent the whole day talking, and before you know it, I'm in love. We've been married ten months."

"Congratulations, Waylon," we both say.

"Thanks so much. You really should come by the bar. A round of drinks will do you some good. Everyone is just so sorry for your loss, man." Waylon means it, but the rote language washes right over Luke. His gaze narrows, just for a moment. Enough for me to see the ill ease.

"It was lovely to meet you, Waylon, but lunch calls." I lift my Happy Meal up like any adult should be proud of their kid-sized lunch.

He chuckles and bows out of the conversation.

Luke pulls out of the lot, and our smiles fade.

We haven't spoken to each other since we left the house. As the car bumps back toward it, I have to say *something*.

"Did you know there's an extra attic space off of your mom's bedroom?" Is it the most elegant way to ask? No, but I got it out there.

The car slows, the speedometer dropping ten miles per hour. Luke lifts his chin, but remains focused on the road. "An attic?"

"Yeah. It's...where I found that box with Cassidy Warren's name on it." Worry thickens my voice, like I'm a child waiting to be reprimanded. That's not our dynamic, and I hate it.

"I wouldn't worry about it." He slows for a stop sign but doesn't fully pause.

He wasn't the one finding doll parts or having to face a wall of boxes in that hidden room. "Part of that doll was in the backyard last night."

Tension radiates from Luke. His knuckles have gone white where he grips the steering wheel. The muscle in his jaw is ticking like a bomb in the final throes of countdown. "Are you certain it was that doll?"

"Well, unless you dumped more dolls in the trash that night." I try to laugh, but it's just a halfhearted whine. Because there are more dolls. So many more.

The speedometer jumps back up ten miles per hour. "Sorry about that. I'll make sure the lids on the trash bins are firmly closed."

"Not your fault at all, babe." The distance between us billows until it's bigger than the center console of the rental car. Do I tell him about the marbles too? Katy's doll? His intense glare out the windshield smacks of punishment for the question.

I want to ask why he doesn't want to talk about this, why it's clearly stressing him out. I should be able to talk to him. "Did you know about the attic? Are there others that we should plan for in the house?" I try again.

He huffs with derision, but his fingers tighten on the wheel. "Oh, there are crawl space doors in some of the upstairs closets. It's just to give access for insulation and the like." It's such a plausible answer.

Only this isn't that. "I thought I'd check it out again this afternoon. See if I can get the boxes there pulled out so we can go through them."

"No," he snaps.

"Excuse me?" I sharpen the question. We don't yell, but that was too close.

Luke rubs the back of his hand against his chin like I've shocked him. "I just want to be done here. To go back home." It's exactly what I want to hear. He continues. "I don't think we need to worry about going hands and knees into crawl spaces. Let's get the bedrooms clear, the office, the dining room. Let's make some charities happy before we start stressing about what might be tucked in with old insulation."

I hadn't seen a tuft of pink or yellow fiberglass when I'd been up there, but I had been firmly focused on the sea of cardboard.

I agree with him, because it's not a hill to die on. Yet bitterness claws the back of my throat. Katy's injury. Cassidy's disappearance.

The chill that bit me in Barb's home. The only way to shake it all, to feel safe, is to understand it. I'm going back in that room. Even if I don't want to admit it now.

At the house, Luke types furiously on his phone while I scarf down my McNuggets and fries.

"Are you solid? Work okay?" I ask.

His furrowed brows smooth when he lifts his attention to me. "Oh, yeah. It's nothing important."

"Glad nothing is on fire." Only now I'm curious as hell.

Being in a room with one other person who is on their phone is deeply isolating. They have a connection you're not privy to, and it underscores their priorities. I hate being the third wheel in my own home. Turns out I hate it in this house too.

"Who are you chatting with?" I blurt.

"No one. Just replying to Facebook comments." He punctuates this supercasual comment with a long sip of his soda. He thumbs the lock button and then places his phone screen-side down on the table. "Everyone is reaching out about Mom since the scholarship information went live."

Right. They'd announced that a couple weeks ago. Barb had a small trust that she'd funded for a scholarship to be made in her name at the local high school.

"Well, I'm glad people are excited to celebrate her good works." Rockside Bay needs more funding like that. "Do you think we should do an estate sale and add that money to the scholarship trust?"

Luke's upper lip pulls back, like he must flash his teeth at me to warn me away from his spoils. He schools his features quickly, but I spy the disgust all the same.

"Mom funded it fully. So we're good to use my inheritance as we see fit. I'm sure you'd love to do more with our local causes." Luke has been pulled between his mother and me for years. The reminder that Barb's estate can help Luke and me build our community is a kindness from him, and yet everything about the rules with the money makes me uncomfortable.

I dip my nugget in sauce. Charity work and chicken nuggets. It'll be okay. "You know me well."

"My bighearted beauty. You're the reason I won't go to hell." It's not the first time he's made this joke, but it hits differently today.

I blow him a kiss anyway.

His phone vibrates again, and then he's texting.

"You might have to go on Do Not Disturb mode to get anything accomplished today."

"I'll mute Facebook after this one," he says, still staring at his phone.

Facebook almost always meant Kim. His high school sweetheart has been posting her little cheerleader-y messages on his wall since Barb died. Nice messages about his mom, who she'd "cared for deeply."

It shouldn't sting, but holy shit does it.

Five minutes later I'm alone on the second story again staring at the mountain of paper I'd unearthed next to Barb's elliptical trainer. I could see the Marketplace ad for it now. "Like-new elliptical. Never been used. Vanity piece. Great for fitness or storage.

Any scuff marks are newspaper ink and will wipe off with a Magic Eraser." Not that Luke would let me sell anything of his mom's without scrubbing it to perfection first.

Scooping an armful of old newspapers against my body is a tricky undertaking, and several editions slip to the floor. Something small and shiny peeks at me from amid the newsprint. I stoop down. My earring winks back at me. It's a diamond stud in an antique cut, part of a pair Luke bought me two Christmases ago. They'd been my everyday wear for months. I look for the matching partner, but it's nowhere on the ground. *How odd.* An unfamiliar tendril of fear slips down my center. Is the other earring in a box in the attic? I close my eyes tightly and will the thought away.

Focus on your task.

I tuck the stud in my pocket and gather the papers again. I drop this first set in the hallway. There's no way I'm reading hundreds of local newspapers as part of getting the house cleaned. There is a big recycling bin outside waiting to be filled.

I snag the ones I dropped earlier and place them on top of the stack. August 1981. I shake my head at the date. No wonder the pages are yellowed and curling. The headline is a sad one, too. *Fisherman Bert Wall Missing.* At least it wasn't a story about another member of the Warren family. Between seeing Cassidy's name on that box and Kim probably posting more support for my husband online, that family was under my skin.

My fingers itch to grab my phone, to look at Luke's social media. Only I trust him. There's never been a risk of him cheating. *There isn't now.* This is loneliness talking, I tell myself. And yet I still conjure an image of Kim's face. The one that keeps popping up in my pending friend requests, which she has ignored for the last four years. It shouldn't razz me. I have no reason to be friends with anyone from this town, much less someone who used to date my husband. That's drama I don't need in my life. And yet her smooth blond hair, her perfectly contoured features, her ruby lips challenge my ego.

Luke is different in Rockside Bay. That is the trouble with us coming here, beyond Barb. People change, a little bit, when they return to their hometown. Part of your brain reverts to a younger version of yourself. It's like rewatching an early season of your favorite show and suddenly you catch all the foreshadowing but can't help but fall into those expected emotional beats all the same.

I don't doubt that same thing happens to me when I return to my dot of a hometown in West Texas, but there, everyone still knows my sister. They know what happened with our parents. If you're going to school hungry and in threadbare clothes in a small town, people notice. The kids remembered the times Mallory went to school dirty before I realized I had to tell her to take a bath. Even now when I come back, the people I grew up with whisper about how I don't do enough for Mallory. As if anyone knows what I do for her, what her kids need.

Fixing others' crises is a skill I came by naturally. And yet Barb's house has rattled something in my marrow. A phantom itch flickers between my shoulders. I stretch my neck muscles and make myself ignore my stupid phone and the unhelpful information I'd find on it.

"All right, room. Let's do this." The invocation does it for me, and I grab the next stack of papers. A little gust cuts through the hallway whenever I drop a new stack out there. I'm thankful that Luke must have opened a window.

The dates on the papers span decades. The oldest ones are from the late 1960s, and then there is one from just two years ago. There's no organization to them—and why would I expect any? While I refuse to read these things—*eyes on the prize, Addison*—the headlines are *right there*. For such a tiny town, this place has seen tragedy hit over and over. Or Barb was cataloging the worst moments in Rockside Bay for posterity. Some last names appear frequently, which I suppose is common in a small community, but I can't help but commit each to memory as I heft load after load of newspapers to the hallway and then down to the recycling can out back.

Taylor.

Meints.

Borden.

Warren.

It's the last batch that has a story about Cassidy. The final papers I find are beneath a table lamp on a small marble stand at the far side of the exercise equipment. If Luke had joined me, I could have asked the purpose of putting a little reading lamp next to the gym equipment, but he isn't here, and Cassidy Warren's name is in front of me again.

I sit on the newly cleared floor and gather the paper to my lap. The pages are slick. My skin is already marked with inky battle wounds from the newsprint.

LOCAL TEEN CASSIDY WARREN STILL MISSING

The headline is direct, but it's the smaller second heading that is the real sucker punch:

MOTHER PLEADS, "PLEASE HELP US FIND OUR BELOVED DAUGHTER"

A tear splats on the page, blurring the words. Then another. My sadness is immersive. I am sorrow in the moment. I'm breathing grief. Those simple words, the standard copy when a person goes missing, crack me. The fissure behind my sternum is raw. There is always something about mothers and daughters that does this to me. When we lost our baby, I didn't know if it would have become a daughter or a son, but I imagine that mother's heartache. And it becomes mine. I shove the paper away.

Too much sadness in this town.

In this house.

Accidents and tragedies happen everywhere, but at least in a bigger city, they could feel more spread out. Less likely to hit you. Here, they've already found my family. We will recover, but Luke and I need to leave Rockside Bay to start that process again.

We cannot become the next Warrens who befall bad luck. I refuse to become a headline.

I fold the paper and throw it on top of my recycle stack.

Redoubling my efforts, I find a desk with drawers full of my husband's report cards and old phone bills for the house line. Detailed call records for when Luke was in college.

"Barb, you were one hell of a weirdo," I say under my breath. The drawer slips from the track and crashes to the floor. I jump back just in time to avoid yet another bruise. Not that it would have been my fault. Not that it stopped the contents from scattering around me, making more work.

CHAPTER 12

LUKE AND I BOTH FELL INTO BED EARLY LAST NIGHT, EXHAUS-tion pushing us into restful hours quickly and not because we were avoiding awkward conversations. Definitely not. This morning, I wake before him again. At least I'm not dripping in sweat and mired in panic. That's something. I repeat what is quickly becoming my comfort morning routine: joggers, blanket selection, coffee, and out to the back deck.

A hazy orange cuts across the top of the fence line, but the deck is still cool in the shadows.

The crows are already in the yard. It seems unfair that a group of them is called a murder when they bring me such joy. I bring out a bag of peanuts still in the shell—the internet told me this is the most precious treat.

I climb down the four steps from the deck to the grass and sprinkle three handfuls into the yard. Immediately, Eddie's attention is on me. I thought the bird would look to the snacks first, but he's watching me. I retreat back to my chair.

Eddie caws at his feathered brethren. A moment later, six crows are strutting around the lawn feasting on the goodies. Each of the birds has sharp, beady eyes and the signature deep-black feathers, but they move among one another in a display of personality. One of the larger ones hops from spot to spot. Another keeps checking her tail feathers after each treat. They chatter to one another, presumably about the meal. I am effectively invisible. And that's fine. I've been swimming in loneliness at this house, but watching these birds is comforting, even if I'm a mere observer. I drink my coffee, and it's like sharing a companionable breakfast with new friends.

Eddie and the tail-feather crow hop toward me. They remain down in the grass though. I'm calling the pretty preening girl Selene, I decide, meeting the crow's gaze.

"There are more peanuts closer to the driveway," I say, pointing toward my right.

Selene follows the gesture. She doesn't go for the food. Eddie merely watches me.

"Are you okay?" I wish someone would ask me that.

Eddie comes a little closer. Is that his way of asking?

"We're cleaning out this house." I pause, but the freedom of telling someone who can't talk back or be invested in it or have their feelings hurt is freeing. I continue. "Though it's clearly not going as quickly as I'd like."

Selene bobs her cute little head.

"I know, right?" I toss a couple more peanuts her way. "We're all on the same side."

I twist in my chair to look through the window. Lights are off. No Luke. I turn back to my crow friends, leaning in like we're conspiring for me to join the murder.

"I'm fairly certain Barb felt the same way about you that she felt about me." The birds click and caw at my late mother-in-law's name. "Exactly."

Another crow swoops into our conversation. Or, I guess, my opining to the birds in the backyard. When I think of it that way, this might not be the healthiest choice. But telling Luke how much this house is rattling me is off-limits. He wore his fatigue on his face last night. I'm not surprised he's sleeping in again.

"What was her problem with you guys? She didn't think I was good enough for her son. As if anyone could be." Though if I believe Kim's latest post on social media, Luke's ex would have been Barb's prime pick for his wife.

Small-town society type. Conventionally attractive. Smart but not likely to outshine Luke.

"I should have ticked her boxes for approval," I tell the crows. "I graduated college in three years. I'm a damn good CPA. I'm cute and curvy. What's wrong with me?" I can't make myself say the answer aloud, though it screams in my mind. My family is poor. It didn't matter that I worked hard to find success, to help support my sister, to help her have resources to learn and provide for her kids. Barb had only ever seen me as beneath her.

"There's nothing wrong with you either, my lovely friends. Whatever reason you're guarding this place, I appreciate you."

Eddie and Selene take this as an invitation, apparently, and fly up to land on the little bistro table.

A warning rises in the back of my mind. Luke swore these birds dive-bombed, pecked, injured. Should I be this close?

The crows talk among one another. Such intelligent birds, but I have no idea what they are conveying to each other. It feels like it is about me, but my body eases the longer I'm in their presence. I roll my shoulders, stretch, let them have their moment.

Selene flies off around the side of the house. The uncanny presence of the hidden attic behind me and up to my left presses harder and harder against my top vertebrae, like it wishes to slice down my spine and overwhelm my nervous system.

Eddie raps his beak against the table, and I jerk my head up. *You've got my attention, friend.* He taps his black beak against the table again and looks at me expectantly.

"What do you need?"

His only reply is to stare at me harder. And OMG, crow stares are piercing.

"I'm doing my best here. Luke is gutted, and there is so much in this house that I don't understand and unnerves me." Why am I saying this aloud? It's like Eddie is making me affirm my feelings. I shake my head. "Have you considered a career in counseling?"

Before the bird can ignore that question too, Selene returns. She drops a red bead on the table and flies off beyond the garden fence.

I exhale all the relief I garnered this morning, my body deflating in front of yet another tiny bead. This one has the letter *S* on it.

"Did you find this bracelet by the trash cans?" It's the only plausible answer now. Luke pitched the Cassidy Warren box. The bracelet must have slipped from it. Probably how that rogue arm ended up beneath the dahlias.

"I don't need prizes in exchange for the peanuts. I just like having company in the morning," I tell Eddie, like he's going to get that I don't want another one of these beads messing with my mind.

The crow pushes the bead closer to me, raps the glass table again, and then flies off. The "take it" is clear. I pocket the bead. The fresh chill cutting a path down my back is because of the wind and not anything else.

I wait nearly five minutes before I walk down the steps again and over to the trash barrels. There's no bracelet anywhere on the ground. Maybe there were just the two beads? Maybe the birds took it to a safe place?

I swipe my hair off the back of my neck, looping it around my hand and up into a makeshift twist. I hold it there, high on my head, and let the crisp morning air cool my skin. I close my eyes and focus on the shushing of the water in the distance and the rattle of leaves in the tree nearby. When I open my eyes, I take in the side of Barb's house. Tall, white, stalwart. Vines still lashed to the wall. Here they practically appear to climb down from the rooftop. I'll ask Luke if he found the tools to remove them. I start to turn back to the deck when I see movement upstairs. At the third-floor window, there's a flash of sharp features and blond hair piled high. Barb Lowe is very dead, and yet I can't stop seeing her.

I blink a dozen times, tears dotting my lashes, and when I gaze up again, the window is empty. The chill gripping my heart remains.

I don't wait for Luke to stumble into the kitchen. He needs rest, but I need to act. I head back upstairs and start hauling everything I can out of the rooms and into the hallway. This morning's bounty includes more newspapers—good lord, this lady liked periodicals—several tote bags of men's dress socks with the tags still on, as if she picked up a pair for Luke every time she bought something for herself and then just never gave them to him. Finally, there is a corner packed with towers of paperback books. The piles were well over four feet tall but had the stability of a Jenga game with only center blocks remaining.

Luke had expressly said we should review every book title before deciding to donate. There might be first editions. There might be ones we want for our collection. Special titles from his childhood. Except if there's a beloved book in this room, he already has a copy in our house.

We need to donate these. Flat out. I grab my phone from the charger in the bedroom. Luke is snoring even at nearly 10:00 a.m. I should wake him. His help means going home faster. But there are cracks on his lips, a sallow tinge to his skin, and even in sleep, his brow is drawn under the weight of everything. I kiss his forehead and leave quietly.

The local library's web address redirects to its Facebook page. I verify the hours. We can drop books off for donation anytime today before five. If I can get Luke on board. I suck my lips, but it doesn't help with decision-making. I can move everything into the hallway, pack it into boxes, and let Luke review it this afternoon. That'll give him a task that isn't the office. He stayed in there with paperwork until nearly nine last night.

The notifications tab in my Facebook app has two updates for me. I can't resist the dopamine hit of clearing the queue. It's like inbox zero for social media—satisfying.

There's nothing gratifying about the updates. "Luke Lowe commented on Kim Warren's post."

I should not care. It's Facebook. It's probably a simple thanks for whatever motivational quote she'd posted to help him with this "trying time." That is the phrase she uses in most of the posts. I've been through loss, and I'd never label it as a trying time. We're not trying; we're surviving or grieving or processing. There's no halfway with emotions. If there was, I would have found it by now.

Properly riled, I click on the stupid link. There's Kim's perfectly made-up face. She'd reposted an update from the Rockside Bay Food Bank announcing an opening on their board of directors, specifically a fundraising chair. Kim's addition to the post tagged my husband. Because that's what he needs.

"No one can fill the amazing—and stylish!—shoes of Barb Lowe. I feel her absence throughout our community, but I'm eager to raise my hand to help the food bank. I hope others will follow in Barb's footsteps and offer to help them with service or support. @Luke Lowe."

She didn't even talk about him. Merely pinned his profile to her thoughts with a tag like they're linked and not exes from more than a decade ago.

No wonder he looks so grim holding his phone lately. It's sending digital flares to view another's thoughts about his mom. He has his own feelings to deal with. This house and its memories are more than enough without the locals invoking Barb's name to make themselves look caring, *Kim.*

I scroll down to view his reply. Luke is too kind to say, "Don't tag me," but I want to be that person for him.

His reply isn't about Barb or the unnecessary tag. "The food bank would be lucky to have your efforts. You have my vote, Kim."

He's not on the board. We have our own food bank to support back in Austin. And we do. I write letters to get donations for their school backpack program. A percentage of our paychecks goes straight to them. I love this kind of work, so why does this rankle me so much? He's being kind. Supportive. It's what Barb would expect of him.

But he didn't mention any needs of the local charities to me beyond the scholarship and trust requirement generalities. Why hide this? Why not tell me he cares about supporting causes here? He's not leaning on me for support; he's sleeping and replying to Facebook posts.

We need to go home. It's the only thought it my head. We can't heal here. This house sets my teeth on edge, but being here is pulling him down and away from me. And I want out. I load all the books from this pass into the back of the car. They fill the entire trunk. I'm tempted to grab a few of the totes of books from Barb's bedroom too, but if I go up there, I'll fall into clearing things and delay.

It has nothing to do with that small door at the back of her closet. Nothing to do with the beads still in my pocket.

I hate lying to myself.

The note I leave for Luke in the kitchen promises my speedy return. I sign it with a big heart and take off for the library.

CHAPTER 13

WHEN I RETURN FROM THE LIBRARY, LUKE IS LOUNGING IN the kitchen. I have never seen anyone *lounge* in Barb Lowe's home. He rises smoothly and meets me.

"Hey, beautiful." He slips his hand low on my waist and presses a kiss to my temple.

The delectable scent of his crisp soap beneath the clean cologne I'd bought him for his birthday envelopes me. It's this perfect heady combination that hits all my buttons, which is good since I'm married to the man.

I curl toward him, slipping my hand over his shoulder and toward the back of his head. He takes the hint and leans in for a proper kiss. Heat and focus and that electric zing lighting my skin in the way only Luke can capture my everything. It's almost enough to make me forget where we are, but exactly what I need. No matter the place, we're Luke and Addison. We're the power team. We're one. He's mine and vice versa. I secure this belonging tight in my chest. Other feelings have their own boxes, but my love for Luke has earned its prime position at my core.

He pulls back first but keeps his forehead against mine. "I needed that this morning."

I don't correct him and say that it's nearly noon. "Anytime," I say, infusing as much of myself, my need, and my thoughts into it. "Why does it look like you're leaving though?"

He sighs and steps back enough for us to have a conversation. "I've got lunch plans today."

He's in a button-down, and I'm in a T-shirt one hundred percent marked with sweat from my manual-labor morning. "Guessing they aren't with me?"

Luke cringes, and my gut clenches.

"No worries," I add quickly. I am all worries, which makes it easy to let others hold none of them. "I've got so much to get through. Making good progress this morning."

"You could come—"

"It's fine, Luke. Go. You deserve a break." Getting out of the house is good, promising. It's certainly better than hiding away in Barb's office for yet another afternoon.

He takes my hand, fingers loosely entwined with mine. "Don't haul boxes out back while I'm gone. If anything needs to be carried downstairs or outside, make a pile. I'll do it for you."

Bless him. My arms are already sore from this morning's jaunts. "Oh, there will be plenty of work saved for you."

His dimple appears, and I grin at him.

"I should be back in a couple hours at most."

I nod, and then we stand there in silence verging on awkward.

Finally he says, "I need the car keys."

"Oh, shit. Sorry. Here you go." I hand over the rental's bulky key ring.

He doesn't even ask how I did with driving the car. *Surprisingly well.*

And then he is gone, and I am left to my own devices inside Barb Lowe's house.

My mother-in-law excluded me at every opportunity, unless that meant leaving me in her home alone. I'd never been permitted to sleep in if she and Luke wanted to take an early hike. I could never be the person who stayed behind while others ran errands. Luke had told me it was about underscoring that I was part of the family. More like Barb didn't trust me not to touch her things. Or pocket them.

"Bet you couldn't have imagined a scenario where I'm the person assessing your possessions for value," I say, like the woman is here.

Wind rattles the windows on the western side of the house, but otherwise silence reigns.

"I'm going to touch every vase, book, and picture frame, and I'm doing it for Luke. So he doesn't have to face the wild amount of unnecessary shit you accumulated."

The first floor continues to be mostly inoffensive, but I am making progress on the second level. I return there and try to open the bedroom door next to the one Luke and I are staying in. The handle sticks. I jiggle the knob. It clicks but doesn't open. I fidget with it until the latch releases, and the brilliance on the other side of the door would tempt a dragon. Crystal is stacked left, right, and center, each item cut with precision to catch the light from any angle. Reaching for the light switch might be dangerous, but I shield my eyes and flip the toggle upward.

After my eyes adjust, I step into the room fully. Where books sit in stacks on floors and crammed in tote bags in other rooms, here the walls are lined with crystal on built-in shelves. Clear tote bins form miniature mazes in here. Did the local closet storage place know my mother-in-law by name? I groan. Barb hadn't let anything go, but this required thought. She'd planned to house all of this. Why? A tacky layer of pity settles on my shoulders, slowing my movements and making me look at the bins more closely. Heavy wool blankets press against the plastic in places, like a child who can't resist smushing their face against a window.

Sorting the heavy cut-crystal items goes slower than my book binge earlier. I place seven vases in the hallway. There are goblets and candy dishes and serving bowls. Not a one that has ever made an appearance at a holiday meal I've attended. I start moving the next round out into the hallway. We have no use for a crystal rooster at our house. Much less nine of them. Piece after piece has the retail tag attached. The prices make *me* uncomfortable, and I'm not afraid of a solid "treat yourself" day. I take a deep breath, but the inhalation of dust has me sputtering. I press the back of my hand to my mouth, like I can quell the coughing fit through will alone. I turn my back on the crystal and step out into the hall. It's darker here, but I'm steadier. My lungs catch up; my knees are solid. *You're fine*, I reassure myself. Someone has to.

I look past my shoulder to the room, to everything I need to review and set a destination for. The light chases toward the door; it's like the stack of bowls has rolled closer to me in the last few seconds. I give the room my back again and let the normal stagnant air fill me with some sense of familiarity. All that crystal will raise so much money for good causes if we auction it off. That's the plan, I decide. Luke will like that, I tell myself.

I stare at the glistening glass. The sheer excess of it all flips my stomach. It's a collection of the demonstrable difference between who Luke had been as a kid and who I had been. It's not just the wastefulness of Barb's weird collecting. I don't come from money, but Luke truly doesn't understand that he did, despite living in a house so huge there could be rooms *forgotten*. It'd been a point of contention for us in the past. It's possible his mom hadn't hoarded crystal when he was a child, but he didn't know what poor looked like. His mom allowing him to make name-brand mac and cheese on the weekends was not a sign of financial strain. Moments like this underscored how different our lives were twenty years ago. We'd grown up in separate worlds and with vastly different support structures. Would he have dated me in high school? Would Barb have let him? A heavy laugh punches from my chest. *Absolutely not.*

She hadn't wanted him to date me when we met, much less marry me.

And yet the idea bothers me a lot. I continue cataloging the crystal, unwrapping enough dainty teacups to serve high tea to an army battalion. Bin after bin after bin of imported Czech Republic crystal. At least I'm not smudged with the ink of sad newspaper stories. The reminder doesn't ease my concern as much as I'd like.

I break for food and bring one of Barb's fancy goblets downstairs for my Dr Pepper. Luke is out to lunch, but I can be fancy too. Only I must bump the lid of my soda bottle against the rim of the glass, because it topples right off the counter. The cup breaks cleanly into two pieces. The precious twenty-three-flavored beverage spreads across the counter like an oil slick and drips onto the pieces.

"Oh, come the fuck on," I grumble and pick up the broken crystal.

Once again, I'm reminded that I don't belong here. I didn't push to go to lunch with Luke and whatever friend he's meeting, because I'm not really meant to be here. The weight of my overwhelm pushes me until I'm seated at the kitchen table with the pre-made chicken wrap I picked up earlier.

Probably better food wherever Luke went, I mutter to myself.

Across the table, Luke's iPad lights up. I shouldn't glance at it, but the screen is bright, and Luke's high school sweetheart's face is there. I grab the device and read the alert.

can't wait to see you!!! running late but buy me a beer u know what I like

Having lunch with a friend is great when that friend isn't Kim Warren. Luke knows her flirty little comments on social media rile me. He's well aware his mom used to invite Kim over every time we were in town. Find any excuse for his ex to be in the same room as me. And he has said nothing.

I'm his family. We don't hide things from one another.

Fire licks my cheeks, my throat. I clench my jaw and stare at Luke's screen until it dims. And then for another minute. There's no reason to be jealous. He's not interested in Kim. She may have been Barb's pick for him, but not his. He's never taken time away from me to meet her before. To talk to her alone. Perhaps it's that Kim understood his mother in a way I did not.

Well, we could rectify that now.

I bolt up the stairs. One flight. Another.

Barb's bedroom door is closed. Had I done that? The knob is cool beneath my palm, but I twist and shove the door open without care. The walkway I'd cleared around the bed is empty still, as is the pathway to the closet. Dust bunnies cluster at the corners of boxes. A few leap in the wake of my entry. I sneeze hard, like it stops them from burrowing in my sinuses.

Many people tuck their beloved objects in dresser drawers. Or they hide their secrets in the nightstand. Barb's whole house is like that—the top layer of a wedding cake meant only to be eaten at home. I don't think the old lady was strong enough to move the items she'd shoved in front of the dresser drawers. But then, she had the hidden attic.

The one with the tiny door she'd kept unhindered.

The boxes that disappear if you look the wrong way?

That had to be the real Barb. And I will get to know her my own way.

I don't know all of my husband's secrets, but I sure can dig into his late mother's.

The carved feather on the door calls to me, my fingers skating over it. The texture ripples right up my arm, centering me. No hesitation. I open the small door and crawl through. The switch is where I remember it, and I rise and flip on the overhead lights.

What? I stagger with the new view. There are boxes, but the walls stretch on and on endlessly. I can't see a back wall, a corner, anything. I step forward on unsteady feet. There's this pull at my core. It's beyond the need to see whatever Barb was hiding; it's as though I'm being sucked into something.

Swallowed.

I close my eyes, and the sensation slows. I count to ten until it ebbs further. When I open them, I'm standing between two stacks of boxes. The walls continue their elastic optical illusion, but it's surely the shifting of the boxes.

I laugh at myself. Loudly. "They're just boxes."

Creeeeeeeeeak.

I whirl on the sound in time to see the attic door slam shut. The click of the latch ping-pongs around me, the sound so like every lock in the house latching.

My heart punches in my chest. Darkness looms in the corners. Coming here was a dumb idea. I rarely am impulsive or jealous, and this is what it gets me. Locked in an attic that shouldn't even exist. Working my way back to the door is slow. I weave between the stacks of boxes. It's now a maze that goes on for miles. The air thickens, softens, like a cloud made of spun sugar. So like my dream the other night; my body is disconnected. It's mine but slower. As though I'm trying to race to the exit, but my physical form is making me stop and look at the boxes. There are so many, each with a woman's name scrawled on the side. I bump into the boxes, sending everything shifting to the side. Each container is light. Nothing falls out. Nothing breaks. It's not like Luke's ass taking out the ceramic elephant. The urge to straighten them is hard to resist, but no one is here to knock them over again. Hell, Luke didn't even want us to deal with the contents of the crawl space. I look up. Even if I stretch my arms high overhead, I can't reach the pitched ceiling here.

Soft white light outlines the doorway. It's not the siren's call I heard before from the other side but a welcome relief. That's the boring glow from an LED bulb. Nothing dreamlike about that.

I pick up the closest box, unwilling to have come in here for nothing. Its flaps are tattered, and yet instead of the musty scent of age, I only catch a hint of cotton candy on the air. My mouth waters in full Pavlovian response, and I hate myself a bit.

I only have cotton candy with my sister or her kids. It's only for good memories and only with her. Mallory would never be in this attic. Not that I'd given her the opportunity to tag along. She'd ask too many questions, pressure Luke too hard.

I take the box with me to the door and set it at my side. I flex my fingers, readying for a chill or another tricky latch that requires a proper yank at the precise moment. But the knob turns smoothly, the latch release barely audible.

Pushing the box through first is necessary. Whether it's instinct, awkwardness, or an unwillingness to have the door shut without me pulling the thing free, I'm not sure. What matters is I get both me and the box out. I need to see what my mother-in-law was hiding up here, and I need it to not be tied to a dead teenager. Truly, I need less answers in my life that involve someone being dead.

Zero death, please.

When both the box and I are out, I move to Barb's bed. I've done enough crouching on the floor for a lifetime in the last few days. An unfamiliar name is written in the same looping script as on the previous box—*Wendy Owen.*

Don't think her name.

Cassidy Warren.

Damn it, Addie.

Sitting next to the box, I'm wary to open it. I need to look inside, not for the dark thrill of poking at Barb's secrets when she clearly loved to poke at my life. Okay, a little of that. But more because I had to see that Cassidy Warren's box is normal. Nothing. I'm not sure what I want there to be in this box. I'm not sure if the contents matter. I just need it not to scare me.

I lift the flaps, dust littering my knuckles and the bedspread in the process. Inside there's another doll. Another feather. Pale-pink buttons. Unease roils in my belly, and sweat dampens my clothes.

That little brown-eyed doll stares at me. Ruby cheeks. White collared shirt with pink buttons down the front. My heartbeat threatens to choke me. I close my eyes, but the doll's gaze presses against my skin. A shiver shakes my spine, and I inch backward.

I don't touch a fucking thing in that box. I flick my middle finger toward the open flaps, only knocking each closed with the tip of my nail.

Another doll should mean that Luke is right. His mom was into crafts. If making eerie, "Why are her eyes tracking me?" dolls is a hobby. Only nothing about Barb had been hands-on. She liked to control a party, don't get me wrong. But the copious backups of backup items stashed through the house prove she was a buy-not-build kind of woman.

This doll and Cassidy's weren't gifts. Will Luke still hold the "craft" line once he sees this? He is hiding from so many of his feelings right now, and apparently hiding reconnection with old friends, but is it too hard to ask what his mom was doing with this stuff hidden away?

I'd wanted to find Barb's secrets, but this feels like so much more. Whatever is locked in that room, I am not about to let it be a part of the inheritance. At least Luke and I agree on that part.

I can wait for Luke to get back. I linger on the bed, the closed box next to me, counting the minutes until Luke returns from his lunch with Kim. Cleaning might move my brain along, but I'm too unnerved. Can I tell Luke about this doll? Is he solid enough right now to handle this, or am I pushing him away if I question his mother's creepy belongings?

It shouldn't be a question, and the reality that it is burrows doubt into my gut.

I hope Luke has never seen this doll before. I believe he truly had no idea these boxes were tucked away in hidden alcoves. Barb put him first in all things. I understand that instinct. My husband is hurting. I want to flatten the hill of mourning for him. But lying to him isn't the path.

An hour ticks by, and he's still not back. He's been so raw, so hurt. Maybe today doesn't have to be the day I unveil another of his mother's unnerving dolls. I can give him another day to show me he's stable before I confront him with yet another doll and bring up Cassidy Warren again.

I leave the box with the doll on the bed. If he gets brave enough to go in here on his own, he'll find it.

But my softness toward him wanes as the minutes tick by. The longer he's with Kim Warren, the more tinder lands on the fire of my frustration. I'm not taking care of him for the appreciation, but I also am not doing all of this to have another person be the priority.

I'll give him a reprieve on talking about Cassidy today. Her sister though? That's another story.

CHAPTER 14

WENDY OWEN'S NAME DOESN'T CLING TO MY BRAIN IN THE same way as Cassidy's has, but I can't forget her either. Who was she? How had she known Barb? Had I met her at the funeral? Why would my late mother-in-law have crafted a doll for this person?

If I believe Luke—and I always believe Luke—then the doll for Cassidy had been intended as a gift. Had this one been a present too? Was Wendy a young girl waiting for this doll? The box had been so dusty. If she had been a child, she'd be an adult now, going by the wear and tear on the box alone.

There are so many boxes in the secret attic. What other weird shit had Barb stuffed away there? Half-done projects? Toys for children she didn't have? I understand both of those situations. My attempt to teach myself crochet resulted in one little frog from a kit and four more kits of varied completion tucked in my bottom desk drawer. But Barb trying hobbies that she'd work on alone is too far for my mind to stretch.

An engine hums nearby. Perfect. I hotfoot down the stairs. Spiderwebs of anxious energy stick to my skin. The engine dies outside, a door slams. Luke will be inside soon. Back from his lunch with Kim Warren. *His ex*, a sharp voice hisses in my mind. The one who lost her little sister. The sister that Barb apparently had affection for. The longer I wait, the more the itch of inaction digs at me. I slide my fingernails across the pad of my thumb. The pressure isn't enough to leave a mark, but enough to hold me in the present.

Luke taps his shoes on the bottom step of the back porch. He comes into the house all smiles. He holds a travel cup from the little drive-through coffee shop. He extends it to me. His shirtsleeves are rolled back. Forearms don't have any right being sexy, but they are. Bet Kim thought so too.

"It's decaf, but I saw they were open and couldn't resist picking up a white mocha for you." He waggles the cup.

I accept it, but the ire simmering in my belly sloshes at the thought of being doused in sweet bribery coffee. Maybe this is the prelude to a confession?

"How was your lunch?" I ask, nibbling the words instead of snapping.

"Good." He steps around me and sits down at the kitchen table. His loafers clunk against the floor a moment later. He nudges them under his chair. "I didn't mean to be gone for so long, but we got to talking."

I nod. Talking. Can he tell I'm gnashing my teeth?

"You know how it is," he adds. So, yes, he's reading me.

"Sure. You didn't mention who you were with." I open the door for the truth.

He does not walk through. "Just an old friend."

I fold my arms, the mostly warm coffee heating my elbow. "You can say it was Kim."

All humor leaks from Luke's face. He licks his lips and then leans in, like we're in this together. Slowly, he says, "Yes, I had lunch with Kim. I didn't realize that was a problem."

"Then why didn't you mention it?"

"I honestly didn't think about it, Addie."

"Setting a lunch date with your ex didn't seem like a thing to share with your wife? That tracks." I hate this jealousy spicing my tongue, my heart. The fissures in the emotional lockboxes in my chest are widening. Bolts are melting; buckles are springing free. My feelings aren't staying in their places, and it's making this conversation messy.

I fucking hate being messy.

"You have nothing to worry about." He's on his feet now.

"That line doesn't help the lying." I can't even look at him.

We don't do secrets. We don't do lies. This is both. He could have punched me in the gut for how deeply this hit me, which only makes me madder. I don't want to feel this way. I don't want to have to open a door on sadness or even touch the latch on betrayal.

Luke's hands are heavy on my shoulders. "Babe, I didn't lie." Before I can refuse him, he moves closer, his nose near mine. "I should have told you I was with Kim. You've taken on so much in helping me deal with all of this, I just didn't want to add any extra strain."

I swallow hard. This is not how it works, but it'd be really wonderful to believe his choice was truly one meant to make my life easier. Only right now we've both been making Luke the priority.

"I appreciate that, but I don't think that's the whole reason you chose not to tell me." The hurt leaks all over my words.

Luke steps back but takes my hand in his. He's always been good about keeping us physically connected. It does make these types of conversations less confrontational.

My anger is alive in my chest, roasting on a bed of anxiety coals, each breath a bellows keeping it ablaze. My brain whips through a series of potential conversations, the ways he'll dismiss my feelings about Kim as irrational and then dance over to how gentle he's had to be with my feelings since we lost the baby. As though potential motherhood made me delicate. I've been galvanized by my loss. I'd cradled the joy of who I *could* be in my body, let my mind bathe in it. I'll do anything to get back to that feeling, to be back on the path to building our family and moving forward—including taking a breath to stop my mind from spiraling.

Luke isn't that person. He'd never throw my pain in my face. Our marriage is built on trust, and he gives it to me.

He leads me into the living room. We sit on the cream upholstery, which would be a wine magnet in any other home. He maintains his hold on my hand, rubbing his thumb in circles.

"I needed to talk to Kim," he starts.

"About?" Certainly not the local charity needs.

"First, a reminder that I have zero interest in Kim Warren. I love my hot wife and her brilliant brain."

"Yes, I'm a bombshell," I indulge him. "What brought you to lunch with Kim?"

He hesitates, and after a couple false starts, he says, "When I was in high school, Kim's little sister died."

"Cassidy Warren." I say the name and swear the temperature dips in the room.

He doesn't repeat her name but nods. "We talked about it a little the other day, but that happened when Kim and I were dating. Her family was broken. Cassie went missing, and the whole town was looking for her. I was out with her dad combing the beach and the woods. It was day after day, Ads. Just coming home and not having this girl back. I had been there for Kim and her family for the searches, and I stayed when it was clear Cassie was gone." He looks away, jaw clenching. "When they ruled her dead, it hurt everyone here."

I squeeze his hand. The pain of the past is made fresh in the room with us. Being in this place, in mourning, would reopen a wound like that, but perhaps so did finding the doll.

"Kim remembered how I'd been there for her family and wanted to offer the same. And Cassie's death was fresh in my mind after the other day. I owed it to her to let her try to help. She only wanted to talk about Mom and good memories with her. I swear, Addison."

"I believe you," I say with full confidence. "Secrets cut me though. Can you be up-front next time?"

He leans his side against mine. The corner of his mouth quirks in a weak attempt at a smile. "Finding that box the other day knocked my knees out. I'm sorry I reacted so poorly to it."

"Do you think your mom kept a box like that, the doll for Cassidy, for a reason?" It's close to asking about the other dolls, to acknowledging that something is off here.

He shrugs it off. "Sentimentality? Mom kept a close relationship with the Warrens."

Luke dodges any other attempt I make to talk about the dolls, pivoting to how much he misses Barb and how sad he is that our kids will never get to meet her. A fresh wave of grief washes over me, and I stop pushing.

Maybe having extra support for Luke is a good thing. And I was able to clear more of the house while he was out. It won't be long until we return to our happy life in Austin, and we can work on building the family we want.

CHAPTER 15

CLEARING OUT THE THIRD-FLOOR ROOMS IS A FAR MORE enjoyable experience than I'd predicted. While a large part of me wanted to yeet boxes out the windows, the thick vines trapping the shutters closed would have made it difficult. I hold on to this as the only reason I'm sitting on the tufted round rug at the center of the loft space, opening each box, and checking each item with care.

It has nothing to do with the fact that Luke is only two feet away doing the same thing. It takes so much longer with him here, but there is a weight lifted when he's with me.

But not just for me.

His movements are lighter. His shoulders are square again—his natural state. Some men puff their chests for attention, but Luke's confidence is intrinsic to *him*. It's a natural power that drew me to him in our college days. The harsh lines that gouged his forehead earlier have eased into echoes of their former ravines. His phone is staying pocketed, too. Separating him from paperwork has historically resulted in more stress for my workaholic spouse, but his mother's documents twisted him differently. Pulling him from her contracts and *that office* cured his worries.

"I can't believe she kept this," he says for the tenth time in as many minutes. Awe wraps him with each uncovered item. The mementos and keepsakes and random clothing items that act as touchstones captivate him.

Luke is on a treasure hunt where everything is gold.

It's such a better way to approach the emptying of the estate than my disdain.

"What did you find?" I set my own box aside. Full attention on Luke.

He holds a VHS tape aloft. It's sealed in one of those hard black cases, a handwritten label slipped into a clear sleeve. "Fourth grade class project."

"You made a film in fourth grade?" My school didn't have a video recorder to lend out until middle school. And even then, it was only the one.

He turns the video tape in his hands, eyes shimmering as if he's watching the tape's contents in his mind's eye. His chuckle is distant but delighted. "Yes. It was terrible."

"Let's not be too harsh. You were in fourth grade." My cheeks ache from stifling my humor. A self-deprecating Luke is a rare delight.

He waggles the tape at me. "If I can find a VHS player, you'll agree with me."

Oh, this has to be good. "I would not mock a kid."

"You haven't seen me with a fake beard and a top hat flexing my nonexistent acting chops as Abraham Lincoln."

"You know, I'm game for you to dress up if that's what brings you joy." I gesture widely, as though open arms somehow say I'm down for whatever, for him, and I guess for our sixteenth president?

He drops to his serious, deposition voice. "Got an untapped presidential kink there, Addison?"

I shrug and give him my best coy smile. "Not all presidents."

"Just Honest Abe? It's the hat, isn't it?" He's already snickering.

"Beards and wigs. Founding Fathers or get the fuck out." I have to make my joke through gasping breaths. Tears track my cheeks.

"It's not *that* funny, babe." He says that, but he's laughing hard too.

"Funnier than you dressed as Abraham Lincoln?"

"Thought we weren't mocking kids?" He clasps his hands to his chest, faking offense.

"Oh, I meant picturing you all grown now and stovepiped up."

"You're going to regret that when I find a hat like that here." He pounces on me. Lips at my ear, half talking, half kissing.

This is the magic of our dynamic. Chemistry and connection and *understanding*. This man gets me to my core.

I'm still giggling even with him on top of me. We're both shaking from my laughter. "You find that hat, I'm down."

When we finally part, the loft is sweltering. While so much of the house is chilled, this space is thick with wet heat. I pull the elastic from my hair and retie my curls up in a sloppy bun. Like a fresh topknot will magically cool me.

This sticky space is stacked with small boxes. Little keepsakes. Luke has made a surprisingly large pile of school art projects he wishes to keep.

"Our kids might like seeing what my school projects looked like when they're in the thick of it," he says defensively.

Yearning spears my chest. *Our kids.* Instinct pulls my hand toward my abdomen, like I can conjure connection to the past or the future or the life we're supposed to be living simply by pressing my palm against my body. I grit my teeth and force my hand toward another box.

"I love that you're thinking that way." My voice goes watery, but no tears are shed.

I pull a white shirt box free from the closest pile. One corner is worn, as though the box is only ever opened from there. I do the same.

White tissue paper billows inside. A gift for someone else, or one Barb received and never bothered to unpack? My stomach twists, and my fingers hover over the packaging. This box is too small to have a porcelain doll in it, but if I'm wrong and move that paper, and creepy lifelike eyes are staring at me, I can't be held liable for my actions. *Should I warn Luke?*

He's here. I'm not alone. This is not one of the boxes from the hidden attic. The box is blank and thin. It's light in my lap. Not a sweater like the ones we pulled free from the boxes we've now shunted toward the door.

Addie, you're overthinking it. Again.

I glance at my husband. He's thumbing through a pile of Little Golden Books. *The Poky Little Puppy* already at his side. His presence, steadiness, nearness, it all helps.

I peel back the paper, and my heart squeezes. I suck my lips in, holding them between my front teeth and slowly run my fingers over the delicate white fabric inside.

"Luke." I choke on his name. This shouldn't have overwhelmed me, but the longer I stare at the little blue collar, the tighter my chest gets.

The books plunk to the floor, and he is on his knees at my side. "Addison?" Panic weaves through my name.

"Look," I eke out. I can't stop petting the baby clothes.

His arm rests heavy on my shoulders. He reels me in until my side slams into his solid chest. Grief is tricky. It's fresh for Luke, and that's where my focus is. Where it should be. But this tiny outfit—so clearly a luxe dress-up onesie for a newborn—has shot me into the past. To the agony of losing the potential of a little one of our own. To saying farewell to being called *Mom*. To my own heavy loss hardening my stomach, shifting me to stone.

Luke rests his head on mine. Can he tell I'm turning into a statue?

"We'll have a baby." He is resolute.

"I know," I reply, because I'm supposed to lie.

He squeezes me hard enough it hurts. "You will be the mom. To our baby. It'll happen."

A sob shakes me. "When?"

It's not fair to ask, but Luke kisses my temple.

"It's not up to us when it happens, but I hope we will go back to building our family when we get home." There's no anxiety piercing his promise. Has this always been his plan?

"It's okay if you're not ready," I say, because I should, because it's right, because I love him and we both have to be in the proper headspace.

His arms loosen enough for me to be comfortable, but he doesn't release me. "This place is a good reminder of family. I get that you had your differences, but I think you'd be an amazing mother just like my mom."

It hits like a backhanded compliment, but for Luke it's ultimate praise. "Thank you," I whisper, eyes still on the delicate little outfit.

"That was mine," he says.

"What?" I give him my attention.

The apples of his cheeks are pink, a wistful smile plays at his mouth.

"The outfit," he explains. "I'm sure we'll come across the pictures, but Mom had me in that for some of the first baby pictures."

"I thought you wore a sailor suit?" He'd made me vow to never put our kid in one.

"She did that, too. There were a lot of outfits, Ads." He plays like he hated it, but Luke acquiesced to his mom with gusto. For all her faults, she raised a hell of a son.

When I'm steady, we move on. But I keep peeking at the baby clothes. Had Barb kept them because she loved remembering Luke as a tiny being, or had she held on to them for our baby?

For the first time, I relate to Barb Lowe. Her infinite love for Luke drove her forward. I love him, but at my core, I'm aware that I will be like Barb in putting the care of our children first. If only she could have seen that being kind to me, accepting his choice were signs of her love, it would have been a zillion times easier. But I was not her child.

I try to imagine myself in her shoes. Worried about my child moving several states away. Being alone. Them being without me. It had to be a mule kick to the chest. What would it have taken to make Barb trust me with her son?

I try not to dwell. It only doubles my stress and doesn't solve a damned thing. Instead I work through a mass of keepsake clothing items from varied stages of my husband's life.

"We should keep that," Luke says as I toss a pair of corduroy pants into the donate pile.

"Babe, I hate to break this to you, but they won't fit."

"What if our—"

"No," I stop him. "Cool things we can't buy for them again we can keep, but we can buy cords if they come back into style for our kids."

"If? Harsh there, Ads."

"I'm ruthless," I laugh. "That's why you brought me with you."

"No, I brought you because I love you and my home is wherever you are."

Heat surges to my cheeks. I open my mouth to offer some sappy sweetness.

Luke grins. "The fact you're ruthless is a bonus."

"So the cords go." I throw a second, chocolate-brown pair onto the pile.

"If you find a leather jacket though..." He narrows his gaze like it's a test.

"They're always cool. We keep leather jackets."

Luke wears that playful smile I know and an affable ease as he moves around the room, but I catch the dip in his shoulders at my words. He needs to keep things almost as badly as his mother had. I'm here to keep it reasonable.

If I can.

CHAPTER 16

I'D HALF EXPECTED LUKE TO JOIN ME FOR COFFEE THE NEXT morning. We'd had this blissful day of reminiscing and surprises and laughter. He slept like a stone, and when I wake, he is eerily still, in the same position he'd been in when I got up at three for water. Emptying the hoarder's den is exhausting, even in the brighter moments. My body aches in a way it hasn't in years.

There had been a time when I trained for obstacle-based marathons. The kind of physical endurance event where you were covered in filth by the end. Getting an actual medal for perseverance did more than stroke my ego; back then I'd needed the prize to keep it together. Funny how a decade changes us. In those days, I wouldn't have even stretched in the mornings. Idiocy of youth. Now I try to quell the cries in my thighs and shoulders with a quick run-through of my favorite yoga moves. When that doesn't cure me, I pop a trio of ibuprofen and venture downstairs for coffee.

I have no proof that caffeine makes pain relievers work more quickly, but it certainly isn't going to hurt me. While the pot brews,

I head to the pantry cabinet and reach behind a box of rotini for the canvas tote bag I took with me to the store last night. It is ridiculous that I'm hiding a bag of peanuts from my husband. Luke has continued to get worked up any time I mention the birds in the backyard. In fact, I've now caught him twice stomping toward them, and once I'm pretty sure he tossed rock salt from the garage at them. Salting the earth is a good way to melt ice, ruin your garden, and probably drop the home value here. It did not, though, scare away my new friends.

I pour a healthy plop of creamer into my coffee and take the mug and the stash of peanuts out to the back deck. Eddie, Nixie, Selene, and the gang are all there. There are seven birds in total. This feels like a large murder, but then we so rarely have them around our house in Austin. There is a group of three I sometimes see from my office window downtown. I should bring them snacks when I get back home. Crow friends everywhere.

Eddie cants his head toward me.

Birds can't hear your thoughts. That's ridiculous. And yet I still think in his direction, *You're not interchangeable. I'm sure I'll miss you when I go back home.*

Another of the crows caws at him, and he turns away. Guess I won't know if he heard me. *Mind-reading birds, Addie? Really?* I shake my head. I might need to see about talking to more humans soon.

I scoop a handful of the peanuts and chuck them into the yard. The crows linger where they are.

I throw another handful. I researched this. These are prime treats for crows. There is a venerable feast now in the yard, and not a single bird gives one fuck. Did I offend the crows?

Eddie and another of the crows begin chattering, their *caw-caw-caw* cries getting louder, more agitated. *Are they the same ones I'd heard in the attic?* Eddie flaps his wings sharply. The other bird, Nixie, flaps back. The two are bickering as best I can tell. Nixie flies up to the fence perch, a feather fluttering down atop the fullest part of the garden, and caws directly at me.

It's pointed, and while I can't tell if it's admonishment or a cry for backup, I can suddenly see why my husband would be wary of the crows. They are smart. They're planners. And they don't mess around.

I grip my coffee mug tightly. My god, I'm a crow. The peal of laughter that escapes me startles my bird friends. But once it's out there, I can't rein it in. Good problem-solving skills, a bit of a territorial nature, thoughtful gift giving, appreciation for a good snack. It's no wonder I'm friends with Eddie and the gang.

"I'm just a crow in a human body," I say as if it'll make more sense aloud.

The murder turns its attention on me. Seven sets of black eyes, seven sharp beaks, seven smart birds, all focused on me. Eddie's caw is short, clipped, and almost like he's sighing in resignation.

Selene disappears over the fence. My humor evaporates. The other crows continue to watch me. A vise locks around my ribs, and the longer we stare at one another, the tighter it cinches.

Nixie taps her beak against the metal flashing of the garden bed. The sound is eerily unnatural in this verdant space. I look to the driveway, but only our lonely rental waits there, the edge of one of the trash bins peeking from the side of the house. *Pickup is tomorrow,*

I remind myself, as though focusing on the mundane order of things will counteract the tension between me and the crows.

Selene returns, white poking from her beak. She drops her prize at Eddie's feet and cocks her head in question. There's an element of "Are you sure?" in the way she looks at him. I don't know why Eddie's in charge, but then I don't understand any sort of avian hierarchy, much less that of birds that I'm somehow friends with.

He hops onto the square of white and then backs off. And then both birds are flying toward me. I pick up a few peanuts. I want to say it's only to treat them, but that anxiety vise is pinching my torso so hard, it should crack a rib. Are the peanuts for protection? I don't know anymore.

They land silently on the table. My coffee doesn't even slosh in the mug. *Smooth, birds, smooth.* Eddie drops the object of much discussion and then caws at me.

Has the vise locked me in my seat, too? All my muscles are tight, my earlier fatigue forgotten. Am I supposed to just *take* it from them?

"What did you bring me?" The peanut shells are digging into my palm.

Selene dips her head and nudges the found treasure toward me but only, like, a millimeter. Her confidence, though, carries through. These are my crow friends. Thoughtful, beautiful, and clearly protective. Why else would they all perch on that back fence like guardians?

I look more closely at the proffered item. It's paper, but it's more than that. It's folded paper. A thick square of a ripped notebook page. The red rule down one side has faded, and the blue lines even more, and the ragged edge from a former connection with a metal coil is so familiar I can practically hear the *pffffft* of it being torn free.

It's a note. The realization strikes my chest like a hammer on a church bell. It's the kind passed from hand to hand between desks at school. At least, as it had been when I was thirteen. Do teenagers actually still write notes by hand? Don't they have Snapchat or another far less trackable option for chatting with their friends?

"Is...is this for me?" I hesitate to reach for it. The folded paper is still between the two birds, and while they have been of the gift-giving nature, I also don't want to misread them and get pecked. *Luke would lose it if I had a crow injury.*

I empty the peanuts from my palm onto the table and spread them out closer to the birds. Eddie hops closer and takes one. From back at the fence, the other crows caw. Eddie's attention doesn't waver. Selene walks to the middle of the table, right next to my hand, and then nudges my knuckle with her beak. It doesn't hurt, and it's far from a peck. She's being gentle with me, but at least the intention is clear.

"It's okay to take it?" It comes out as a question, though my hand is already moving to grab the note.

The little packet of paper is folded over and over until the square is barely two inches wide. The exterior is marred with dirt. How long has this been sitting on the ground? How long have the crows had it? Both birds continue to watch me, though I can tell Eddie is debating cracking open the peanut shell.

"Why did you bring me this?" It's unique, certainly, but this isn't like the beads. They'd come from the box with the doll. The one Luke had thrown out. Weren't crows like magpies and supposed to collect shiny things? This is old paper. Dull. Matte. Dirty. By all accounts boring.

Selene caws at me. I flinch. I'm not sure how I know she's exasperated, but there's a clear urgency in her song.

"Right. Right. Thanks for the, um, gift." I pinch the note between my thumb and forefinger and hold it aloft. Showcasing how I'm taking it.

Eddie caves and cracks open the nut. Snack Town, population: 1.

Selene stares at me. Hard. Or maybe normal. I reach for my coffee cup, but she takes a step forward, and I'm not here to piss off my only friends.

"I'll open it, but it feels weird to snoop on teen gossip." As I tilt the note in my direction, claiming it, I catch the handwriting on the other side.

It's not the looping script I've seen on the boxes upstairs. Thank god for small favors and all that.

The pencil lines have smudged, but Luke's name in all caps remains legible, as do the two giant hearts drawn at either end of it. I stare at it for a long time. Too long.

"Eddie. Selene." I say the crow's names like I'm chiding children. "Did you really bring me a love note for my husband?"

Selene flaps her wings once. Did she just call me a bitch?

The vise at my center eases. This isn't from the box upstairs. It's not part of a doll. This is paper. Old paper, at that. Not even a page that belonged to Barb. I set the still-folded note down.

I flatten my lips. I'm letting go of my jealousy of Luke's high school ex. Even thinking it makes me want to cringe. I hate disappointing the crows, but I still say, "I don't think I can handle reading some missive from Kim right now."

Eddie lifts his head, but both he and the other crow simply watch me.

"They had lunch, but it's fine. We talked about it, and it's all normal. He loves me. And this?" I gesture at their gift. "It's only going to get in my head."

Eddie leaps forward and snatches up the note. I jerk backward, but my chair catches on the deck. I go flying. My feet kick the underside of the table. Coffee is everywhere. My ass hurts, my pride even more so.

I pull myself out of the debris. Neither bird moves to help or to avoid the pooling coffee on the table. I step inside to gather a towel. Still no sign of Luke. Guess my fall wasn't *too* loud. When I return to clean up, the crows have opened the note. It lies on my fallen chair, a peanut shell resting in a crease like a signature.

I drop the cloth, the mess forgotten.

I look out toward the yard. All seven of the birds are perched on the fence. Facing me. Waiting.

I inhale slowly, but I have no words. My hand shakes as I pick up the decades-old note.

Only Kim's name isn't written at the bottom of the 1990s-era letter. Instead, it's signed with another big heart and the name Cassie.

I read the note over and over. It's a love letter to be certain, but the obsession of a little sister. Which I guess she was. She talks about how she knows Luke isn't really happy with Kim. About how her sister is boring and doesn't really listen to him. *Your taste in music is better than hers. You deserve more.* Each line reads like it was written from the bleachers while watching him work out at track practice. My heart hurts once again for Cassidy Warren. Kim's little sister had a crush on Luke. She'd captured it in pencil and handed it to him? Bold moves for a freshman.

Why would Luke have kept this? Hell, *where* had he kept it? I'd cleared a whole lot of junk in this house, but nothing that Luke had tucked away. So how had the crows come across this missive from so long ago? It hadn't been in the box with Cassidy's name... had it?

Unease twists my stomach, and the wicked blend of coffee and stomach acid splashes the back of my throat.

"Addison?" Luke calls from deep within the house. Is it late? How long have I been out here with the crows and the note and, oh hell, the mess?

I stagger away from the crime scene I've made of the deck, crumpling the note in my hand.

Luke calls my name again, closer this time.

"Out here," I say before I can think better of it.

The storm door whines as he pushes it open. "Oh, Addie. Are you okay?"

I appreciate that his first thought is for my welfare. Am I pale? Does my face showcase how rattled I am? The crows wanted me to read this note, and that's strange enough. But it keeps coming back to Cassidy Warren and my husband, and my head is spinning.

"Yeah, I'm not injured." No lying to my husband, I remind myself.

"What even happened here?" Luke picks up the towel from the ground and tosses it onto the coffee-covered table.

I hold out the crumpled note toward him. "I found a love note to you."

Luke stiffens, a momentary lapse into statue mode. When he turns though, his brows are drawn tight in confusion. "Ads, I told you there's nothing going on with Kim." The exhaustion in his voice, the patronizing tone grates on my already frayed nerves.

"It's from when you were in high school," I say flatly.

"Oh." He has the good sense to look abashed. He takes the note from me and skims it. "Where did you find this?"

That's where he goes? Not a funny story about the kid with a crush on him? I tell Luke everything as a rule, but I'm not about to narc on the crows. This is important to them, and that matters to me. There's this flash of darkness in my husband's eyes that makes me worry he'll run the birds off. My heart clenches at the thought.

"Over by the trash." The lie comes quickly, smoothly, and dries my mouth. "Did you pitch a bunch of stuff from when you were a kid?"

Luke looks toward the ocean in the distance. The waves are quieter now, but perhaps if you grew up in this place, the hint of their crashes is calming. "Must have," he mutters. "Sorry for my reaction. It's strange to see something in Cassie's handwriting. It's been a long time."

How did I not even think about that? *Because you're too busy fretting over dolls and crows and your inadequacies.* Guilt softens my stance, my voice, my resolve. "I totally get that."

He opens his mouth but then closes it again without saying more.

"What is it?" I prod.

"You really didn't find this in the house?" His face scrunches up like he's repulsed by questioning me. Good.

I try to give him the benefit of the doubt. I'm keeping the crows a secret, but I think it's his own memories that are pushing him to ask. Not mistrust. "Really. It was out here in the dirt."

He makes one of those deep noises in the back of his throat, like his thoughts are so heavy, they've settled in his chest.

"Are you all right?" Asking him this while we stand around the spilled coffee, the toppled chair, and the overall mess of my chaos should feel backward, but the muscle in his jaw keeps flexing in a way that tells me he's on edge.

"No." He huffs. It's a mirthless laugh. "I'm not. Being here has always been complicated, but it's like everywhere I go, I'm reminded of how different—better?—life is away from here."

Well, that's nice to hear. "Is that bad?"

"Not at all, but... I don't know, Ads." He rights the fallen chair and then clings to the back of it like it's what's holding him steady.

The crumpled note is still clutched in his hand, but we've both mostly forgotten it. I press my palm to his back. Luke only divulges when he's ready. So I wait.

"Life is good in Oregon. You get the ocean. You get great people. This was my home." He pauses for so long, I think that's all. Finally, though, he sighs. Shoulders crumpling forward, head dropping to hang low. I slip my fingers up into his hair, running my nails on his scalp.

"It was easier to forget about the sad parts of this town when we were just popping in to visit Mom. Seeing Cassidy's name on that box was strange, but now reading a note she wrote?" He pulls in a shaky breath. "I'm sure it's the rawness of Mom's passing, but Cassie was a good kid. When she went missing, it wrecked me."

"Losing a friend is always hard," I say softly. "But losing one so young? Having to deal with death while still in high school? All those feelings are fair. Did you ever see someone about it?"

Luke lifts his head and looks at me like I've lost my mind. "You met my mother. Do you think she sent me to therapy?"

It makes me smile, the thought of Barb in therapy. "No, I'm sure she had hang-ups about it, but I meant the school. Usually they bring in counselors..."

"Not here. But it's fine." He rights himself and wads the note up in his palm. "It was a long time ago." He takes the steps down from the deck two at a time and tosses the paper into the big barrel.

When he comes back up, I've finished cleaning the coffee mess. "Ready for another day of curating Luke's new art gallery?"

My attempt to lighten the mood falls flat. "Actually, do you mind if I work on sorting through all that crystal? Uncle Stan reached out and said there are a couple pieces that he wants."

Stan lives four hours away and didn't offer to come help, but he still wanted dibs. That tracks.

While Luke sets up in the de facto crystal shop, I return to the school keepsake section of the house in the loft. It'll go faster without Luke there, I tell myself, like the reason I pick it isn't to try to find more notes from my husband's high school days.

CHAPTER 17

APPROXIMATELY TWO DOZEN RUNS FROM TOP FLOOR TO backyard, and I have emptied most of the loft space, only to spot another hallway tucked at the edge of the room. I've cleared the collections stacked on either side of a heavy bookcase, and on the left, there's a tiny gap in the wall. The opening is only half an inch, if that, and when I lean close to peer past, all I can see are endless inky shadows. Emptying the bookcase is enough of a challenge, but I'm not up for hauling furniture to the side to see where the open space behind it goes. The opening has no molding or frame. It's nearly identical in size to the bookshelf, which is ornate and mahogany and not like the IKEA ones Luke and I used to make the built-ins in our living room.

It is, thankfully, way the hell heavier than its some-assembly-required brethren. It's a good excuse not to peek into dark spaces.

I take a water break and find Luke planted on the living room sofa. His jaw is slackened in bewilderment.

"You hanging in there, handsome?" I ask.

He jumps like I shouted boo.

"Didn't mean to startle you." I tiptoe through a crystal maze to reach the couch. I sit next to him.

Luke relaxes, but his eyelashes flutter like they can clear the tears waiting in the corners of his eyes. "I'm solid." He's reassuring himself, but I still nod.

"How is the search for Uncle Stan's crystal going?" Focusing on specific tasks is Compartmentalization 101. If you want to hold your emotions at bay, staying busy is the cheap cure.

"Surprisingly easy. Mom had amassed a hell of a collection." He gestures at the rows and rows of pieces laid out on the floor as though this is news. *Bless his heart.* "But he really only wanted the globe with celestial maps etched into it. There's only one of those. It stuck out."

"I'm glad, but then why are you surveying the fancy dishware like it's an indemnification clause from an insurance company?"

Luke turns toward me slowly, eyes wide. "One time, Addison. One time that happened."

"Yes, and I think we should be quite proud of me for remembering a phrase like *indemnification clause.*"

"Don't undersell yourself. You understand contract terms better than most."

"Perhaps, but I handle the books, the taxes, and making sense of how businesses run."

"Math queen." He bumps his shoulder with mine.

I shouldn't let him derail the conversation. I want to know why his gaze sought to shatter a punch bowl. But if coping means dodging my question, I can let him.

"So, I have boxed and bagged up most of that loft space. No more President Lincoln fantasy goods but solidly sorted."

"Wow. You really are a wonder at this stuff." Luke pauses, hesitation tugging at his mouth. He goes for it. "You didn't just throw it all away, right?"

It smacks of judgment, but I try not to take it personally. Mostly succeed. "I promised to be compassionate to your mementos."

"Right." He nods, again convincing himself. "Sorry. Thank you."

"Lot of short replies there, Mr. Lowe."

He laughs. "Who's the lawyer here?"

We tease each other for a few minutes. Muscles easing. Smiles coming easier.

"Oh, so I might need your help upstairs." Asking for his help is tricky. Luke has helped me countless times, and while I know this is supposed to be me making his life easier, some furniture is harder to move than others.

His nostrils flare. It's the only outward sign of his discomfort. He so rarely schools his emotions around me that the act stings. *No, he's not hiding from you, dumbass. He's keeping the floodgates locked.* Chiding myself only conjures memories of my own mother—well, the lack of her. She pulled the multiple-job gauntlet for years. It wasn't neglect, never ever that. It was determination to feed us, clothe us, protect us. It just meant she was gone, and I ran the house. I solved the problems. I fielded my sister's emotions. I hadn't felt safe around Luke until we'd been together over a year. Not enough to cry. Not enough to be vulnerable. And he'd been patient with me. Kind. Considerate.

I don't want him to have to box it all up, but I get survival instincts. He's not holding back from me but from himself. It's how Luke moves forward, and I respect it.

Luke dips his chin. The simple controlled move is all I need.

"There is a huge bookcase up where we found your Founding Fathers tape."

"You make it sound like it's lewd." He snickers.

"Babe, I'm not here to judge." My playfulness dissipates the tension in the room enough to go forward. "But *anyway*, I cleared the shelves, and there's actually like a hallway or another room behind it?"

I make it a question, like I don't know full well that there is yet another surprise pathway in this house.

Thankfully, Luke nods. "I'm surprised you didn't move the bookcase yourself. You've been hauling boxes these last couple days like you're going to sign up for CrossFit when we get back home."

"Oh, no. My mornings will remain dedicated to coffee and comfort, but I like the idea that you think I could hang with them."

"I can tackle what's up there." There's a softness in the way my husband speaks now, that kind of distant tone when memories flood back and thicken the tongue. "I should have told you it was back there. It's been years since anyone has been in there."

He isn't hesitating to go to this room, but the surprise attic we leave alone?

"I didn't expect the loft to keep going," I admit.

"Hmm?" He shakes off whatever cobwebs remain in his mind. "Oh, it's just another storage space."

"It's like this house was built to collect," I mumble.

Never discount my attorney husband's ability to catch every aside. "It kind of was."

"Wait? How long has this house been in your family?" And why am I only learning of it now?

"Always," he says like he, too, finds it odd I don't know this. "My grandfather built the house. It's always been in our family."

Silence sits heavy between us. Any earlier giggles have been gutted. The wicked chill that cut through me in the night is back. Slicing at my ribs, making me squirm.

A question pierces my mind, the idea covered in spines and making me wince. I hold it back. Because I don't want the answer. Don't need the answer.

But perhaps the same thorns prick Luke, because he breaks the silence. "I hate the idea of giving this house to someone other than a Lowe."

I loathe the idea of living in this house. It isn't that I'm not built for regularly rainy weather—but to be fair, I am not—this house is *off*. Barb's bad vibes have tainted it.

Carefully, I suggest, "You could reach out to your uncle."

"He won't come back here," Luke says immediately.

"Right." This is the same uncle who was supposedly injured by the black birds in the yard. He also has been in perpetual poor health, if you trusted updates from Barb over the years.

I bite the inside of my cheek and try to ignore the pinch at the back of my neck. "Given all the collectibles, we could reach out to a local preservation society. See if this could be kept as more like a museum in her honor?"

I say it like it wouldn't horrify Barb. People in her house, touching whatever they wanted. The prick at my neck sharpens, twists until I yipe like a puppy. I clap my hand to the back of my neck.

"Addison? Are you—" Luke scrambles to his feet. He isn't solely focused on me though. His gaze is flitting around the room, like he's looking for whatever could have caused my behavior. "Are you okay?"

I press my palm firmly against my nape. Wetness seeps beneath it. "I'm fine," I lie.

Luke takes a step backward and knocks over a tall candy dish. It clunks against the rug but doesn't shatter. "Damn it."

"No harm, no foul," I say, sounding steadier than I am. I pull my hand from my neck. Blood smears my palm. *What in the actual hell?*

Luke lets out a heavy sigh. His back is still to me, hands on his hips. "I'm going to head upstairs. I can get that bookshelf moved and deal with the storage behind it. Less likely I break anything Mom loved that way."

Another day I'd inject some positivity, but there is blood on my hand, and I didn't understand how I got injured in the first place.

Neither of us said no to the museum idea aloud, but somehow the moment has passed with a finality that we would not be doing so. Fair enough. No Barb Lowe Memorial Museum means an easier road to healing.

I blot the small cut on the back of my neck with a washcloth after Luke disappears up the stairs. The cut keeps welling with fresh blood until I finally cave and put an adhesive bandage over it.

Minutes have passed since Luke went up the stairs. Long enough that I can't hear him now. How long will it take him to clear yet another "storage space?" In this house, that could mean everything from a nook with shelves to an endless supply of boxes sealed and mislabeled.

I want to tell myself it's the silence and knowing Luke is participating now that pushes me to Barb's bedroom. Or that it's that I don't want him to have to tackle his mother's room. Or blame it on my need to get the hell out of here. But once I'm there, this urgency to clear it resonates in my chest. Each time I return from toting a box or an armload of clothes out into the hallway, down to the trash, my gaze goes right to the closet.

I shut the closet door. No shimmering golden lure if the door is closed. Only as I fold yet another blouse, the whispering cold plea of the attic space reaches me. There are no words—which, I suppose is a good reason to assume it's in my head—but this *thrum*. My body vibrates with it.

The silk blouse in my hands is a pale cream. It's my size. Luke would tell me Barb bought it for me. Why else would she have a shirt two sizes too big for her in her room? I roll the fabric between my fingers, luxuriating in the waterfall sensation of it. When I turn to fold the shirt and place it on the donation pile, the call from the small door smacks me solidly in the sternum. My bones hum with the twist of a C-sharp note.

"If Luke's clearing a storage space, I should too," I say, like I need the universe to approve of this choice.

The note the crows had given me this morning fills my thoughts. I step closer to the closet door. Cassidy Warren's name in her own hand—Cassie—flashes in my mind. If Barb planned to gift her the doll, wouldn't she have known the girl went by Cassie?

Inside the closet, the small door shimmers. The carvings sharpen. Or is the steady buzz growing in my ears making me see things?

Had the note been in the box for Cassidy? Maybe Barb threw the old notes in for sentimental reasons after the girl died? The birds had simply found it among the rest of the garbage.

This idea propels me forward. Maybe other notes spilled on the floor in there. Luke would want to see them. Who am I lying to? It's my own curiosity pushing me forward. I need to understand more of Luke's past. He's peered into the darker corners of mine. Knowing these secrets will let me support him better, be a better wife, bring us closer. But also a tiny filthy part of me also wants us to be even. Our match makes a deeper sense if we both were broken and repaired ourselves.

The sludge of disgust seeps down my chest, plopping in my stomach so heavily as to set me off-kilter. *It's not a competition. We're a team. He loves me.* All these facts run in a loop in my mind, but none of them stop me from gripping the cold knob and opening the small door.

I tumble into the secret attic, more Alice in *Through the Looking-Glass* than *American Ninja Warrior.*

CHAPTER 18

AN ATTIC—HIDDEN OR OTHERWISE—SHOULDN'T CHANGE shape or size. Yet each time I creep through the miniature door, the space has altered in some way. It'd been practically vaulted last time. Huge, endless. Today, the ceiling is lower than I remember, and the walls are practically pressing against my skin. I stretch my hand up, but my fingers are far from grazing the wooden beams overhead. The shadows in this space are tricky.

We'd had an attic in my house growing up. East Texas soil couldn't support a foundation for a generation, much less allow for a basement. But we'd had overhead storage aplenty. Windows had speared light over Christmas decorations and leftover baby gear that my mother kept under the guise of helping some family member with a surprise pregnancy, but really because she thought my sister or I would one day need them. Pretty sure they all were now safety recalled. I shake away the wandering thoughts. *This* is the house I am tasked with cataloging and clearing. Dark corners and all.

Only what am I even doing in this attic again? Notes. Right. Calming nerves. All of that. I plant my hands on my hips, like a power stance can force answers to manifest before me. It does not.

I bite my lip until it twinges. Where had Cassidy's box been when I'd first found it? The floor in front of me is empty, save a sprinkling of dust. If other notes had fallen out of the box, they had to be wherever the box had been originally.

That's a stretch even for you, Addison. Oh, hell, now even my internal thoughts are sounding like Barb. I need out of this house.

I stomp forward, because I'm unwilling to let even the idea of Barb hold me back. Thin tendrils of the green vines that snake the exterior of the house have pierced the floor along a center aisle. I step past them. Cassidy's box had been right up front. Was it the first row or the second? I skim my fingers over the boxes I reach first. There's no dust here. So Cassidy or Katy's or Wendy's box must have been here originally. A pulse of ick shakes me. *So many women.* There aren't any high school notes unfurled or piled neatly waiting for me. I kneel, the hard floor biting at my skin even through my pants. It's hard to see much of anything. The overhead bulb doesn't cast more than a haze in this direction. I pat my palms over the floor. Wood. Wood. More wood. Nothing.

A hint of softness tickles my fingertips. I jerk them back to my chest. My hand heats; my heart races. I freeze, clutching my hand for ten shaky breaths. Why am I so freaked out? Soft is good. Soft is safe. Hell, this is an attic, not a dungeon. There should be soft things. Winter wardrobes and tree skirts.

I slowly lower my hand and ease forward. The blast of cold air that rushes in from my right, from the back of the attic, tosses my hair across my face. The strands slap me. I pull my elastic hair tie from my wrist and swipe the locks back. Secure them. The chill doesn't abate. Howling gusts cut through the hidden attic.

I should leave. I should go find the opening letting this weather in. I should warn Luke. The ideas rattle rapid-fire in my skull, but I do none of them.

I've never been much for woo-woo beliefs. But if anyone were going to find a way to cling to the mortal realm just to tell me I'm cleaning out her house incorrectly, to tell me to leave, to screw with me while I do her a goddamned favor, it would be Barb.

So if this icy blast is her, I'm middle-fingering it. I reach into my pocket and free my phone.

No signal. Of course. That's fine. I press the flashlight icon for a couple seconds until a brilliant beam illuminates out the back.

There in the cold, clear light is a solitary black feather. Icy pain wraps around my wrist, though I see nothing there when I angle the beam of light at it. The invisible grip tightens, it burns, but instinct makes me pick up the feather.

Silence.

Warmth.

Calm.

The pain at my forearm is gone. The wicked wintery air abates. My heart continues to gallop. The feather is such a deep black that it's almost blue. I roll the end between my fingers, letting the feather twist in my light. It's at least eight inches long. Is this Eddie's? Or

Selene's? Have the birds been in here? Maybe there is a hole in the roof? That makes more sense than them digging in the trash, now that I think about it.

Only there had been a feather like this in Cassidy's box. And Wendy's too. Corvids are clever as hell, but they still don't have thumbs. They couldn't have tucked the box lids closed the way I'd found them. The birds haven't been storing excess feathers in these boxes.

I rest on my heels.

"What is this room?" I ask aloud. "Barb, what were you doing here?"

I twist to my right, with the phone light lifted, and survey my surroundings. Boxes, of course, but the stacks go on for rows and rows. Are there hundreds in here? Do they all have names on them? There aren't enough crows outside to have donated feathers to all these boxes, so maybe it's a fluke?

I'm overthinking it. It's a part of the whole being-really-good-in-a-crisis thing. I can solve problems well because I imagine every possible terrible outcome.

I rise and walk toward the back of the room. The wind has to come from here, and if there is damage to the house, I need to know. Also, I need a little sanity check. Clearly. Only the deeper I go into the attic, the wider and taller are the stacks. The boxes reach far overhead, the mazelike path becomes downright labyrinthine. I peek at my phone. Instead of showing me the Wi-Fi icon or how many bars of service, I just see "SOS." *Wonderful.* If I trap myself in Barb's creepy attic, will Luke even look for me here?

There are a lot of dumb ways to get lost, but this would be by far the most embarrassing one. I start working my way back toward the door, because I will not have this be a story my children someday hear. Although better than whatever stories Barb would have told them about me.

The names on the boxes are harder to miss with the extra light. Bold black permanent marker labels most of them, but some bear a finer blue ink. Like the kind that could fade but somehow didn't. Every letter regardless of color or size or boldness of line is in the same looping cursive. The same handwriting that filled countless birthday cards sent to our home. The same one that left canary-yellow sticky notes on the bathroom mirror whenever we visited this house. The handwriting that loved to remind me that I should keep my belongings in a toiletry bag.

I wasn't rifling through your medicine cabinet back then, Barb, but I'm sifting through your secrets now.

My steps slow. I'm supposed to be leaving, but the names—why are there *so many names*?—slow me down. Are there even this many people in Rockside Bay? Who knows this many people? I mean, maybe over a lifetime?

Could all these dolls be "injured" like Katy's had been? I close my eyes and picture Cassidy's doll. Her delicate face had been perfect and far too real. No fake blood or bruises.

I glance over my shoulder. Shadows and boxes loom closer. I right myself quickly, checking my elbow into the boxes on the other side. They tumble. Bows and bracelets and candles with burned wicks scatter across the floor. Black feathers flutter down more slowly, landing atop the spread of memories before me. I don't know who these belonged to. Had Barb actually been a kleptomaniac? That would make more sense than her not being able to find anything to do with her money but buy endlessly.

Manic laughter bites the air. *My laughter.* I sputter. Humor punches itself into coughs. And finally gasps.

Finally, I let out a long sigh. "I actually made more of a mess." I shake my head. "Nothing like making bonus work for yourself."

I snag the nearest box and right it. I hold my phone over the opening to make sure I didn't miss anything. There's gold glitter at the bottom of the box but none on the lid. My new goal becomes leaving this room without being caked in glitter. *My dead mother-in-law is trying to give me craft herpes.* I try to swallow another sudden fit of laughter. Water wells at my eyes. Luke says his mom had a secret passion for crafting dolls or whatever. Her inflicting glitter on me—the ultimate craft crime—as her final act would have tracked. I pick up the spilled items one by one.

I find a playbill from a local community theater production of *Our Town* circa 1986. Had the glitter in the box been from the stage production, or had Barb kept this memento for a papier-mâché project? Whatever. I drop the item back into the box and scoop more of the random bits into my palms and dump them back in too. My hand glances one of the feathers. It's delicate like the other one I touched, but the sensation jolts me. My mind is muddy. I inhale sharply, earthy moisture and cedar rushing in. I blink and blink and blink until the room is blurred and tears track my cheeks. The overwhelm hits solidly at my center, but it claws up my throat, the path familiar. I try to swallow, but there's too much here. Too much wrapping around me. Too many boxes. Too much pressure.

Too.

Much.

It squeezes.

I drop forward, catching myself on all fours, palms smacking the wood. A crow feather is beneath my fingertips. I curl them in, taking the bird's gift with it. My breaths become steadier. I swallow the panic. It shouldn't have broken through its safe little box. Maybe I need a bump in SSRIs while I'm here. I grip the feather in my left hand. I don't have to pick this up now, I realize. Luke didn't even want me to clean out this room. So why do I care?

"You're being petty, Addison," I chide myself. Knowing Barb's secrets won't change the past. They wouldn't have made me like her while she was alive; why would I expect them to change who she was in her death? She raised a good man, and that's all I'd needed from her.

I rise and try to leave my hope of understanding Barb there on the floor.

I pick the half-full box up from the path and turn to set it back on its stack.

From the ground, half a step away, two dark-brown eyes watch me.

The doll tracks my motion, its thin lips painted in a tight smile. Permanent judgment on its mouth. Its hair is pulled back in a fancy double twist of some sort—not usual for a baby doll, even a porcelain one.

With the box on the stack of its contemporaries, I spin it until I can read the name.

The doll watches me. Its facial features can't change, but I swear it's leering at me. There's a challenge in the depths of its too-humanlike eyes.

You don't see that.

It's not real.

That's a doll. Sometimes dolls are unnerving.

Get. It. Together.

On the box is a name I recognize. It's not Cassidy Warren or Wendy Owens. But Kathryn Wall.

That last name made headlines. The fisherman. The one who disappeared. Are they related?

My stomach twists, because I know they are. Just as I'm certain that if I ask Luke about her, there'll be some tragic story, and I'll get another brush-off. Not because my husband doesn't care, but because he only wants to see the good. Because he's too mired in his own emotions to open the gate for more.

Only I need closure. And distraction. And to understand what the hell Barb was up to in this place. Because tragedy had struck me too. Just like these women.

The thought sobers me. I lift my phone again, but not for the light this time. I flip open the camera app and snap a picture of the name. And then toggle on the video, pausing every few steps as I work my way to the door.

I need to know who these women are. Why Barb would be making dolls for them...of them?

CHAPTER 19

DOWNTOWN ROCKSIDE BAY IS LUSH AND LIVELY. THE DEEP greens of the woods surrounding the town are carried throughout its center. While there are trees aplenty, it's more about cottages-turned-shops and the green lawns rolling between them. The hand-painted signs hanging near the road are emblazoned with the store name alongside a nature image. A sockeye salmon. A horned owl. A copse of dense trees. It's like every person had to post an apology and a thank-you to the land for being here. It's charming.

Walking around here, which has more pedestrians and bikes than cars, is like home. Austin has vehicles aplenty, but it clings to its artist's voice. Murals splash building walls. Music spills on the streets. Independent restaurants allow cultural roots to blossom. It's vibrant. It's weird. It's home.

And while this coastal community is not my beloved weird home, walking toward the community center lawn fills me with fresh hope. The salt air is strong enough to remind me where I am, but mild enough I'm not worried my hair is going to spring free of its elastic any minute.

I chuckle to myself. Guess I really did need to get out of the house.

Luke had side-eyed me a little when I grabbed his mother's yoga mat. Probably more because I'm not the seasoned yogi she was, and less because I held one of Barb's possessions. But he'd seemed genuinely happy that I was stepping out to exercise.

"All the dust and cleaning agents in here can't be great for you," he said, like he wasn't also captive in the never-ending cleaning project.

Around fifteen women in Lycra and loose sweatshirts are gathered on the lawn. This was Barb's yoga group. The community center offers the outdoor yoga sessions free of charge. The fact that they are right in the center of town and visible from a number of restaurant patios had been a bonus for my mother-in-law. I, however, try not to note the people brunching nearby. I didn't come here to put on a show. I'm here to gossip.

Which makes me more like Barb than I care to think about.

The others have noticed me. Their glances are careful, and the soft whispers of conversation don't reach my ears, but I know they're about me all the same. They must recognize me. Barb, I'm sure, ran her mouth about her terrible daughter-in-law. So these women think they know me. Well, they only know Barb's version.

That's okay. They don't need to know the real me. I only want them to talk, which they clearly wish to do.

So instead of rolling my mat at the back of the group like I might have back home, I stride toward the instructor. She's in her early fifties.

She's pulling a *plant-based person* T-shirt off and going for sports-bra mode, despite it being only in the low sixty degrees outside.

"Hi, I'm Addison. I'm in town visiting, but I heard this class is open to everyone?" I introduce myself loudly enough that none of the women behind me can miss it.

"Absolutely," the instructor says with quad-shot-espresso energy. "I'm Marie. Today is a recovery flow."

Marie delves into the particulars. I smile and nod at the right points, but my attention is on the soft chatter behind me.

"That's her." The first voice is far from a whisper.

"Barb said she didn't care for fitness." The next is a little louder.

"She has Barb's mat. That's distasteful." I can almost feel the spittle as the backbiting gets going.

"You know that Barb's son wanted to move back here. Maybe that girl will let him now."

"If Barb couldn't make it happen, it's not happening."

Ah. So I'm the reason Luke lives several states away. I resist chiming in that we *met* in Texas.

Correcting them doesn't matter. They've confirmed what I need. These ladies live for the tea, and while they may be predisposed not to like me, there's no question they love gossip.

The need to spill it, to drink it, to spice it with their own half-truths. There is more than salt in the air for this yoga group.

I roll my mat out toward the front of the group, trying to stay in the center. There's a little bit of huffing about my choice.

"Am I stealing someone's space?" I ask, willing my body to flush with embarrassment I don't feel.

"You're fine, honey," says the woman on my right. She's wearing head-to-toe purple. Even her silver hair is pulled back in a violet scrunchie. "We'll work around you. I'm glad you came."

"Thanks." I glance toward our instructor, who is pairing her phone with a Bluetooth speaker. Might as well open the door. "I've been cooped up inside the last several days."

"You're visiting and not out eating or touring the coast?" Her attempt to be surprised is halfhearted, but the glimmer in her eyes tells me she knows exactly where I've been.

"My husband and I are preparing my late mother-in-law's estate for sale. Lots of clearing out the house. Determining what to keep, what to donate."

"Oh, I'm so sorry for your loss. And for all those decisions. They do come in droves after a passing of a loved one, don't they?" There's experience in her words.

"They do," I agree.

The instructor is back on her mat. Instrumental Celtic music plays softly. *Not what I would pick for yoga, but okay.*

I need to plant the seed for us to talk more later. "Well, and I keep finding items she'd labeled for people, but I didn't grow up here. So it's hard to know if they're meant as gifts or bequeathments. I don't even know if these women still live here."

The fit seventysomething next to me should have dollar signs flashing in her eyes for the greed that emanates from her.

"I'm Evelyn," she says, clearly hoping that it's one of the names I'm looking for.

"Nice to meet you," I say.

The instructor shushes me at the perfect time. I nod at her and give a conspiratorial smile to Evelyn. She beams. Oh, this lady thinks she's getting fancy crystal or fur coats. I don't recognize her name, but if I did, it'd just mean I'd found whatever strange amalgamation of items Barb had from her. And maybe a doll.

For the next forty-five minutes, I follow the yoga flow. The stretching is welcome after hauling boxes and crawling on the floor. The instructor's voice is soothing throughout the workout, but I can only dedicate half my attention to her. My mind hums with how I'm going to get the rest of these women to speak with me. Would they all act like Evelyn and want to hear the names simply to know if their own is listed? And what if it is? Should I give them whatever box in the creepy attic has their name on it?

Last night I passed a half dozen labeled *Kathryn Wall*. Why are there so many? Had Barb been close to her at some point? The number of boxes with one person's name on it makes me feel like my sticky-fingers theory has legs.

By the time I roll my mat up, I have a plan, a contingency plan, and a contingency for the contingency.

All unnecessary.

Evelyn waves the other women closer. "Has everyone met Addison?" She points at me like the regulars wouldn't know I am the new person.

While she gets questioning looks and those eye-contact-only conversations going with a couple people, I shake hands with a few of the other yoga attendees.

"She's Barb's daughter-in-law," Evelyn announces.

"I don't think I told you that," I say slowly, like I'm surprised. I'm not.

"Oh, sugar, this is a tight community. I put it together." She pats me on the arm.

"Of course," I demur.

"Anyway, Addison here was telling me she has been going through that big house divining what Luke will keep, what to donate. You know."

There are five women who stay to chat. They nod and offer general platitudes. If they were Barb's friends, they don't say it. The youngest of the group is only a decade or so older than me, but the others are all much closer to Evelyn's age and want me to know they've "seen a lot." They claim to know the histories of every person in Rockside Bay, and I am a source for fresh gossip.

I take it at face value, but it doesn't help.

"Come get coffee with us." Evelyn doesn't wait. She slings her bundled yoga mat over her shoulder and starts walking to the closest restaurant. They promote a bottomless brunch mimosa on a small banner at the hostess stand.

"No one would judge you if you want to go with a mimosa this morning," a woman named Debbie tells me. She's stayed at my elbow since we left the lawn.

"Booze this early would just make me nap," I say honestly. "And while I'm taking a break from the estate duties, I'll need to be back at it this afternoon."

We get a large table on the patio. Two of the women go for the mimosas, but everyone else gets coffee. Danish appear at the center of the table, but my anxiety is barely tolerating the espresso in my cappuccino at this point.

Evelyn is eager to tell the others about my need to know who people are for the purposes of doling out goods. Which isn't what I said, but whatever fuels the gossip flames.

The women quickly introduce themselves. Robin is the only name that is familiar, but I don't recall the last name on the box in the attic. I'll review the video when I get home. Not here, though. I'm not trying to let these ladies see the weird attic space. The goal today is to learn who the women from the boxes are, not start a fresh pot of tea about Barb. That doesn't help anyone. Not even my petty side.

"If I see anything for you, I'll make sure to come find you." My promise soothes them.

A woman on the other side of the table named Debbie offers to come to the house and help review items.

"The girl's got it under control," Evelyn chides, and then leans forward with her own agenda. "Well, is there anyone in particular you're looking for?"

"I'm not quite ready to *find* anyone, but I was wondering if any of you knew a Kathryn Wall?"

"Kathy Wall? Oh, well, of course. Her family has lived in Rockside Bay for as long as I can remember." Evelyn ignites the conversation.

As soon as she acknowledges knowing Kathryn Wall, the others chime in.

"Odd that Barb would have anything for her," Debbie says.

Heat dapples my chest. I'm not alone in being hated by my revered mother-in-law. I take a sip of my fancy coffee, and then nudge, "Why is that?"

Debbie tips her champagne flute toward me. "Kathryn doesn't run in the same circles as Barb, for one."

"So no charity work?" That's all I really have. I'm not about to ask if this is a money thing and kill the candor. Or remind myself I don't belong here either.

"Well..." One of the women is barely hiding a joyful sneer on her face.

So, yes, tax brackets. My espresso turns acidic in my gut. Entitled rich ladies did that to me.

"Be nice," another of the women admonishes. "It's not *that*, but the Wall name is almost synonymous with *bad luck* here."

"Bad luck?" I'm pretty sure Barb had been one of those "you make your own luck" types.

"Oh, it's a sad story. Kathryn used to be real popular. Bartended at Frankie's while her husband was at sea. He was a fisherman." Evelyn says.

I'd read an article about the presumed death of a fisherman named Wall. "What was her husband's name?"

"Bert," she says briskly. "Real sad, but at least she had her work family."

I swallow hard. Bert Wall, Kathryn's husband, was the one I'd read about. Headlines like that are hard to forget.

"Bartenders usually stay popular. What happened?" *Stay the course, ladies. Who is this woman?*

"They do. I heard she had been popular with more than one husband that wasn't her own."

"Now, Debbie," the other mimosa drinker gives Debbie a playful slap on the wrist. "That was just talk."

"Talk comes from somewhere," Debbie mutters.

I file this all away, but who was Kathryn Wall and why did Barb have boxes with her name on them stored in a hidden space? She'd loathed me too. I wriggle my toes to release my anxiety. Is there a box with my name on it too?

Hunger for answers sharpens my tone. "So what happened to Kathryn?"

Evelyn nods solemnly. "Her husband disappeared. Taken by the ocean."

"Oh." I press my hand to my chest. I know this already, but hearing these women speak of the loss stings.

"It went down from there. She lost most of her hair. Probably grief. It's hard on the body, you know." Evelyn says this like I should be moisturizing five times a day. Like I'm wearing my own sadness.

"Remember she wore those terrible wigs for years?" Debbie snickers.

I don't laugh. Evelyn watches me and then more softly continues. "After her husband disappeared, she had one small sad thing happen after another."

"Did Barb know her at all?" None of this makes sense.

"She was a house cleaner for a stint," one of the women says. "Barb might have hired her to clean before a party?"

"Oh, I'm sure she did," the women agree.

Their conversation spins onward about the bad luck of those who marry men who work on the ocean. The bad luck of fish. How kind Barb was to donate time and energy and money to the community.

I try sharing another round of names. The stories involve two broken legs, a bicycle accident, a headache that lasted a year, and an allergy to all jewelry that manifested in the middle of a community theater stage production. Strange stories surround each of the names I share, but none of them have a thing to do with Barb as far as her yoga group knows. And I have no doubt that these women would divulge any secret given to them within twenty seconds for a good mimosa and a chance to pilfer Barb's belongings.

Almost makes me feel better about choosing to trash so much of Barb's stuff. These ladies clearly don't have a need for any of it.

CHAPTER 20

THERE ARE SO MANY STRANGE THINGS I COULD HAVE returned to at Barb's house. The collection of crows—it feels wrong to call them a murder, even if it's accurate. Too much like snitching on a friend—should be weird, but instead, seeing the feathered collective eases the apprehension that twinges my nerves every time my late mother-in-law's home comes into view.

The local sanitation department had dropped off a debris dumpster in the driveway while I was off downward-dogging it. The gravel path beside the house is plenty wide enough for both the giant blue bin and our rental. I've only ever seen a bin that big when people were getting a new roof, which is a surprisingly common occurrence where we live.

The birds, the giant refuse bin, and even the thick forest-green vines slapped to the eastern side of the house no longer flip my uncanny switch.

But hearing "Dancing Queen" emanate from within sure does. I open the back door slowly, but the sound shoots out. It curls a finger in my shirt, like it seeks to pull me in, to make me spin and sway.

"Luke?" I shout instead.

No response. I move farther into the house, following the Swedish pop music into the formal living room.

Luke is bent over the coffee table. His near-perfect ass is in the air, shaking it like he's practiced in a mirror. I don't want to take years off his life with a jump scare by smacking his rear, but it's like he's asking for it. The temptation manifests in a cackle, giving me away.

Luke quickly rights himself and spins toward me. Embarrassment floods his cheeks and heats the sides of his neck. It's hard to fluster my husband, but I rather like seeing him this way.

"Hi. I didn't hear you. Um. How was your workout?" He fumbles. Luke has a bottle of Pledge in one hand and a microfiber cloth in the other. He still tries to put his hands in his pockets. Bless him.

The absurdity of it pricks at my eyes. "It was fine. Good to get out of the house," I admit.

"I'm glad to hear it." He sets the dust spray on the table.

"Although I think I missed out on the ABBA dance party," I tease lightly.

The redness on his cheeks deepens.

I close the distance between us, cupping my palm to his face. "I'm only joking. I love seeing you have fun. It's good for you."

Good for us, for that matter.

Luke leans into my hand, and my chest constricts with the warm knowledge that I'm not screwing this up.

"I couldn't get my phone to pair with her stereo," he says like he needs the excuse.

"You don't have to explain."

Luke straightens himself, no longer letting me hold his cheek. "I do if I don't want you gifting me a 'Best of ABBA' set."

Now it's my turn to be bashful. "I want to say I would not do that, but..."

"You already have it in the Amazon cart, don't you?" His playfulness is a balm.

"I admit nothing. But Luke?" I wait for those hazel eyes to catch mine, to see the glimmer of my lighthearted husband in them. Then I add, "I find it hard to believe the only music your mother kept in her home was ABBA."

I keep a straight face, but Luke doesn't. His bombastic laugh rattles the chandelier overhead.

"Fair enough, gorgeous." He gives me a bear hug that is on the verge of painful, and yet I don't want it to end. This house is fucking weird. This town is a tragedy magnet. But Luke? Me? When we're together like this, hope pools in my chest, insulates my heart. He's going to be such an amazing dad someday.

The thought is errant and sudden, but it only warms me further. He will. He'll dance with our kids. Will they mock him for the songs he picks? Or will they find whatever their father loves to be the best they've heard simply because it's something he loves?

The emptiness in my belly aches. My hand slips to where a baby could be again someday. Luke catches the motion.

His hands are on my shoulders, steadying me like he has so many times before. The humor is gone. He's all determination. Gaze sharp, brows furrowed, he's mapping my face. I can tell. He's watching for whatever flicker gives away my thoughts. Because Luke always knows. My spouse is not a mind reader, but he is an expert in me. "It'll—"

"I know," I cut him off before he can give me the standard "we'll have a baby when it's time."

He nods once and then slips his hand over mine. "We'll build our family, Ads. And soon."

I force a smile and then lean forward to peck his cheek. "We will. I heard you the other night and don't discount this moment as doubt."

He narrows his gaze but doesn't challenge me. The music continues to jingle and pop around us.

I tuck my chin. It's easier to say the words without looking at him, but when they still don't come, I close my eyes. I need to not think about being in Barb's house. Finally, I tell him, "It's okay for me to miss what could have been. I'm still excited for the future. For us. For what our family will be."

"But?" he nudges.

"But I also know I could have been getting ready for a baby shower right now." *Instead of standing with an empty womb in my dead mother-in-law's house.*

I don't say that last part, but it's almost like Luke heard it. "This all would have been so much harder though."

"The hauling boxes?" I look up at him. This detour from my life plan is hard enough.

His jaw flexes, but he subtly shakes his head. "The grieving."

"But with hope on the horizon?" I think it would make it all so much easier.

"We have that now too." He pulls my palm from my stomach and links our fingers together. "I appreciate you. Your help gets me to focus."

I get what he's saying, but it still hits like a slap. "I don't quite see it that way."

"You don't have to." He squeezes my hand. "But know that having you here for me now means so much. When we get home, we'll be able to move forward."

"Forward." I agree, because I need to hear the word aloud to have a chance at believing it.

"And I promise to order in the best takeout every night for a week when we get back."

"I will very much hold you to that."

The moment ends, and we return to the tasks at hand. Luke made progress while I was gone. The formal living and dining rooms are down to just furniture and mostly polished up. He's found a collection of travel "memorabilia" (his word) that he wanted to go through this afternoon.

"I also put a few stacks of newspapers and *Harvard Law Review* editions on the kitchen table."

I hadn't even noticed them when I came in. "You want me to pitch them before I head up to shower off the yoga funk?" I offer.

"No," he says quickly, like I'm about to torch his childhood blanket. "Mom liked to annotate articles. I want to see what was special about these."

Given the sheer volume of items in this house, it isn't a stretch to believe Barb just hadn't thrown these out. But I bite my tongue.

"Of course. That does remind me, I saw some newspapers the other day too. There was a fair bit about someone named Wall?" I say this like I don't know half as much as I do.

"Oh?" Luke steps to the stereo and halves the volume.

"Yeah. I wouldn't have thought anything of it, but I had coffee with the yoga women after class, and a few were talking about a Kathryn Wall? I wonder if your mom knew her, since she had those articles?"

Luke lowers himself slowly onto the cream-colored sofa. "That's a name that never gets spoken in this house."

I flinch at the snap in my husband's voice. He's in on at least one of Barb's secrets.

"What? Why?" Gossip had never been off-limits in here. Barb could backbite with the best of them. What had this woman done to be worth Luke's mom refusing to hear her name?

"It's a long story. A complicated one." Luke shakes his head like he's sifting through important memories. "I doubt she kept a single article about Kathryn."

"Maybe I misread it." I shrug. But I hadn't misread it. It'd been about Bert.

"That's a possibility. Mom may have kept those papers for another article too."

"So why is that lady's name verboten here?" Because that is a special kind of grudge. Even for Barb.

Luke is quiet for a long moment. He looks at his fingers, digs one nail under another. "I really don't want to talk about it here."

It shouldn't grate, but my insides twist, because there's at least one thing Kathryn Wall and I have in common: Barb hated us. Only Ms. Wall has boxes for or about her stashed in the attic, and I'm the one forced to find them.

Boundaries are healthy though. He's trying to process all of this. I remind myself of all these things, but also, I need in on the secrets. It's like an itch on the sole of my foot. Unnerving, unyielding, and unreachable.

The weight of the room settles on my shoulders. The vibe has shifted in the same way it had when my mother-in-law would breeze into a room. Her momentary glower determined to make me shy away from conversation. But that's not how this works. Barb isn't here. This is just us. Me and Luke.

"Where do you want to talk about it?" I ask, because I can have boundaries too.

Luke stares at his knuckles. They're turning white. "Just not here."

He's not saying no. It's not about secrets then; it's about respect to him. I can't begrudge him wanting to honor his mother's wishes, even if I can't relate.

I slip onto the couch next to him and lean against his arm. "Not here," I say aloud so he can hear the agreement.

"We should go to dinner tonight," he calls across the newly formed chasm of awkwardness between us.

"I'd like that. It was good to get out of the house earlier." More than the gossip, the fresh air focused me.

Luke heads toward the kitchen for his reading project, and I tromp up the stairs for a quick rinse before getting myself sweaty again pulling the backlog of bills and receipts from the upstairs secretary's desk and closet. We could swing by the shredding place on the way to dinner tonight if I can get all the papers in boxes or trash bags beforehand.

It's only when I turn down the hallway that I catch the soft whistle of a breeze. My steps slow. Luke wouldn't have opened a window up here. I turn back to check the window over the stairwell, but it's sealed shut. I edge forward and flip myself right over another of those vines. We'd cleared the house repeatedly. Luke told me he'd made sure there were no openings for them to even grow into the house. Yet here is another one. The end curls around my ankle possessively. These vines are literally the only part of this place that wants to keep me here. I kick and kick but can't dislodge the damned plant. I bend down and peel it away; the stalk is sticky and leaves my fingers roughened. I toe it to the edge of the hallway. Its end stretches toward Barb's bedroom. I can bring Luke back up here to deal with it. He'll find out how it got there.

That sparks an idea. If the yoga group all knew Kathryn Wall, could any of their names be on the boxes in the hidden attic? I hadn't recognized them, but then the slapdash video I made while leaving last night is exactly that. It's blurry and has a bad angle. I missed so many names.

I pause at the doorway to Barb's bedroom. The closet door is open. *Did I leave it that way?* The wind whistle is louder here.

I'll pop in and look for Debbie and Evelyn's names. Then I can shower, and before I know it, I'll be off to dinner with my husband. Away from here.

The breezeway-style *whoosh* escalates as I step into the closet. It claps my ears and dulls all other sound. I blink away tears that shouldn't be welling. I grip the handle on the smaller door in the back wall, and the empty sound falls away. The air stills. The quiet bump of bass from downstairs returns.

I pull on the knob, but the door doesn't budge. I turn it from side to side, but there's no latch, no click, no *give*.

The attic door is locked.

But how? There's not even a keyhole.

CHAPTER 21

BEING BARRED FROM ENTRY ONLY INCREASES MY DESIRE TO get inside. This was true when I was twenty and trying to get into bars on 6th Street. Vigilant bouncers made me believe those bars were the epicenter of cool. Once I'd finally hit twenty-one and had the legal go-ahead, I'd waded across a sticky floor to elbow my way to a bar for a shitty amaretto sour.

In other words, I'd had a mediocre time but refused to admit it, because I'd yearned to be allowed past that threshold for so long.

Will I feel the same after I get through Barb's hidden door in the closet again? Because my inability to open the door is a black wave breaking against my skull.

I don't need to go in there. It doesn't change anything.

Yet leaving the room is harder than I expect. I make it to the hallway but am reeled back. Did I turn the knob to the left? I better try right.

It doesn't give.

Which is fine. There are boxes out here that need my attention. The ones I can reach are the ones that matter. These are the ones I have to purge. The ones that stand between me and returning to the sunny expanse that is Texas.

The tide keeps pulling me back into the closet.

"I need to finish this room," I say aloud, like that makes it a choice borne of logic.

I start working through Barb's dresser. I've cleared enough away to reach the drawers now. It's a classic oak piece with two columns of three wide drawers. I grasp the crystal knob and pull the top right drawer open. Scraps of black-and-white and red fabric fill the drawer. I lift one.

"Oh god." I recoil, letting a thong fall from my grasp.

I've found Barb's underwear drawer. There's some solace to be found in that the dresser has been blocked for so long, there's no way my mother-in-law had worn these panties in years.

I grab a black trash bag and spread it open wide on the floor.

"I knew you wore underwear, Barb," I mutter. "Or at least I hoped you did. But I didn't want to ever see it."

I grasp the sides of the underwear drawer and pull it free of its track. The bin is so wide it's unwieldy in my arms. The wood digs into my biceps on one side and pinches my fingers on the other. Better than touching Barb's thongs.

I tilt the bin awkwardly and let the undies flutter down into the bag. The few that miss the mark, I push in with the toe of my sneaker. Kicking them much like I did the vine in the hallway. *Should I tuck that in this bag too?*

I wedge the drawer back in place and question my next step. Do I run these to the trash can outside now to put as much distance between myself and the lacy panties as possible, or am I an adult who will continue to clean this place out and fill the bag first?

There are five more drawers that need to be opened. Are they all clothing? That'd be normal. It'd make it easy to fill this bag and be done. But some people also store vibrators in their sock drawers. Is the next one I open going to be worse?

"Really would have preferred to be in the attic searching for a box for Debbie." I'm not sure who I'm talking to, but speaking aloud makes this less frightening.

Screw it. I stalk over to the little door in the closet and yank on the knob. Still locked.

I eye the dresser. Luke would crawl out of his skin if he ran into the sexy undies. Holding this thought—and what is clearly a kindness I am doing out of pure love—I open the next drawer.

My mind blanks. My ears buzz. Panic licks my chest, my throat, and then squeezes my chin with a fiery grip, forcing me to look at the contents of the drawer.

"Why couldn't it be sex toys?" A tear slips down my cheek.

I'm frozen to this spot. I can't close the drawer. I can't flee. I'm stuck meeting the gaze of a doll. Well, just the head of one.

Her hair is a wild array of brown and auburn curls. Freckles spatter the bridge of her nose. The doll head isn't attached to a body, making this whole thing a hundred times worse. The porcelain face is turned toward me, as though she has been waiting for me to free her from this wooden prison. Her honey-brown eyes match my own. The other features are close, but the eyes? They're mine, and they're tracking me.

"Why?" My whisper echoes in the bedroom.

The doll head doesn't answer, which feels like it has more to do with the fact that her mouth is painted shut than the fact that she's an inanimate object.

The heat of panic pushes into my cheeks drains as dread drips down from overhead. I'm soon covered in the sludge, but at least I'm mobile.

I shove the drawer shut.

The wave of curiosity rises before me, readying to shove me backward.

"They aren't gifts. The detail she put into that? Definitely not for my benefit." I'm shaking my head, but it's only twisting the knob on a burgeoning headache.

Click.

The drawer remains closed. Okay. I pivot slowly to look past Barb's bed to the closet. The small door built into the back wall, the one I have been fighting to open for the last hour, calls me forward.

Because it's open.

I tiptoe closer like if I make one wrong step or sound, it'll slam shut and I'll be barred from entry again.

It doesn't waver. There's no wind humming from the opening. In fact, the only things I hear are the bass from whatever Luke is listening to downstairs and the clank of the furnace kicking on.

Wrapping my hand around the edge of the ornate door makes this all more real. The wood is hot beneath my palm. My breastbone vibrates at such a pace that I'm certain if I open my mouth, a low drone will slip free.

I close my eyes and inhale slowly. You'd think a morning of yoga would make centering my mind easier. But that was before I saw the doll head in Barb's dresser drawer. Why would my mother-in-law keep a porcelain head in her bedroom? Why does it look like me? Tears collect on my eyelashes. They'll fall as soon as I open my eyes again. Am I ready to cry? I'd wanted Barb's secrets. This is the price of being petty. Because I no longer want her secrets, but I'm too far in to just *not know*.

Is there a box in that room with my name on it? How many of her friends from yoga have a dedicated box hidden away in Barb's secret room? What had she stolen from them? From me?

I squeeze my eyes tighter. It's a childish move, and while it feels akin to yanking the covers over my head, I'm not ashamed. An image of a crow in profile flickers in my mind's eye, or maybe I've stared at the birds so much it is imprinted on my retinas. The beak is sharp, the tail feathers nearly to the ground. I don't know that it's Eddie or any of the other birds from the backyard. In fact, it's likely the general idea of a crow. My chest tightens, the vibration accelerating. That note from Cassie had rattled Luke. The birds had been insistent about my reading it. *Why?*

I open my eyes and let the tears fall in heavy splats against the oak floor. I said I would look for more notes but never found them. I had taken that hurried video that ended up being less helpful than I wanted it to be—gossip about Kathryn Wall aside.

The need to know what Barb had stolen from others is enough to get me through the passageway. It's enough to dry my tears. I turn on the light and stand, waiting for my eyes and my heart to adjust to the room.

The A-frame beams overhead are reddish brown. Cedar. They amplify the sense I'm inside a keepsake box. There are girls where I grew up that had hope chests from the day they were born, the warm, shiny wood protecting their most precious memories.

"Is that what this was for you, Barb?" My throat is tight, my voice reedy. "Is this a treasure trove? Or just a way to make you feel more powerful than these women?"

The dead woman doesn't answer.

Not that I expect her to.

Shimmying my shoulders does not loosen a single muscle. I pull my phone from my pocket and open the Notes app. I can make a list of names while I look for Debbie's and Evelyn's...and, I suppose, my own.

My fingers shake, but I begin adding names to the list. Open the box with Meg Haltom's name. *Is this the same Meg who stopped by the other day?* I lift out an ornate baking dish. The edges are crimped and painted a brilliant red. Cherries have been hand-painted all over the interior and the bottom. Barb had stolen the family's coveted bakeware. What a bitch. I keep moving forward; I can get the pan back to Meg later.

Focusing on these other women keeps the tears from welling at my eyes, but finding a freaky doll version of my head in my dead mother-in-law's dresser isn't the kind of thing I can just shake off.

My body won't let it go. My muscles are too tight. My tongue sticks to the roof of my mouth. Even my every inhale of the cedar-scented room barely registers in my lungs. I will my mind to focus on the boxes, the names. That's safer than thinking about the *why*.

The first few rows have a smattering of different members of the Warren family. All women. None of them Kim.

If Luke is right and the dolls were gifts, then why wouldn't Barb have made one for the girl she liked? I push a box to the side so I can read the label on the next one. Only it's heavy enough that it doesn't want to budge.

The sloping roof is lower here than in the center of the space. I'm already hunched over, but I go ahead and squat. My quads whine. I tilt my phone so its light can illuminate the name on the box.

But there is none. Instead, the box is marked with an *X*. The lines are thick—not the same markers and pens used on the other boxes—and the black ink is so dark, it mimics being branded into the box.

Only I'm pretty sure a cardboard box would go up in flames in that situation. I drop my knees toward the floor. The smack of bone against wood echoes up my legs and into my hips. They'll bruise, but what's a few more?

The sticky humidity of the attic dissipates quickly. There's no breeze, but the air chills around me. Still. Stagnant. Dry. Bitter cold bites from beneath the floorboards. I tilt my phone light down. An icy snake spirals up my spine, both keeping me in place and making my body shudder. Frost slickens the wood around my knees.

I reach for the unnamed box. My fingers grow stiff, but I still tug the box off the pile. It thumps to the floor next to me.

"It's not for you." The words come from far away and right behind me in the ethereal way of dreams. Only I'm awake. The sharpness in my knees is real, the phone still clasped in my hand is real. Barb's creepy-as-hell dolls are real. And this box before me is real.

Lifting the flaps takes more strength than it should. The cardboard is weighted somehow.

"Not yours. You don't belong here." The words are sharp. The sensation of talons at the back of my neck, pinching and piercing, are even more so. The pain only encourages me.

"No more secrets," I say, as if this room needs to know my intentions.

I open the box and am shoved backward. My shoulders hit the floor; my head collides with the next row of boxes. Everything scatters. My phone goes sliding across the icy floor, its beacon of light shooting up toward the ceiling, but the room yo-yos. It's long. It's short. The walls are miles away. They're pressing in on me. *Did I hit my head that hard?* I sit slowly, but the room still ricochets.

A pulse that isn't my own beats at my temples. *Ba-ba-ba-bump. Ba-ba-ba-bump.* Half beats shaking me. I press a hand to the box with no name, and the sound stops. The room is once again long but just an attic.

It has always been just an attic.

I hold the thought in my mind as I grip the top of the box.

Dragging the cardboard container to the center of the room, next to my phone, isn't difficult. The box isn't *that* heavy, but the growing fatigue in my limbs makes me sluggish. Did I overdo it today? Is this stress? Have I drunk enough water? Am I turning to ice like the fucking floor?

I reach my phone and pick it up. I cradle the device to my chest like a beloved childhood stuffed animal. My emotional support device, I guess. But it's my line to reality. This room—this *house*—is playing with my head. It's being around Barb without her being here. I know that. This is some trauma response. And yet I can't let it go. I need to know why she has endless boxes here. I need to know why she made dolls. What had she collected or stolen from the other women in this town over the years?

This box, unlike the others, is not worn. The edges show no creases or fraying. It's as secure as the day it was produced.

Were the dolls part of Luke's childhood? Had he seen his mother making them before? Did he know about this room, even as a "Mom says never go in there" type of place? He'd been so dismissive of a *secret* room. He didn't want me in here.

Did that make it a rule that had never been broken?

There is so much inside this three-story house—beyond the accumulated junk—that could expose who Barb was when Luke was young. Luke would be heartbroken if his mother's memory were tarnished, and his happiness is more important to me than most anything.

But there's this granule of doubt in my gut. This tiny pellet that sifts against my insides and says I need to understand who Barb was to fully know her son. Which is ridiculous. I know Luke. And yet, I need to see in this box. I can't let it go.

I tilt my phone to look at the list of eighteen different women's names I've found in the room. Barb had kept this hidden for a reason.

I begin to lift the flap, and it's as though another hand—invisible and frigid—is on top of mine, slowing the motion. It doesn't stop me though.

I take a deep breath before looking inside. I can handle another doll. I ready myself for sharp eyes looking directly at me.

I am not prepared. A small glass mason jar sits in the center of the box, almost as if it's been glued in place. There's no lid, but seven shiny black feathers sit within, the sharpened ends poking free of the container. There's a ball of brown twine. A folded cloth of crushed red velvet is on the other side. Two fine paintbrushes rest on top of the fabric, but there is no paint in the box. There are no doll parts and no keepsakes from Luke's childhood.

The box is organized in a way that makes me feel like these are treasured craft tools. Only since when are crow feathers considered art supplies? And if this was such a passion of Barb's, why would she keep them tucked in this room beneath other boxes?

I turn around. I'm missing something here. Something more than my late mother-in-law's secret hobby of creating porcelain dolls that she never gifts.

The light overhead flickers. The floorboards creak. I open the camera on my phone. *Photos it is.* I lift the device to do a quick 360 in the room before hauling my ass out, but my thumb brushes the flip-camera icon and the front-facing camera turns on.

My face fills the screen. Skin so pale that even my freckles are pallid. I raise the phone and move to toggle back to the regular camera, but my hands freeze. Over my shoulder in an ocean-gray haze, a hand hovers. The fingers are folded down aside from the index finger. A ghastly number one. The hand drifts backward, to press against two blue lips. A scream catches in my throat. I choke and sputter.

There is no face I can see. Only slithering vines and blue lips flattened together, urging me to stay silent.

Whether that means not to scream or to never speak of this room, I don't have time to worry about.

I bolt for the door. I crack the top of my head on the frame on the way out. The pain is nothing compared to the panic ripping my stomach open. My belly is tight, acid churning hard enough to kick bile up my throat. I swallow the bitterness and slam the tiny door shut behind me. It bounces back open.

"You can't fucking lock now?" I yell at the door. I push it closed and lean my back against the carvings in the wood. I don't need to see the door, think about the door, or anything behind it. Especially not *whatever* that was.

CHAPTER 22

I'D ONLY BEEN IN BARB'S SECRET ATTIC FOR FIFTEEN MINUTES. At most. But when I reemerge into the bedroom, the glow through the windows is a low, smoldering amber.

I plop onto the rug at the center of the room. It's one of those oval braided affairs. Not plush or particularly kind to bare feet, but well insulated. A narrow, faded path bisects the carpet, leading to the bed. The rest is the original captivating cerulean.

Sprawling on a floor that hasn't been vacuumed or mopped since the last Bush administration is concerning, but I flop back on the freshest parts and hope for the best.

I can't fathom walking out of the room now. Going *anywhere.* Stepping out of this bedroom means either admitting that surrounding myself with Barb's garbage is addling my brain or the far more likely but way weirder truth that I just saw an apparition in the attic.

Holding my hands before my face doesn't show a single hint of frostbite. My knuckles are stiff, but I probably squeezed my fingers into fists in fear. *Did I?*

Why would there be a ghost in the attic? Why am I so certain it's not Barb? Because she didn't talk to me? Didn't try to shove me out of her secret den of dolls? I close my eyes tightly, but the woman's hidden face—no, the *girl's* hidden face—is burned into the back of my eyelids. There's no relief. Only the slight frame, the clawlike fingers, the vines fat and slithering across her face. Her touch would have been colder than any ice. I'm certain of it.

Is she the cause of the chill that has pinched me in this house? Is she the reason the crows are dropping me gifts?

I open my eyes and stare at the fan overhead. It spins slowly, methodically. If only I could be mesmerized by the motion. My lungs only fill halfway on each inhale, like my body is preparing to hyperventilate, but I don't feel winded. Just...fixed here.

What was with the jar of feathers in the attic? Why were there so many dolls? Who were all those women? I'm tempted to look at the list, like reviewing their names again will make this all make sense. Like I'll read a woman's name aloud, and the ghost girl will flash in here and be like "That's me!" and depart.

I try to take a steadying breath, but it's like I've been strapped into a corset, my Elizabethan ass unable to take a proper breath and collect myself. Dizziness pushes in at my temples.

Don't close your eyes. Don't close your eyes.

Darkness edges my vision, and I cave. I lower my lids. And she's there. Behind me. Around me. With me. Though she loomed at my back in the attic, she's smaller in my memory. Shorter than me and rail thin. Everything about her is frigid—the icy tinge of her lips peeking from between the vines encasing her, the steel blue of her skin on the gnarled hand that begged me to stay silent.

Had I screamed? My head throbs.

"Babe? You pass out?" Luke's honey-and-whisky voice pulls me from the dwelling deep.

When my vision refocuses, I lock on him like he's a tether. He's leaning against the doorframe, shoulder first. He's got one hand gripping the top, like he's keeping himself from falling into the room.

"It's all fine." The rote lie is thick in my mouth and hides none of its falsehood.

"You've been stuck in here too long." Worry creases around his mouth. "You've gotten so much done."

I survey the room. We're down to what one would expect to purge—dresser, nightstands, an armoire. Not that most people needed all of that, but sure. "I suppose so," I agree. Except I'd mostly pitched his mom's panties and then dug around in her attic until I got freaked out. Not exactly a prime use of my time.

"This room is getting close to being done," I say more for myself. "I can knock this out before the afternoon is done."

Because then I won't have an excuse to come back in here.

Luke chuckles and shakes his head like he's moderately amused.

"What?"

"It's already five thirty, Ads. You deserve a break. I promised dinner out." He dangles the escape.

I try to focus on the out. The option to leave the house, because *ohmygod* do I need it. Only I can't let go of the time. "I don't understand."

"Dinner. Restaurant. With your husband?" He waggles his brows, and normally I'd giggle. But I can't. He frowns, then tries again. "Why don't I start the shower for you? Take a long one, and then we can go get food. You'll feel like a whole new woman."

Is he staring at the closet? I left the main door open. He could see the carvings in the back wall, the little door that leads to his mother's secret stash of boxes and klepto trophies and freaky dolls.

But he's pointedly *not* looking there. In fact, he's watching me too closely. Like he can see the panic that encases me, like he can see the ghastly image that now haunts me.

I push myself into a seated position. "That would be awesome. I hadn't realized how long I'd been in here."

"You do lean into tunnel vision when you work."

Yeah, when I'm in a ledger or QuickBooks or Sage or with numbers. Not while logging the women's names in your mom's collection. The bitterness in my thoughts is quickly doused by guilt. "I'm just glad we both can get out of the house together."

At least that's truthful.

"Always, beautiful." Luke's mouth softens, and his tone soothes. At least one of us can let go of worry. "I'll get the water heating up for you, but I also found something in Mom's craft room that I think you'll appreciate."

"There's a craft room?" I've been to this house countless times and never once have I seen craft supplies, unless we're counting the doll head that stared at me with replicas of my own freaking eyes, and I'd only encountered that today. Except the box in the attic reminded me of treasured craft tools...

Luke releases the doorframe and steps backward into the hallway. The lithe way he moves pulls my gaze to all the spots on his body that I love—which are pretty much all of them, but especially his forearms and hips. He slips his hands into his pockets. He knows what he's doing, but why distract me now?

"It's upstairs. I doubt she used it while others were here." He doesn't mean that dismissive tone, I'm certain.

"Was it behind the—you know what, it doesn't matter. What did you find?" No need to beg for more concerns about this house or the way Barb stashed things in it.

"I have to show you." Delight sparkles in his eyes, and Luke extends his hand toward me, inviting me to join him.

It's a kind gesture, but it's not like he's trying to help me stand. I post my hand on the rug and push myself up. My knees protest loudly, and I groan.

"I'll make sure the water is extra hot if yoga is making you that achy." It's meant as a kindness, but a tiny, terrible part wonders why he's not sore too. But then I remember my role here—tackle the big stuff, move through Barb's things, and get both Luke and me home with minimal emotional damage.

I might have failed that last part for myself, but I can still protect him. If one of us is stable, then we'll both make it. Because we're partners and we can take turns being broken.

"It's from the floors. It's been a big kneeling day." Why do I need him to see my sacrifice? I press my teeth into the inside of my cheek and hold tightly until the pain centers me. *You're better than this, Addison.*

"Oof. Now I'm particularly glad I brought what I found down into the kitchen. Less stairs."

"Can it wait until after the shower?" Because now that I'm upright, I don't want to do another down and back up before dinner.

Luke deflates a little. "Oh. Yeah. Sure. Let me go start it."

I stand in Barb's room and wonder if I should take something now. Should I empty all her drawers quickly into trash bags and keep myself from seeing another doll part? Before I can decide, Luke is lumbering back. The floorboards in the hallway announce his presence before I see him.

I join him in the hallway. He smells of bergamot and cedarwood, and I go a little heady. Maybe it's a lingering side effect of the dizziness. I lean into him, and he wraps his arms around me.

"You too tired to do dinner tonight? We could hold until tomorrow," he offers.

I push up on my tiptoes and kiss him. "Oh, you're taking me out, Mr. Lowe."

His hand slips low on my back, and he presses me more firmly against him. "Good."

That one word sends me into a sea of want. I kiss him again. Take in the warmth of his body, the aftershave that smells like home, and the strength in the connection. My eyes are closed, but my mind is blank. Thoughts swallowed by the physical moment. It's enough to forget where I am. Perfect.

He pulls away too quickly, clearing his throat and adjusting himself. "Right. Shower. Dinner plans."

I roll my eyes at him. "Come show me what you found quickly, so I don't miss out on the hot water, and then I'll get cleaned up, and you can take me to the fanciest place in town."

"I was actually hoping we could go to Frankie's." The apology is silent.

"Not fancy vibes, but okay. The food is outstanding." It's hard to go wrong with any restaurant here. Even the pub food is farm-to-table.

Luke doesn't give me time to change my mind. He leads me down the stairs with the bouncing footsteps of a man who ran these steps for years. He ducks as he turns past the landing, the ceiling grazing his hair. I slow here though. I check the floor for errant greenery, but there are no vines. None on the floor and none wrapped around a ghostly face.

He's at the ground floor before I've even started the last flight. "Addison?"

"Just slow. Body aches and all that." The forced playfulness in my tone hurts my heart. Luke deserves better than me pretending. "And I have to admit, being here, seeing all these new sides to your mom, is a lot for me."

He calls back up to me, voice tight, "I'm glad you're getting to know her now. I wish she hadn't kept you at such a distance."

This is the most honest we've been about Barb and my relationship. The first time he has voiced his hurt about it. I suck my lips in and hobble down the remaining steps. *This* is good. He deserves my truths as much as I deserve his.

Except the sorrow tightening the corners of his mouth fades quickly when he sees me. If he can shut it off that fast, does he really need me to help him through this?

"Luke." His name is heavy on my tongue. "I found something… unnerving today."

He holds up a hand, his smile widening by the second. "I'm sure it'll be fine in context."

Doll heads and ghosts. Totally cool in context. The brush-off stings. I'll share more when we get home. When we're both steadier. We can process somewhere safe.

And I would like that to be several states away.

My husband proudly slaps his hand atop a hatbox. It's big enough to handle the most robust Sunday church hat. My stomach hollows.

"What do you have there?" I ask carefully, because Barb participated in many community events, but none of them were religious. And she went for subtle displays of wealth over ostentatious accessories. Big fancy hat? Not on Barb Lowe.

"You're going to get a kick out of this." Luke is beaming as he pulls the large circular box toward him.

Maybe it's mementos? Or it's all the high school notes his mom collected when cleaning his room one year? Only she never purged this house. Dread sludges through my veins. I swallow hard, even my insides moving in half time.

"What's in the box?" My nerves tighten my throat. I've already found so many items I never wanted to see today—and that he didn't want to hear about. I focus on Luke. His cheeks are bright with joy. He flutters his fingers at the edge of the lid.

"Okay." He pauses, the box still unopened. The anticipation might possibly stop my heart at this point. "I'm learning more about my mom while we're here. Like a new side of her."

Yes. I have told him this is normal. To be expected. What did he find that pleases him so much, and why are my intestines knotting themselves right now?

"Luke? The water is getting cold," I prompt.

"Right. Sorry." He lifts the lid and then upends the hatbox onto the table. Four small bottles of paint *thunk* in quick succession against the table. Luke jerks forward to stop one from rolling onto the floor. Two paintbrushes flutter out too. They match the ones I found in the unnamed box in the attic. Forest-green handles and bristles that transition from black to a delicate gray at the tips. But it's the doll at the center that punches my chest. I collapse into a chair.

"See?" Luke is *beaming*. Must be nice.

The body is wrapped in a luxe scarf. The kaleidoscope purples and blues are all the brighter against the unpainted porcelain. The face is still blank—no eyes to watch me—but the hair is in place. White and bobbed at the shoulders. This must be Evelyn. My heart throttles my rib cage, as though it is screaming.

"Do you know her?" I ask, as I imagine the way Barb would have painted Evelyn's wry smile and her pale eyes.

"Who?"

I lift my chin toward the doll. "Whoever that's...for." I almost say "supposed to be," but then I'd open more conversations than we are ready for tonight.

Luke shrugs. "Maybe a gift for a friend." He leans a little closer to me, like we're in on a discovery. "But, Addison, I told you she made that doll. And here's a new doll she was making. She had a passion outside of charity work. Outside of the parties. And it's art. I mean, how cool is that? Now it all makes sense."

He's in awe of Barb and her doll making. Of course he is. It's his mom. Why would he find this unnerving? What would he say if I told him about the head I found, the one that looks curiously like me?

"You didn't know she crafted?" The question tumbles awkwardly from my mouth, like I'm trying to choke down undercooked eggs.

"Not like this." Awe radiates from him. The smile on his face is wholesome, the tears glistening unshed are all love and grief.

He deserves this delight. This wonder. This new facet of his mother. A positive should come from this trip—beyond being done with Rockside Bay.

There are *so many* dolls upstairs though. He'd brushed off the hidden attic as a crawl space. He'd told me to leave it be. If Barb had been making these dolls for decades, how had her son not known?

I peel my tongue from the roof of my mouth. "I thought you said she made that doll for Cassidy as a gift?"

I'm not saying he's a liar. Luke doesn't lie to me. Ever. But the aftermath of loss twists our minds, our memories. It's perfectly reasonable for him to remember the dolls before in the heat of being faced with the name of a dead friend and not remember them now in the discovery of his mother's painting tools. I tell myself this. Even mostly believe it. But even when Luke winces, I can't make myself take it back.

He sputters an uncomfortable staccato laugh. "Yeah, I did."

And? I wait, but Luke doesn't look at me. His gaze is on the plain porcelain between us. It's on Barb's paintbrushes.

A tendril of fear winds across my back, from shoulder to hip. My ear burns, the one closest to the stairs. It's more than the superstitious concept of someone speaking about me making my ears ring. A breath of a whisper brushes the shell of my ear. My earring grows hot. I have to yank the back off and pull it free.

The move jerks Luke's attention back to me. "Are you okay?"

But I'm looking over my shoulder. Toward the stairs. I can't say why, but I swear there is a tiny version of my face turned toward me. The doll knows we're talking about it.

Luke's hand lands on my shoulder, grounds me, and pulls me from the spiraling thoughts.

The dolls are just *dolls*. They aren't malevolent. They aren't alive. Urban legends make them unnerving. This is what I get for watching all those Annabelle movies.

I blink rapidly like I can flutter away the mental images. "I'm fine." I pause. "Well, I guess I'm a little confused."

Luke's brows furrow so tightly he's verging on monobrow territory. "I'm sorry about that. I don't want to give you reason to doubt me."

"Doubt you?" The phrase jars me enough to stumble from his touch. "I trust you with my everything."

"Oh," he says, punctuating his clear concern with a heavy sigh.

I move closer, slipping my arms around his waist. I rest my head against his chest, loving how our height disparity gives me access to his heartbeat. It's racing.

"I only meant I thought you already knew she made these..." I'm not saying *dolls*.

"Mom was great at making people feel special. She'd put together dolls like that one we found before, sure, but it was an assembly."

"Assembly?" That's some word choice from Mr. Attorney at Law.

He squeezes me more tightly against him. His heartbeat never ebbs. Its gallop would be more appropriate after running the stairs. "Just she'd buy a doll, pick an outfit, dress it. That kind of thing."

"You mean like how my sister's chili recipe is just combining prepackaged things?" He'd called her out more than once. For a man not originally from Texas, he carries vigilance for proper chili.

"Exactly." Relief slips down from his shoulders, muscles softening beneath me. "I can't believe she took up painting. And now I wish I'd kept that doll she'd made for Cassidy. I could have given it to Kim, at least."

"You think she painted that one too? All those years ago?"

"I hope so," he says, his breathing becoming steadier. "She was so talented."

I nod and try not to think about the fact that her talent included stealing crow feathers and making creepy renderings of women throughout this town. Including at least one that was dead and another Luke wouldn't even discuss inside the house despite Barb no longer living here.

"Anyway, I thought seeing this would help you too." Luke lets me go and repacks the art supplies in the hatbox.

"Help me?"

"Finding that box bothered you, and since *this* box showed us more of who my mom was, I thought it might also help you see her intentions."

Intentions. Yeah. Whatever Barb had been doing with her doll collection, it hadn't been about delighting others. The woman I'd seen in the attic. The vines that encased her. Whoever she was, she didn't care for Barb's collection. And even if she is only in my mind, I trust her more than anything Barb left behind.

CHAPTER 23

LUKE'S FAVORITE PLACE IN ALL ROCKSIDE BAY—IF WE DON'T count his mother's house—is Frankie's. The pub is perched on a cliff overlooking the Pacific. Windows set in the hewn-wood walls reveal the perfect view of choppy sea breaking over gray stone. It's gorgeous and dangerous and my favorite part of coming to this bar.

The food-and-beer joint is on its second generation of ownership. The original Frankie is a gruff man who has posted himself at the end of the bar every time I've been in the place. Tonight is no exception. White stubble speckles his chin, and a worn 49ers ball cap shields his face. His daughter, also named Frankie, now runs the restaurant.

Luke knows them both, naturally.

We make our regular stop with Old Frankie first.

"Hell. Look who finally decided to stop by," Old Frankie says, clapping Luke on the back hard enough for him to hip check the bar. "And he brought the pretty one." He is very much a charmer.

"Like I'd miss my chance to say hello."

Old Frankie kisses the back of my hand, leaving an echo of whatever beer he is drinking. "Frankie," he yells to his daughter. "Get Luke a beer!"

He never orders for me. Old Frankie has a lot of rules—how people should talk, who they should greet (everyone), and the importance of community. Respecting all of that doesn't change the burden that comes with this pub. There is no opportunity to simply sit at a table and enjoy a quiet meal with my spouse. Every person to come through the door will be told Luke is here. They will all say hello. They will buy him drinks.

My husband drinks two or three beers on a date night. He doesn't watch football. But in this pub? Every time he suddenly needs to talk sports and test the strength of his liver.

It's a Wednesday though. I hope that means quiet. Inasmuch as a bar is ever quiet.

Luke gathers the pint Young Frankie pours for him, orders me a glass of pinot noir from a nearby winery, and then leads me to a booth next to the seaside windows.

I zip up the hooded sweatshirt I've worn as a jacket, my cute jean jacket having gone missing in the house's chaos. Cold air pulses from the window and permeates the walls here, but it's not the scratching cold that pierces me at Barb's. Just the chill from the wind off the ocean hitting the poorly insulated building. I can handle that.

"You want to sit somewhere else?" Luke asks, though he's already passing a menu my way.

I accept the menu but don't bother looking at it. "I'm cozy in my hoodie. The chill is always worth it for that view."

Evening is on the horizon. We timed dinner perfectly. Orange light ignites the end of the world. The water blazes endlessly as the sun slips lower and lower.

I take a sip of my wine. Cherry warms the back of my throat. Picking out the notes in great wine is not a skill I have, but I know what I like, and cherry in a medium red is it.

"This is so good." The wine, the view, and the freedom from Barb's house.

Luke holds his pint glass toward me, and I tap the lip of my glass against his.

"Cheers," I say.

"To you," Luke corrects.

I raise my brows and keep my glass toward his.

He eases back into the padded booth. Body languid, confident, and still entirely focused on me. "To you, Addison," he says again, this time more firmly. "For keeping me together, for overseeing the chaos in that house, and to our future."

I lower my gaze as heat rushes to my face. I look at the princess-cut diamond on my left hand. Not an antique. Not a jewel his mother picked out. A symbol of our love, of his devotion, of him putting me first.

Love has a way of overwhelming me. The steady simmer boils over. My lower lip trembles, but I eke out, "Always to our future."

"Oh, Ads." Luke sets his beer down and slips around from his side of the booth to mine. "I didn't mean to upset you."

"I'm not upset. Not at all." I'm perpetually on edge in this town, but *he* hasn't upset me.

"You're shaking." He states this fact like it means more than it does.

"It's the comedown. It's relief." And I mostly mean it. This is us, and the reminder of it is how I shake off the anxiety bending my nerves.

"From what, babe?" Luke settles in next to me.

"From the disconnect, I guess? I know we've been in that house together, but I also don't feel like I've seen you." Or been me.

He nods once and kisses the top of my head. Luke's arm becomes a fixture around my shoulders, fingers drumming the beat of each random 1970s rock song played on the overhead speakers.

We both order the special—because that's what you're supposed to do at Frankie's. Today it's an ancho chili–crusted salmon with an arugula salad and red potatoes. This town even makes pub dinners fancy. Not that I'm complaining.

The sun blinks out of view, leaving the window dark. The waves continue a steady shushing beyond the panes, now cloaked in shadow.

Luke and I haven't sat on the same side of a booth in too long. Having him this close after days of separation by stairs and memories heartens me. Despite the chill from the nearby window, warmth fills my chest. My breaths come more easily than they had on the lawn during yoga. I bet I could nail those eight-count box breaths now.

"Do I want to know why Debbie Thorne is waving at you?" Luke can mask his emotions better than most anyone I know, but he doesn't with me.

Which is why I elbow him to shake that smirk from his face. "Yoga and brunch, baby," I tease and then lean forward to spot Debbie four tables over waving like she's directing air traffic. Get that lady a Day-Glo vest.

"Is she always this enthusiastic?" I wave to the woman from brunch and then ease back behind Luke's shadow.

"When she wants something," he mutters.

Oh, hell. "She's not coming over, is she?" Can I melt into the seat? I'd told Debbie about finding boxes with people's names on them. Not exactly information Luke would love being made public.

I just needed answers he's not ready to share. Or can't. I cling to these thoughts and sip my wine.

"No." Luke bites out. "Mom wasn't a fan."

"Doesn't sound like you care much for her either." Luke has only ever spoken kindly of the people of Rockside Bay. And, I suppose, technically that's still true, but the muscle flexing at the hinge of his jaw suggests he'd really like to try a bit of shit talking.

"If it makes you feel better, she didn't say anything unkind about your mom," I offer, though I'm struggling to remember if Debbie said anything about Barb directly. Mostly she'd leaned in about the opportunity that there might be something for her in the Lowe house. Much like Evelyn.

"Of course she didn't." The dismissal doesn't sting. It's not about me.

"Do you not want to talk about it?"

"No, no, it's fine." He takes my hand, gives it a squeeze, keeps us linked under the table. "This town tries to pull me into the past every time we're here, but this trip it's succeeding." He sighs, and I look more closely at him. He'd shaved before we left and put pomade in his hair. Luke carries his effortlessly cool, put-together look well, but there are dark smudges beneath his eyes. Not the deep wells of nights without sleep, but the echo of them. Only he's been getting more hours here than he does back home—and my husband is a strict 8.5-hours-per-night, use-the-sleep-tracker-app kind of guy.

"It's okay for it to be emotional letting it go," I say softly.

"It's okay because you're here." He plants a small kiss on my forehead.

"I try."

"Since Debbie isn't needling, I'll tell you that she kept trying to set me up with her daughter. I wasn't interested. Not that her daughter isn't a nice person, but at the time I was twenty and Becky was sixteen."

"Gross."

"Exactly." Luke finishes his beer. "I politely told Becky no, but Debbie pushed it. Every time Mom ran into her at the market, she'd push about how I'd be so happy with Becky. Irritated the shit out of my mom."

I stifle the urge to smile at the image of Barb flustered over matchmaking. "She must have eventually gotten over it."

"Well, I am married."

"That you are." I squeeze his hand for a long moment. "But it took legal documentation for her to let it go?"

Maybe I shouldn't have let Debbie know there were goods to be had. Were we about to be hounded until we left town?

"Nah. Becky had a wakeboarding accident her senior year. Caught a rogue wave. Broke every bone on the right side of her body," Luke says this all to the small amount of amber liquid in his pint glass. "Scary shit. Debbie shepherded her straight through therapy. Really put her priorities in order."

My god. My free hand went to my chest, like I could still the sympathy pain in my heart at such an image. The poor girl, her poor mother. This town's list of tragedies is endless. It's a miracle Luke made it out unscathed.

"That's terrible," I whisper, horror stealing my voice.

Luke shakes his head. "And terrifying. Becky made a full recovery, but I don't think anyone in town went to the beach for years after that."

"Did they close the area to wakeboarders?"

He looks into the distance, thoughtful. "No, tourists still came. And now people go. Even though it was a long time ago, it shook the whole community."

I could relate. The longer I'm in Rockside Bay, the scarier the place becomes. I'd believed I hated this place because of Barb, but perhaps it is just a bad luck breeding ground.

Yet another reason to get the house done and leave.

"Do you think we'll finish getting the second floor clear tomorrow?" I ask, hoping his mind is on getting out of here too.

Luke slouches against the vinyl booth. He's still holding my hand, but with the other, he clings to the now-empty pint glass. Finally, he answers. "I want to say yes."

"But?" I prompt.

"I need to finish a few more tasks in her office, and I only started getting the craft room cleared."

"Is that your way of saying you can't help on the second floor with me tomorrow?" It shouldn't bother me. Divide and conquer. That's the plan.

"Getting the office done means first floor clear." His words are bright with optimism.

I'm going to be finishing his mother's bedroom. Her private bathroom.

I'm going to end up in that attic again, even if I tell myself I'm not opening the door. I don't need boxes and vines and mirages of dead girls in my life. But even now, the four carvings on the door are crisp in my mind. I could draw them on the bar napkin from memory. Closing my eyes will only bring the pale-gray visage of that woman behind vines or possibly a lifelike doll head that looks way too much like me for any sort of comfort.

"Addison?" My name drips from Luke's mouth like molasses. "I can put it off a day if you want, but the sooner I get the documentation off, the sooner everything closes."

There is an apology in there. An explanation. But mostly it's Luke speak for *I know best, but I'll ignore it if it makes you happy.* Nothing about this project makes me happy.

"Of course you should finish up in the office," I say, because it's what he expects. "Are you sure you don't want me to help there? I am our household numbers queen."

"I've got it covered, but hopefully we can wrap everything up in the next couple days." The hollowness in his tone belies any implied promise. *Damn it.*

I'm going to drop it. There's no point in pushing now. We're out at a bar. We're having a nice time. Mostly. The slap and slosh of the sea beyond the darkened window is slightly less soothing now that I've heard the story about Becky, but I shove it from my thoughts. I'm not going in the water. I'm letting it lull me.

CHAPTER 24

"LOOKED LIKE YOU COULD USE ANOTHER BEER," A HIGH, perky voice jerks my attention to the end of the table.

Come on. Kim Warren stands there, bright and tiny and eyes locked on my husband.

"Oh, we're wrapping up." Luke's baritone goes sharp.

Luke's high school sweetheart doesn't notice, but then she'd spent time with him back before his voice dropped.

She slips into the seat across from us and slides a fresh pint toward my husband. He accepts it.

"That one for me?" I ask of the second beer in her other hand.

"Oh, goodness!" Kim straightens her spine. Her blond hair is longer than in her Facebook profile picture. It's dagger straight and down to her boobs. Kim looks, in a word, fantastic. She wears a fitted red sweater that dips low enough to tease cleavage but not so low as to be attention seeking.

"I didn't see you back there, Allison."

"Addison," Luke corrects.

"Gosh. Yes. *Addison.*" Her mouth fouls my name.

I hate the envy rising in me, like a jealous monster is about to overtake my body. Because there's no reason for it. I'm merely off from spending too much time in Barb's house.

"I thought Luke was here all on his lonesome," Kim says.

"Nope." I lean into him. "We're a package deal."

"I figured you were waiting for a friend," she says to Luke. "Being back here must be so comforting. Being around people who knew your mama and loved her."

None of them really knew Barb. Not even Luke, I suspect.

"It doesn't hurt," he says, but his fingers tighten on mine. The only tell of his lie, but a reminder that I get to be his comfort.

Kim drinks from the beer she brought for herself. I'm both thankful and disappointed that my wineglass is empty. "I'm glad. And if you need to talk again, you have my number. I know how hard it is to not have answers." Her button nose scrunches, and she tilts her head in that pity move everyone makes. Like sympathy can only be delivered at an angle.

"I appreciate that." Luke's attention flits over the growing crowd in the bar. Faces familiar even to me are chatting up Old Frankie.

Kim could be the first in a parade of high school friends hitting our table. We need to wrap up quickly, or I'm going to have to roll my husband home.

"I really appreciate you telling the food bank committee that you'd support my bid to carry on your mom's efforts." She beams at him but casts me a quick glance. "Barb was a treasure in this town. No one could live up to her fundraising skills, but luckily she'd been letting me help her for years. Just the most generous woman with her time. Well, I'm sure you know that, Addison." She flashes her red fingernails dismissively in my direction.

"She supported several worthy causes," I agree, because flies and honey and all that. "Luke and I actually do the same thing back home."

Kim blinks at me like I've uttered profanity. "What do you mean?"

What part of that was confusing? I turn to Luke and hope he can read the plea for help in my eyes.

"She means back in Texas," he says to Kim.

She shakes her head. "Goodness. Of course. I forgot you're from Texas, Addison."

"Not only me," I reply quickly. "Luke's lived there long enough now that even the other partners at his firm classify him as a Texan."

"Oh, *pssh*. You'll always be from Rockside Bay, Luke." She doesn't mean it as a threat, but my stomach girds itself for fight or flight.

"It's like dual citizenship," Luke jokes. "But we'll be heading out soon. I appreciate the beer."

"Sure, sure. I didn't mean to intrude on your date."

"No worries," I say, entirely full of worries.

"I really did think you were meeting up with one of the guys. It was nice to talk with you about Cassidy the other day, and your mom, and...well, I enjoyed it." Kim's already rosy cheeks drop a shade darker.

Luke lifts his chin in agreement. "She was as good as they came."

Whether he is talking about Kim's sister or his mom isn't clear.

I'm not about to ask. Luke squeezes my hand, like he can sense my discomfort. That's something.

"She was." Kim nods. "Oh, I also wanted to let you know that I have reviewed all your mother's finances and the last two tax returns, and everything is solid. I'll email you the summary and a punch list, since I assume the trust went straight to you. You left that document out of the pile."

Each statement out of Kim's mouth lashes a tourniquet around my center. The longer she speaks, the tighter I'm squeezed. Anguish bucks against the bonds, bile churns inside, but Kim just keeps talking.

I rip my hand out of Luke's grip so fast, we should both have a friction burn.

"Excuse me?" My shrill question turns heads. I do not care.

Kim leans toward me over the table, like that will somehow cool the situation. "Luke needed a good line on Barb's finances and tax liabilities. I'm a bookkeeper—did he tell you that? I handle the books for most everyone in town these days." She's brimming with pride, and I'm seething with betrayal. "Anyway, that lends itself to taxes, and so I agreed to take a quick run-through to help Luke—and you—out."

I blink and then blink again. Maybe if I make myself tear up, it'll wash away whatever is happening here. Luke reaches for my hand again under the table, and I slide closer to the window.

So low that I almost can't hear him, Luke says, "It is not what you think, Ads."

"I think you asked another person to review your mom's taxes." It's a fact. Not even just what I *perceive*, but Kim literally laid this out.

"I can see you two are having a moment. I'll just see myself out." Kim slides from the booth so quickly, she doesn't even take her beer.

Condensation pools beneath the glass; it'd be easy to throw. Luke follows my gaze and pushes the pint farther from me. "It's not Kim's fault."

Bitterness fills my mouth and clogs my sinuses. "Oh, I'm not mad at Kim."

"It's really not a big deal." Luke already has his hands up like he needs to defend himself, like it'll keep me quiet.

The pub patrons are watching us. Fine. I don't know these people.

"Let's go home, and I'll explain everything."

"You can explain here."

"We don't want them gossiping about us." No, *he* doesn't want them to talk about him. I am used to it.

My back is pressed to the chilled window, but my ire has engulfed me in cruel warmth. "They were going to do that regardless. What I want to know is why you would hand *anyone* other than me our family's finances."

"It was my mom's." Like that's an answer?

"Are we not family?" I snap.

"You are my family." He is resolute. I even believe him.

It doesn't change what he did. "Then why?"

"Mom would have wanted her..."

"Yes, I'm well aware that Barb liked Kim and found me fully lacking."

"She didn't—"

My turn to hold a hand up. "Oh, she did. Your mom had no issue letting me know my status and her feelings about my place in the family. She was my family too, even if she didn't like it."

His shoulders roll forward, the hint of frown lines framing his mouth. "I just thought it would be easier to let Kim help."

"How?" I'm not here to argue. I'm here for an explanation. I fold my arms and wait.

Luke fidgets with a napkin, tearing tiny pieces off it like it's the most interesting paper he's ever encountered.

"Luke?" I prompt loudly enough to make an older gentleman nearby chuckle.

"Mom didn't want you to be a part of the trust," he blurts like this is some revelation.

I shrug. "And?"

"And I figured it'd make everyone happier if I used Kim as the accountant for it."

"Everyone." I lift my brows and watch him with a gaze I hope cuts.

"Well, sure." It's rare to see my husband scramble, but he's backpedaling like he's on a stationary bike. "Because we want to get out of here quickly. And you're already doing so much. You've gone through so many of her things and had to handle messes and even birds."

I refuse to be distracted by the lure of the crows. "Are you our family's lawyer?"

He hedges, fully aware it's a trap. "Yes."

"And if I were to solicit services of another lawyer, what would you think?"

"I'd be worried they were a divorce attorney."

"Because?" I ask like I'm his college ethics professor and not his wife.

"Because with any other legal matter, I would have your best interest at heart."

"Right. So tell me why you'd have another person—particularly one that your mother would have greatly preferred you marry—handle the taxes and finances for our family when your wife is an exceedingly talented CPA?"

I'm getting loud. Any other day I'd be embarrassed, but there isn't space in my body for those feelings right now.

And then Luke shushes me.

"Wow." I push against him. "Let me out of this booth."

Luke scrambles, apologies falling from his mouth. I care about none of them. The bars of betrayal banding my belly squeeze tighter. Hurt bubbles in my chest, fizzing up my throat.

I rush toward the front door, my sneakers squeaking on the polished floor. I shove the heavy wood door open. Cold, wet air rushes at my face. I welcome the slap.

Luke's apologies trail me—some for me, some for the Rockside Bay locals filling the pub. I catch him tossing a few bills on the bar near Young Frankie, and then he's hurrying toward me.

I've been holding my fears to my chest for days now. I'd come with him to this house I hated, to treat his mother's possessions with the care she'd never shown my *person*, to hold his hand and shepherd him through his misery. I would do anything for Luke Lowe, but would he do the same for me?

It was supposed to be Luke and Addie against the world.

I'm such an idiot. I came here to clean, while he chatted up friends and apparently entrusted them with parts of his life I wasn't privy to.

How are there parts of my husband's life that he wouldn't trust with me? He'd seen me at my worst, and I hadn't thought it'd changed a thing. Perhaps I was wrong.

I let the door close and run. Not to the car. I need air. I need space. I need to reassess my damned life.

CHAPTER 25

THE PARKING LOT IS HARD-PACKED EARTH COVERED WITH commercial rock. The uneven surface and my soft shoes slow my steps, but I still stomp toward the metal handrail jutting up to the south of the building. A set of stairs has been placed beside the cliff and creates a winding path down to the water.

Small lamps loom at each landing. Enough light to guide me but not enough to make me comfortable running the steps in the dark.

I move as quickly as I'm comfortable. *Ha.* What's comfort? The salty air surrounds me, but I can't get a deep pull of the steadying scent into my lungs. My fingers tingle; my tongue clings to the roof of my mouth.

How did this day get so bad? I'd thought what I'd seen in Barb's house was the epitome of terrible, and then *this*.

Luke is the one person who knows my secrets. He's the one person I trust without a doubt.

And I was wrong to do so.

He's yelling my name. No longer worrying about attracting the wrong attention.

"Addison!" he shouts again as he reaches me on the second landing.

I grip the rail. The metal is damp and cold against my hands, but at least he can't see them shake. The moon is slender in the sky but gives enough glow for the sea to appear as a separate abyss from the night sky.

Can I just walk into it?

A crow caws in the distance. Coincidence, but enough to give me pause.

"Addison." Luke turns my name into a plea.

"What, Luke?" I snap.

"I just want to explain."

I whirl on him, keeping one hand on the rail. "Do you have an explanation that is going to make me feel better, or is it about you? Because I can handle a lot of things being about you right now, but not this."

He places his hand atop mine.

"No." I put distance between us.

He nods slowly. He turns toward me, letting his hip bear his weight against the cold steel. "I'm sorry."

"I'm sure you are." It doesn't fix anything.

"Ads..."

"Don't 'Ads' me now. You cut me out. After all those long conversations about how vital I am to you getting through this. About how you couldn't *trust* anyone else with your raw feelings."

"That's still true. Do I seem like my normal self around these people?" He gestures wildly back toward the pub.

"So I'm worthy of knowing the real you but not of seeing your mother's tax records?" I did taxes for everyone in my family, and of course for Luke and me.

"It's not about worthiness—" he tries.

"I never pushed about why your mom hadn't wanted me to look over her taxes. I assumed it was because we were in Texas." I let out a sharp breath. White puffs between us. "It was never that, was it?"

His answer is so quiet, I have the sense I'm merely reading his lips. "No."

"Well, go ahead. Tell me why I'm not good enough to help you with this, but a *bookkeeper* is?" I shouldn't shit-talk the profession. Bookkeeping is complicated, and a good one makes all the difference for an accountant. But this isn't truly about taxes, and the pain of being rejected, dismissed is cinching me like a corset. If I don't deal with it soon, I'm going to damage organs.

More than my heart, which is already bruised and bleeding from this conversation.

"It was something my mom asked for." The crashing of the waves pauses so I don't miss a single word.

"She asked you to exclude me?"

He won't look at me. Suddenly he, too, is enamored with the abyssal waters. "Yes. She had clear directions about parts of her estate."

"And those directions were to cut out your wife? And you were fine with it? What other information am I not allowed to have? What other parts of our life have you decided I'm not capable of participating in?"

"Addison." His voice breaks on my name. The orange glow of the overhead lamp disguises the redness around his eyes, but the tears begin to fall. "Don't do this. Please."

A flash of anger sears my center, splitting the bindings of betrayal and freeing me to inhale, if only to spit fire. "Oh, I didn't do *anything* other than meticulously review and sort and clean your mother's house. I definitely didn't care for her son when he was broken or sick. I didn't do shit. I'm clearly not even here. Addison? She's a ghost."

The longer I speak, the sharper my tone. I think of my dreams then. Of being beside the water. Of being bound in vines, locked in Barb's hellscape of a house. Of the fight between fleeing and the fear of the fallout that comes with it. I get it now, the way Cassie looked at me in my dreams.

Luke throws up his hands. "You're everything to me, Addison. I love you. More than anything. But you can't expect me to ignore my mother's dying wish."

"Her dying wish was about her taxes?" That is the most ridiculous thing I've ever heard. I almost laugh, only I'm not capable of humor right now.

"Kind of," he hedges. His gaze ping-pongs around us. From me to the cliff to me and then to the sea, round and round.

"There's no one here but the Lowes," I tell him.

He rolls his shoulders back, and I wonder if he can sense his mother's memory with us. If that's what unnerves him so greatly. But then I look inward at the pain slicking my insides. I can help him through a lot of things, but only if I can trust him.

He sniffles. My pain doesn't ebb with his emotions, but that doesn't stop empathy from rising. I care, even if I don't want to. Even if he doesn't deserve it.

"She made me promise to keep her finances private from you." He's careful with his words. More than usual.

"She didn't phrase it that way, did she?"

He shuffles his feet. "She did not."

"She didn't want me near her money. Not before, not now."

"My mother wasn't perfect—"

This time I do laugh. Loud and dark and cutting.

"I know you two had your differences, but this was one thing that was important to her. So I was trying to honor it."

"Let's say that it made sense that you didn't tell her your wife is excellent with money, that growing up poor doesn't equate to a lack of understanding, that we don't need her money, and that I would only look at her books as a kindness to family. Let's pretend you said all of that—though I doubt you did."

Luke sputters, but I shake my head sharply and continue. "Let's say you couldn't sway her. You still could have told me. You could have shared your hurt and discomfort. You could have prepared me for someone else being involved. Hell, you could have chosen someone other than Kim."

"Kim—"

"Isn't the problem. She just wants to help. I get it. She liked your mom, and it was mutual. Regardless, *you* made a choice to cut me out. Not your mom. You."

He swears, but the vitriol is for himself. "God, you're right."

"I know." Did I need to say that? Yes, I did.

"It's all so complicated, Ads." Luke lowers himself to the ground. As if sitting on the concrete will help.

I remain standing.

"Help me understand, Luke, because right now all I have is you keeping secrets from me and then letting those secrets slap me in the face in public." I might not know these people, but I still don't care to be the entertainment for the evening.

Luke stays quiet. I watch the ocean and ignore the chill that skates over my skin when the spray is carried ashore on a gust.

Finally, he speaks. "My mom blamed herself for my dad's death. Like she could control a heart attack."

I glance down at him. He's crumpled himself to the ground in such a way he appears small for the first time.

He continues. "So since I was six, she focused on helping me make good, safe choices."

"That's all moms."

"Yes, but it was really important to her."

I don't bother pushing back again.

"And for the most part, that worked out. She cleared my path so I could excel in school. I honestly think getting the scholarship to UT was huge to her, even though she was mad about it not being within driving distance."

"I get all this, but how does it impact me not helping with the financial side of the estate?"

"Sorry. I'm getting there. This is…uncomfortable."

"More uncomfortable than finding out your husband hid things from you with his high school girlfriend's help?"

"Point made." He flexes his fingers slowly, like he's readying for a fight. *Great.* "Mom expected me to come back home after law school. In fact, everyone did."

"By *everyone*, do you mean Kim?"

"I mean everyone here, but my mom had certainly assured Kim I was returning."

"But you weren't with her when we met."

"No, I wasn't. I broke up with her before the end of senior year. We were both pretty wrecked by Cassie's disappearance."

Odd that he was as hurt as she was, but when you spend years with a family, I'm sure deep bonds are made. Barb and I are the obvious exceptions.

"Help me here, Luke, because none of this is making me feel any better." In fact, the more he talks about what these other women wanted, the more grounded I become in my hurt. He can clean his mother's room. He can finish the house.

"I met you," he says like this explains everything.

It doesn't. "And?"

"It ruined all my mom's plans."

"Nothing like being the monkey wrench in a well-planned life," I deadpan.

"I'd never met a woman like you. Brilliant and kind and could see through my emotional shield like you were freaking Superman." He brightens, eyes glistening as he looks up at me. "Don't you see, Ads? I met you, and you're everything. You're who I need."

"Then why keep this from me?"

"*Because* you're who I need. My mom was not kind to you. I talked to her about it over and over, but you weren't her choice, and she struggled with that. Even, clearly, at the end."

"I'm aware of her feelings, but what I don't get is you."

"It was a dumb mistake."

"That's an understatement."

"Perhaps. I just know you're my touchstone. I can't do any of this without you. We've only just come out the other side after losing the baby. You're rock steady, but your heart is still raw. I could see it, and I just couldn't add another layer to it."

Bringing up the baby is a cheap shot. "So you didn't tell me because you were trying to protect my feelings?"

"I mean, yeah. Being here was going to be hard enough for both of us. I didn't want to add the extra angst of knowing how strongly my mother didn't want you involved even after all these years."

Even after she was dead.

"This is just like the Porsche," Luke says under his breath.

It's like he's snuffed a flame. "Are you kidding me right now?"

"No, it's the same." His voice is solid now. "Hear me out."

I'd rather not. "Me telling you that I didn't think spending a bunch of money on a sports car was a solid idea is the same as you asking an ex to review your late mother's finances? Not even the same ballpark, Luke."

"It is in that I let my emotions override my judgment," he says quickly.

I can only stare at him. If he sprouts a second head right now, it'll track.

"I was so mad about you saying no to the car."

I cut in. "I didn't say no. I said we could do more important things with the money, but I didn't tell you what to do."

A muscle in his jaw ticks. "Right. Well, it was part of how I pictured being partner at the firm. I'd been so frustrated not being able to put this final piece in place. Not getting the Porsche. I couldn't see the logic in what you told me."

"Did you tell Barb all about it? Did she side with you?" I just bet she had.

Even in the sallow light, ruddiness is obvious on his cheeks. "Yes, I vented to her and then took it back once I saw the good sense you'd made.

"I wish I could do the same now. Take back this choice that hurt you so much. I didn't realize I let feelings cloud my logic, but I see it now. And I'm so sorry, Addison." The tension of holding back is visible in every line of his body.

But he waits.

"I don't know what to do," I say honestly. My body remains filled with anger and hurt.

He pushes up from the ground and steps toward me slowly. When I don't retreat, Luke slips his arm around my waist. I fall in against him.

"Usually you're the one who has a plan for how to handle the feelings stuff," he says. "I can interpret rules and live by them, but there's no guidebook for this."

"Technically our wedding vows are guidelines. You are to love and honor me, as I do you." I speak into his shirt. The cotton can diffuse the distance between us.

Luke kisses the top of my head. "I stumbled. You deserve better; I'll do better."

We linger there together, watching the tide crash its way inland. The darkness slipping closer and closer to our perch on the safety of the stairs.

Luke coaxes me back to the car. A few people smoking on the patio outside watch us, but none wave. Even they sense the fragility of the moment.

Once home, we head to bed. The weight of the day makes me sluggish, but Luke has a point to prove. We've never had sex at Barb's house. It would have been disrespectful, and honestly, the thought made me uncomfortable as all get out.

But when I climb into bed, Luke is already naked. My soul needs the makeup sex, and so I don't deny him. The closeness, the intimacy, the prioritization, it all builds and builds between us. I'm wrung out before he is, but when it's over we're a pile of loose muscles and sweat.

He whispers, "Love and honor you, gorgeous," before falling asleep. Which he does exceedingly quickly.

My body is toast from all the *ahem* activities today, but also I'm emotionally drained. My mind deserves rest. And yet, I lie there, glued to my spouse, and will sleep to come. Which has never worked in my thirty-two years. But I have limited tools in this particular toolbox. Goose bumps march over my legs and then my arms. I yank the covers up, bundling both Luke and me in the comforter. He huffs but doesn't move.

I close my eyes, and a vine-wrapped visage erupts in my mind. I open my eyes in a flash, holding them wide like I'm about to get the glaucoma puff test. Much preferable to thinking of whatever sight I thought I'd witnessed in that attic.

I stare at the ceiling and try to count the revolutions of the fan as it chugs around on low.

Eventually drowsiness tugs at my eyelids.

"You need to know." I don't recognize the voice that resounds in my mind, but it wakes me fully.

"Who's there?" I say, pressing myself more firmly against Luke.

His arm drapes over my stomach. He pulls me closer, but the move is automatic, as his soft snore proves.

"It's not safe unless you know."

I sit upright, letting Luke's arm slip to my lap. I scan the walls, the doorway, and the armoire on the far side of the bedroom. There's no one in here with us.

I hold that thought as I lie back down. Only the sense I'm not alone—beyond Luke—doesn't ease. I let him pull me in as a little spoon and eventually fall asleep. No one else whispers unnerving things to me tonight.

CHAPTER 26

A TACKY FOG ENVELOPS ME. WATER SLAPS AND RETREATS nearby, but I can see nothing but gray. Waving my hands before my face only underscores how little I can see.

I take a tentative step forward. Cold sand bites my bare feet, the granules seeking every crease in my skin and gouging as though they were corners of folded sandpaper.

"Hello?" I call, but my voice is snatched by the low clouds. The sound diffuses, disperses, and then disappears.

Light emerges overhead. I pivot to see it more clearly, tilting my chin up to let the pale glow cover my face. Like I, too, can be illuminated if I absorb enough of it.

I close my eyes, and thick arms wrap around me. Squeezing. I gasp, but the salty air doesn't so much as touch my tongue. My eyes go wide, searching for the source of my pain, but then it's gone. The fog too.

I stand on the beach in the same place I was in the last dream. Only my body is my own. I scrunch my toes in the sand, as though they can root me despite the coarseness. I spot the scar on the top of my right foot I got from a curling iron when I was in elementary school. It's me. This is real.

Or as real as a dream can be.

I recognize this place. Not simply from the nights when I've been the other girl, from beyond Frankie's pub. I turn and see the stairs ascending the rocky cliff. They disappear into a smudge of darkness, which I assume is my tired brain not wanting to fill in all the blanks.

But why dream at all? Could tonight have been a reprieve? Why am I here?

This is my dream, I remind myself and walk toward the water. It's brackish, and the closer I get, the more pungent it becomes.

"I wouldn't go in there," a voice calls from behind me.

I don't move. Not into the water. Not away from it.

"Who are you?" Even my dream self is scared.

"It doesn't matter," the feminine voice says. It's not me speaking. It's no one I know, and yet it's intimately familiar.

"It does to me."

"I can see why he chose you."

If I walk into the water now, I'll wake. This knowledge chills my bones. Why am I afraid of the waking world when the dream carries such apprehension?

What does she mean? None of this makes sense. My thoughts tumble atop one another, a tiny whirlpool of dread eddying above a burgeoning headache. Maybe that will wake me too.

Do I want to wake?

"I mean Luke," the girl answers, as though she's heard my thoughts. A tiny laugh trills around me. "Of course I heard you. This is all in your head."

"If that's true, then you're me," I say, finally relinquishing the sea view and turning to face whatever figment of anxiety my mind has conjured for the night.

A short blond teenager stands before me. Half her hair is pulled up into a high ponytail; the rest flows over her shoulders and frames her round cheeks. She has shoved her hands into the front pocket of her maroon hooded sweatshirt, which pulls the garment taut to show her slim frame.

I've never seen this girl before, but I know her immediately.

Her sister's skin is warmer and her eyes brighter, but the resemblance is too obvious to ignore.

"Cassidy Warren?" I sputter.

The girl shrugs. "Bingo."

I stare at the girl. There's a coldness to her, like the charred clouds overhead have stolen all the rosy warmth from the beach and those standing upon it.

"Though my friends call me Cassie," she adds.

Luke calls her Cassie, I think. But not her sister. The box in the attic hadn't said Cassie.

"Barb had a doll for you." I say the words slowly, like even in my dream they're dangerous.

Cassie's mouth opens, but it isn't humor that spills out. Dirt—dark and teeming with worms—falls from her lips. She huffs a disgusted chuckle, the kind reserved for idiots who don't see how bad the world truly is. My mother used to employ the same sound. Soil flies at me like spittle. It lands on my chemise, the same one I'd worn to bed.

You're dreaming. You're dreaming. You're dreaming.

"Barb never offered a gift she wasn't obligated to," Cassie says, the soil smudging her chin.

My mother-in-law's house is a den of withholding. She purchased trinkets and prizes, and hoarded them like no one was worthy of her spending. Aside from Luke, of course.

"I didn't know how far she'd go for Luke," Cassie says. Her body is fading.

"Wait. What do you mean?" Whether I was talking to my subconscious or this was semi-real, I needed more out of this.

"Barb Lowe didn't stand for anyone ruining her plans." The statement vibrates in the air. It more than lingers; it settles over me, into me. Until the truth of it pinches my very bones.

"But I'm still here." And she's dead.

"Unexpected." The way Cassie twists the word, I can't tell if that's a good thing.

"We're almost done in Rockside Bay," I say, because I want the fact spoken.

"Sure, but you're not done with the darkness of the Lowes."

"I'm a Lowe," I say sharply.

The corner of Cassie's mouth turns up. A worm wriggles free from her pale lips. "Not in the way that matters to them."

"To who? Luke?" I sputter. "He loves me."

Pity makes her head bob, attention never leaving me. "Love isn't enough with the Lowes, but I hope it's enough for you."

She says this like she's not me. Is this actually a memory of Cassie suffused into my dream?

She continues, her voice quieting. "Find me. Please."

"What?" Grit grows in my own mouth. I cough against it.

The maroon of Cassie's hoodie dips to black. It clings to her body as though soaked. "I don't want to be left behind again. Forgotten."

I realize she's crying. My need to help overcomes my fear. "No one has forgotten you."

She nods once, sagely. For a moment she wears the years, her fourteen-year-old body carrying the weight of decades. "Open the door again. Protect yourself. Please."

She turns, leaving me. I rush forward and grab at her arm. I need to stop her. I need to make sense of this dream, but my hand collapses around nothingness. Soil, weedy roots, and a spindly finger of a vine are all that remain in my palm.

The tide trips in, faster than it should. It licks my heels.

I go under.

I wake gasping. Luke snores at my side. The sun hasn't even considered winking at the window. I tap my phone screen to life: 4:12 a.m.

I flop back down onto my pillow. It's wet. I touch my chest: dry. Had I cried? I dab at my eyes. I haven't wept in my sleep in months.

What had dreaming of Cassie done to me?

I give up on sleep and head downstairs for coffee and a game plan. It's only when I've turned on the kitchen light that I see the dirt smudging my cami.

CHAPTER 27

OKAY. SO THERE'S A SMUDGE OF DIRT ON MY CAMISOLE. Plausible reasons why are plentiful. I'd moved Luke's shoes to the side of the door before going to bed. Perhaps I'd gotten dirt on my hand from it and transferred it to the silky top. Or maybe it's from Luke's hand. Maybe we simply aren't fastidious enough when washing our hands. Even my rationalizing self must admit that last one is a stretch.

I'd dreamed of Cassidy Warren. She'd been more than a frail teenager in my sleep. She'd been broken, rotting, and determined. Not that Cassie—could I call her that? Were we friends if she was in my dreams?—had cared about the dirt falling from her mouth or what lived within it.

Perhaps the version of her I dreamed of had made peace with death? Ha. No one does that. Least of all the living. I have yet to find any peace here, and given the way my husband keeps secrets and deposits his feelings in deepening grooves on his forehead, neither has he. But this house did that to people. I'd never come to visit Barb and not left ten times more exhausted than I had been before the "vacation." The woman had been walking stress. She entered the room, and the collective anxiety level shot up 50 percent. Yet this version of Cassie has no fear of Barb. She wants to be found; she wants me to protect myself.

I grip the back of the kitchen chair for balance. Cassie pleaded for me to "protect" myself, but what did that even mean? Barb is gone. This house will be too, in time. And I could be done with Rockside Bay, and eventually Barb could be re-formed into only the memories Luke had of her. He'd tell our children of special moments, and they'd be true and the only version that mattered. Because she wasn't going to show up and treat their mom cruelly.

Open the door. Open the door. Openthe door. Openthedoor.

Cassie's rasp grates my ears, my mind, until I gnash my teeth.

"C'mon, brain. You have to give me more," I mutter, pretending I truly believe this is all the work of stress and limited sleep. Lying to myself is a coping mechanism I don't hate.

Only I don't get an answer from myself or any ghosts. Does the door I'm to open *lead* to Cassie or protect me? Both? I lift both hands as though I can ward away bad thoughts. I definitely don't need to see a dead body, so it better be the latter.

The coffee smells good. I inhale the warm aroma while the pot brews. It'll sober me and clear my head of this ridiculousness. My stomach aches with a hollowness I haven't experienced in months. It's the burn of loneliness sloshing in the barren sea of stomach acid.

I make one of the bagels Luke insisted on buying, even though neither of us ever ate them. Decorative breakfast foods are coming in handy now. Condiments are slim, but I manage a makeshift meal.

I dig my teeth into my lips as I cradle my breakfast in my arm and pivot to push open the screen door. Whatever the crows decide to bring me today can't be more unnerving that last night's dream or, ugh, the memory of Kim dropping that truth bomb at dinner and having to cry it out with my husband.

Honestly, I could use a shiny little gift now. Even if it ends up being a stolen trinket from a random person in Rockside Bay.

There is no comfort at the table though. It's frigid outside. I need my sweatshirt or an extra blanket, or both. But a sharp pang of panic cuts into my side, lodging itself between my ribs.

The crows are gone.

I gasp hard, but the air won't fill my lungs.

The crows are gone. Even in the dark, I can tell the yard is empty, save a scattering of black feathers along the garden perimeter.

A fire-iron-scalding scream for oxygen burns the middle of my back, and I fold forward. I gulp at the air, like a beached fish begging for water. The wind slaps my back with an icy fist. The air trickles in, prickling as though the molecules have grown barbs and are seeking purchase on every alveolus.

The moon hides behind streaky clouds, casting the yard in ash. Even my quaking hands cupped to my knees have been leached of color. I'm living in black and white, but this is not a wholesome

1950s TV show. The sludge of dread clogging my veins puts my mind firmly in Norman Bates territory.

I hold that thought, trying to imagine Luke in his late mother's clothes. I sputter a laugh. More air eases into my body, my breaths evening out. Barb had been more likely to pretend to be Luke than the opposite. And while so many people in this town found her charming, there's no way she could have ever duped me.

I ease myself upright, letting early-morning air harden my skin. Willing it to do the same to my bones. To make me stronger, fearless. Or at least freeze whatever frightens me from my mind.

I sip the coffee, still hot enough to scald the roof of my mouth. It's the jolt I need. Bad dreams can't ruin everything if I don't let them.

I slip back into the house to retrieve one of Barb's coziest blankets. I drape it over my shoulders and tuck it around my knees. The sun won't wake for nearly two more hours. It's just me and the darkness out here.

"Eddie, where'd you go?" I ask, like the crow will pop up from the other side of the fence and answer me.

All I get is more still night. I nibble on the bagel and stare at the garden. I've gotten accustomed to seeing black birds decorating the foliage; it's odd to see it empty. Though the moon is bright, the clouds' dispersal of light brings the shapes of the plants into view. Tall stalks. Curled petals lie atop one another, forming big heavy balls of softness. Like petticoats come alive. Doll-sized petticoats.

Ugh. My asshole brain *had* to go there. Frigid fingers press at my neck, as though a gnarled hand is trying to hold me down. It pushes at my nape, sharp, cold, like it's heard my thoughts. I slap behind me, but there's nothing. My neck aches, but that could be anything. Poor sleep. Not drinking enough water. The air in Oregon. Who knows?

I drink my coffee fast enough I nearly chug the thing. It doesn't warm my throat though.

An anxious tendril of thrill rushes through me in being alone here. Like I'm about to be caught doing something naughty. When Barb was alive, I wasn't allowed to be unaccompanied here. Having now seen her hidden collections, I wonder if the only person she's ever trusted is her son.

It's only now that I understand I am still being watched. That itch in my shoulders, that chill down my spine might have been vibes, but the crows have been a constant presence since we arrived. Perpetually perched on the back wall and overseeing the garden like night watchmen. But now they, too, have fled.

Leaving me alone with my thoughts. Memories crawl out, tiny spiders scuttling free from an egg sac. They spread and they tickle. Stirring up thoughts I want to keep buried.

My mother died eleven years ago, though I still say *a decade*, because if you aren't specific, people tend not to ask follow-up questions. Not that there was much to say. *Car accident.* It isn't the remembered grief that grips me now; it's the guilt.

My tears sear my chilled cheeks. I flutter my eyes, focusing on the outline of the dahlia in the garden.

I had stepped up when Mom had worked double shifts. I'd practically raised Mallory. And that was fine. We all had our parts to play. But it also meant Mallory and I were never close in the way of sisters. I was the one who held her when she cried and made sure she was fed. So when a teenager reaching for his phone from the floorboard T-boned Mom's car, my first thoughts weren't of my mom. They were of my sister. I hadn't acknowledged my own sticky feelings about my mother's death until nearly two months had passed. Long after the sympathy cards stopped arriving. I should have been grieving my mother instead of fretting over my sister back then. I should have wept for her and not focused on shielding Mallory from the decisions that come with death.

Squeezing my coffee mug doesn't warm my fingers. They're the gray of spent charcoal in this ghastly light, the moon offering no path to distraction.

What kind of child doesn't crumble when her mother dies? The insidious thought hisses in my ear. And I know that where there is one, there is another.

A shiver slices through me. I tug the blanket tighter, but the guilt is rotting me from the inside out.

I blink once, twice, and soon I can imagine black spiders on my arms, marching down my legs. Crawling in places they have no business. I want to scrub my face, to confirm the sensation is merely a trick, but my muscles are tight, locked. Hands on my mug, body quaking.

"You expect to support Luke when your heart was so cold as to not cry for your mother?" The voice takes on Barb's tone, but it's my own regret.

"I cried for her," I whisper to the silent night. "Alone like this, I cried."

Only that hadn't been for weeks.

"Luke lost the woman who loved him most in this world. The one who would do anything for him," the cruel voice spits.

That might be true. The last part anyway. "Giving someone anything they want isn't parenting." There is love in boundaries. And in respecting them. Luke and I could do that.

"You aren't a mother. You don't know."

The unfairness twists my stomach, and bile splashes my throat. I swallow, but the stench of sickness is cloying. My mom's car accident wasn't my fault, and neither was my own.

I press a hand to my abdomen. "I will be."

"Women always think they know what motherhood entails. They think they understand unconditional love. You aren't ready for it." I can practically picture Barb shouting the words at me from the lawn. The visual, though, pulls me from the darkness. Because while Barb had been capable of spewing vitriol, she wouldn't lower herself to making a scene. No hollering in the yard for her.

Maybe that changes when you die.

I nod slowly, to myself. Fatigue swallows me, and my muscles soften enough to let me move.

"I don't expect that I understand motherhood, but I do know myself. When I become a mom, I will do everything in my power to teach my children kindness." I say the words aloud, to the empty yard, because I need to hear them. "I deserve to be a mom as much as the next woman."

Barb raised a magnificent man. I love Luke with every part of me. But there are moments when he's hurt or worried or scared, where a flash of Barb pops up. A judgmental comment. A fascination with what my mom would have called "rich-people shit." An expectation that I'll do the work with or for him.

But he is not his mother. We are not our parents. Unpacking the parts of ourselves we don't like—inherited or otherwise—is a journey.

"Leaving here was a good choice," I say. This town teems with tragedy. It's nothing but dark memories—even in Luke's childhood home. Abe Lincoln videotape aside, there were news clippings packed with heartache that Barb had stockpiled. Luke didn't even know the full extent of his mother's collection behind the small door in her bedroom.

I sip my coffee; it's cold. I drink it anyway. As if caffeine can center my thoughts on a more comfortable topic.

The crows would do that for me. A fresh pang of heartache hits me at their absence. I stand and pace a few circuits on the deck. The itch to take action wriggles beneath my skin. It does not, however, provide a helpful task. I pour another cup of coffee and pick up the packet of peanuts from the pantry. A snack will lure my feathered friends, right?

I settle back into what I'm thinking of as my chair. This little coffee setup is perfect. If not for my memories and the circumstances, I can see how this part of the day would be so appealing. The air crisp and brined to wake you, the distant shush of water, and, on every other morning, the fascinating show of crows living their best garden lives.

Luke hadn't run them off, had he? I dismiss the errant thought. Luke might have kept the accounting secret from me, but after last night, he wouldn't skimp on divulging. Besides, if Barb couldn't keep them gone, I doubt Luke could either. Why had Barb bothered with this deck setup if she hated the crows so much?

A hazy yellow glow appears on the horizon, and like that, the gray veil lifts. The violets and mossy greens of the yard come into view with a brilliant reveal that makes the natural feel supernatural. Barb had loved that garden. It shows. The flowers are varied, the soil sparse enough to allow for growth while still creating a full display. The scattered line of black feathers at the perimeter only makes the colors brighter.

I squint at the lawn. There's something blue and crumpled lying in the center. I rise slowly from my coffee perch, blanket slipping down, chill biting my back.

I pad to the edge of the deck, toes tipped over the first step. It's a heap of denim in the yard. Where I'd imagined my dead mother-in-law shit-talking me.

I rush out there. The grass is dewy, saturating my socks. The cold ground numbs my feet, but it's my heart that ices over when I reach the clothing. It's my jean jacket. The one I'd wanted when we went to dinner. The one I hadn't seen since we arrived days ago.

I pick it up. It's wet and heavy but very much mine. The wind couldn't have taken this. I haven't been walking around the yard. Luke had been in the garage, but he wouldn't steal my jean jacket and then dump it in the grass.

The wind whips my ears, a dull whistle wrapping my thoughts. I spin, but no one is there. It's me, the rising sun, and a soggy denim jacket.

"Barb?" I whisper her name.

There's no reply. *Of course there isn't. She's dead.*

The blossoms wake and unfurl in the distance, but I can't shake what I've seen. The nightmares may be my subconscious, but the boxes are real. The doll head bearing my face is real. The names in this town, the stories of what has happened to them, that is all very much real. Did I see a ghost in the hidden attic? In the morning light, I'm no longer certain. If I ever was.

I won't ever be able to make peace with this unless I go back into the attic space. Not with nightmares telling me to open the door. Ignoring intuition never ends well. And I intend to put everything at this house behind us when we leave.

My favorite crow, Eddie, flies past me. He enters from the east, like perhaps he'd been hanging out on our rental car the whole time.

"You didn't leave this for me, right?" I ask, like the birds would be strong enough to heft the jacket.

Eddie merely circles overhead until Nixie joins him. The two birds slip from my sight again, but at least they haven't fully abandoned me.

A girl needs friends, even if they're the avian kind.

I walk across the yard to peek at our rental. No additional birds there. But I catch the tail feathers overhead. The crows have landed atop the house. A couple are digging their beaks into the green vines on the side of the house. I rush back inside before I can think too hard about what creatures they might be hunting for in them.

Starting the day with the certainty I'm not alone bolsters my resolve. I'm not going to let this house break me. Barb won't get that satisfaction, even in death.

CHAPTER 28

GETTING READY FOR THE DAY RALLIES ME. IT'S A DO-OVER for the morning, and I'm focused. I use the time in the shower not only to replenish the warmth I'd lost out on the deck but to craft a plan. I've been approaching Barb's secret stash room all wrong.

Making a list of names hadn't been a bad start, but every time I go in there, I lose my senses. Time ebbs. Space stretches. My sense of self is even distorted. Ignoring the room helps no one, despite Luke's refrain that the "crawl spaces" are not a priority.

Luke's puttering around on the first floor. The swinging door between the kitchen and dining rooms click-clacks, and occasionally his muffled voice reaches me on the second floor. He's talking to himself down there, but I stall out heading down to give him a good-morning kiss. The worn wooden step holds me steady, as though this is the natural halfway point where everyone questions why they were heading up or down the stairs. Only I know why I'm on the move—I'm going to open the small carved door in Barb's closet.

"Ads?" Luke calls.

"Yeah?" My throat is tight, my reply squeaky. Am I lying by omission if I don't tell him about my plan?

"You've got to see this." Without the cues of his body language, I can't discern if he's awestruck or freaked out.

Green-gold light cascades overhead. A shadow splits the window at the landing, the textured glass there almost creating a trick of the mind when you catch it wrong. The shadows stretch onto the stairs above, up to the ceiling and away from me, gnarled fingers pointing to Barb's bedroom. A threat, an omen, a guide? I'm running on empty. My heart rattles in its cage.

"Addison?" My full name in the air makes the choice.

Downstairs it is. "Coming."

When I arrive in the kitchen, Luke is standing at its center. His gray sweatpants are slung low on his hips, his navy-blue T-shirt slightly wrinkled from sleep. His arms are folded across this chest, and he's just *staring* outside.

I step close to his side. I press my hand against his bicep; the skin is cool. As though he made the same move this morning that I had and went outside first thing, coat free.

"Luke," I say his name low, careful.

His brows furrow, but he remains focused elsewhere. His throat bobs. Luke isn't fast to reply generally, but his silence now jangles a warning bell deep in my mind. I lean into him, making my presence undeniable. I'm there to keep him upright, to hold him steady. The hidden doorway is no longer my priority. I wrap my arms around him and squeeze tight, tighter, tighter.

"Babe, you're kind of scaring me." My whisper has nowhere to hide in this quiet room.

Luke flinches, and slowly he turns to meet my gaze. His eyes are wild, bloodshot. Darkness smudges his cheeks. If I hadn't endured hours of his snoring, I would believe he had insomnia.

"Please tell me you see them." A soft-spoken Luke is alarming.

A heaviness settles in the room, around me. The weight of his moment, of his fear, slows my motions, but I make myself turn and follow his gaze. Brilliant light from the rare sunny day spotlights the backyard—a yard teeming with crows.

There's a sea of inky black from fence to fence. Shiny eyes all turned this direction. Dozens of the birds simply watching the home.

They aren't chattering. Or feasting on the insects surely active early in the morn.

"I see them," I assure Luke.

"It's never been like this," he says, like there's a history I should know about.

But I don't. "I didn't know murders this big were even possible."

His attention snaps to me, hand seizing my wrist, eyes wild. "*That* is not natural."

I press my free hand against my thigh, digging my fingertips into the fresh bruise there. I need the physical pain to dull the threat of more feelings than I have depth for. "It's unsettling," I admit. This isn't the gathering of friendly crows watching over my morning coffee ritual.

I edge closer to the door, like if I can see better, I'll understand the message. I have no doubt there is one.

And I'm not going to like it.

"That's an understatement," my husband mutters. He inhales sharply before continuing. "There's a reason my mother chased them off."

"Don't tell me the story about your uncle again, please. There was not a backyard of birds watching him." Having now met the crows, I rather suspect Luke's uncle had earned the comeuppance.

"No, but they..." Luke grows quiet. That makes him far more curious than the corvid wave outside.

"They what?" My entire face hurts from the pinch of holding back fear. Though I'm not sure whether the threat is outside the house.

"They hold grudges," he says finally.

I lean back, trying to see the lie on him better. "Come on."

"They do—"

"Oh, I'm certain they have great memories, but your beef can't be that a bird doesn't like you. There's more." When he doesn't confide, I push. "You wouldn't have hesitated if the reason was a fact I could learn with a three-second search query."

Luke releases me and stares at his palm as though he is viewing the appendage anew. His lips part and then close. His hands move like he is gesturing for emphasis, though he says nothing.

"This place twists you up. I get that, but after last night I thought we weren't going to do the whole holding-back dance again." My exhale is more than a sigh; it's a deflation.

I shake my head slowly, disappointment dripping from me like droplets from wet hair. The floor would be slick with it. I open the back door and step onto the deck.

The crows say nothing. Not a one of them has ventured up here.

"I don't think I have snacks enough for all of y'all," I say, fear unleashing the drawl I squashed long ago. I sounded too much like my mom.

Two more crows fly in, landing on the bistro table beside me.

"Eddie? Nixie?" I scurry forward as if I'm going to hug them.

Nixie juts her beak toward me, bouncing the tip in what I take as both acknowledgment and a "Please do not touch me, strange lady."

Luke blasts out onto the deck behind me. The door claps behind him, and a gust of wind curls around the house to catch my face.

"You named them?" The incredulity on his face is cranked to peak.

I lift a hand as if I can still the panic washing over my husband. His nostrils flare, and he simply stares at me.

Before I can reply though, the ocean of black winged creatures caws. First one cry, then another. Soon their symphony boxes my ears, and the sound redoubles on itself. The constant caws bury my thoughts.

Eddie isn't singing. He taps his beak against the table, though the sound is lost to the cacophony.

I lean toward the crow. What has Eddie brought me? Luke's hands are hot on my shoulders, pulling me back against his body. "What are you doing, Addison?"

His fear is palpable. His heartbeat is tempting hummingbird territory for speed and hits with the wallop of a kick drum. His body is shaking mine, not purposely. He's beyond quaking; his whole body is locked and ready for battle.

It's enough to open the gate on my own fear. Had I miscalculated this whole time? Was there more happening here than I realized?

Barb had black feathers in her freaky little attic space but hated the birds that provided them. None of this makes sense, but the birds have only been kind to me.

I stare at Eddie and the prize he's brought me. A simple ring. Two thin silver bands coming together to hold a small pearl.

"Do you see that?" I ask, knowing he'll hear me despite the noise.

Luke jerks backward, and then his whole body locks. The muscles in his forearms twitch against me, cranking my anxiety.

"Luke?" I prod. "Look what he has."

"It's nothing." He speaks so quickly, I almost misunderstand him.

His dismissal slashes my center. My heart should fall out. No more secrets. He'd promised. And yet I could see the terror gripping him, *feel* it. He'd just lied to me.

Again.

"No, it's a promise ring." I free myself from his protective embrace and pick up the jewelry.

The crows take flight.

All of them.

Eddie is the last to leave. His onyx eyes lock on Luke for a long moment, but then Eddie departs too.

And it's just me, Luke, and a promise ring.

The fine hairs on Luke's arm rise in a wave, as though the ambient air has dropped a dozen degrees. "You named the crows?" His lips barely part, making this question tight with accusation.

I already explained this. "Not a full yard of them."

"Addison," he chides.

"Dial it back there, counselor."

His mouth flattens.

I edge toward him, refusing to let either of us look away now. "I'm not a child, and I've done nothing wrong."

His tone says otherwise. "I told you to avoid those birds—"

"Which was, frankly, weird."

He doesn't back down. His words shake with authority. "They are dangerous."

"Not to me." I'm not here to dismiss his fears, but even after the flood of black birds in the yard, I can't say I'm afraid. "They've kept me company in the mornings."

"Kept you company?" His incredulity would be more appropriate if I'd said I'd met three of them in a trench coat.

"The ones that stay here? Yeah. I give them snacks, and we chat." I want to share this cool experience with him, but every word I speak makes the whole conversation more contentious.

Luke's scowl hardens by the second. "No wonder the whole mass of them was here. You've been feeding them."

"I've been feeding a few crows. Not dozens of birds, and *it's fine.* Nothing disastrous has happened. They chatter. They're cute. They bring little trinkets."

Trinkets. Is Luke trying to distract me by being mad about me giving Eddie and Nixie and the others names?

I lift up the promise ring, pinching it between my fingers. I hold it aloft between us. "Now, this seems like a more worthwhile point of discussion," I say.

Luke's gaze locks on the dainty ring. "They brought you someone's jewelry. Okay. They're thieves." He shifts his shoulders; his fingers flutter at his sides. It's this ring making him nervous.

"Do you recognize it?" I ask plainly.

"What? What use would I have for that?" he sputters.

We're fighting. Our voices aren't raised, but that's what this is. Holding the ring between us is pushing us to opposite sides. It's separating us.

"Luke." I pause. Sorrow slaps my cheek, tears well. "It's okay."

"What's okay?"

"It's okay if you recognize it." I lower the ring and set it on the table. Use my free hands to take his. I can help him now. "I think the crows have been using our discard pile beside the house to find treasures for me."

"Of course they're stealing from our garbage."

"Not sure it's stealing if it's been pitched in a dumpster, but that's not the point, babe. Our past only hurts us when we let it."

Luke's brows furrow, and his hands tighten on mine, the coldness around us forgotten. "It doesn't matter," he says finally.

We won't move forward if we avoid this. Maybe my compartmentalization plan isn't as effective as I'd hoped.

"It does matter." I leave no room for doubt. "I love you, but whatever that ring means, it hurts you. I need to know why."

"Talking about it will only make it worse. Can't we just go inside and take a shower together?"

Luring me with warmth and intimacy is a dirty trick, but I'm beyond it right now. We both need to work through this. It'll make it easier when we get back home.

"I showered already. I want to know why it upset you. I love every part of you, Luke, even the dark bits."

"Now I have darkness?" He guffaws.

"I sure as hell do."

He pulls me in against his chest. "Fine, but let's go inside. I'm freezing."

I bring the ring with us. It's meaningful to Luke and to my crows. Dismissing it isn't a choice.

The box with Barb's craft materials is still on the kitchen table. After we sit, I nudge it back against the wall, as far from me as it can go. Luke pretends he doesn't notice. Thankfully. I toss the ring on the table too, like it hasn't shaken us both. It slides across the surface and bumps into Barb's hatbox.

Silence stretches between us, but I refuse to let distance grow in the gap. "So tell me about this ring." My tone is light, my attention on him, and I really hope he'll answer.

His nod releases knots in my back. I rest my elbow on the table.

Luke's tongue darts out to wet his lips, but that's his last delay. "It was Cassie's."

Screw knots in my back; my muscles damn well braid themselves with that. "*Cassie?*" I clarify. "Not Kim?"

"I never gave Kim a promise ring," he says.

"Were you a promise-ring kind of guy?" I find it hard to picture.

The corner of his mouth ticks up, but he shakes his head. "Not even a little. And my mom was even less so."

Interesting. "So this was Cassie's promise ring." I can't make the dots connect. "But why is it here? Who gave it to her?"

"I don't know." Luke slides down in the hardback chair, his knees bumping mine. "This whole week has been a flood of memories about Cassie. I haven't thought about her or what happened in so long, and then we're back here and everything is in my face."

"That I get." It's in my face too. And around me. And haunting my dreams.

"The Warrens carried a lot of trouble," Luke says, gazing at the ceiling.

The phrase is one his mother loved to use. "Trouble for who?"

"Me, mostly," he grumbles.

I can't fight the scowl twisting my face. "Your mom wanted you to marry into that family. It couldn't have been that bad."

"She..." He decides not to deny it. "The Warren family did a lot of good in town. Still does."

"And?" Oh, he's going to have to spell it out.

He drops a heavy sigh. "Mom didn't appreciate competition."

"But you and Kim were so close; weren't you practically a part of the family for a few years?" He'd talked about it minimally, but it'd been a complicated and tragic part of his life.

"Yes, I spent most of junior and senior year at the Warrens' house. Just coming home to sleep."

"I'm surprised Barb liked Kim so much then," I tease.

Luke winces. “She didn’t like people in our house unless she’d invited them. So spending time at Kim’s was easier.”

Had Barb ever actually *invited* me here, or had I just been Luke’s plus-one?

“So this ring...” I incline my head toward the promise ring. “Cassie wore it all the time?”

“For the last few months before she disappeared.” He choked on the last word, coughing hard enough he had to get a glass of water.

“How did it end up here?” I should not be thinking out loud.

“I don’t fucking know,” Luke snipes.

“Sorry. Really, babe. It’s just weird.” Far stranger than my jean jacket finding its way to the yard.

Luke wipes a hand over his eyes. Sweat glimmers at his brow. “I’m sorry, too. It’s all jarring. I’m not used to all this.” He gestures in a circle at his chest, like it can encompass the feelings.

“Do you need a break?” From this conversation or this house?

He offers a lone nod. “Can we finish the second floor today?” He’s asking if I’ll finish Barb’s bedroom. It’s taken the longest of any in the house.

“I hope so.” It’s an honest answer, but a beacon from upstairs, that hidden space, calls to me. I need to know more. I need to go in again. And I need to do it today.

“Did you want to come help me wrap up the office first?” It’s an olive branch. Luke’s eyes widen, pleading with me to see this is him putting me first.

“Let me pour a cup of coffee, and then yes.”

CHAPTER 29

THE OFFICE IS TIDY AND BORING. A CAN OF PLEDGE SITS ON one of the built-in shelves. And yet Luke manages to find one thing after another to show me. Items that should have already been packed away, papers that should have been shredded. Busywork. For the next three hours, every time I try to head to Barb's bedroom, Luke has another important item to show me. He's dismissed what he calls the crawl space, and yet it feels like he's purposefully keeping me from it.

Finally, I suggest we break for lunch. "And afterward, I really want to get upstairs."

"If you feel like this is okay." He's faking nerves, and I don't get it.

"It's buttoned up," I say firmly. "I'll review everything when we get home. Besides, didn't you say you wanted to get the second floor done today?"

"That was before I realized I hadn't had the best CPA review the trust documents and the bank accounts."

After I'd found Cassie's promise ring. After the crows had flooded the yard. This morning had freaked my husband out. I don't blame him. It's all eerie.

But why stop me from doing the things that will get us out of this house fastest? Things he *says* he wants done?

And why does every part of me *know* that he needs me to stay away from Barb's hidden boxes?

In the kitchen, our provisions are running low.

"I'm not exactly excited about a peanut butter sandwich," I say.

Luke stares out the window, like he's looking beyond the fence, beyond the sea. I follow his gaze, half expecting to see more birds. There are only a handful in the garden. At the very back. They're watching him too, but their gazes are harder to track. Perhaps they're waiting for me. Or they just had a snack.

"Luke?" I have to say his name a couple times to get his attention.

"Hmm?" He comes back to the kitchen with me.

"Please don't make me prepare a lackluster sandwich." I lift the bread and peanut butter jar.

His attention flits around the room, like he's going to spy some ingredient I didn't. "We can snag those roast beef sandwiches you love from the deli over on Montrose."

My mouth waters already. "Oh, that's perfect."

"Let me grab my keys," he says, already brushing past me.

"Actually, babe." I hurry after him. "Do you mind picking it up for us?"

"Why? I mean, sure." Confusion has a way of making Luke pace. His weight is already shifting from side to side.

"I've got a bit of a headache. I'm going to pop some ibuprofen and lie down for a few while it kicks in."

"Food will probably help." His shuffling slows.

"I'm sure you're right." I hand him his keys and hate that he doesn't see my deception for what it is. Hate that I'm doing this after railing at him about honesty. I'm going to the hidden attic. I just want a few minutes in there. Enough to heed the warning from my dream, enough to convince myself there isn't another box up there with Cassidy's name on it that could have held a promise ring.

I move slowly up the stairs. Luke is lingering below. I close the door to the bedroom we're staying in and shuffle around, taking off my shoes. Two minutes later, the back door claps shut.

The deli Luke is driving to isn't far—few things are in Rockside Bay—but it also isn't a fast-food establishment. I likely have close to thirty minutes before he returns. And I don't really want to be inside that attic all that long anyway.

The small gateway into Barb's secret box storage is gilded again today. Like it was the first time I'd glimpsed it. The gold handle beckons me. Each carving quadrant pulses and moves, an optical illusion of the light, I'm sure.

My dream version of Cassie said I need to do this. Why am I trusting my sleeping self more than anyone else right now? Gut instincts count for something, I suppose. I pull the door open soundlessly. There's no breeze today. No roar as I crawl over the threshold.

A jaundiced light settles in the room. The boxes are stacked as ever; the switch near me doesn't work at my first flip. But the ambient glow is enough to see the rows are parted today. There is a wide center aisle now. I didn't reorganize the room, but it's no longer the same.

The wood floor emanates heat. The light switch works on the third try. The box I'd left open on my last foray here waits at the top of the stack on the right, its bold *X* turned toward me.

I did not place it there.

The flaps are lowered, like they've been tucked back in place. Fear grips my chin and my jaw trembles, my teeth clacking together. I clench hard, but biting away the chatter doesn't swallow its source.

I peek over my shoulder toward the doorway. It's open, alight, and not too far away. *You're just in an attic. You're only steps away from that bedroom. Luke will be back soon.*

It's that last thought that centers me. Luke will be back soon. He'll either find me in here, or I'll be done. Either way, there's an out.

I step forward; my sock clings to the floor a half-second longer than it should. I don't look at the big *X* to my right. It remains in my periphery. Just a box.

They're all just boxes. They may be filled with pilfered goods or eerie dolls, but they were all simply objects. The dolls are strange, but the unnerving part of them has to be one of those societal things. Like people say clowns are scary, and then it becomes a type of trope that we all just buy into. Only not every entertainer with a big red nose making balloon animals is a creep. Probably. The doll reaction is the same.

Past the first row, my attention is back on the boxes. The names. While more are familiar this time, I'm not seeing the names I want to see most. There must be more Warren women in here. How could Luke have been so embedded within the Warren family and Barb only taken items from the youngest daughter? Only made a fancy poppet for the one?

Barb liked Kim. Photos on Kim's Facebook of late proved that. But I don't think those with the compulsion to steal skip over those they like. There are boxes labeled with the names of other childhood flings of Luke's. Kim had been his only serious paramour, but the names of girls I'd heard stories about sprinkle the boxes here. The stories about these women had been about how Barb helped them after a tragedy.

This cursed town. I need to move faster. My socks continue to cling to the floor, as though a layer of molasses has been used to wax the wood. Though the warm oak looks dry and pristine, a hint of green peeks between the boards.

I want to find another box with the verboten Kathryn Wall's name or one with Cassidy's. The people Luke doesn't want to talk about. I'm running out of time. Wasting time. I'm here because of a *dream*. Whatever Barb did while alive doesn't matter now. And yet I can't stop stalking deeper into the room. I consider turning back, but icy fingers grip my nape and urge me onward.

At this point, I'm not even fighting them. My stomach twists at the thought of not knowing more. The promise ring shouldn't unnerve me like it does, but I didn't find anything like that. I would have noticed a pearl ring in the boxes I'd taken from here. But then I hadn't known about the notes. There had to be another box. And, I don't know, maybe the crows nest in here? I gnash my teeth together harder until a headache actually blossoms at my temple.

"What was it about Cassie?" I whisper my question, like if I speak too loudly the boxes might answer.

Needles prick my back, sharp and urgent. Fear cascades down my body, pooling in my legs. I stagger forward, dread sloshing with each uneven step. But the piercing push at my back only lessens if I keep moving. There is no other choice. At least that's what I tell myself, because I can't look back now.

She's there. That same bound face I'd encountered before. Looking back will only add to my nightmares but won't confirm anything. Dirt unfurls from the floorboards in front me. I walk through it, over it, going and going. The ceiling dips lower until it's grazing my hair. I hunch forward, because I can't go back. Tears tumble down my cheeks and fall to the dusty path, leaving a heart-broken trail back to the exit.

The boxes press closer on each side. The ceiling slopes downward further. There's another doorway. It's a golden square of light. Bright and warm and welcoming.

"*You need to see. To save yourself.*" The voice from my dreams is here. My heart quakes in my chest. Cassidy's voice.

And still I hesitate. The only way through this passage is on my knees. To lower myself onto this dirt and crawl into yet another of Barb's secret spaces. Can Luke find me here?

I inhale slowly, taking in the scent of amber and moss in the air. I need to know. I can't let this go, this place, Luke's lying by omission; I can't do it without seeing what his mother hid.

I'm running out of time.

"You need to see. To find me. To save yourself," the memory of Cassidy hisses with urgency.

"Find you?" I ask, like this is the right time. I keep finding her belongings, but I simply don't believe Barb stashed a teenage girl up in her weird attic. Also, this place does not smell like death.

"Go," is all she says.

Why I'm listening to a dead teenager who is likely manifested in my brain, I can't explain, but hell, I'm getting down on my knees. I crawl through the opening. The room beyond is bordering on hot. The cloying scent of roses and lilies and gardenias makes me swim for a moment. It's like every lotion my grandma ever owned had been put on a wax warmer. My tongue sticks to the roof of my mouth, the palate gluey, like it's covered in petals. I sputter until my mouth feels like it's mine again.

I rise and immediately regret coming into this room. In fact, I regret coming to this house.

I back up until my butt knocks into the wall. I flatten my hands at each side, like holding on to the drywall will protect me. Like I can meld into the surface.

Hundreds of eyes are on me. Brown and green and blue and hazel and black. Glassy and bloodshot. Sharp and determined. Sad but cruel. Every set watches me. Stares at me. Judges me.

I hedge to the side, but they track me. Not their bodies. Only those watchful gazes.

The dolls are stacked on a miniature riser. Like someone had placed them to watch an event.

Oh shit.

At the center of the room, beneath the dolls but where their eyesight reaches, is one box.

It's newer than the ones in the rest of the attic. There are no creases on the corners. There isn't a name written on the side facing me.

Is this Cassie's? The box isn't big enough to hold the actual girl, but is this where the ring came from?

I relinquish my grip on the wall. None of the dolls rush me. *Because they're inanimate objects. You're fine, Addison.* Even my inner thoughts are shitty liars. I'm not fine. None of this is fine.

I take one half step forward, and that frigid pinch I'd felt so often downstairs takes hold of my wrist. It wrenches it back and toward the entrance. I yank my arm away from the invisible grasp. My pull is hard enough to escape, hard enough to send me backward and onto the floor. I bump against the box; it shifts to the side, but not far, contents clinking. A gasp fills my mind, an attempted scream. Mine or Cassie's or the fucking audience of dolls, I have no idea. All of us, none of us. I stare at the doorway, but there's no one there. No ghastly girl. No malevolent threat. Just a plain wall and an empty doorway.

My wrist is another story. It more than whines when I rotate it, it screams. My forearm is a mottled purple and mauve where I'd been held. The finger marks are obvious. Someone gripped me. An invisible someone.

What the hell have I done?

I get to my knees and try to ignore the sea of eyes watching my back with intensity. I open the box.

"Find Cassie's stuff, get an answer, and you can go," I tell myself. And I guess the dolls.

The flaps are stiff, but fold back easily enough. I stare into the box, and my tears return. One splats on the doll's face. And then another.

The porcelain face that matches mine.

CHAPTER 30

BARB HAD CRAFTED A DOLL THAT LOOKED LIKE ME. HEAT rushes up my chest and over my head like a hood. How many times had my mother-in-law done this? I spin to face the audience of miniature women. Faces repeat throughout the crowd. I recognize three versions of Cassie. Another doll appears almost a dozen times, different clothes, but the same face. I don't see myself in the lineup, but then Barb had kept a backup head in the bedroom. Perhaps she simply needed more time.

My doll lies on top of the box's contents. I reach in and lift her out. The miniature version of myself is heavy in my hands. She watches me—or I watch me? This is too much. Her hair is curly and has the same frizz I battled this morning. There's a sadness in her gaze. I can relate. She's in a tiny orange sweater and stonewashed skinny jeans. Her feet are bare.

"Sorry about this," I say as I set her on the floor. Why I'm apologizing to her, I'm not sure, but it feels right. Important.

I pull the matching human-sized orange sweater from the box. I'd worn it here last Thanksgiving. The burnt hue amped up my freckles, and Luke had very much been a fan. I'd wondered how I'd lost it.

Barb snatching it and making a tiny version for a doll had not even been a consideration.

The rest of the box held a receipt from the coffee shop nearby, a lone earring—matching the stud I'd found in the home gym—and the Advil bottle I'd put my prenatal vitamins in for travel because the other bottle had been massive. I had not told Barb about taking them. None of these things were meaningful. They weren't precious notes from childhood, jewelry that came with a vow, or really anything treasured. They were merely things that had belonged to me.

So why did this feel like so much more than Barb simply stealing from me? She had filled a box with my things. She'd crafted a doll-like version of me. This room and the one connected to it meant something to her. Placing this box—my box—before these dolls of other women, at least one of whom had died, all of it feels *ritualistic*. Only why would Barb want to do this with me?

Barb didn't want me in her house in the first place. Why make a version of me that's here all the time? Unless it made her feel good that she could shove me in this terrible room, contain me? Was that it?

Hating me was one thing, but this is another level.

I turn toward the dolls. "Did she hate all of you?"

It's not even plausible. To have this many dolls, she would have to have hated every person in this town. Yet the longer I stare at them, the more I see. The red at the wrist. The bruise at the cheek. A knee cracked, the leg jutting to the side, but posed like a curtsey. A ruby tear pooling at the corner of an eye. These dolls are painted to have been injured in some way. I grab my doll self from the floor, a fresh wave of panic building in my belly. The tide of my anxiety was rolling in, and a storm isn't far behind.

I look to the dolls for answers. Cassie's face is obvious in the sea of painted porcelain. Her bow of a mouth is split on the left. Dark brown smudges her brow. I walk closer to the collection. Sweat trickles down my back. This close, the dolls pulse with an intense energy. Looking away from them for even a moment is now impossible. I need answers; I need to know I'm safe from the same disaster. Only...am I? Am I just lucky that I'm not tucked on Barb's shelf here?

The uncanny valley carves into my chest the longer I stare at them. They're dolls. Children's toys. Creepy ones, sure, but toys all the same. And yet... I squirm, shuffling back a half step. The room is full, and not in the way boxes and bags and bins have been shoved inside closets and up against walls in the rest of the house. I'm not alone now. The sense that each of these tiny faces is *aware* of me has my hands shaking, my toes curling against the tacky floor.

Cassie's face appears again in the back row. Her hair is brushed forward, as though Barb had tried to hide her face. The doll's sad eyes stare into the distance, a black-and-blue ring haloing her orbital socket.

Cassie's doll isn't the only thing I notice in the sea of tiny girls. One is that there's another face repeated far more frequently here.

The porcelain nose is sharp, cheekbones high, and regardless of the red, black, or purple paint marring the doll, the mouth on each has a mischievous upturn to it. Like she knows something. But given the number of boxes I'd seen with Kathryn Wall's name scrawled on them, there is no question that has to be her.

Kathryn's dolls are spread throughout the lifelike crowd. Her hair is twisted up on some, a red gash where an earring ripped free. On other of her dolls, her hair is nearly brushing the slingback shoes the doll wears, brown curls skimming patent leather. The porcelain version of Kathryn closest to me has its eyes downcast; four red marks strike across its chest. Its white blouse gapes, making the mottled wound—layer of paint atop paint atop paint giving texture—even more garish.

Barb had made doll after doll of a woman whose name wasn't allowed to be spoken within the house? These had never been gifts. You didn't stash presents away like trophies or bad family secrets. But why make a doll of a woman you hate? Why make it over and over?

And why had the little sister of her son's girlfriend been worth making a doll of in the first place, much less—I pause to count—four of them?

Barb made dolls of people she didn't like. It's honestly a surprise that I'm not on the riser here. I'd pissed her off simply by existing.

I stare at these echoes of the women they represent and notice one more thing. Black feathers are bound to their backs. Each one. The smudges of darkness behind each are trimmed in a way so as to not distract.

The boxes in the other room had feathers. The supply box I'd found had feathers. Did the crows help? They'd dropped so many feathers at the garden. Is this why they hated Barb? She'd been stealing their discards or taking feathers from the living birds?

"The feathers do..." No, I cut that thought off. Feathers are feathers and dolls are dolls.

"Yes."

I spin toward the voice. Half a face is visible in the corner. Gray blue and covered with vines.

My knees are rubber. I wobble but manage to whisper. "Cassidy?"

Behind me, the closest of Cassie's dolls crashes to the floor. I look away for a moment; the shards are spread in a perfect circle. Green vines sprout from the center.

"My friends called me Cassie." Her words snap me back to attention.

Adrenaline pours into my body by the bucketful. It floods my joints. It squeezes my shoulders. It lights my neck with a tingle of anticipation. Ready to run or puke or both.

"You're running out of time. He knows. The feathers prove it." Cassie's visage dissipates. A small pile of dark-brown dirt remains in the corner.

He knows? Is she talking about Luke? What would he know? Maybe that his mom was fixated on the crows? The unspent adrenaline shakes my core. It's not fear, I tell myself.

Wait. The feathers. I sprint to the box with my in-progress doll. I unload it all onto the floor. Upturn the box and let every scrap of paper and thread fall to the floor. A small pot of red paint rolls toward the dolls.

God, I hate this.

But there's no feather in my box.

Whatever that means, it dials back my terror enough to take a breath.

I sniffle and realize I'm crying. Of course I am.

"What *are* you?" I ask the dolls.

I'm only half happy when they don't reply.

Putting the items back in the box meant for me is unnecessary, but going through the motions should help. Routine calms the nerves.

Except it doesn't when you have hundreds of eyes on you, watching, examining. My fear is set on fire, made molten. Smelting my terror into a more tenable option: anger.

And that's when I grab the bundle of thread from the floor. Smooth nylon is mingled with coarser strands. Familiar ones.

My hair is in this box.

"She took my hair?" I'm incendiary. Even the dolls appear to flinch. "Was stealing a cute sweater not enough? Was making some weirdo tiny version of me not worth it if you couldn't make it really me? What the fuck was wrong with you, Barb?"

She doesn't answer, but then when had she ever answered my questions before? If living Barb didn't give a shit about my feelings, why would the recently departed version?

My rage boils over, scalding ire spilling down my arms. The dolls are before me now. The closest one is a likeness to Cassie Warren.

The doll's cheeks are round, a blush of purple kisses her jaw. But it's the long blond hair hanging past the shoulders that I care about now. My earlier worries evaporate, and I touch the shiny yellow strands.

Soft. Slick. Too real.

My eyes widen, tears flowing more freely, each droplet filled with anger and shock and exhaustion. Barb had never been kind to me, but this is a whole extra level of bad. How could a woman capable of caring so deeply for Luke be able to do this? To steal from women and children? To make trophies of these people—what they meant, I didn't entirely know. But I'd heard the stories about the run of bad luck Kathryn Wall had. The number of dolls bearing her likeness here and Barb forbidding the lady's name being spoken in this house couldn't be coincidences.

Barb fooled everyone else, but I'd seen her cruelty this whole time. It wasn't that I wasn't a good enough daughter-in-law. She'd been whatever the hell this was. Scary. Cruel. Controlling.

You don't get to control me anymore, Barb. Not me. Not these women.

Dead people don't get to keep ruining our lives.

She'd made this trip harder for me by creating boundaries for Luke, by trying to keep me out of this house, of his life.

I can take away things you like too, Barb.

My carefully erected emotional barriers are incinerated, anger taking down the walls blocking off my loneliness in this house, trapping my lingering grief at losing a potential family, my self-consciousness that I might truly not be good enough for Luke. It's all open. Flooding every synapse with a miasma of hurt and loss and ripe anger.

Everything in this house was for show. The crystal. The carefully curated books. The stacks of high-end purchases in boxes that still carried shipping labels. But the garden had been for no one but Barb.

The need to destroy a beloved possession of Barb's consumes me. These dolls might have been her treasures, but even the thought of harming them raises a caterwaul in my mind. But I have to act or my body is going to self-immolate.

The crows might not like me wrecking the garden, but they'll forgive me.

The wood bites my knees as I drop to all fours and crawl back through the entrance to the doll room. I scuttle and then run back to the door into Barb's closet. I don't stop there. Or at the stairs. Or even the back door.

Luke hasn't returned yet. Good. He would try to stop me.

The garage is neatly organized. *Thanks, Luke.* There are shovels hung on the wall. One to scoop snow, a handheld spade for Barb's digging in the dirt, and a long narrow one that has a job I'm unfamiliar with. All the tools have specific tasks, but I just want a regular one. Finally, there is one with a grip meant for my hand, a long wooden handle, and a wide metal spade.

I snatch it from the wall. "Barb, I'm going to fuck up your garden."

A series of sharp pains nick at my neck. Like a mother tiger is trying to nip my nape, only I'm not her cub. I storm from the garage before I can overthink my decision.

There's a warm trickle down my back, teasing my spine. It doesn't slow me.

Barb's garden is gorgeous in the midday light. The flowers are at their apex blossom, petals floppy and bright, bees and butterflies dipping in for nectar. I hate to screw over the pollinators, but they don't need to feed from Barb's tainted land.

I slam the spade into the soil. It sinks in easily, like the dirt wants to be tilled. Seven crows are perched on the fence lining the back of the garden. I stomp my foot down on the handle, popping a huge clump of dirt free, plants going askew on either side.

I throw the dirt behind me and plunge the shovel back in for more. Roots sever, petals plummet, and dirt sprinkles everywhere.

And I keep digging.

And digging.

The crows watch over me silently. If they have a problem with me uprooting their favorite feeding grounds, they aren't making it known.

Stab.

Barb had to control everything.

Lift.

This house.

Toss.

Every holiday.

Stab.

Who her son dated.

Lift.

Except for me. You couldn't get rid of me, Barb.

Toss.

The plants are gone now, but I can't stop digging. Won't stop. I plunge the shovel down like I'm stabbing a sword into a corpse on a battlefield in one of those war movies Luke loves.

Why did she have that box for me in the attic? What was her plan for my doll? Was it to be painted bloody and bruised too? Was she going to shatter it or stage it with the rest of her trophies? My gut clenches. What was that room? Why *dolls*?

I keep digging. The hole grows deeper. Sweat slips into my eyes. I swipe at the sting but then keep slamming the spade back into the soil, my fury more potent than the salt in my eye.

"I was going to give you a grandchild. I'm going to have Luke's kids someday. Why would you want me gone?" My stomach sinks. Had Luke told her I was pregnant? Was I so abhorrent to her that she wouldn't have wanted me to mother her grandchildren?

I stab the shovel down once more, as hard as I can. Like I can punctuate my pain with a proper thrust. It kicks back at me, the metal resounding against a hard object below.

A flash of ecru peeks from within the dark dirt. Horror washes over me at the textured off-white object I can see. There is probably some perfect tool for digging up whatever is buried here, but I use the tip of my shovel to pry under it. When it pops free, I fall back onto my butt.

A femur.

Oh god oh god oh god. My stomach pitches, and I heave into the grass. I have handled darkness and death in a lot of ways, but not with body parts lying in the dirt.

Why the hell is there a bone beneath Barb's garden?

The crows caw. I push myself back to my feet, looking down at the bone. Eddie, Nixie, and the others are loud. They see what I see, right? Only their calls increase in urgency. Demanding attention. A car door slams behind me. *Luke.*

These sweet birds are watching my back.

I'm not going to stop. Not now. Not when I'm certain I'm looking at a part of someone's leg. I shove the spade into the soil to the right of the deepest part of the hole—the part with the bone.

Luke is yelling. A high-pitched ringing fills my ears, drowning out whatever he's saying.

His hand grips my shoulder. I jerk free, whirling toward him. Luke leaps backward and narrowly escapes an accidental shovel to the shin.

"What the hell is going on, Addison?" The words are harsh, but panic squeezes my name.

I'm sweaty, caked in dirt, and have been working through the Lowes' fucked-up family memories. I don't doubt it's a terrifying sight. *Welcome to the club.*

"I'm digging up the garden." Bitterness curdles my words.

"You can't just destroy this—"

"Oh, but I can." I turn back and pitch another shovelful of dirt his way. "I'm trying to find out what is buried here."

"Why would you think anything is buried in my mother's garden? It's for flowers—"

I step aside and gesture down into the hole I've made. "Why is there a goddamned bone here?"

Luke is on his back foot. He stumbles but doesn't stop staring at the off-white object peeking from below. "It's probably from an animal."

There's a distance between us now; where my mind has gone and where his has retreated to are different places.

Terror leaches color from his face with each passing moment.

But all I am is rage. "It's not an animal." Saying the words makes them real.

"What else could it be?" My husband doesn't want an answer. "It's an animal. I can clean it up."

He tries to take the shovel from me.

"No. Stop right there, Luke Lowe. I've done so much for you in this house. The whole time feeling like I was being watched and judged despite Barb not being here anymore. And I'm not about to be brushed aside again. I need to know what's in this garden, and either you can help or you can bail, but I'm not moving until I unearth the whole thing."

"Don't you dare." Luke rushes forward and grips the shovel between my hands.

Panic surges beneath my breastbone. I tighten my hold. "Let go, Luke."

"No, Addison, you need to go back in the house. Now." He's using the courtroom command voice on me.

But I've done nothing wrong. "Why don't you want to me to know what's here?"

"Go inside, Addison." He keeps saying my name through his teeth. He's on the verge of snapping.

I'm already there. "I can go in and call the cops now and tell them I found human remains in Barb Lowe's garden, or you can let me dig this up."

His nostrils flare, and a half-second later, he wrenches the shovel away. His elbow catches my shoulder, throwing me back. I land in the dirt next to the exposed bone. My fingers itch to grab it, throw it at him. Like if it literally hits him in the face, he'll see what a fucked-up situation this is. What I've gone through. Why his mom *was not perfect*.

He throws the tool to the side, eyes going wide. "Addie. Oh, shit. Addie, I'm so sorry."

I cradle my shoulder, the pain still sharp from the collision. "If you're sorry, then dig it up."

He shakes his head slowly, like the weight of the situation has finally landed on him. "Let me help you up."

"I don't want you to touch me."

He staggers back. "Ads, I didn't mean to—"

"To what? To hit me? To put me in the fucking dirt next to what is probably a dead body?"

He blinks rapidly, no longer looking at me. "It can't be."

"Well, where there's one bone..." Darkness coats my tongue. I push myself up and out of the garden bed.

"Okay, but I can see this is looks bad." When I glare, he corrects himself. "It *is* bad. Just... You can let me handle this for you."

I snatch the shovel from the yard and plummet it back into the garden, the move answer enough.

He starts pacing behind me. "This doesn't make sense."

At least he has the good sense not to try to stop me again. He's muttering and then yelling, and then—*thunk*—my shovel sings with more bad news.

Luke goes quiet.

"Don't you want to see what's buried here?" The nastiness in my tone isn't for him. It's for this house. It's for Barb. It's for being forgotten. Unworthy.

"It's nothing," he blurts.

But he's seen the femur.

We both know better.

CHAPTER 31

AN AVALANCHE OF DENIALS FALLS FROM LUKE'S MOUTH. None meant for me. He's pacing again; this time his arms are folded across his chest, and his right hand has crept up to cover his mouth.

But I'm not stopping now. I've held back while we've been here. There's a limit though. And apparently it's when I find a human skeleton buried in my mother-in-law's garden. The skull isn't completely unveiled, but I don't need to dig more to know this is no animal. The rounded cranium, the orbital arch around an empty eye socket. That's more than enough.

"Luke." I don't lock a single feeling away this time. The demand to assuage my anger and fear is laid bare. "Make it make sense."

He shakes his head. Luke stares at the roof of his mother's house, his childhood home. Eyes wide, jaw slackened.

So quietly a gust could steal the words, he says, "She said she wouldn't. She promised she didn't know where she'd gone."

The coastal breeze is gone. It's as though all Rockside Bay is holding its breath. The crows still too, their sharp gazes locked on my husband.

He's trembling, but I don't move closer. I can't. My own limbs are locked in a war of good sense. I'm mere feet from a dead person. A murder victim—no one who dies from natural causes gets hidden beneath the begonias.

"Who?" I ask like I don't already know. I'm standing over Cassidy Warren, and I need to hear him say it.

"It can't be." His eyes are on me now, wild, pleading.

At least he's surprised. "A human was buried in your mother's garden. How long has it been here?" The last bit is an accusation.

The tips of his tennis shoes are suddenly fascinating.

I wait him out. My heart thudding against my chest. My mind spinning. If Barb had been capable of this, what had she done to the others she'd crafted into dolls? What had she planned for me? And why? I get I wasn't her first choice, but come on.

"The garden has been here as long as the house." There's no defensiveness from Luke, only regret. "But she overhauled it the year Cassie disappeared."

"Before or after the girl went missing?"

"Right around the time." He's hugging himself so tightly, his fingertips are turning white. "I-I-I thought she was distracting herself. She loved the Warrens."

No, she loved *Kim* Warren. The rest of us could go jump in the ocean for all she had cared.

His gaze finally connects with mine. Panic makes him appear both younger and older. There's an openness I only see from him in sleep right now, but the harsh lines on either side of his mouth only come with age.

"I had *no idea*, Addie." He staggers toward me. "This… I didn't think she was capable of this degree of…" He trails off, like even now he can't speak ill of her.

I can. "Depravity?"

He stays silent. Must be nice to have that privilege.

I reach in my pocket, but my phone is missing. "We need to call the police. Give me your phone."

I hold my palm out and wait.

"What?"

"My phone is inside." Hopefully it didn't fall out in that creepy doll room, because if so, I'm getting a new phone.

"I can call them." He inhales sharply, like if he breathes fast enough, he can burn his sinuses with brine.

Ill ease creeps between us as he dials. I see him closing the shutters on his emotions. His breathing evens out; he licks his lips a few times, clears his throat. When the operator answers, he's collected. It's only the sweat at his temples and the redness ringing his eyes that show how shaken he is.

A trickle of relief pours into my chest. He didn't know. I couldn't have fallen for a man who would hide a girl's death, much less a girl he knew well.

My mind flits back to the note from Cassie. Its familiarity. How well did Luke know her?

Wariness and worry wage war in my head. Luke speaks clearly and swiftly with the police. He doesn't use Cassidy's name, but he is up-front with what we found.

When he hangs up, he looks to me again. "I don't know what we do now."

"Why would you? We've never been in this situation before, but we'll figure it out." Because I need to understand.

He nods solemnly. "The police are sending a unit over now. I think I have to go sit down for a moment. We should ice your shoulder too."

He turns toward the house, but I don't follow.

"Aren't you coming?"

"I can't leave her here like this. Alone." She's been alone for so long. Hidden. Locked beneath roots.

"I understand," Luke says, but I doubt he does. Even if he entered the room off his mother's bedroom and crawled through the passage into the golden space filled with dolls, there would be no threat to him. He wouldn't find his face among them. He wouldn't have to question himself, his family, his place.

But I do.

Cassie sure had. How had she ended up here? The other names I'd found weren't linked to missing persons files or a label of *presumed dead.*

They were linked to tragedy though. Accidents. Broken bones. A barren cherry orchard. Lost family members. Runs of extreme bad luck for years on end. If that had been Barb somehow, why would a fourteen-year-old girl have been the one who died?

Luke retreats to the deck. He says he won't leave me alone, but also clearly can't take being so close to Cassie. He may need to sort through memories, but I need to see this through. She'd begged me to find her. And I have, but there is no peace washing over me.

A crow caws behind me. I turn back to find only Eddie holding vigil now.

He cocks his head to the side, and I can only give him a wan smile.

"Eddie, was this what I was supposed to find?" I ask the bird.

He hops twice, coming closer.

"I think I'm starting to understand why Barb hated you." Eddie immediately puffs his feathers up. I lean in, head low. "*I* couldn't have survived here without you, and I suspect Cassie's memory might have crumbled otherwise too. You saw right through Barb, didn't you?"

Eddie does not answer me. He seems to be monitoring my husband closely.

"Where has the rest of your murder gone?" Will they all leave now that we've found Cassie?

Two short caws later, and Nixie perches at his side.

"Well, thank you," I say to them. "For me and for her."

Gravel crunches behind me, and the birds fly to perch on the peak of the garage. The police car rolls into view a moment later.

Both police officers know Luke. Of course they do.

But when they learn I'd found the bones, they take my statement without any deference to my spouse. Not treatment I'm accustomed to in Rockside Bay but appreciated nonetheless. I tell them about the dolls too. About Barb's attic and that I'd found boxes with women's belongings.

Luke stands stalwart at my side the whole time. Never contradicting. His fingers flex on my back with each fresh fact. Like the truth about his mother's possessions wounds him. I suppose they do. This new side of her is so different from his hope that she'd had this secret crafting passion.

But there is no flash of surprise from him upon learning the number of boxes. No questioning the veracity of my statements. Boxes full of items that seemed to belong to other people? Not weird to him.

He admits to the police officers that we'd pitched a box with Cassidy Warren's name on it into the garbage.

"Why would you do that, sir?" The younger of the two men asks. His older brother went to school with Luke.

My husband exhales harshly, all put upon. "We're cleaning out my late mother's home. While I prefer to keep the particulars of her private life a family matter, the truth is my mother collected many things. We've been purging the home."

"We saw the dumpster, Luke," the older cop says. He'd grown up with Luke and Kim. Probably knew Cassidy too. "But you still have to answer."

"I threw it out because there was no point in keeping it. We thought giving a doll or Cassie's lost things to her family now would only add hurt. I believe this town has had enough of it," Luke says with authority. "And, quite frankly, the doll unnerved my wife."

"That so, Mrs. Lowe?" the older cop asks. Little notebook at the ready.

I fold my arms across my chest. Cold from the inside out. "You haven't seen the doll collection yet, but yeah, the dolls freaked me out."

"*Dolls?* Plural?"

The police call in a forensics team and additional units. And then ask me to lead them to the attic space I'd found. They need to see the boxes, the dolls, they say.

I ignore their placating tones and their apologetic looks at Luke. *Luke, yes, she found a dead girl in the yard, but clearly your wife is having* a time.

But they do their jobs. They follow me. Their gazes miss nothing. They take in the dust lines on the floor outlining where boxes had been stacked. The clutter in the hallway waiting to be carried down to the big bin outside.

They kneel and crawl through the tiny door with me. It's the first time my body doesn't sense the hum as I enter. Luke follows at the back. He clings to the wall, as though his mother will know he's entered a space she'd forbidden.

The men are overwhelmed. There is a salty vindication in that. Even as I crawl under the doorway into the doll room, part of me worries the eerie porcelain creations won't be there. Not that the dolls would have fled, but that my mind isn't as solid as I believe. Grief twists our world, and even though I don't feel the loss of Barb acutely, I do still mourn what could have been for my family.

But the rows and rows and rows of dolls are there. I watch the policemen straighten their uniforms, as if a crisp line will remove the ill ease in this room.

Luke does not enter. He's still pressing his back against the beams supporting the doorway back into Barb's closet, as if he could disappear into the woodwork.

"Holy shit. It looks just like you." The younger officer releases the box with my doll as though the cardboard has seared him.

I move to the side of the room, giving them space to do whatever they need. I stand where I'd last seen Cassie. Cold curls up my legs, twisting and coiling around my thighs like the vines outside. They haven't sneaked back in the house in the last two days, but I still expect to see one ensnaring me when I look down. There's nothing. Just the pile of dirt where a dead girl had spoken to me. There's something in the soil here.

I crouch and spread the dirt out, revealing another of the carefully folded notes with Luke's name on it.

Fear seizes my chest. I cast a quick glance at the others. The cops are examining the dolls, but they don't touch a single one. The same innate warning I've sensed around them must be trickling through their bones now. *It's not just me.*

This note is like the last one. A tiny heart next to Luke's name. I slip it in my pocket and then excuse myself.

"I wouldn't want to stay in here any longer than I had to either," the younger man says.

Luke is eager to leave the attic when I arrive back at the doorway. We retreat into the house, and I go directly to the guest room.

Luke follows. "What did they find?"

"Exactly what I told them they'd find," I bite back.

"Sorry. I didn't mean it like that. I just... I hoped there were answers about Cassie." He stumbles on the girl's name. He's thinking of his mother now. I can see it in the way his jaw ticks and how he fights the urge to go back to her room.

Barb hated anyone in her bedroom. She wouldn't want strangers in there. *Probably because of whatever horrible shit she was working on in the hidden attic.*

I start packing my things back into the suitcase.

"We can't leave now, Ads." Urgency underscores his every word.

Ha. "I am not staying in this place a second longer."

"But we haven't finished everything here, and don't you want to know what they find out there?" He points toward the back of the house, toward the garden, toward Cassie.

Yes, I want to know what happened to her, and I need to know what Barb did. But I don't have to learn any of that while sleeping in her creepfest house.

"Luke, we don't have to leave town. We can go to the B and B in town or the motel, but I'm not staying *here*." I draw a circle in the air to make it clear I mean anywhere in this house.

He is nodding fast, like he's flipping through excuses or plans. "Not the bed-and-breakfast."

"I usually hate those places, but I'd make an exception." I don't like staying with strangers on the whole, but having extra people around wouldn't be terrible.

"The family who owns it will gossip. If you don't want to have to talk about this, we can't stay there."

"Motel it is." I brush past him to get my toiletries from the bathroom.

CHAPTER 32

LUKE AND I BARELY SPEAK WHILE HE PACKS. WE GIVE THE police an update, Luke hands over a spare key, and then we're in the car, bumping on over to the Rockside Bay Inn. I stare out the passenger window for the entirety of the drive. The ocean is on Luke's side of the car, but I'd rather watch the bungalow residences and cottage-style shops skip by than look at him.

Love for Luke is staked in my heart, but that only increases the intensity of this fresh hurt.

The quiet unfurls between us. It fills the car with heartache. It's heavy and solid and pressing me further into my seat. I don't want to run from Luke, but this unspoken fear is locking us on opposite sides. I hate it.

And yet...

He pulls our rental under the portico at the inn. Luke is out of the car before the engine fully dies. I wave off his questioning look. "I'll wait here," I say quietly.

He nods and slips behind the dingy glass door.

I should be able to breathe better alone, but the *waiting* crushes me.

I pull the note I'd found in the doll room from my pocket. Luke's name is written in a smudged pencil, but the big looping script is the same as the last one I'd found from Cassie.

I found her body; I could call her that.

I shoot a quick, panicked look at the door. Luke is leaning on the counter. It's going to be a minute. Might as well rip off the bandage.

The paper is stiff. Like it's only been unfolded a time to two.

The note is shorter than the last, but the pencil lines are darker. The print leans to the right like Cassie needed to jot it in a hurry.

My sister doesn't know. I promise.

An echo of a droplet of water punctuates the sentence.

I know you don't believe me, but she would have told Mom. She tells Mom everything.

She underlined this fact like it carried more weight.

Please talk to me. You made a promise to me. I never take off the ring. Even when I shower. Hope you like that.

My sister will get over it. Your mom will too.

Just talk to me.

The letter is pleading. This isn't the ghastly girl who spat dirt and demanded I find her. But perhaps death does that to a person.

I'll come to our spot tonight after everyone else is asleep. Please be there.

She'd written *please* enough times for me to *feel* her crisis. Cassie had signed her name beneath a big heart.

There had been more between Cassie and Luke. This wasn't a girl with a crush. What had my husband done?

The bell over the motel's front door rings loud and crisp. I crumple the note and shove it back in my pocket.

"We're in 104." Luke drops a key labeled with the same number into the cup holder.

We park outside the room, but I don't move. I can't. My teeth are locked on the inside of my cheek, like if I were to release them, I'd scream. And even after everything, I can't let myself make a scene here.

"Addison?" Luke questions, low and concerned.

"Tell me about Cassie." My lips barely part, but the breathy demand is still that.

He rests his hand on the back of mine. "It won't help."

"It might not help you, but it'll help me." I meet his gaze. Let him see the water welling on the edge of my eyelids.

Recognition flares in his gaze. "Whatever you need. Can we go into the room or"—his voice breaks—"or do you need to do this here?"

"I'm not leaving you, Luke." Not yet anyway.

His body is shaking. Leftover panic or fresh, I don't know. "It's all too much to ask of you." He's staring at our hands. His words low.

"I'm in my own head, and you're dealing with Mom's stuff, and now *this*? It's understandable to be uncertain."

"Uncertain? There's an army of dolls in a hidden room in your childhood home. A girl you had some type of relationship with is buried in the backyard. I have big fucking questions."

His head snaps up at having the truth laid so plainly. "What did you just say?"

I shrug one shoulder. "Are we doing this here, or do you still want to go inside?"

Breaking this toxic energy is appealing, but honestly I want Cassie's secrets to be private. And I don't know that whoever is working the front desk isn't peeking at us through the window sheers and relaying the blow-by-blow to a group chat.

The motel room is tidy but plain. Luke sits on the bed, looking at me expectantly. I take the chair instead.

When I pull the notebook paper from my pocket, shame swallows my spouse. His head lowers, as though in supplication, his shoulders slump, and his top teeth dig into his bottom lip.

But Luke says nothing.

"I found another note to you."

"Another from Cassie?" He speaks to the floor.

"She said her sister doesn't know. She's begging you to meet her."

He lifts his head slowly, confusion screwing his features tight. "I don't remember that one."

"But you remember others?"

"I was a teenager," he says like it's an explanation.

"We all made shit choices in high school, Luke, but one of yours ended up dead in your yard. Tell me what happened. Were you dating Cassie too?"

"Dating?" He sputters on a dark laugh.

"She says she never took off your ring," I snap.

His nostrils flare. "I never dated Cassie. But I slept with her."

I take a long look at the man I love. "You slept with your girlfriend's little sister."

"She wasn't that little," he says like he should get a pass.

"She was a freshman in high school," I correct.

"I'm not making excuses. It was a terrible thing to do. Mom wanted me to be with Kim, but she's never been a match for me. Wasn't then and isn't now."

"I know you're not fucking Kim. Don't dodge this." The more he tap-dances, the tighter my tummy twists. The thought of him sleeping around *ever* gives me the ick, but doing it with a young girl? Double ick. A sibling of his girlfriend? Fucking A. Would he sleep with my sister Mallory if the opportunity arose? I gnash my teeth together until it hurts.

"I liked Cassie. She was funny and clever and cute. It just happened." He stops there, but when I don't reply, he tumbles forward with another take. "It shouldn't have."

"There's more," I prod.

"No," he says quickly. "We were still sleeping together when she went missing."

"Tell me what she was so worried about then?" I hand him her note.

He reads it again and again. He wets his lips. Reads the letter again.

"My mom had this note?" Luke's knee bounces with excess energy.

"It was in the attic." He doesn't get to know more about Afterlife Cassie now.

"She—she knew?" Befuddlement gives way to denial.

"Knew what?" I need to hear him explain this.

Luke's disbelief is sliced away, panic leaving shavings on the floor. "I've never told anyone this, Addison. Not a friend. Not my mom. No one."

Is that supposed to make me feel special? "I'm the person who you share secrets with. Remember. Vows?"

Slowly, he lifts his head. There's a starkness to his face. Like hope has drained from his soul. "Cassie was pregnant."

"What?" Luke was going to be a dad back then?

He jumps up from the bed. Pacing isn't going to solve this. "She'd told me the day before she went missing. I was eighteen and freaked out. Cassie was almost, like, excited when she told me. Like I'd dump Kim and we'd make a go of things."

A coldness pools in my chest. "And you wouldn't have?"

"I don't know. We were kids. I needed time to sort it out." He lifts the letter again. Then, to himself, mutters, "Mom had this?"

"What is it?" I push. "If we're making it through this—and I swear, Luke, I'm willing to do a lot for you—I can't have you hold back now. Not about Cassie. Not about your mom. Not about your past. Nothing."

He drops to his knees before me and takes both my hands. "All of it," he vows. "I didn't know about this note. But we used to meet behind the garage at Mom's house. At the time I thought I was clever whenever I snuck out, but now I know better. Mom had to have known."

"You think she met Cassie in your place?" Even saying the words disgusts me.

"I think she'd already been making a poppet of Cassie to get her out of my life."

My breath hitches. "Excuse me?"

"I know what the dolls are." He presses closer, like if he gets close enough, I'll have to believe him. "You said no secrets. So here it is. Every one of those was my mother's way of directing bad luck. Falls, accidents, losing a job, you name it. Mom would make the likeness of a woman and bind her intent with a feather."

"And you knew this?" No matter how slowly I speak, the whole thing *feels* bonkers.

"I wasn't supposed to. The one time I'd seen it, she'd made me swear to never tell another soul." For him, breaking this promise is the ultimate demonstration of his trust.

I'm going to vomit any minute. "So every doll..."

"Mom controlled this town."

"She had more than one of Cassie." I say pointedly.

"Fuck."

"So why is the girl buried in your backyard if it's just bad luck?" I swallow the taste of sickness.

"Mom never told me. But..."

I stare at him so hard he should burst into flames.

"If she had this note and had already made dolls…then my mom is the reason we found Cassie in the ground." This is as close as he's getting to labeling his mom a murderer.

But Luke's mom killed a girl. She killed… "But Cassie was pregnant with your child, right?"

"I've never said it aloud." He pauses, and I don't give him the out. He finally admits it. "Yes, Cassie was pregnant with my child."

Barb would lose a grandchild to control Luke's path? I sprint for the bathroom and heave past the sanitization strip on the toilet.

Luke follows me. "Are you okay?"

"Not even a little," I say from the most obvious place of not-okay-ness.

"I'm sorry." He doesn't say for what, but then there's so much to pick from.

"Your mom was making a doll of me." I shift onto my bottom and pull my knees up.

"She wouldn't—"

"There was a ready-to-go Addison head in her bedroom and an in-progress doll in the attic. She had my hair in the box. My. Hair."

He swears again, harsher. Luke drops to his knees and starts running his hands over me like he'll find fresh wounds.

I push his hands away. "I'm fine. Physically."

He retreats to sit on the thin carpet outside the bathroom. "None of this was supposed to happen."

"We can't control it." Though apparently Barb sure tried.

"What do we do now?" he asks like I'm still in the problem-solver seat.

"You went to law school. You probably know better than me." It isn't a fair thing to throw at him, but now is the time to protect myself.

He's spared from further sparring by a knock at the door. I let Luke answer it and stay on the cool tile. My stomach is settled enough, but I'm just done.

"Hi, Mr. Lowe." I recognize the voice of the younger police officer.

"Brady. What's going on?" Luke uses the guy's last name but drops the honorific.

"We're still working through the house, but we would like your permission to excavate as much of the yard as we need."

"Do you have a court order?" Luke curtness surprises me.

"We can get one, sir. Sergeant Wilson said you were keen to get back home, and we thought this could expedite things." Plausible.

"I'm sure it would, but I'd prefer us to do everything with standard processes." Luke's flipped on his lawyer voice. No hint of his earlier breakdown.

"Asking for permission is a normal practice," the cop replies.

"Legal processes are important." Luke holds his line.

"Fair enough. We'll bring the warrant by later. Please stay in town until we've finished up."

Once the officer has left, I poke my head from the bathroom. "You couldn't just let them in? The sooner we can go home, the better."

"I don't know what else my mom has hidden there." He leans back against the closed door.

"But you don't want to just have it over with?" I did.

Luke slides down to the floor. We're both sitting on the floor of a motel room, wallowing. Hurting. Drowning in emotion.

"Cassie had secrets, and maybe she should get to keep them. I don't know." He says that, but he does know. He knows he wants *his* secrets to stay buried.

But I'd found her. The authorities already had her. The truth would be apparent soon.

I hope I can make it that long.

CHAPTER 33

THE LOST GIRL'S REMAINS ARE COLLECTED FROM BARB'S garden. Luke begs me not to tell the police I suspect it's Cassie. It only takes one day for the reason to keep the secret to become "doing things by the book." Luke leans into his legal training, even when speaking to me. "Never give the police information unless compelled to do so by a court of law." Any other day I could follow that, but now it feels like we are hiding. Hiding Luke's secrets, hiding Barb's. Being stuck in this town razes my nerves altogether.

Guess it's not only Barb's house that I hate about this place.

Hunger comes for us quickly in the bare-bones motel room. Neither Luke nor I want to try a meal at Frankie's or another local spot tonight. If last time had been uncomfortable and the people nosy, it'd surely be ratcheted to eleven now.

"There's a vending machine in the lobby?" Luke's idea comes out as a question, but it's one he should damn well know the answer to.

"It's been too long of a day for a chips-and-Snickers dinner," I say lightly.

"There are sandwiches too."

"If you want to puke in that toilet too, you go ahead and eat motel vending sandwiches, but I need something more health inspected."

We settle for McDonald's. Another fast-food run. Another out-of-our-routine night. And to extend the shift in dynamic, Luke doesn't want to leave the motel.

"I can't face them, Addison. Even at a drive-through, they're going to ask about what's happening at Mom's house. Ask about Cassie. Ask what I know."

They were fair questions for me or the police, but I understood this need to bury himself. One of the things Luke and I had in common when we first met was the appreciation of going to the grocery store and not running into a single person we knew. Small towns meant people seeing you at your worst, and Luke controlled what people saw. He's beyond that now.

"I'll pick it up for us." And get a reprieve from the tension in this motel room.

"They're going to recognize you."

"And?"

He nods. "Thanks, babe."

I grab my purse and the keys to the rental and venture to the golden arches. The drive-through line is long and unmoving, so I park the car and head inside to order. I'm filling up my soda cup when someone nudges my elbow. Coke splashes my knuckle.

"Would have thought you'd have hightailed it out of town already." Evelyn's smile is bold, her gaze sharp.

"If only," I say far too honestly.

"I heard about poor Cassidy. Right there in Barb's..." She trails off when she catches the glare I'm attempting to slice her with. That news definitely hadn't been released. "Sorry about that, sugar. This town has had its share of drama, but this is more than one could imagine."

I nod like I agree with her. Barb had conjured much of it, from what I can tell. "I don't know much, but I hope those who need it get answers."

It's the safe and honest option. Evelyn purses her lips, though, like my truth has lit another within her. Her hand captures my arm. All that yoga makes her strong, I suppose. "Can I borrow you for a moment. In private?"

She doesn't wait for an answer but tugs me around the side of the soda machines. We linger in silence over the trash bin, until she finally speaks. "You'd asked about Kathryn Wall that day after yoga."

"I had," I hedge.

"Given what I'm hearing around town, I think you need to know about her."

My stomach plummets. Are the cops going to find a second body in the backyard at Barb's? "Please."

Evelyn checks her surroundings like another gossip is going to creep up behind her and call her a snitch. Deciding it's clear, she says, "Kathryn Wall had an affair with Barb's husband. A long one. Then he died suddenly, and Kathryn couldn't hold down a job, couldn't keep a man, her hair was falling out. The stress after he died just ate her up."

"Wait, Luke's dad cheated on Barb?" Oh, hell. There's no way Luke knew that, but had he guessed?

Evelyn nods, somberly. "If you believe Kathryn, it went on for a few years."

Years? Why would anyone do such a thing?

They're calling my order number, but I'm sure not leaving this conversation for McNuggets.

"Where is Kathryn now?" My whisper cracks. *Please don't say* dead. *Please don't say* missing.

"She's living the next county over. Still working as last I heard. Still no man." Evelyn shrugs like this information is unimportant.

She's alive. So Barb didn't kill everyone. Just the girl who might have gotten her son to skip college or get married young.

I thank Evelyn—and don't mention the doll in-progress I'd seen that reminded me of her—and grab my order.

The whole drive back to the motel, all I can think about is how Barb Lowe had tormented Kathryn Wall for years, but when it came to Luke, she acted swiftly.

She must not have hated me as much as I thought if she didn't whip up a doll upon our first contact. Or maybe I simply hadn't seen *that* box.

The police are quick to confirm the remains as Cassidy Warren. This would be great if it also didn't coincide with daily trips to the police station for my husband.

The sun is low in the sky the next day when Officer Brady brings Luke back to the motel room. He's kind to me, though Luke has taken a particular distaste to him.

The police officer remains at the threshold and tips his hat toward me. "Mrs. Lowe, I wanted to let you know you were right about the dolls having human hair. We have collected all of them and will be running any DNA against the missing persons database."

I come closer to the door, but Luke half blocks my passage. "I appreciate the update, Officer Brady."

There is small comfort in his update, but at least the lies of that house won't be inherited by my children.

"Goodbye, Brady," Luke says. He doesn't wait for a response before closing the door.

I cock my head toward him. "That was unnecessary."

"You didn't spend the entire day having them question your integrity." He's seething.

I press my hand against his back. "I'm sure that's not the case."

Luke flops back onto the bed. "It really was."

I sit next to him, and the bed dips, tilting him closer. "We can do this together," I repeat our new mantra to him. He's been the one so emphatic about it, but I too cling to the hope we'll weather this storm.

"It's all just a head trip, Ads." He's staring at the ceiling, but that makes the moment more intimate somehow. "Every girl I ever even thought about fooling around with in high school had a doll."

It takes my brain several seconds to process that. "That can't be true."

Luke pushes up onto his elbows. "All of them. Even the one-off bad choices at a bonfire party on the beach. There's a doll for each of them."

"That room wasn't about you alone though." I don't begrudge my husband his past, but one high schooler couldn't have been that busy.

"No, but I never thought I was putting girls in harm's way by making out." He hesitates like that's not the limit, but that's not what matters to me.

"Why would you have any reason to believe your mom would do anything? You didn't know the extent of the dolls or the luck back then, right?" He'd said he'd only seen the dolls once, but he also knew how they worked. What had Barb told him? What else had he witnessed?

"No, but I should have put it together."

"You were a teenager." I give him the obvious out.

"Yeah, but the list they showed me..." He deflates, flopping back onto the bed. "Anyone who threatened my reputation in any way..."

"Did you tell the police?"

He snorts. "Of course not. I don't need more attention, but truly, it wouldn't change anything."

"It might help them close the case sooner? Get us home?"

Luke shakes his head. "The dolls go back nearly fifty years. They aren't getting answers about those from me or girls I dated."

Girls you secretly got pregnant. My thoughts are loud, but he's right that Barb's wrath had targeted women in Rockside Bay far before Luke was born. It wasn't all about him, at least. That provided the thinnest balm.

Every person, though, had had a run-in with the Lowe family.

Except for me. I *am a Lowe.*

"But your mom was making a doll of me."

"My mom had issues with you. I'm not saying she didn't, but..."

"There were practice heads, Luke. Heads just lying around the house that look like me."

He has the good sense to cringe.

"What was she trying to do to me?" I ask.

He answers too quickly. "If she didn't finish them, then I'm sure nothing."

"How can you be so certain?" My mind spun to every clumsy bump, every broken bowl, and the one time I poured expired creamer into my coffee. Were those coincidences or Barb fucking with me?

Luke swipes his hand over his face. "Ads, she wouldn't want to hurt me, and when you're hurt, I'm hurt."

My husband hides no pain from me now. His brow is pinched, his upper lip twisting. Except I've had accidents that made no sense.

"I lost control of our car six months ago," I say quietly.

Luke stills.

"The accident never made sense. I had no reason to drive that day. The other cars were all fine, but mine skids right off the road and into a tree. I couldn't explain it. The cops couldn't either."

Luke swallows, and the sound shoots through the room, into my heart.

Softly, I ask the question I hate the most. "You didn't tell your mom I was pregnant, did you?"

She'd figured out about Cassie by intercepting a note, but it's not like she'd tapped our phone calls.

"You said there wasn't a feather in the box," he says, like that's an answer.

"I didn't see one, but… Luke, did your mom know I was pregnant?" Panic leaks into my voice. I fist the bedspread, hoping to keep it together.

"Yeah. That's why she stopped making the doll, I think." He *thinks*? "She was flustered when I told her about the baby but excited."

It all clicks. "You knew the car accident was her, didn't you?"

"No." He is emphatic. "I couldn't have imagined she would ever try to do something like that to you."

But she'd done it to so many other women. "You knew about her ability to make accidents happen."

His eyes are wide, imploring me to see his earnest soul. "But hurting you is hurting me. She wouldn't do that to us."

To him, he means.

"Then why was there a doll of me in that room? Why did she pilfer my sweater? My earring? Why had she collected *my hair*, Luke?"

He opens his mouth like he'll deny it again. The protest is ready, but then color drains from his face. "You had that sweater at Thanksgiving."

I nod slowly.

The cavalcade of profanity that pours from his mouth would be impressive if it weren't so damning.

"Tell me." No more dodging the truths that hurt us. It's time for him to explain.

"The Porsche."

"What?" Now is not the time to change the subject.

"I'd vented to her about you not wanting me to get the Porsche." His admission is flat, like he has to hide all his emotions or they'll overwhelm him. Must be nice to pick and choose right now.

A tingle begins in my fingers and shoots up my arms, my neck, my head. My whole body is buzzing. My voice is electric, cutting. "You called your mommy because you wife didn't like the idea of you buying a specific car?"

"Ads—"

My laugh is cruel. "Wow, Luke. Just. You knew she crafted cruel accidents for fun—killed people—and you hadn't considered that she might, I don't know, do that to me—who she absolutely hated?"

"It wasn't that."

"What part? That you gave her the ammunition to move forward in making a doll of me, or that she would find me saying no reason enough to make sure I crashed my car?" I'm seething. I stand, but I still have nowhere for all the anger and hurt to go.

"I shouldn't have said anything to her, but how was I to know she'd go there? Addison, I love you with every part of me. I put you first, and Mom understood you are my priority."

Was that why she'd hated me so much? I roll my shoulders and hope the errant thought dissipates. It doesn't matter why Barb hated me. It matters that her son made this happen.

"We lost our baby because of her."

"We don't know that." His hands are on me, trying to hold me, trying to pull me close.

I stagger backward. "The doctor said the fetus hadn't been viable, but we don't know if that's because something happened in that accident."

"You can't think like that."

"Like what? That your mom put this all into motion?"

"She wouldn't have." He's so certain.

"She killed Cassie knowing full well she was pregnant with your kid."

"That was different."

"Not from where I'm standing."

"Mom learned to stop fixing things for me. I didn't know she'd been doing this while I was in high school. Making sure I had a good path forward. I didn't *ask* her for any of that."

"You didn't ask her to make a creepy, cursed doll of your wife, but she sure did."

"Without my knowledge." He's spiraling. Mouth flattened, looking to the ceiling, he inhales slowly. "Addison, I swear to you, the only thing I want in this whole world is to be with you, to build a life, a family with you."

Apparently he'd also wanted a stupid sports car. "It doesn't feel that way."

"I'll show you. We'll get home, and I can make this better. I will."

"This isn't the kind of thing you bring home flowers and the perfect coffee to fix, Luke." I wish our problems were so easily solved.

"I know that, Ads, but I would never have let my mom hurt you. Never." He's emphatic, but it doesn't change the truth.

He let her hurt so many others. He'd known what she was capable of. "Did you ever consider I was in danger?"

Tears well on his lash lines. "If I had, I never would have brought you here."

I love Luke Lowe more than anyone in this world. I wish his words convinced me, but there is only hollow hurt in my chest. "I hope so."

CHAPTER 34

EACH NIGHT IN THAT MOTEL ROOM, LUKE TELLS ME STORIES of his youth, his regrets. He holds me, and we cry together, and in those moments, I believe him. Luke may have known what his mother was capable of, but her meddling had never been at his behest. How had he become so capable back home with a mother fixing his problems all the time? Did I fix his problems too? That's what I'd been doing the whole trip.

We get permission to return to Austin as long as Luke's free to fly back as needed. My belly is full of worry instead of food for days on end.

Once home, Luke goes back to work like nothing has happened. Like the girl he'd cared for—loved?—in high school hadn't been found in his backyard. Like his mom hadn't killed not one, but two of his potential children. All this time, I've believed I was the master in compartmentalization in our house. He locks up his feelings so quickly, like he can leave our loss and my fear back in Oregon with his late mother's estate. He discusses his cases in broad terms over coffee, he orders in the best takeout for robes-only movie nights and dotes on me at every spare moment. But he also takes the first inheritance payout and buys the Porsche he's long coveted, like it isn't the reason we're a family of two instead of three.

He's back to normal. He *shouldn't* be. I can't let go of what I learned in Oregon. No matter how many times Luke tells me to.

My skin crawls anytime I look at an item Barb gifted us. I try moving them to other rooms, but Luke keeps returning them to their original places.

"She was still my mom. We can't throw out the good memories because of this."

I did not have good memories. "You mean like the time I found out she was making a cursed doll of me and might have tried to kill me? Those kinds of good memories?"

Luke soothes his hands down my arms. "I'm sorry," he whispers. "It's just complicated."

For him it is. For me, keeping anything of hers is a hard sell. I pitch every terribly ugly scarf my mother-in-law gifted me. They're too drenched in terribleness to risk donating.

Three weeks later, the police call.

"Mrs. Lowe?" the caller asks.

"Yes? This is she."

"Mrs. Lowe, I'm glad I caught you. It's Officer Brady." He lets out a big breath like he'd had to work up the nerve to call.

"What can I do for you? Luke isn't here." My husband had mentioned refusing to take the cops' calls and directing them to another attorney.

"I know. I mean, I just spoke with him at his office."

Strange.

"I need to let you know that we've concluded our investigation into the death of Cassidy Warren."

"Well, thank you, but I didn't know Cassidy." At least not while she was alive.

"Luke has been cleared." His tone sharpens. "But we are finding quite a bit about a feud of sorts between his late mother and his late father's mistress. There's a lot of leads to track down from that attic. We...well, I wanted to make sure you're okay."

I can imagine how much they've found and need to investigate. I'm not normal yet, but it'll pass. Being back home has helped. "I appreciate that, but is there a reason?"

"We found some items here that reminded us of you, and I...I can't explain it, but it felt like we should check on you." Hesitation laces the police officer's tone. He's not going to say *doll heads*, but I know.

"Everything in that place is eerie," I agree. "But I really am fine." Trying to move forward with my life like I haven't learned what my mother-in-law was capable of or that a magic like that existed.

"If you need me for anything, here's my number."

I took it down because it sounded important to him.

"Cassie was my cousin."

"I'm sorry for your loss."

"It was a long time ago," he says. "But I'm glad she has peace." He says this like her ghost haunted him. Maybe we'll both find freedom.

"We may be calling Mr. Lowe back up here with more questions, but I'd understand if you stayed home." It's an odd thing for a cop to say. It's like he's trying to tell me more, but I can only focus on the way his voice grinds Luke's name.

"Thank you again, Officer."

I hang up, call in sick to work, and marinate in the anxiety itching beneath my skin. What does the cop know? What should I know?

I trust Luke. He's come clean with me. We're trying to regain our footing. I'm timing my cycle because we're going to try for a baby again. If I can just keep my fears locked away.

Except I think about the pain in Cassie's voice every time we spoke. In the secrets Luke had been forced to divulge.

We all had those deep, dark ones that we'd rather never see the light of day again. But I need to know if there's more.

My search of our house starts in his office.

It ends in his closet.

Tucked in the back corner on the top shelf is a jar of black feathers. A small woolen poppet lies beside it. The miniature version of Barb stares at me, lifelessly, a feather tied around her neck.

Luke said he would do anything for me. He promised what mattered to him most in the world was me and building our family. For the first time since Oregon, I truly believe him.

And I'm terrified.

KEEP READING FOR AN EXCERPT OF

THE FARMHOUSE

BY CHELSEA CONRADT

CHAPTER 1

THEY'D TOLD ME THE CORNFIELDS CARRIED A CURRENT IN the summer, but no one said it could pull me under. No one told me I could drown here. In the middle of a field. Alone in a sea of green stalks.

It'd started beneath the summer sunshine, warmth and welcome washing over me. My husband Josh and I were three days in and eighty-seven miles out from our destination: mile marker 116 on Route 136.

The address read like a clue in one of those murder mystery delivery boxes. We'd tackled one early on in our perpetually at-home life, but the grisly nature unnerved Josh. Or maybe he didn't like that I was *really* good at solving crime. Probably intimidating to have a potential crime-fighting hero in your home. The destination, though, had zero death, ghosts, or sickly memories for us: a farmhouse.

Our farmhouse.

Even with speed-limit signs that read more as a challenge than a limit, the drive from California to Nebraska was into day three. We'd researched ahead of time, of course, but I wasn't certain knowing the state was No. 2 in cybersecurity and also the home of Kool-Aid counted as prepared.

My mother would never have let me live down this move, but if she were still alive, I might not have needed the clean slate it provided. I'd grown up between the brightly painted Victorian homes and the sticky punk rock shops of Haight-Ashbury—San Francisco's best neighborhood, if you had asked my mother.

But then Penelope Wagers had been a paid arbiter of cool for decades. Her voice, sweet and salty, with too little sleep and two sips of liquor, enveloped me.

"Emily, the Bay is in your blood," she'd say, probably flinging her arms wide like the drama could encompass everything she loved about my hometown. "I raised you with far too much style to waste in a field somewhere."

Mom had a way of delivering compliments that snuck a jab around back afterward. *Style* had never been my area. *Aesthetic*, yes. It's what made me land in graphic design and not fashion. Even imagining her distaste for my decision didn't make me miss her less. It'd been six months since she passed—the nice way the hospice workers described the quick decline from thriving fifty-eight-year-old to gone.

She'd liked Josh, but I suspected she would have blamed this move on him. When he'd crashed out after two cups of Mom's signature eggnog, she'd teased, "He wouldn't have made it a night on the Haight in the seventies."

"Good." I'd lifted a glass in salute to her. "I want a man who thinks I look hot in lounge pants and is happy to snuggle on the couch with me."

She'd tapped her glass to mine, but her attention flitted to everything in the room that wasn't me. "All I want is your happiness."

I needed to quit letting my thoughts, my heart linger in her memory, but all attempts had failed. There was value—and hope—in this journey. I had to cling to that, to the future. I had Josh, a job I could do from anywhere, and a new life waiting for me whenever our GPS led us to the turn toward the farm. Our new mailbox's little flag waved hello. This was my path back to happiness, and I was determined not to get lost.

The land here was beautiful. Yellow fields waved from either side of the moving truck, welcoming us to the Heartland. Water towers stretching white or blue in the distance, marking other small towns. Not that I could see much in the way of buildings. The last half dozen towns we'd passed through had populations less than three hundred. There were more people who took 6 a.m. workout classes at Lifetime with me than lived in those entire communities. Nebraska was nothing but glorious space and freedom, and Josh and I deserved them both.

Loose pebbles pelted the underside of the U-Haul. I'd already tapped Josh's arm a half dozen times to slow down. I'd expected dirt roads, but there was more gravel than anything else on this last stretch to our new home.

Our new home.

Hope bubbled bright beneath my breastbone. Nebraska was the

start of something big. This bumpy road was the kind of precipice that lifted your belly with flashes of future freedom. I'd felt it when I'd left for college. When I'd found a creative job that was distinctly corporate. If you needed graphics for a white paper about accounting or human resources software, or a style guide for your attorney's website, I was your girl. Going corporate had given me that same tinge of fear, but it turned out health benefits were rad. Being the reliable graphic designer at a behemoth agency meant people only cared enough to tap the party horn icon on Zoom when you announced you were buying a farmhouse in the middle of nowhere. The specter of my mom tried to resurrect, all effervescence fizzling. Six months wasn't long enough to dull the pain of losing her. Would six years? Six decades? Would I be alive in sixty years if my mother died at fifty-eight? Those other moves had been leaping to new adventures, but if I was honest with myself, this time I was fleeing the past.

Plink. Pli-pli-pli-plink. "Those rocks are going to wreck something."

"It's a rental." Josh thrummed his fingers against the steering wheel like the jostling was more massage chair than a puke-over-the-edge boat ride.

My stomach was less convinced.

"Our car is hitched to the back." Had memory swallowed him too? Or was he simply drinking in the expansive scenery?

Josh swore and slowed the moving truck. "We're here though."

A simple white mailbox marked the driveway. We turned onto a dirt road. Dust whirling behind us in the side mirrors. Fields stretched on either side of the path. Green and thick and structured. The road arced hard to the right, revealing our farm.

The house's exterior was picture-perfect, which made sense since we'd toured over FaceTime. Good to know our Realtor wasn't working camera angles on us. It was a single-story ranch painted white. Two steps led up to a porch nearly as long as the house. A wooden bench swing hung at one end. Like, the Waltons would be jealous of this style. Not that the house was big enough for a TV family like that. It was only Josh and me, making the three-bedroom setup perfect. One room for us, one for a home office, and one to set up for guests, because eventually people might visit. (Okay, we were putting gym equipment in next to a pull-out couch. But *if* someone decided to visit, we'd move it.)

"This is good." Josh slipped his arm around me, my constant home. "Everything you thought?"

"Even better." My gaze skipped from the daylilies blooming in the front garden to the endless blue sky surrounding us to the barn. "Did they show us the barn?"

While the house was ready to be submitted to some home and garden magazine, the run-down barn would not be allowed in the background of a two-page spread. The walls were a mishmash of peeling gray and red paint. Darkness speckled the corners and eaves. The window over what I expected was the loft had only one of the four panes of glass still intact. At least the eyesore was a healthy distance from the house.

"There were pictures. Remember, it's part of the farm?" Josh's attention locked solely on me. Seven years in, and he could still make me feel like the center of the universe.

"Right. The farmers have access to it." We weren't trying to change careers here. I knew exactly shit about gardening or grains or working a tractor. The folks who had sold us the house wanted to keep the fields and tend to them. So we got the house and leased the farmland back to the people who actually knew how to use it.

Josh rolled his shoulders. I pressed my palm to the center of his back and slowly rubbed. We both would feel that car ride tomorrow.

"We can use the barn too, for storage or to park the car when storms hit."

I squinted at the barn, and my stomach lurched. When had we last eaten? "It's far from the house."

"That's why we're parking up here, Em." Josh leaned over and kissed my forehead.

I clambered out of the moving truck and took in a noseful of country air. "You smell that?"

"Clean air?" A dimple flashed in his right cheek.

"I totally thought it was bullshit."

"You thought people made up fresh air?" He wasn't even bothering to hold back his laughter.

"I understand air pollution and smog, and that some days it's gloomy because of selfish, climate-change denying assholes driving big SUVs in rush hour, but I didn't think it actually *smelled* different." I inhaled, saturating myself in the fresh euphoria.

"You're ridiculous and I love you." Josh pressed his lips against my forehead once more and then offered me a proper kiss.

I surely smelled like fourteen hours in a moving truck, but Josh wrapped his arms around my back and lifted me. And everything was freedom during that kiss. His body supporting mine—which, God, I'd let him do so much the last year while I tried not to fall apart in grief—but now he held me with only excitement behind his eyes. I slipped my hands up the back of his neck, letting my nails graze him. His smile forced my own. All I cared about now was the clean air in my lungs, the man before me, and our fresh start.

When he finally released me, we were both breathless. A fresh start indeed.

Our Realtor had left the key out front. A heavy black rubber mat with the bold red *N* of the University of Nebraska's Cornhuskers—a logo I'd seen on billboards, in store windows, and on T-shirts at every stop within the state—had been placed before our front door. Its center hid the brass key. The mat was crisp on the white wood of the porch, but the big yellow sunflowers and "Welcome" in looping script on the coir mat I'd brought were far homier. I could move this one to the back entrance. The grooves would be good for cleaning mud off running shoes.

Josh unlocked the door and stepped through first. "It looks huge without furniture."

"It's bigger on the inside!" I couldn't resist the joke.

Josh groaned, continuing to pretend he hated *Doctor Who*—even if I caught him watching it every time he was sick.

He was right though. Not about the Doctor, but about our new home.

Our apartment in Mission Bay had two bedrooms, eight hundred square feet, and zero space. This house tripled our living area.

We had an extra bedroom and a kitchen with counters for days. And the mortgage cost less than half our monthly rent.

"We're going to have to buy more stuff," I said, stalking across the oak floors into the empty living room.

"Or we could enjoy the extra white space."

"White space is useful on a website, but in a home, it just makes it feel cold."

Josh leaned against the counter marking the entrance to the kitchen. "We don't need to fill every corner..."

ACKNOWLEDGMENTS

Writing *The Secret Attic* was a process unlike any other for me. The book is a bit of a fever dream, and writing it was much the same. It wasn't until I finished the first draft that I realized just how much I needed to stay with this novel. And I am so lucky to have Rachel Gilmer as my editor on this journey. She understood exactly the kinds of statements made by this novel, what was important, and what made it fun too. Also, thanks for enduring me writing about dolls, Rachel. I'll try not to do that to you again.

Thanks to my agent, Cheyenne Faircloth, for designating me as her crow lady and championing all my ideas. Even if they're bonkers.

A huge thank-you to the remarkable team at Sourcebooks and Poisoned Pen Press. Y'all are absolute rock stars, and I'm so happy to get to work with you on making books like *The Secret Attic* happen. Specific thanks to: Dominique Raccah, Mandy Chahal, Aimee Alker, Mary Wheelehan, Angela Cardoz, Sarah Brody, Hartley Christensen, Almeda Beynon, and Jenna Jankowski.

Simon Mendez, you are a magician at bringing my words to life in your art. Thank you for the remarkable interior art yet again.

To my audiobook queen, Brittany Pressley, thank you for narration so captivating that even I get caught up in the story!

Writer friends are the best friends. Big thanks to bestie Cathlin Shahriary. All the love for my author chats that keeps me sane: Lish McBride, Kristen Simmons, Jaye Wells, Molly Harper, and Jeanette Battista. And extra thank-yous to Rachel Harrison, Ande Pliego, Christa Carmen, Brian McAuley, May Cobb, Darby Kane, CJ Dotson, Alma Katsu, Bonnie Jo Stufflebeam, and Amanda Casile for being rad, kind, and the most fun at parties.

To all the amazing independent booksellers, I am so grateful for your support. Your stores build community, and I'm so thankful to get to be a part of them.

Last, and most importantly, the biggest thank-you to my supportive husband, Matt, and our amazing son. Thanks for helping me make the dream happen.

ABOUT THE AUTHOR

Chelsea Conradt is the *USA Today* bestselling author of twisty speculative thrillers. Her books are packed with both murder and kindness, because we can be more than one thing. When not writing stories that make you question what's real, she is likely watching a baking show or a true-crime documentary. She is nothing if not on-brand.

Chelsea lives in Texas with her husband, son, and two big dogs.

Website: chelseaconradt.com

Facebook: ChelseaConradt

Instagram: @authorchelseaconradt

TikTok: @chelseaconradt